VAMPIRE'S KISS

"Antonio," I whispered.

"What is it," he said quietly.

"I . . ." I began, and then swallowed. "I want to be a vampire."

"You have no idea what you ask for."

"Please, Antonio! I understand what I'm asking for. I even know what I'd be giving up."

"Do you?"

"Of course," I said. "I know that I would never see the sun again. I know that—that I would have to live off the blood of others. I know those things. But I also know what I'll gain. Strength. Power. Immortality!"

"Theresa—"

"Make me a vampire and I'll be your disciple," I said.

He turned to face me, placing his hands on my cheeks and staring long and hard into my eyes. I stared back and could have sworn his eyes were beginning to glow red as embers.

I remember hearing his voice, but not the words. Then his lips pressed against mine, and I kissed back, until his lips glided away to touch my cheeks, and chin, and all along my neck. I shut my eyes and let my head sink back. The last thing I remember was a tiny sting and then a chill racing from my head to the tips of my toes as a rush of warm blood flowed from my veins.

TRACI BRIERY

ZEBRA BOOKS
KENSINGTON PUBLISHING CORP.

ZEBRA BOOKS

are published by

Kensington Publishing Corp.
475 Park Avenue South
New York, NY 10016

First Printing: April, 1993

Printed in the United States of America

For Mike and Ma Payne, Fred, Mark, who reminded me of the historical facts and left the rest to my sense of duty, and of course, to my mother.

Chapter 1

I wanted to call this "My Turn," but that title was already taken. But then, I won't be wasting my time refuting everything that was said about me in another autobiography, which shall remain nameless. And speaking of that unnamed autobiography, those of you who might have read that vampire's book might remember someone in it who vaguely resembled me. According to that version, I am dead and buried. Needless to say reports of my permanent death have been *greatly* exaggerated.

I just think we all need to take a break from whiny, self-pitying treatises and hear someone who *hasn't* sold out to the humans. That must mean I'm not a human myself. Well, no, because I'm a vampire, and rather content to stay that way.

I was born Maria Theresa Allogiamento, but I don't go by that name right now. Before that I always went by Theresa. I was born about two hundred years ago—and never mind the exact date—in Sicily. As a young girl I spent most of my time trying to be a good little Catholic and not worrying about the real world. Mine was an old, prominent family—prosperous even under foreign rule. Mother had eleven of us children, two of whom died when I was rather young. I was child number eight and considered most likely to become a nun. That may be why my parents waited longer before seeking a suitable husband for me. But that's getting ahead of things.

Two things characterized my childhood: a love of reading and a love of men. Ironically enough, it was my love of reading that provoked my parents' wrath and not the more obvious sin. When I was a little girl I wanted to go to school, as my brothers did, but I was always told not to think of such things. It wasn't my job to learn facts, except when it came to cooking. Actually, I did enjoy cooking and helped my mother quite a bit with it. I also wanted to learn how to read, though, so I could read such things as the family Bible. That turned out to be beyond me, as it was in Latin, but I did manage to steal one of my brother's primers and copy down some pages in secret before returning it (without his knowledge, of course). It turned out that his teacher had given him a good lashing for not having it with him several days in a row.

From there I learned some of the basics and stole and copied more advanced writings as the years went by. One of my sisters once caught me with a sheet of paper, but I convinced her that I didn't know what it said.

Before any trouble came of the reading or of boyfriends, I was blessed from early childhood with a reputation for being the ne'er-do-wrong good little girl. As far as Mother and Father were concerned I was destined for nunhood and could do no wrong. Most of my brothers and sisters knew otherwise, but I had the sort of angelic face that led Father to lash my siblings after *I'd* been the one who slugged *them.*

In true Catholic fashion, Mother and Father also wanted me to be married at an early age and have fifteen or so children, if the nun thing didn't work out.

Before I learned otherwise, though, I wanted to be both nun and mother of many and *really* be the perfect Catholic.

The many children would have been no problem; from an early age I had a rather healthy libido. Never in front of my parents, however. Even then I knew it was best to keep my saintly reputation for as long as I could. This necessarily led to my leading almost two separate lives. An angel at home but a tigress in private, so to speak. I can't remember exactly when I became interested in men, or rather, when I *wasn't* interested in men. In spite of my early interest I didn't have a secret boyfriend until I was twelve or so. After that I had something like sixteen—yes, and one at a time, thank you.

The reason for the secrecy should be obvious. My husbands were supposed to be picked for me, not by me. Keeping the boyfriends secret wasn't as much of a challenge as it may seem; I'd already had years of practice hiding my reading from everyone, so the boys were just another little game for me. My first was Vittorio, a fifteen-year-old volcano who wanted me to marry him and live in the mountains with him. We met every day for two months in all sorts of secret places—a different one nearly every day—and hugged and kissed and other romantic things. In spite of all this I was reluctant to go further, as I was, after all, a good Catholic. I might have ended up marrying him after all if my brother Leonardo hadn't caught us and chased him away for good. Then Leonardo gave me a good lashing in exchange for not telling Mother and Father.

Ever after, it was Leonardo I had to be especially careful around. In a way, that made things far more exciting for me. After all, sneaking around with my boyfriends was one of the only thrills I got out of my later youth. Oh, I still fully intended to be the perfect mother of fifteen, or a nun, whichever came first, but at the time it didn't seem worth bringing to confession. I was still a virgin, so none of the stolen kisses and flirting mattered.

I tried to brag of my literacy to some of my boyfriends, except that they laughed until I proved myself. Four of them actually broke up with me for that very reason—that I could read! It was soon after the last one broke up with me that I started thinking about my situation. Women's situation, actually. Until then I'd been so caught up in the thrill of hiding yet another little secret from everyone that it hadn't occurred to me how unfair it was. Here I was being dumped by boys who couldn't handle an intelligent girl. Understanding why was beyond me at first, until I finally opened my eyes after the last boy. It wasn't until then that I began to be more observant of the world around me.

I'd been so used to being able to read that I overlooked the fact that I probably wouldn't ever be allowed to put it to any use, except to write down recipes, maybe. Or poetry, which I really don't like much. Being able to read also allowed me to know pretty much what men knew, except I couldn't possibly tell them whenever they got their facts wrong. I'd have to name my sources. For a time I did get the secret satisfaction of knowing when my boyfriends were wrong, and let them think I was a dumb brunette. Unfortunately there did come times when their arrogance became almost too much, and I almost read them the riot act.

My parents finally started noticing these subtle changes in my personality when I was about sixteen. I started voicing my opinions, for one thing, which was a bad thing for any of the children to do. Fortunately none of the changes was so harsh as to warrant a sore bottom, but they were enough to weaken my well-protected angelic reputation. Then, all hell broke loose when they discovered me in Father's library reading none other than Cervantes. It had long been my dream to read one of Father's naughty stories, and I became so engrossed in it that I didn't even hear him enter behind me. He tore the book from my hand in anger, and then *really* flew into a rage when he saw what it was. From there he blasted me with every foul and vicious accusation he could imagine, even going as far as to call me a slut and a whore. It wasn't until years later that I could laugh at *those* names; a slut and whore because I could read? It's just as well that I hadn't been reading his translated Chaucer.

Mother was called in, and of course was horrified that her favorite daughter was . . . was whatever a daughter who could read was, but naturally it was a bad thing. Almost my entire family was crowded in the doorway, watching me get it good for the first time. I have no doubts most of them were thrilled with that. Finally Father grabbed me by the ear and dragged me from the library to my room, where he flung my things all over the room in search of more books. He found enough of them—including one of those original primers—to warrant tanning my hide. After that I was confined to my room for a week straight and absolutely forbidden ever to enter the library again.

I lost one of my boyfriends because of my confinement. He thought I was being a typically fickle little girl, and my explanation didn't make things much better. After this last boy I swore off men for a time, which strengthened my parents' resolve to make me a nun. That way I was more likely to be forgiven for my sin, whatever that was. Oh, yes, intelligence. They sent me off to a monasterial convent. By that I mean these were not the sort of sisters who worked in hospitals and comforted children; these sisters stayed indoors and prayed. All the time.

Cloistered life is not for everyone. My mistake was believing in the glamor of being a nun without realizing what torments awaited me in the convent. I knew nuns took vows of chastity, obedience, and poverty—all of which I misunderstood before taking them. I knew I was supposed not to have any money, but to give away or sell all the things I had *before* that time? I had sisters that I didn't want even *looking* at some of my things, let alone owning them. But I was stuck. Since I'd sworn off men, chastity didn't bother me so much—at first, and obedience basically means following the rules.

More culture shock set in when they cut off most of my hair. I had always loved my hair long, still do now, and probably always will. The drab clothes were tolerable, if lice-infested, but the food was no more than functional at best. I admit that life with Mother's cooking had spoiled me beyond hope there.

The turning point for me in the monastery was when I realized that I did not love God as much as I thought I did. Or at least, not so much that I wanted to pray to Him all the time. Almost all free time there was spent in prayer or quiet contemplation, which for me became increasingly spent on men and what they had to offer me. At next-to-worst, the priests started looking good. At the end, the nuns did. It seems my vow of chastity had been taken prematurely, but even then I had no outlet. Self-educated or not, I still believed those old horror stories about masturbating and going blind and whatnot. There wasn't much I could do.

Cabin fever started setting in, and I couldn't help but mutter things under my breath during inappropriate times, which got me a crack on the knuckles. Sometimes I answered questions in not-completely-obedient tones, and got more cracks. The final straw was when I couldn't take any more of those wretched periods of silence (for prayer, of course!). I'd been putting up with this for too many years now. Everyone there was oh so serious at all times, and I must have started thinking about my private joke about how the sisters had all taken vows of misery, when I started giggling. I stopped myself, but the abbess came over to me and cracked my knuckles in front of everyone, which made me cry out a little, which got another crack. From there it wouldn't stop. I'd make a noise in protest, she'd hit me, and I'd complain louder. Soon it got to the point where I completely lost it and threw my food at her, then let out a string of curses that would have melted a church. Then things got messy. In fact, I probably passed out at times from the beating I got. I resolved soon after that that I was going to get myself thrown out of that place if it killed me.

Finally, the abbess called Mother and Father in to confess that even they couldn't help such a wicked girl as I. She said the Devil had too great a hold on me, I was too wicked, and so on. My parents were flabbergasted, but Mother Maria was quite serious and even suggested an exorcist, which I've been told Mother and Father argued against at first. Not very convincingly, it seems.

I was tied up, bound, and carried into the catacombs by the burliest sisters. From there I was left with just the priest. He untied me and then spread out my limbs and bound them to the bars on a cell door. From there he pulled out his Bible and began shouting various prayers and rebukes at the demons in me. My ears were ringing throughout, and then he began throwing holy water into my face, some of which got into my nose. And we mustn't forget that demons are guaranteed to flee when their host body is beaten repeatedly.

The entire experience was so ridiculous that I should have laughed throughout. But I didn't. I was genuinely terrified this time. After a time I even started to believe that maybe I really *did* have demons in me, and called out some prayers during the ordeal to help the priest. The priest saw this as inspirational and yelled even louder for the demons to leave me, over and over, in Latin and Hebrew and other bizarre languages. By the end I had been reduced to hysterics and screamed long and loud, and then collapsed into a sobbing heap. The priest's shoutings stopped, and after a time I heard him calling my name quietly, and I answered through tears. Then he told me that I'd been cleansed and that no demons would ever bother me again. He also said something about how both of us could rest now from such a draining ordeal. I felt drained, all right, but not because of any cleansing. I'd been traumatized, not saved.

At last I was sprung from the convent and was free to go home. There began my silent period. I walked around in a haze for a year or so. I hadn't read anything for some time—not even in the convent—nor did I have any desire to. I helped Mother around the house and eventually did most of the cooking for the family, which gave me some sense of purpose. Meanwhile the family treated me differently. Most of my brothers and sisters had been married off by this time; only I and the youngest were left. I became more or less the black sheep of the family—the wayward one, the sick child. My parents perceived my silence as progress, as I was on my way to becoming wife material.

Because of my time in the convent, my parents were forced to begin my husband-hunting late. I was practically an old biddy already—twenty-one. Whenever Father returned from his business trips, he told me about some young man he'd come across who seemed just right for me, until some terrible flaw had been discovered. Father would tell me about these men, and then shrug and promise he'd find someone for me soon. Then I'd go into the garden and walk around, usually. I spent a lot of time in the garden then.

About a year later Father told me about someone named Frederico that he was rather impressed with. Naturally he was the son of some wealthy man in Naples, but he couldn't come down to meet me for another few months or so. I thanked Father and took more walks in the garden. I should have been plotting ways to make Frederico hate me when he arrived, but I decided to see if it was possible for that to happen on its own.

Chapter 2

Frederico came with his father and other businessmen. Apparently he was part of some huge gathering of families visiting our house to do their business. I was drafted into service to help look after the gentlemen. We had plenty of servants, but there were only so many of them, and even Mother had to wait on some tables. She was much happier when she was able to supervise the food preparations, but I wasn't allowed to help there. Personally I would have preferred being very far away from this whole ordeal, but of course I had to be around to meet my future husband. On the first day we weren't even introduced, so I had no idea who he would be. After everyone arrived I hoped he was one particularly handsome gentlemen who arrived late at night and with only a few men with him. I didn't see him all the next day, but he did appear at our second banquet. Not everyone there could stay at our house, so he must have been in town.

It wasn't until the second night was almost through that Father formally introduced me to Frederico. My heart sank a little when I learned that he was *not* the handsome latecomer. Worse than that, I'd learned that the latecomer was from Rome, a city I'd wanted to see for years. I'd read much about ancient Rome but had heard that a lot of the buildings and landmarks were still there. Oh, to visit the Coliseum, empty though it must have been. As far as I was concerned, Naples had nothing to offer me. Yet here was some other man that Father had chosen for me, and I must admit that I was not at my most gracious when we first met. Later that night Mother came to my room and lectured me about keeping in my place if I ever expected to have a good husband. I wasn't exactly rude to Frederico, but I wasn't quite as warm and charming as my parents had wanted me to be.

The next night I spent a lot of time stealing glances at the Roman visitor, who seemed to be stealing them at me, too. Later on Father approached me, telling me how pleased he was that Frederico had also been stealing glances at me. I hadn't been paying a bit of attention to him. Then Frederico came over, and Father nudged him and left us alone to get acquainted. Well, not entirely alone. I caught glimpses of Father watching us every now and then. Meanwhile Frederico seemed to believe that our wedding date was as good as set, as he talked about all the things he had planned for us. Most of the time I just smiled and nodded and tried not to stare at the Roman gentleman. Finally Frederico had his fill of me and made to rejoin his father, but not before discreetly taking up my hand and kissing the inside of my wrist. I rubbed the spot while he rejoined his group, and quickly searched for the handsome one, who seemed to have disappeared. I was then called back into service for the rest of the night.

I was also one of the people who had to see everyone safely to the door. Father would declare the evening over, and everyone had to leave fairly soon after that and not dawdle. Only those staying at the house could remain, of course. I was seeing the last of them out, when I glimpsed a figure in the shadows. I knew it was simply a leftover guest, so I stepped outside to bid him a final goodnight. He was leaning casually against a wall, apparently watching the stars. I approached him silently and remained just behind him. Eventually he stood up straight and finally seemed to notice me. He turned around, and only then could I see that he was the Roman. I gasped quietly and stepped back a little, as I honestly didn't expect to be face-to-face with him like this.

"Ah, good evening, *signorina,*" he said casually. "I didn't mean to stay behind."

"Oh, it's no trouble, *signore,*" I said, my courage returning a little. "I was . . . simply bidding you good night. It was I who disturbed *you,* I think."

"Not at all," he said, smiling. "I was only admiring the heavens. But . . . I ought to be returning to my men now."

"Yes," I said, "And . . . I ought to return inside. Farewell, *signore.* Until tomorrow, that is."

"Farewell, *signorina,*" he said, and started to turn away, but stopped. "Ah, *signorina,*" he said.

"Yes?"

"You are our host's daughter, aren't you?" he asked. For some reason I felt my cheeks warming, so I smiled and nodded.

"Yes," I said.

"Good," he said. "That is, you have a splendid home. And, is that a garden I keep seeing peeking out from behind your house?"

"Um, yes," I said. "Do you mean as you approach us?"

"Yes," he said.

"Yes, we do have a garden," I said. "A beautiful garden. Perhaps . . . you'd like to see it sometime?"

"I'd be honored to."

"Wonderful," I said, "And I would be honored to show you. If you wish."

"I . . ." he began, and I leaned forward a little expectedly, "You will be serving us tomorrow night, also, *signorina?*"

"Oh . . . yes," I said. "Yes, of course. And you'll be here?"

"I will," he said, "But until then," he added, and touched my chin, "I must take my leave of you. *Arrivederci, signorina.*"

He took up my hand and kissed it gently. I didn't want him to let go, but he did, then turned abruptly to leave. I watched him as if in a trance, until he seemed to disappear into the very night. Then I was snapped back to my senses by my sister, who was chastising me for leaving the door open. I headed back inside, but not without a last backward glance to look for the handsome Roman whose name I again had failed to learn.

Some of the families had already finished their business by the next night; a lot of our visitors had left. I silently thanked God that the Roman still had matters to attend to.

I can be quite subtle with my flirtations if I so choose. This time I had no choice, so I made all the times that I touched the Roman seem like accidents. A brush against the cheek here, a gentle nudge there—but nothing that would arouse his suspicions. Still, I found some pleasure in it, however small. Frederico was trying the same sort of thing with me, only he was much more noticeable. Since we were pretty much engaged, Frederico didn't have to be subtle. It did help to draw attention away from what I was doing to the Roman, though.

My progress was hampered when, during a break in the festivities, Father summoned me to him. He stood between Frederico and me and held his mug high, and with great joy and enthusiasm, announced our engagement to all present. There was a lot of applause and cheering followed by many women standing in line to kiss and congratulate me. Frederico congratulated me quite a bit, too.

Chapter 3

The next day was the last for the gathering of families. That afternoon Frederico said his goodbyes to me and promised to return in eight months for the wedding. I was upset that the gathering had finished, which Father mistook as sadness for Frederico.

"Father," I said once everyone had left, "does this mean there will be no more festivities tonight?"

"No, Daughter," he said. "I'm afraid you won't see him again until the wedding."

"Oh," I said, and looked down. Father turned to leave, when I called to him again.

"Father," I said, and he listened. "Um . . . was there not a man from Rome here, during the dinners?"

"Er, yes, there was," he said slowly.

"Oh," I said. "I thought there was. I've wanted to see Rome for many years now. Um . . . do you remember who it was?"

"Yes, that was . . . da Clovino," he said. "Signore Antonio da Clovino."

"Clovino?" I said. "I don't know that place."

"Neither do I," he said, and made to leave again.

"Well . . ." I said, and Father stopped again, "Perhaps . . . Frederico will take me to Rome sometime."

Father watched me a moment before stepping forward and holding my shoulders gently.

"Daughter," he said quietly, "I have spent a great deal of time finding the right man for you. Frederico may be young, but he knows his father's business and stands to inherit a lot of money. A *lot* of money."

"I know, Father."

"That, and . . . he likes you," he continued. "This is even better."

"I know, Father."

"Then I suggest you try to like *him,* too," he said. "You should consider yourself fortunate you're getting married at *all;* you're nearly twenty-three."

"I know, Father. I do consider myself fortunate."

"Then of course you'll make an effort to be a good wife. And I think you know what I mean, Theresa."

"I . . . perhaps I don't, Father," I said. "Besides being . . . good and obedient, that is."

"I mean . . ." he began, and then continued in a lower voice, "You haven't been . . . 'educating' yourself still, have you? And you *do* know what I mean *there.*"

"Yes, Father," I said. "I mean, no, Father. I haven't been 'educating' myself."

"Good," he said, patting my shoulders. "The last thing he needs is a wife who argues every fact with him."

"I won't, Father."

"Of course you won't," he said. "You just leave the facts to us men and worry about your home and children."

"Yes, Father."

"Well, Daughter," he said, kissing my cheeks, "I must return to my study. Go back to cleaning up now. And you keep your mind off Rome, understand?"

"Yes, Father," I said, and went back to clearing off the lunch tables.

The next eight months were spent preparing for the big day. Mother had the seamstress make me the biggest wedding dress I'd ever seen. Mother and Father worked for about a month getting the guest list ready. I tried to make some suggestions, such as maybe Signore da Clovino, and listed others, of course, but was always sent away. At least I got to choose some of my bridesmaids. But only some. Father made up a huge dowry for my future husband. I was the second to last of us children who was getting married, but we still had plenty left over to make dowries fit for royalty. Unfortunately we weren't royalty, but we were still rich.

Mother spent the entire eight months telling me what was going to happen during the wedding, and I would nod and wait for her to plan the other parts. I had plenty to do, of course, but the planning was up to Mother. It was just as well, because the closer the date came to my wedding day, the more depressed I became. It was nothing I could pinpoint. I was happy that I was to be married, but tradition or not, I was increasingly distressed that I literally had nothing to do with it. Essentially my job was to stand before the altar and be married, then ride off and try to fall in love with someone I barely knew. Or fall in *like,* if love was impossible. This was nothing new. Marriages weren't to be based on love and romance for at least a hundred years, so it's not as if I should know what I was missing. Still, in retrospect I think that deep down I did know what I was missing.

Needless to say the wedding was glorious and magnificent. Thousands of (well, not *thousands)* of bridesmaids, several hundred guests, High Mass, bishops, singing, vows, and all for a little peck on the lips at the end. Before Mass, that is. I must admit that I was quite swept away by the whole experience. Like many brides, I stood through the wedding in a trance and barely remember any details. Not out of unspeakable bliss, I realize now, but simply because the wedding was glorious and magnificent. I soon discovered that the real part of a wedding is the reception, though. Mine lasted for a few days. Several hours were spent standing at the receiving line as it was. Mother bawled her head off almost the entire time, and Frederico's mother cried every time she looked at my ring, which had been her mother's. Even Father shed a quiet tear for me, but in his case I wouldn't be surprised if it had been a tear of relief. Married in the nick of time, as it were.

The second night of the reception was eventful. These were all day affairs, mind you, but it took me two and a half days to discover that Signore da Clovino had indeed been invited—invited to the wedding or to the reception only, I couldn't say. Nevertheless I caught several glimpses of him while mingling. He seemed to be keeping to himself, except that I couldn't find the opportunity to break away from Frederico and go talk to him. A brief opportunity did arise when my new husband and I were strolling past him, and da Clovino confronted me himself.

"Ah, *signore* and *signora,*" he said, taking my hand. "I haven't had the opportunity to congratulate you until now." He kissed my hand gently, then took both of Frederico's into his own and shook them firmly.

"Congratulations, *signore,*" he said. Frederico nodded and pulled away.

"Grazie, signore . . . ?"

"Da Clovino," he said, "With, uh . . . with her

father's guests. May I say you are a fortunate man, *signore.*"

"*Grazie,*" Frederico said, and pulled at my arm a little.

"*Grazie,*" I whispered.

"Uh—I hope I don't seem prying if I ask where you'll be honeymooning?" da Clovino called to us.

"Not at all," Frederico said. "My bride and I will go to my home first in Naples, and from there we'll be off to Rome."

"Rome?" I said rather excitedly. This was the first time anyone had bothered to tell me where the honeymoon would be. Needless to say my heart quickened.

"Of course, my bride," he said, squeezing my shoulders. "One month to see its sights, and then it's back to *truly* . . . the most beautiful city."

"You mean Naples," I said.

"Of course," he said. Da Clovino started asking about our accommodations, which I really wanted to listen to, except that other guests pulled me aside to give their congratulations. They had already done this several times before, but apparently there is no limit to the number of times people should congratulate the newlyweds. That, and plenty of liquor can help people forget what they've done before.

By the time I could break away, da Clovino had already left our side. Frederico smiled and offered his arm to me. I took it and looked around for our Roman guest.

"Oh," I said, "Have you, um . . . has our guest left us?"

"Hm? Oh—yes, he only wanted to know where we were going. He said he was from Rome, too."

"I know," I said.

"Hm?"

"Um, Father told me about many of our visitors the

last . . . well, that time that everyone was here, for all that business."

"Ah, yes," he said. " 'All that business.' "

It was time again for us to dance. We did mostly the rigid, courtly dances, but during one waltz Frederico and I separated to cater to other partners. The bride is the one who ends up dancing the most in such cases. My partners came and went so quickly that I was becoming dizzy, until into my arms glided Signore da Clovino. I looked into his eyes—as I did with all my partners—and time itself seemed to stand still. An invisible bubble formed around us, blocking out all sight and sound, even the music. I'm not even certain if we were still moving. The thoughts running through my mind then should have put me to shame, but they didn't. I didn't want them to end.

Another man broke in, but I kept my gaze on da Clovino, who backed away slowly and bowed deeply before I was whirled about some more. The music ended just as I looked into my husband's eyes.

"So many men for you, Theresa," he teased. "What am I going to do with you?"

"Hnh?" I said, still in a daze. He smiled and led me from the dance floor, where we were finally allowed to sit and rest our feet. I wasn't able to meet up with da Clovino again that night, thanks to the barrage of more congratulatory guests.

Chapter 4

I was a good and obedient wife when we arrived in Naples, albeit not a passionate one. We consummated our nuptials on the first night of arrival. Considering how long I had yearned for that moment, I was sadly disappointed, although I don't think my husband noticed. As mentioned above, I was dutiful and obedient, but could not conjure up the level of passion I knew I was fully capable of. I was hoping that our official wedding night would be all that I needed to make me finally fall in love with the man, but it was not to be. The longer I've been on this earth, the more convinced I am that men can fall in love after good sex, while women must be in love first. I have since had plenty of sex with men I wasn't in love with, but never—I mean never—have I fallen in love with one just because he was good in bed.

The next morning we were treated to a sumptuous banquet prepared by Frederico's own mother. Family loyalty forbids me from saying whether or not her cooking was better than my mother's, but I could probably say without retribution that I haven't met a Sicilian woman yet who isn't a master chef.

I would give you a sweeping description of the wonders of the capital of the kingdom of the Two Sicilies, except that I didn't see much of it before we had to leave for Rome. I did get to visit the Caglionis—my new in-laws—alone now, meaning without hundreds of other wedding guests competing for my attention. One of the sisters, Rapphaela, and I were close to becoming good friends by this time, as she had already been one of my bridesmaids. The day after our arrival I was only allowed a one-day tour of Naples before repacking. At least the dowry would be left behind; this would be the first time I'd be packing on my terms. I vowed to travel light.

The wonders of the local Neopolitan shops would have to wait until after I'd seen what I was certain was *truly* the most beautiful city. We traveled there by sea as we had to Naples. To say that Rome is a magnificent, glorious, and beautiful city does it no justice. The popes had done wonders for the place over the years. I defy anyone to attend High Mass at St. Peter's and not be inspired by the beauty of the ceremony, and by all the artwork within. I would have loved to see the Sistine Chapel, but that's inside the Vatican, and ordinary mortals weren't allowed inside at the time. Almost all of the ancient landmarks I wanted to see were there, but most of the city had been completely built up and decorated by the greatest artists of the times. If only I'd been born a few hundred years earlier, I might have actually met Michelangelo. He sculpted his men well.

Frederico could hardly keep his hands off me while I could hardly keep my eyes off of the sights. We were staying at the house of an old family friend. He was a Sicilian businessman who, like most, lived in Rome and collected his money from Sicily. My father was one of the few who'd insisted on staying in his homeland. Fortunately for us, he continued making his fortune anyway. I was sad about leaving my homeland for the foreign capital, but I certainly had no qualms about honeymooning in Rome.

Our host treated us to yet another banquet. The only person I knew there was Frederico; our Roman friend was nowhere to be seen. Not surprising, considering that he'd been my father's guest, not the Caglionis. Most of the table conversation centered around us newlyweds. I still wanted to have plenty of children, but not as many as I'd wanted as a child. At worst I think several hundred had been my goal. Now my expectations were more realistic. I couldn't say that blissful happiness was what I felt at this point; acceptance of my fate was probably more accurate. Obviously I wasn't in love with my husband, nor did I think I ever would be. Frederico was not a bad man. He was going to be a more than excellent provider. In fact, now that he was married, his father was going to retire and hand over everything to Frederico. I wasn't going to lack for anything. Nothing material, that is. It's simply that I knew somehow that if I got any satisfaction from our union at all, it would be from the children we were bound to have. I could live with devoting my life to my children if it came to that.

One of my greatest thrills while in Rome came from the marvelous symphonies we attended. We were privileged to hear Haydn's latest, not to mention a Vivaldi concerto or two. *Le Quattro Stagioni* was my favorite of his. I only wish that the composer had lived to conduct the performance himself, but the musicians performed more than adequately without him. Most of these events occurred from afternoon to evening, but several symphonies began at night, and we attended almost all of them.

One of my pleasures was to take the opera glasses

and spy on the audience,—especially on the people in the boxes opposite us. And one night I stifled a gasp when I discovered the one and only Signore da Clovino in the fifth box. From then on I hardly heard the music, so intent did I become on my spying. Frederico tried to attract my attention sometimes, saying I was rude to stare at others, but this instance couldn't be helped. Besides, it's not as if there was dancing going on; there was only the orchestra to watch. It wasn't until near the end that my good Catholic upbringing surfaced, and I became ashamed of my thoughts. But only a little bit. After all, I was frustrated that not once did da Clovino turn his head towards me. At least he didn't discover me that way.

The same thing occurred during some other performances. I noted that he always missed the early performances but I came to no conclusions about this. As the theaters emptied, I tried to find him, but almost every time he escaped my view. Besides, Frederico usually ushered me very quickly through the crowds and into our carriage, leaving little opportunity to see anything, or anyone.

Until the last night, that is. As usual my husband was in a hurry to get out and get home, and there were few people outside, when from the corner of my eye I spotted a figure walking away from the theater and into the dark streets. His movements and clothing told me that it had to be my Roman friend. Our carriage had just arrived when da Clovino stopped, looked around slightly, then seemed to melt into the shadows. I stared more intently just as Frederico was ushering me into the carriage, and saw a big, black, shadowy thing fly straight up from the exact spot where da Clovino had been. The light from a passing carriage lantern revealed nothing now in that spot, and from there Frederico shoved me all the way inside.

I was silent most of the way home. Frederico made a comment about this, but I eased his concern with a remark about how thrilling the symphony had been. In truth, the music was still playing in my mind, but only to accompany the memory of that . . . something that I'd just seen that night.

I forced myself to forget what I'd seen. After all, the light had been terrible. Further contemplation of such things could only lead to madness, of course.

Chapter 5

By now it should be obvious that I had failed to be the good Catholic wife. It's taught that thinking of adultery is the same as committing it, and if so, I'd more then filled my quota of sin. I tried in vain to convince myself that I was acting like the silly girl I'd been with all those boyfriends. I then tried to remind myself of my marital obligations: namely, keeping my mind on my husband and not on others. The problem is that I felt guilty only because I'd been taught it was something to feel guilty about. Confession would solve nothing, as one has to be truly repentant for it to work. It's not as if I didn't try to make myself feel guilty. All I learned is that the heart is not easily controlled.

It became obvious soon into our honeymoon that Signore da Clovino had not invited us to visit him while we were in Rome, or Frederico would have told me by then. I could have made certain by asking him, but I wasn't about to take the chance of arousing his suspicions. Even worse would have been if I'd asked Frederico to invite him over to our host's house. He was supposed to be my father's acquaintance, not mine.

I was getting nowhere fast and had to face my demons myself, even if it meant having to sneak off into the night looking for the man. Unfortunately it took some time to get even a clue of his whereabouts. This I'd discreetly learned during one of our hosts's many social gatherings, most of which were in our honor. During the brief moments when Frederico was not all over me, I took the opportunity to mingle, and inquire about da Clovino's location. It seemed strange that no one seemed to have heard of him; perhaps he wasn't as prominent as I'd thought. Nevertheless I found one person who had heard of him, but could only suggest that I look around in the northeast.

I would have preferred going in the daytime, but my husband might have been in the way. Fortunately he'd been drinking all day during another party and retired early. He fell asleep quickly, without demanding favors of me, so I was free to creep quietly out of bed and gather my clothes. He wasn't likely to sleep lightly that night, either.

I had already paid a driver plenty to bring a carriage around at night. I climbed in and spent the entire journey reminding myself of the foolishness of my actions. But this was something that was not going to go away.

I would describe the estates in the northeastern section of Rome, except I couldn't see them at this hour. I instructed the driver to keep going, however, as I had the feeling I would know the da Clovino residence when we passed it. And coming upon us from the distance was one house with faint lights coming from within. All other places were pitch black.

I ordered the driver to stop and debated having him stay there while I tried the door. Eventually I decided to trust my instincts, and sent him away. After the carriage disappeared into the night, I swept through the gates and walked along the long path to the house as fearlessly as I could. It was a full moon out, which made me nervous, for I'd heard that full moons caused madness, but at least it made things easier to see.

I reached a section of thick bushes and some trees, when a door opened at a balcony, so I ducked behind a tree and watched. A figure stepped outside, silhouetted from the light behind it, but the moonlight let me see that it was a man. I watched him step all the way to the front of the balcony and lean forward. He seemed to be taking in his surroundings before he—before he—well, I wasn't sure then, but it appeared to me that the man suddenly leapt from the balcony, and I heard something flapping in the breeze. I began to stand up from behind the tree, when a huge bird or some other great, flying creature shrieked by me. I almost screamed, but instead leapt off into the bushes and cowered there for only a moment. Then I bolted for the supposed safety of the city streets as though the gates of Hell had opened behind me. I slammed the gates shut behind me and clenched my fingers onto the bars, hoping for some reason that I could espy the—the whatever it was.

This time I cried out when a great black shape shrieked by me again, and I could have sworn it was a bat, but I'd never heard of them being so big. I turned tail and ran for dear life until I could run no more. Finally I found a good wagon to hide under, terrified that whatever that was had seen me and now wanted to hunt. After some moments I managed to catch my breath enough to be sufficiently quiet. I lifted my head ever so slowly, and peeked out—the coast seemed clear.

Reason demands that I should have gone straight back to the Caglionis, but I convinced myself that I was just being a frightened little girl. Once again I moved with purpose towards those gates, through them, and up the path all the way to the door. There were still faint lights coming from within, so I knocked quietly on the door. After a moment I gathered the courage to knock very loudly, when the door swung open. A tall blond woman was there.

"Yes?" she said.

I curtsied briefly.

"Good evening," I said. "I . . . I hope you can forgive me for coming at so unnatural an hour, but—I was wondering. Would this be the house of Signore Antonio da Clovino?"

"Yes," she said, after some time. "Do you have business with him?"

"I . . . um, actually, h-he is a friend of my father's, Signore Alfredo Allogiamento," I said. "H-he attended your wedding. I-I mean *my* wedding. He attended *my* wedding."

"I see," the woman said. "And . . . your business with him is . . . ?"

"Uh—well, actually, I have a—brief message from my father," I said. "He asked me to deliver it, as I'm here on my honeymoon, you see."

"Oh. Congratulations," the woman said woodenly.

"Grazie," I said. "Uh—might the *signore* be here? But then, he must be asleep now—"

"He is not asleep," she said. "In fact, at this time he's on an . . . errand. But he will be returning soon. I can show where you can wait for him. This way, *signora.*"

"Oh! *Grazie,*" I said, and followed her within. His foyer was paved wall-to-wall with mosaic tile, and I momentarily lost my concentration while looking at it and bumped into the woman.

"Oh! Forgive me," I flustered. "I was just admiring this—"

"Quite all right," she said. "Come with me."

I followed her along a hallway, where she stopped at a door and opened it for me.

"I will tell the *signore* you are waiting for him here," she said.

"Grazie, signora . . . grazie," I said, and bowed slightly.

"Yes, go on," she said, and I entered. She shut the door behind me before I could say any more.

It looked much like a receiving room, which it was. There were some comfortable couches and chairs, a painting here and there, and a serving tray off on a small table. No wine on the tray, though. I sat down on one of the couches and fidgeted while waiting, hoping that I hadn't made an enormous mistake.

After an eternity a knock came at the door. I answered, and it opened slowly to reveal da Clovino himself. I started and rose quickly.

"Oh, *signore!"* I said, fixing my dress. "You've returned. I-I hope I've caused you no inconvenience."

"Not at all, uh—why, Signora Caglioni, is it?"

"Aye," I said. "Yes, it is."

"So it is," he said. "Sit, sit."

I sat down again, and he went over to a sofa and settled in.

"So—I'm told you have a message from your father," he said.

"Oh!" I said. "Um . . . there actually is no message. I-I was just trying to get past your servant."

"She's not exactly my . . . servant," he said, "But—there is *no* message? Then . . . to what do I owe the honor of your presence?"

"I . . . um . . ." I murmured, then looked him in the eyes. *"Signore,"* I began, "when you attended the wedding, did you not—well, did you ever suggest to my husband that—well, that we ought to visit you while in Rome?"

"I . . . no, I don't believe I did," he said. "I didn't think it would be appropriate. Unless . . . should I have? I hope that didn't come across as rude or ungracious."

"Uh—oh," I said, "I wouldn't presume to judge you for that, I . . . only thought it odd that you hadn't."

"I see," he said. "Then, this is why you're here now? To ask me to invite you here?"

"Oh . . ." I said, shifting in my seat, "a-actually, *signore,* I—well, in that case, perhaps I ought to invite you to visit us. While we're here, I mean. We're staying with an old friend of the Caglionis."

"Then . . . wouldn't it be more appropriate for him to invite me?"

"Oh, he's been having informal gatherings every other day for us, *signore,*" I said. "And you're a friend of *my* family's."

"Oh . . . really, your father and I have had very minor dealings here and there. Besides, to be honest, I've been very busy these past few weeks. I don't think I could find the time."

"Oh," I said, perhaps a bit too sadly. "Well—I only thought to be gracious." There was some silence before da Clovino broke it.

"Signora," he murmured, and I looked up, "exactly . . . why is it so important that I attend one of your gatherings?"

I opened my mouth, but couldn't speak. I wanted to blurt out a confession, but couldn't. Da Clovino sighed and rose from his seat.

"Why don't you come with me?" he said, holding out his hand. Hesitantly I took it and let him pull me to my feet. From there he escorted me from the room and down the hallway to a large room. There were other people there—about six of them, all gathered around a fireplace, goblets in hand. I think some of the men there had accompanied da Clovino to my father's. There was another tall woman there—also blond.

"Would you care for some wine, *signora?*" da Clovino said.

"Uh—uh, yes, *signore,*" I said. "I'd love some."

Da Clovino gestured to the first tall woman, who bowed slightly and left the room. Then he patted my arm and gestured to the others.

"My people," he said, "May I present Signora Caglioni. She's come all the way from Palermo to pay us a visit."

"Actually . . ." I said, "All the way from Naples."

"Naples? Your family has moved?"

"Oh, no, we're still very much in Palermo," I said. "Naples is where my husband lives."

"And where you live, too," he said.

"Oh, yes," I said, blushing and laughing nervously, "I-I—I'm still getting used to it all."

"Yes," he said, "I know the feeling. So this is your honeymoon, eh? Tell me that Rome hasn't disappointed you."

"Disappointed?" I said incredulously, and was at a loss for words momentarily. "I . . . I . . . forgive me," I said, calming myself. "It's just that never have I seen a more magnificent city. Oh, Naples is beautiful, and of course, so is my home, but Rome—! It takes my breath away!"

He smiled a little and tucked a finger under my chin.

"I'm glad you are a woman who can appreciate beauty," he said. I said nothing, but only looked into his smoldering brown eyes until he suddenly turned away. For a moment I could have sworn my thoughts had no longer been mine in that brief moment.

"So what brings you here, *signora?*" he said.

"Ummm," I began, when the first woman saved me by returning with my wine. *"Grazie,"* I murmured, and was about to sip from the goblet, when da Clovino held out his hand.

"No, no, *signora,*" he said. "We must toast first." I smiled and held up my goblet.

"To our honored guest," he said, holding his drink aloft. The others followed. "To Signora Caglioni, who has traveled all this way to grace us with her presence."

"Hear, hear," the others said, and we drank.

"Grazie, signore," I said, blushing. "And . . . this wine is excellent."

"Grazie," he said, and took up my hand and kissed it. I'm certain I turned as red as my wine. Then he released my hand and distanced himself from me a bit.

"So you truly enjoy Rome, eh, *signora?*" he said.

"Oh, yes."

"Ah. No doubt you wish you could live here, then."

"Oh . . . well . . . I don't know, actually," I said. "But then, even if I could, that would be up to my husband."

"Naturally," he said. "Still, you might manage to visit here often. Do the Caglionis own land here?"

"I . . . I don't know."

"Well, if they don't, they should," he said. "It's quite a place up here."

"Oh, yes, absolutely," I said.

"Yes," he said. "Then . . . your husband, *signora.* Naturally he knows you're here. Yes?"

"Hm? Oh! Oh, of course he does, *signore,*" I said. "He was simply too . . . well, we'd been celebrating, and the wine wouldn't stop pouring, and, um . . ."

"I see," he said, and then turned to the others present. With an unspoken command he sent them away. I looked up to see them putting down their goblets and filing out of the room.

"I-I . . ." I stammered, watching the last of them

leave. "Have I done something wrong? Have I offended?"

"No," he said, "No, you haven't offended. I only thought it was time for us to be alone." He sat in a chair and gestured towards another.

"Sit, sit," he said, and I did so.

"Now," he said, "first of all, your husband doesn't know you're here."

"Why, *signore,* of course he does, I just—" I began, but then stopped myself, bit my lip and looked down, shaking my head slowly.

"I see. So you waited for him to go to sleep, and then rode over by yourself. Correct?"

". . . Yes," I whispered.

"Look at me," he said. "You've nothing to fear from me."

"Sorry," I said, looking up.

"I *would* worry about *him,* though," he said. "Your husband."

"I know," I said. "But he will never know. I . . . I only wanted to . . ."

"Wanted to what, *signora?*"

"I . . . I have sinned greatly, *signore,*" I murmured.

"Have you?"

"Yes," I whispered. "Very greatly."

"I'm . . . sorry to hear that," he said. "But I think you're supposed to tell the priests about that, not me."

"No, *signore,* I—the priests couldn't help me," I said. "Confession won't help me, I know it won't. I—I had to see you, instead."

"Why?"

"Ohhhh . . ." I said, standing now, "You must be able to see, *signore.* I-I have been unfaithful to my husband. Unfaithful because I am here! Now!"

"But we've done nothing but talk, *signora,*" he said. "You haven't sinned."

"But I have, *signore!*" I said, falling to his feet. "I may only speak to you, but my mind—! My heart, it—that is where I sin, *signore.* No matter how much I try I can't make my thoughts of you leave me!"

There was some silence while I tried to regain my composure. Slowly I rose to my feet, unable to meet his gaze until I'd sat down again. He seemed to be in deep contemplation all the while.

"Am I to understand," he said slowly, "that you . . . are in love with me?"

". . . Yes," I whispered after much effort. "And the worst of it is—I don't want what I feel to go away."

"But you just said—"

"I only wish those thoughts to leave because I know they are sinful," I said. "But my heart. It—it—"

There was more silence while I looked down and fought off tears.

"Signora," he said quietly. I looked up. "I . . . learned long ago that it's not wise to become involved with married women," he said.

"I know that, *signore.*"

"Then . . . no doubt you'll appreciate the wisdom of my sending you back to your husband."

"Absolutely, there is tremendous wisdom in that," I said. "But—I don't think it will change how I feel one bit."

"That . . . is not my concern," he said.

"I know that, *signore,*" I said. "I know that this is entirely my fault. Who am I to . . . to tell you this at all? Who am I to disturb your rest and probably keep you from getting a decent night's sleep for some time? But—if you will only grant me this one thing—to answer a question."

"Ask," he said.

"Before tonight," I began, "that is, long ago, when we first met. The way you looked at me, *signore.* At the banquet. That one brief moment, at our front door. Even at my wedding."

"What is your point, *signora?*"

"My point is—my point is that you seemed to . . . think the same of me. Or . . . do I flatter myself?"

"That's possible," he said.

"Oh," I said sadly. "Well, I suppose my imagination has run away from me at times. I . . . I think I was just trying to make things easier."

"Probably."

"Forgive me, *signore,*" I said. "I didn't realize you didn't find me attractive."

"Oh, I never said that," he said.

"Then you *did* think I was—"

"I would be lying if I said you weren't a beautiful woman, *signora,*" he said. "But then, I'm not about to steal away from her husband every beautiful woman I see."

"Of course not," I said. "That would be a terrible thing. But I only meant—I meant . . ."

Da Clovino waited patiently for me to continue, but I began to weep softly instead. A marvelous thing, to feel guilty and not guilty at the same time. He offered a hand in comfort, and I took it and squeezed, but then pushed it away when it sent my thoughts awhirl. I stood up and turned from him.

"Forgive me, *signore,*" I said. "I-I knew this was a foolish thing, to come here. But I couldn't stop myself. I-I thought . . . I thought perhaps that seeing you, and telling you this might . . . might help me settle things, but it's only made things worse."

"I'll tell you what, *signora,*" I heard him say behind me. He placed a hand on my shoulder. "No harm was done here," he continued. "If you wish to go talk to priests about this, then do so, but as for myself . . .

you weren't here. But for both our sakes, I suggest that you believe that yourself. You were never here."

"What of your servants, *signore?*" I asked.

"What of them?"

"Won't they . . . talk?" I asked. I heard him laugh.

"Nothing leaves or enters this house without my permission," he said. "Not even gossip."

"I pray that you're right," I said. "I know that I must leave you. But I also know that even if I never see you again, *signore,* I—I will always love you."

"No more of that," he said. "Go back to your husband now."

"Of course," I said.

"Good," he said, and turned me around to face him. "Now I must ask you to wait here while I have a carriage sent for."

"Yes, I'll wait," I said, and he left. I stood still a moment before wandering slowly about the room. I found one of his guest's goblets. There was still wine left in it, so I look around furtively before finishing it off.

I spat the wine across the room and onto the walls. I gasped and almost dropped the foul liquid and looked around desperately for a rag or something to clean up with. Finding none, I looked down into the goblet and smelled it. It smelled like . . . I collected some of the remaining liquid with my finger and smelled it again.

"Your carriage will be—" I heard before crying out and dropping the goblet. It bounced noisily several times while I scrambled to grab it.

"Oh! Y-you startled me," I said, grabbing the goblet and putting it quickly onto a table. "I didn't mean to make such a mess."

"That's quite all right," da Clovino said, and came over and held my shoulders gently. Then he saw the red stuff on my finger.

"Why, *signora,*" he said, "have you—?"

"What? Uh, no," I said, licking it off quickly, "No, it's nothing. Only a small cut."

"Oh," he said. "Well, if it's nothing serious—"

"It isn't," I said quickly. "Just a tiny prick."

"Ah. Well, I only came to say that a carriage has been called. It'll be around front any moment."

"Grazie, signore," I said. Then he saw the wall.

"Eh?" he said. "What happened there?"

"What? Oh!" I said, and went over to smear some of it with my hand. "It . . . I only thought to . . . well, I had a wine glass in hand, but then tripped and . . . it hit the wall. Please forgive me."

"Um . . . think nothing of it," he said, pulling me away gently from the wall. "Someone will clean it. Don't worry."

"Oh, but I tried to clean it before, but there was nothing to—" I said, and then he held my shoulders again and looked straight into my eyes.

"I said don't worry, Theresa," he said.

"Ohhh," I whispered, unable to look away now. "You called me Ther—"

"Signora," he corrected, "I called you *signora.*"

"Yes . . ." I said, "you called me *signora.*"

"And now . . ." he continued, "I want you to return home. Return to your husband, and go to sleep. Sleep in your warm, soft bed."

"Warm and soft . . . Yes . . ."

"Good girl," he said.

Chapter 6

Somehow I found myself eating breakfast with Frederico without quite remembering how I got there. Naturally this made me wonder if I'd simply had a strange dream the night before. Nevertheless Frederico thought something was wrong because I spent a lot of time that morning stirring my food around aimlessly. I assured him that I was fine; I'd simply been wondering about this dream about a group of pale, thin people at some big house, and instead of wine they'd been drinking blood. I soon regretted mentioning the blood, as then he wondered if I'd been thinking about witches or something. I eased his feelings by saying it had been a horrible nightmare.

It had been a terrible mistake to do what I'd done that night. Had I learned my lesson? If so, then why was I planning on how to get back there? That could not have been a dream. Those people had not been drinking wine, and I could still taste some blood on my finger. Something flew past me that night, and it wasn't a bird. Something also flew away from the theater that night, and that had been no bird, either.

I was hoping I'd be able to use our host's library that day, but Frederico was attached to my hip all day, as usual. Besides, it wouldn't be to my advantage to try and explain why I was so interested in looking up information on creatures who drank blood but looked human—if our host even had any books about them. The answer wasn't as obvious as it may seem. After all, just about every evil creature was believed to be a blood-drinker in my time. All I had to rely upon, then, was my own knowledge, accumulated through the years, of old stories about ghosts, witches, hobgoblins, and so on.

After some time I narrowed it down to a few possibilities. These people were either witches, ghouls, vampires, werewolves, or I was wasting my time fretting about a nightmare. I truly wanted to believe that I'd only been dreaming—after all, I didn't even remember the ride home—but the few memories were entirely too vivid. My dreams until then had almost always been vague, colorless, and rarely with any lasting images. The ones I could remember, anyway. This dream had had purpose.

My husband retired late that evening. That was fine; in a rare moment alone I'd been able to hire a carriage driver to come by at midnight, regardless of when the others were abed. I climbed aboard at midnight, and we were off. I was well armed with all the things I needed to confront da Clovino and his group. The only thing I was concerned about was that the servant woman, or whatever she was, wouldn't let me in this time.

The da Clovino residence came into view, and I was not surprised to see light shining from within. The gates were wide open when I climbed out. I looked around a little, but saw nothing amiss, so I continued along the pathway to the house.

At the door I pulled out the crucifix from around my

neck and held it. I was about to knock on the door but decided to cross myself first. Then I knocked. As usual the tall woman answered. She cocked an eyebrow and frowned at the sight of me. I opened my mouth to speak, but no words escaped.

"Yyyeees?" she said. I regained my composure finally.

"I . . . I would see Signore da Clovino," I said. "It's very important that I see him."

"Very well," said the woman, and she stepped aside. I stared for a moment, wondering if she was really letting me in without a fight, or if it was some jest. I accepted the former and stepped past her wordlessly.

"The master is in his study," she said. "I will announce you."

"Um . . . *grazie,*" I said quietly, and watched her turn the corner before I let out a deep sigh. I shut my eyes and crossed myself again, and gripped the crucifix tighter. I heard the woman coming back around the corner.

"He will see you now, *signora,*" the woman said, and I followed her.

He had some papers spread out on a desk and was apparently writing something when I intruded. At my appearance he rose from his seat.

"*Signora,*" he said, bowing slightly and gesturing to an empty seat. "Um . . . well, I'm surprised, to say the least. Won't you sit, then?"

"*Grazie, signore,*" I whispered, and sat down. I heard the door shut behind me, and turned quickly to look. Then da Clovino cleared his throat, and I whirled back around to face him.

"It's only the door," he said, smiling slightly.

"Of course," I said. "Just the door."

There was silence while da Clovino seemed to be studying me. Try as I did, I couldn't begin speaking.

"So, *signora,*" he began, "As before, this is a . . . surprise to see you again."

"I know that, *signore,*" I said. "I know you must be furious with me for returning, even though we both know last night was a terrible mistake. Yet once again, I am here and without my husband's knowledge."

"Yes, you are," he said, "But—even this can be averted. You can still return to the safety of—"

"No," I said.

"What's that?"

"No," I repeated. "I . . . I won't be returning to Frederico."

". . . Oh," he said. "I see. Then . . . he discovered what happened last night?"

"Oh, no," I said quickly. "He has no idea I was here. He has no idea I'm here now, either."

"Then . . . ?" he said, gesturing for me to continue.

"I-I—don't want to return to him," I said. "I don't want to be married to him anymore."

"Why not?"

"Because . . . because I don't love him."

". . . And? So?"

"So?" I said. "But I don't love him. And . . . I don't think I ever will."

"That's not any concern of mine."

"Of course it isn't," I said, looking down. "It's mine. You need do nothing."

"I'm glad to know that," he said. "But then, how exactly are you not going to be married to him now?"

"I-I don't know yet," I said. "But I will find a way."

"Um . . . correct me if I'm wrong, but—isn't it a bit difficult to divorce one's husband these days?"

"There's no divorce, for me," I said. "But . . . it could be annulled."

"I've heard that's difficult, too."

"Um . . . well, yes, it is," I said. "In fact, I—well, the only way to . . . to obtain that is—well, through unfaithfulness, or—"

"You seem to think you're being unfaithful now."

"I-I suppose I am, but—then, there is the death of the spouse."

"Ah," he said. "An unfortunate but effective—wait," he said. "You're not seriously considering—"

"Killing him?" I said. "No! No, of course not, I—I don't hate him, *signore*. Truly, Frederico is a good man. A . . . good provider. But in spite of this I can't bring myself to love him."

"Because . . . you love me instead," he sighed, and rubbed his nose in frustration. *"Signora,"* he said without looking up, "please consider yourself extremely fortunate that not only am I going to allow you to leave here again, but I am going to let you leave intact."

"What—what do you mean, intact?"

"I mean, that you could use a good slap about now," he said. "Maybe even a spanking."

"A spanking?" I cried, standing up abruptly. "What do you mean, a spanking? I am not some child before you, Signore da Clovino!"

"Then what are you?" he cried back. For a moment I could have sworn his eyes flashed red. "If you're supposed to be an adult woman, then act like one! Enough of this ridiculous little-girl crush on me! Have you no idea what—?"

"Little-girl crush?" I said. "Do my feelings truly mean so little to you?"

"They're meaning less and less with each moment, I'll say that much."

"Well, I never—!"

"Then keep it that way, and leave here now before you're thrown out!"

"You don't even know why I'm here at all, do you?"

"I've got a pretty good idea, now—"

"I am not here for the same reason as last night's, Signore da Clovino!" I cried, and there was silence. Da Clovino was about to point and shout some more, then stopped himself and frowned.

"Another reason, eh?" he murmured. "Please—favor me with your reason."

"I've discovered your secret, *signore,*" I said. "I know . . . I know what you are. I know what the others who were here last night are, too."

"I'm pleased to know that," he said. "So what exactly are we?"

"You are—you are vampires, *signore,*" I said, my voice wavering. "It's the only explanation for what happened here."

I half expected him to hiss and growl and perhaps even bare his fangs at me, but I clung tighter to my crucifix in the hope that it would get me through the next step. I also half expected him to laugh in my face.

At least he had a nice laugh. Full and hearty, but not loud.

"Ahhh, *signora,*" he said after a while, "so now I'm a vampire, am I? Here I thought you'd come back because you still weren't over your little girl crush."

"*Still* you call it that!"

"Forgive me if I try to display a little sense of humor!" he cried. "I should caution you that not everyone would be so amused when accused of being so horrible a creature as a vampire."

"I don't accuse," I said. "I know."

"Oh, really?" he said. "What are your facts?"

"Last night," I said, "I was—as I approached last night, I saw a man. He was coming out of the house onto the balcony. Then, as I watched, he—the man seemed to disappear—as if melting into the shadows—and a huge . . . big, black . . . thing flew by me. A giant bird, or even . . . a bat?"

"And?" he said after a time.

"And . . ." I continued, "when I was here, I—I tasted some of your leftover wine. But it wasn't wine. It . . . it was blood."

"Blood."

"Yes," I said. It was getting difficult to breathe. "It *was* blood, I know it was! I didn't swallow it, of course, I—well, you saw the wall."

"So you're saying that you spit it up."

"Yes," I said. "I spit it up, and—when I returned home—this afternoon I hoped to be able to read of this, but—I had to rely on my own knowledge instead."

"Your knowledge of vampires, you mean," he said.

"Exactly," I said.

"So let me contemplate what you've told me so far," he said. "You saw a very shadowy figure blend into the darkness, and then some large, black thing that may or may not have been a bird, or a . . . what was it?"

"A bat."

"A bat," he continued, "and then later on, you drank some sour wine and decided it was—"

"It was *not* sour wine, *signore,*" I said. "I have had wine as sour as wine can be, but never anything like this. That was blood, *signore.* You and your guests were drinking blood!"

"One of them had probably cut his lip, *signora,*" he said. "But then, I need not justify or explain anything to you."

"Why not, *signore?*" I said. "Doesn't it concern you that I could tell others of this?"

"It would concern me," he said, "but not for my own sake. I worry about what others would think of you if you started accusing people of being vampires left and right."

"Not left and right," I said. "I only accuse you, *signore.*"

He sat back and started pulling at his lip in contemplation. I still had my crucifix in hand and wondered just how much protection it was going to give me.

"Do you fear me, *signora?*" he asked quietly after a time.

". . . No," I said. "Perhaps I should, but I don't."

"That is strange," he said, and then took on a friendlier countenance. "I mean, here you accuse me of being some . . . some horrible creature, yet you're not afraid of what I might do to you."

"I . . . I don't believe that you'll hurt me, signore," I said. "In fact I—I'm certain that you'll end up helping me tonight."

"Oh, I am, am I?" he said, smiling. His smile faded rather quickly, however. *"Signora,"* he began, rising from his seat, "I have been much too patient with you for my own good. Now I—"

"What—what are you doing?" I said, cringing back and gripping my crucifix tightly.

"I'm going to ask you to *leave,* that's what!" he said. "You've done nothing but waste my time, not to mention—"

He placed a hand on my shoulder, and I cried out and thrust my crucifix into plain view. He winced and moved backwards, but that was all.

"What are you—?" he said, and then frowned and snatched it from my hands. "What's this all about? Am I supposed to be afraid of this now?"

"What?" I whispered. "But you—I thought this would . . ."

"Would what?" he said. "Burn me at its touch? Is that something else that happens to vampires?"

"I—I—"

"This used to be amusing, *signora,*" he said, placing the cross on a table. "But no more. This is only wasting both our time. Now this is the last time I will tell you to stop acting like a child and go back to your husband, and *stay* back!"

"I . . . of course, *signore,* I—yes, of course," I said, snatching up my cross without looking him in the eyes. I rose from my seat and made for the door.

"But the blood . . ." I whispered to myself.

"What was that?" he said.

I shook my head without turning around.

"N-nothing, *signore,*" I murmured. "Nothing."

"*Signora,*" he called to me just as I reached the door. I still didn't turn around. "Don't feel too bad. Be glad that I once thought this amusing at all. Besides, for all we know you might be right about vampires. I have no doubts there are people out there . . . depraved enough to feed on blood. And they might even be afraid of God's symbols. But I'd be very careful about who you accuse; for some, your faith might have to be stronger . . ."

"Antonio . . ." I whispered. I heard him sigh.

"What is it," he said quietly, but impatiently.

"I . . ." I began, and then swallowed, "I want to be a vampire."

I heard nothing for a while, and then heard him coming towards me. He held my chin and turned my head to face him.

"Go home, little girl," he murmured. "Or you truly *will* have reason to fear me."

"I—I don't fear you," I whispered. "Because . . . I know that you can help me. You can make me a vampire. Why can't you help me? Why *won't* you help me?"

"Consider yourself fortunate that I've given you more than a second chance to turn back."

"I don't want to."

"You're a foolish little girl."

"I'm not a little girl," I said. "And I am *not* foolish."

"You have no idea what you ask for."

"I do. This is not something I've decided on a moment's thought. True, I didn't realize until today that I wanted to be a vampire, but I've known for a long time that I don't want the life that's been chosen for me."

"Well, life is difficult, isn't it?"

"Please, Antonio! I understand what I'm asking for. I even know what I'd be giving up."

"Do you?"

"Of course," I said. "I know that I would never see the sun again. I know that—that I would have to live off the blood of others. I know those things. But I also know what I'll gain. Strength. Power. Immortality! It's said vampires could live forever, barring any great damage to them. And you—you seem so young, but I wouldn't be surprised if you were hundreds of years old!"

"Theresa—"

"Make me a vampire, and I'll be your disciple," I said. "I—I will join you, learn from you, help you—"

"Theresa!"

"Change me, Antonio," I said. "Please."

He didn't answer for a long time, but first turned away and sighed in frustration. He held the bridge of his nose for a long time as though in deep concentration. Finally he turned his attention back on me.

"So it's the answer to your prayers, is it?" he murmured. "Power?"

"I want to make my own choices, Antonio," I said.

"I know I seem foolish when I say why I don't want to be married to Frederico. But it's more than not loving him, for I could be content just loving his children. My children, I mean. It's—it's difficult to explain, for you are a man, and—men have different choices. I would be lucky if I even had a choice. But for the first time, I do; I *do* have a choice. *This* is my way out. But only *you* can help me, Antonio. Only you can help me be free . . ."

"I see," he said, and nothing else. He scratched his chin as though in contemplation again.

"Well?" I said impatiently. "I mean—please give me your answer. Please."

Again, he said nothing, but turned to face me. He placed his hands on my cheeks and stared long and hard into my eyes. I stared back, and could have sworn his eyes were beginning to glow red as embers.

I remember hearing his voice, but not the words. Then his lips pressed against mine, and I kissed back, until his lips glided away to touch my cheeks, and chin, and all along my neck. I shut my eyes and let my head sink back. The last thing I remember was a tiny sting, and then a chill racing from my head to the tips of my toes as a rush of warm blood flowed from my veins.

Chapter 7

The sun seemed exceptionally bright that morning. I had to hold up my arm to block its rays while I climbed out of bed. My surroundings were unnervingly familiar, however, and I almost cried out when I realized that I was back at the house where I'd been staying. I was about to look outside to see if, indeed, I was back with Frederico, when a knock came at the door. Fending off my growing rage, I rushed to the door and opened it quickly. Frederico was there, and seemed startled.

"Wh—? Theresa, darling," he said, "Is something the matter?"

"What? Uh—uh, no," I said. "Forgive me, I didn't mean to startle you."

"Ah, no matter," he said. "But, I was wondering, is everything all right? You've slept so long."

"I have?" I said. "But—how long *have* I slept, then?"

"Oh, well, I was just about to start lunch," he said. "An hour after noon, at least."

"What? Almost one?"

"Aye," he said. "We were . . . very worried about you. Are you well, my love?"

"Uh—yes," I said, lost in thought. "One o'clock . . . I don't know why I slept so long."

"Then you're not sick?" he said. "You seem pale."

"Do I?" I said, going over to my mirror now. He was right in that case. I also looked thinner than usual. Frederico followed me over and wrapped his arms around me.

"Perhaps it's because you slept through breakfast," he whispered into my ear. "A good meal will get your health back," he added, then kissed my neck.

"Oh—have you scratched yourself, my love?" he said.

"What?" I said, looking back into the mirror. On my neck were two tiny scabs. "I . . . I don't know, darling," I said. "But—I ought to get dressed now, and join you for lunch. Go on now, I'll be along."

"If you say so," he said, and released me. "Just don't fall asleep on the way."

"Of course not, uh, darling," I said, still examining my neck. Frederico left the room, and I checked the other side of my neck, but there were no marks. I thought for a moment, and then went over to the window to look out, but the sun seemed even brighter. It was all I could do to hold my arm up long enough to close the shutters.

I didn't realize how hungry I was until we began lunch, nor how weak I was until I tried to pass a heavy plate. The effort almost winded me, which concerned my husband. I assured him that I hadn't slept well and agreed that I just needed a good meal. I hid my rage well from Frederico, who had big sightseeing plans for us that day.

Why had I been betrayed this way? I offered myself to him, yet he chose to toy with me. I contemplated hiring a covered carriage (shade from the sun) and pounding on his doors until I was given entrance, but of course would have to wait for nightfall instead. And this time, I wouldn't leave until I either got what I wanted, or was dead.

Dinner wasn't very appetizing. The food was probably delicious, but I couldn't seem to appreciate it as in the past. Everything tasted dull, except for the meat, which I kept asking to be cooked less and less each time. Frederico commented that I didn't seem to have any more color in my face than before, but I waved it off as nothing. I felt like hell, of course, and was very enthusiastic about having some choice words with Antonio that night.

Frederico wouldn't be satisfied until I promised to retire early that night, so I made a point of getting undressed and climbing into bed. I forced my eyes to stay open long as I could, but it didn't seem to work. After a time I sat up abruptly in bed, wondering if I was too late, if it was morning again. Frederico had climbed into bed without my noticing and was in a dead sleep. It was to my advantage that he was such a sound sleeper. Meanwhile I noticed that the moon was up, and soon discovered what had woken me up. My name. Someone was calling my name, but I don't think I was hearing it. That is, I don't think my ears heard it, but I'm certain my mind did. My name was being whispered straight into my mind, so without hesitation I slipped on a heavy robe and some slippers, and peered outside. I saw nothing, but felt my name again, and then felt my legs moving. Now I wasn't just being called, I was being summoned, even *pulled* to the source.

A spell of some kind moved my legs from under me, making me walk silently through the halls. I tried to resist at first, until a calming sensation swept over me, a great, soothing wave of pleasure that made me moan quietly and shut my eyes. From there I let my body move itself and began to enjoy the experience.

The air became colder, and I felt lips press over mine, and I let them do their work until they released me. Only then did I open my eyes, and jumped back from the lips' owner.

"You!" I said. "What are you doing here? What have you done to me?"

Antonio held up a finger to silence me, but in vain.

"Don't you shush me!" I cried. "Why have you done this? You toy with me, Antonio."

"I don't toy with you, *signora,*" he said.

"Then why haven't you given me what I want? Why do you only sample my blood instead of taking *all* of it?"

"How do you know this isn't the way it's done in the first place?" he said. "Or do you claim your knowledge of us is greater than mine?"

"I—" I said, and then calmed myself. "Forgive me, Antonio," I whispered. "Then—you are here to complete it, yes?"

"Perhaps," he said, and smiled. "I only thought I'd give you the opportunity to reconsider."

"What? But there is nothing to—!" I said, but he held up a finger again, so I continued to whisper. "There is nothing *to* reconsider."

He didn't answer at first, but waved for me to follow him to a less conspicuous place than the middle of the courtyard. We moved behind the stables.

"Antonio," I whispered, "Why didn't you finish the job? Why tease me like this?"

"As I said, I thought I'd give you the chance to think it over."

"But I *have* thought it over! *This* is what I want! Why, I—I thought you'd be delighted to meet someone who *wants* to join you. I thought you'd—"

"I never turn down those who ask to be converted," he said. "And if this is what you truly want, then you shall be a vampire. But . . . I only thought it might do you good to consider what you'll be losing."

"Frederico?" I said. "So I will lose his wealth. But as I said, I don't love him, so what will I truly be losing?"

"Do you love your family?"

"Of course."

"Then you would mind losing them."

"Why must I lose my family?"

"Well, probably not from becoming a vampire—not if you hide it well enough. But I don't think you'll be very welcome at home when you try to obtain annulment without a . . . suitable explanation."

"Well, I'm certain we'll be able to come up with something."

"We?" he said. "*We* will come up with something?"

"You mean you won't help me?"

"Of course I will, if it's what you really want," he said. "But the consequences are *your* concern, not mine."

"But—"

"If you find that you don't like your new existence, I'm afraid the only way out of it is death. You can't become human again."

"I . . . I must prepare myself for that, then."

"Hmph!" he said with some amusement.

"What?"

"Oh, nothing," he said. "It's just that I don't meet people very often so, uh . . . so passionate about asking for this. In a way, it makes me wonder if there isn't some catch to all this."

"There . . . there is no catch, Antonio," I said. "In

fact I—I even have little to offer you, other than companionship."

"I have enough companions, thank you."

"Obedience, then."

"I have no doubts of that," he said with an odd smile. "Well, then," he said, "It seems you won't mind losing your family after all."

"Oh . . . I will," I murmured. "I will very much. But—this is something I *must* do. This is my opportunity for—for—"

"Freedom?"

"Yes!" I said. "Freedom, Antonio. Freedom to do as I please. To look after myself, to make my *own* fortune."

"Powerful or not, that will be difficult simply because you're a woman."

"I know that," I said. "But I'm willing to try. Please, Antonio; I—I haven't always known what you are, but—from the moment I saw you, I wished it was *you* that Father had found for me, and not Frederico. Somehow, I knew that you were a man that could do more for me than any other man. And I was right, was I not?"

"I don't know," he said. "Perhaps I am. Yet . . . I will give you this gift, Theresa. I'll finish the job, and you'll have the power and immortality you wish for. But I am not willing to nurse the sorrows you'll feel once the consequences begin. Become one of us; but you make your *own* fortune. It is you who demanded this of me; I didn't choose you."

"I . . . I understand," I said. "And yet—you will not even . . . even teach me what I can do? Even if only for a brief time? I am a very quick learner, and—"

"Well, then you can always learn from experience," he said. "Oh, I suppose I could teach you some. One week, then. That's the longest time I can grant you that's safe for *both* of us. For one week only I will give you some basic lessons. But after that time I suggest that you not only leave Rome, but Italy entirely."

"Why?"

"Well, you could always remain and find out why for yourself."

"Is it . . . some consequence of being a vampire?" I asked. "I thought—I thought they could never leave their homeland. Or, mustn't you always bring dirt from there with you?"

"Ummm . . . we'll discuss all that later," he said. "But now—are you ready, Theresa? Are you ready to leave everything you once knew or loved behind?"

"I—I'll be starting a new life," I whispered, then shut my eyes and took a deep breath. "Yes," I whispered, "I am ready."

"Open your eyes, girl," he said, and I opened them to see two glowing embers. They burned straight into my mind, and traveled to my heart, which was now in flames. I could feel, and then hear, my heart beating furiously, working extra hard to pump the hot, red blood now pouring from my body and into his. I sighed long and loud, then drifted into beautiful sleep.

Chapter 8

Somebody was tapping my cheek gently. At first it helped wake me, but quickly became a nuisance, so I smacked at my cheek, and hit a hand. I squeezed, and the fingers squeezed back, so I opened my eyes to see Antonio's face hovering over me. I blinked a few times, and tried to speak, but my throat was too dry. I started coughing and felt my face almost crack when I opened my mouth wide. My skin was so tight; what had happened?

Antonio smiled and helped me sit up. It was then that I saw that I was lying in a coffin, so I gasped and covered my mouth.

"Something wrong, my dear?" he said.

I pointed to the coffin and gestured a bit.

"I'm in a—a—" I whispered, and held my throat.

"Why do they always try to speak before feeding?" he muttered to himself. "Are you upset about this?" he asked me, indicating my bed. I nodded.

"Well, I thought you'd appreciate it," he said. "You . . . do know all about vampires, don't you?"

I almost spoke, but shook my head instead. He smiled and helped me climb out of the box. I'd been in a rather expensive-looking coffin, actually—made of solid mahogany and lined with felt stuffed with down.

Antonio led me from the torch-lit room and up some stairs. There were no other coffins in that room, which I thought odd. I couldn't ask about that until I could wet my throat properly.

He led me through unfamiliar rooms in his house, until we reached his study. Waiting for us within was the servant woman.

"Francesca," he said, "may I present—once again—the Signora Caglioni." Francesca bowed slightly.

"Mistress," she said. "Welcome back."

"Grazie," I croaked, and bowed back, albeit nervously. I coughed some more, which helped moisten my throat.

"Feeding will help that," Antonio said. I nodded while coughing.

"Yes," I whispered. "Perhaps if someone could bring me some water?"

"You won't be drinking water tonight, Theresa," he said. "In fact, you don't need water anymore. Remember?"

"Hnh?" I whispered, and looked up at him. He cocked an eyebrow, and I looked down at my hands and arms. They seemed all right, until I espied a mirror and went to that. I gasped and threw my hands up to my cheeks.

"What—? Wha—?" I sputtered, until Antonio came and took my hands into his. Together we looked at my reflection, which wasn't the beautiful one I'd been accustomed to. This reflection showed a pale, thin, red-eyed wreck of a woman, and when I opened my mouth, long white *sharp* teeth smiled back at me.

"Wh—Wha—Antonio," I whispered. "What is this? Is that *me?* Why have you done this to me?"

"I figured this would bother you," he said, apparently annoyed. "It's only temporary, I assure you."

"Temporary?" I said. "Uh—*how* temporary?"

"A few days, I suppose," he said. "But come; you need to eat."

"But why—? I—I—I'm starved."

"Are you indeed," he said, and guided me over to Francesca. "Now, Theresa,," he said, "I'm afraid you'll have to do this alone. I really have very pressing business tonight."

"Do what alone?"

"Feed, of course," he said. "Francesca will help you. I may see you at the end of the evening, or I may not. That depends on when I'm finished. But until then," he said, taking my hand and kissing it, "I trust you'll be enjoying yourself immensely."

"Um . . . I hope so," I whispered, and he left the room. I stared at the door until Francesca cleared her throat, startling me.

"Oh!" I said, turning around, "Forgive me. I . . . What was I going to do?"

"*Signor* says you're to feed for the first time tonight," she said. "Is that correct?"

"I—I think so," I said. "What does he mean by feeding?"

Francesca smiled coldly. "Sometimes he uses me, but since you've arrived, he wishes you to feed from me. He says my blood is quite good. I hope you like it, too."

"Wh . . . what?" I whispered.

"My blood, mistress," she said. "It's my time now. To be fed from."

"You—your—" I said, then had to sit down. I ran my fingers through my hair and winced when I brushed my tongue against my sharp teeth.

"I—" I began, then held up a hand. "I—I—I have to think for a moment. I have to remember. My throat—it still hurts."

"And it will until you drink, mistress," she said.

"Until I drink . . ." I said, then looked her in the eye. "You—you don't mind? I—it's *your* blood I must take? Does *he* do this?"

"The *signore?*" she asked. "Yes, he does. But only once every two months or so. So I can recover from it."

"You mean, he just feeds from you, but never finishes?" I asked. "He doesn't . . . change you?"

"No," she said. "It's . . . what he wishes of me. And I don't wish to be converted . . . yet. But until then . . ."

"I must . . . feed from you," I said, and sighed. "Yes, I—I suppose I have no right to be repulsed. He—he warned me, or tried to. I knew I would have to do this, but—but it's different when you actually do it."

"I hope it won't be difficult," she said. "For either of us."

"Oh . . ." I said, rising, "I—I don't want to hurt you. But Antonio left me alone here. I don't know how to do this. What if I end up killing you?"

"I'll help you," she said.

"Help me?" I said. "That . . . sounds so strange. I mean, here I have to use you as food, yet you say you'll help me do it."

"It's what he wishes," she said, and held out her hand to me. "Shall we, mistress?"

"I—I suppose I must," I said, and took her hand. She pulled me close to her and tossed one side of her hair behind her neck. Then she put a hand behind my head and pulled me gently towards her.

"What do I do?" I whispered. "I—I don't know if I can do this."

"It will only get worse if you wait," she whispered back. "Come; take some deep breaths, and then . . . then feel my neck." I did as I was told, and reached out to feel the side of her neck.

"Feel it?" she whispered. "Do you feel the blood, mistress?"

"Um . . . yes," I said. "It—it's warm."

"That is my artery, though," she said. "Below that is the vein. Take from there. Otherwise you *will* kill me."

"I don't want to kill you," I whispered. "I—I'm—I'm not sure about this. What if I take too much? Too quickly? Too—?"

"Shh," she said, placing a finger against my lips. "Only enough to quench your thirst. And that will be enough."

"I don't believe this. You're actually helping me eat you."

"You're not eating me. It's only blood."

"Are you sure you don't mind this?"

"As I said, it's what he wishes of me."

"I see," I whispered. "Well—I—here I go, then."

She smiled a little and pulled me slowly towards her. I let my lips rest on her neck, and moved them around until I felt the rush of hot blood under her skin. But I remembered to search below that, so I moved to the base of her neck. There below the artery was another vessel—smaller, but strong, and with a slight grunt I pushed in. Francesca winced and stiffened, and I shut my eyes and held her tightly to me as warm blood rushed from her jugular. I sucked it up as fast as it would come, and Francesca's body became heavier the more I took. Soon my strength alone held her up, but my thirst was yet to be quenched. Whatever repulsion I'd felt before was washed away with her blood. Never had I tasted anything so sweet, so warm, so—good. I had tasted blood for the first time, and I *liked* it, and if I had taken the time to think about it, I would have been repulsed by that.

By the time I'd had my fill, Francesca was unconscious. Carefully I lifted her body and carried it to the sofa, then laid her down gently. I plopped down into a chair and threw my head back and sighed. For a long time nothing at all came to mind—I just sat. Finally, I opened my eyes again and looked over at Francesca, who seemed so peaceful on the couch. Too peaceful, though. I went to the couch and felt her chest. Nothing, so I tried her wrist. She had a pulse, but it was weak. I sighed loudly and plopped down at the edge of the couch.

Now what? I thought. Francesca was alive, but how long would she be unconscious? She could be out for hours, but Antonio had said he wasn't going to see me until the end of the evening, if even then.

I tried to occupy myself with the little trinkets in the room but quickly became bored. Francesca was still unconscious. I tried to shake her awake gently once or twice, each time in vain. I also went to the mirror a few times to try and fix my features, but it usually just made things worse.

Well this is silly! I thought. How was I to learn anything if no one would teach me anything? I rose slowly from the chair and crept over to the door as if afraid to wake Francesca. With a backward glance I opened the door and stepped outside, then shut the door quietly as I could. Once that was done I strode through the hallways, determined to find Antonio. After a time I found him in the main room with some other men. Despite his previous command I went to his side and spoke.

"Antonio," I said, "pray forgive me for this interruption, but I must ask—" Before I could continue he grabbed my arm and dragged me from the room. I was about to protest when we were out of earshot, but he grabbed me roughly and forced me to face him.

"You stupid cow!" he growled. "What do you think you're doing?"

"What? How dare you call me—"

"Did I not tell you I'd be busy tonight? Eh? How dare you run after me, looking like this?"

"But I—!"

"Those are humans in there!" he growled. "Humans, and you come running in there looking like a ghoul! Didn't you remember you don't look human yet? Now go back to Francesca and—"

"Like a ghoul?" I said. "Well, whose fault is that? How could you just leave me looking like—"

"Will you *shut up!"* he said, and I did so. Instantly. In fact, all I could do now was stand silently, calmly, and wait for him to speak. What the—? What has he—?

"Now . . ." he continued, "You will tell me why you came bursting into the room."

"I fed from Francesca," I heard myself say. "She's fainted, I think."

"So she'll wake up eventually, I know this," he said. "Is that it?"

"No, master," I said. Master? What the—?

"Then what is it?"

"I—I was angry," I said. "I—want to learn more. But you won't teach me."

"I've already told you that I would," he said. "Just not tonight. Now go back to Francesca and see that she's all right. When she wakes, she can answer some questions. But stay out of sight, girl! Learning to alter yourself will take some time, now go back to the study!"

"Yes, master."

"Good girl," he said. "Go on now."

"Yes, master," I said, and left him.

Chapter 9

Once again I found myself back somewhere without remembering how I'd gotten there. Francesca was coming around, but preferred to remain lying down while she was recovering. Meanwhile I had a few thousand questions. Unfortunately the answer to most of them was, "You must ask the master." Eventually I grew tired of this master business.

"You, too, eh?" I said.

"Too what?" Francesca said.

"You call him master."

"Oh, that," she said. "Well, he is the master of the house."

"Why not *padrone?*" I asked. "Or is that not enough for him?"

"I can't question his sensibilities, mistress," she said.

"But you insist on calling me mistress, too."

"Do you wish to be called something else?"

"Anything but mistress," I said. "Why I'm not even a *signora* anymore, I suppose. Why not just Theresa, then?"

"Very well, Theresa," she said. "What else do you wish to know?"

"I'm not sure," I said. "Most of my questions you

can't answer, it seems. Except . . ." I said, but drifted off when I began staring at her.

"Is something wrong?" she asked.

"Uh . . . I . . ." I said, then looked her in the eyes. "Francesca, is something wrong with my eyes, or are you glowing?"

"Glowing?" she said, looking at her hands and arms. "I don't know what you mean."

"Well, you seem to be—no, you *are,*" I said. "You seem to have a . . . light blue glow around you."

"Forgive me, but I see nothing," she said.

"But this is so strange," I said, moving back and forth. "No matter which angle I look at, you still have the glow around you. But, it is very faint, so perhaps that's why you don't see it."

"I'll have to take your word for it," she said. "The master has never told me anything about this."

"I've heard that—that some people have a strange light to them, just before they die. Perhaps you—" I said, and gasped. "Oh, no! Francesca, have I—? Are you—?"

"Dying?" she asked. "I don't think so. I'm only a little weak."

"But what if I took too much? Did I? Oh, please tell me I haven't killed you!"

"You haven't—trust me," she said. "I'll recover soon."

"Are you sure?"

"Of course," she said, sitting up now. "I'll only need a day or two of rest. You've done no wrong." That made me laugh.

"Done no wrong," I said. "I've only drunk the blood of a living being. And . . . I must do that for the rest of my life. Mustn't I?"

"I think so."

"Oh no," I said. "And this is what I asked for.

What I *begged* for. What I demanded, even. But he says there's no turning back. I can never see the sun again, either, can I?"

"I don't think so."

"Oh, my Lord, was this truly the only way?" I asked. "Was this truly the only way to gain my freedom? Francesca, how bad an existence is it? Is it bearable? Was this the only way for me not be married to Frederico?"

"I—I don't know . . ."

"Have you been married to a man you don't love?" I asked. "Do you know what it's like?"

"I have never been married at all."

"Never?" I said. "Hmm. Perhaps you're fortunate. But then, you must still be a man's servant, so perhaps you aren't fortunate."

"I am the master's servant," she said. "But—I am other things, too. His companion, for one."

"His—? Oh," I said. "I see. Well, I—I hope you don't think that I mean to—"

"He has other companions, as well," she said. "I also help him with daytime errands. He has a man who helps him with his business, also."

"Oh," I said, "Yes, um—that makes sense. To have human servants, that is. But—that he also feeds from you, and regularly. Doesn't this bother you?"

"It's—one of my duties," she said. "He says he may convert me someday, but—for now, I best serve him this way."

"How did you meet him?" I asked.

"I was very young," she said distantly. "My parents had died. He took me in as his own. In a way I'm his daughter, also. As a 'father' he's . . . stern and distant, but he's cared for me. Even loved me, I'm certain."

"There is so much I don't understand," I murmured. "And he refuses to teach me anything."

"He'll teach you, eventually," she said. "But, as I understand it, you asked to be converted?"

"Um . . . yes," I said.

"That may be it then," she said.

"What do you mean?"

"Oh . . ." she said, "Well, the master is used to being . . . well, the master. He prefers choosing whom to convert."

"Oh," I said. "Yes, I suppose that makes sense. I know of no men who . . . well, forgive me, but men's pride knows no bounds. Eh?"

She wouldn't agree, but did smile.

"Eh, you know," I said. "You can't help but know, eh?" I could see she was trying not to agree, but eventually gave up and nodded. I laughed and kissed her cheek.

"Theresa?" she said in surprise.

"I only mean to show that . . . I can be your friend, Francesca," I said. "I don't think the master likes me, because he *didn't* choose me. But it's not as if he didn't warn me. He told me he wouldn't help me."

"I think he ought to," she said. "But—of course I would never say this to him."

"Hmph," I said, sitting on the couch. "Francesca . . ."

"Yes," she said.

"About some of the things I said earlier," I began, "I . . . I don't wish you to repeat them to Antonio."

"What things?"

"I don't want him to know that I was . . . upset about my . . . condition," I said. "I don't want him to think that I whined or complained about something I'd asked him to do. He would give me no sympathy, I know that."

"I won't tell him," she said.

"Good," I said. "Really I'm—I'm fine now. I don't want him to think I'd been . . . weak. That I'd been an ungrateful child."

"I won't tell him," she said. "But—if I may . . . ?"

"May what?"

"I was only wondering . . . if you *do* regret what's happened?" she asked. I looked her in the eyes a moment before looking down.

"Regrets will get me nowhere now," I said. "I must learn to make the best of things."

Antonio only returned in time to take me back to that coffin room. I asked him if he had his own coffin, and if so, where it was, but he said again that my questions wouldn't be answered until later.

The next night I learned that I had been with Antonio for four days now. The conversion itself had taken three days. Antonio talked me out of going to Frederico and telling him I wasn't to be married anymore. I agreed that we'd need a better plan than that. Correction: I needed a better plan. It occurred to me that Frederico was no doubt scouring the city with a fine-toothed comb to find me. It couldn't have been long before he ended up at this house.

Meanwhile my needs were satisfied by other servants. I thought it odd that Antonio was supposedly feeding regularly from his servants. One would think that they would be constantly trying to escape, but they all took it quietly and obediently. That, and there weren't all that many servants for him to be able to feed from, even if only once every two weeks or so. Besides, a person can't give blood like that all the time and live long. I figured he might have taken from animals or something most of the time.

At last Antonio could set aside some time to answer my questions. One of these was how I was going to deal with Frederico. Antonio would offer no advice, however, no matter how much I pleaded. Matters of the heart were my concern, not his, as he put it. He would only help me survive in my new form, and that was it. He also made it a point of mostly just confirming or denying what I'd heard about vampires. Finally I asked him why he was so against my joining him; why he insisted on making things so difficult for me.

"Life is difficult, Theresa," he said. "Even the unlife."

"Unlife?"

"Just my little joke about it," he said. "Actually, this is even truer living than what mere humans consider to be life. After all, humans are guaranteed to end their lives; we aren't."

"Then . . . we really are immortal?"

"In our own way," he said. "We are ageless. We will never grow old, or withered. We'll never know disease, or hunger."

"But we know thirst," I said.

"True," he said, "But—not in the way humans know thirst. Obviously we crave different liquids, except that humans can die should they not drink, but we cannot."

"You mean we don't have to drink blood to survive?"

"No, not exactly."

"Then, why do we have to do it?"

"Well, you yourself discovered what happens when you haven't fed for a bit. But the troubles only begin when you haven't fed for a *long* time. You won't die of thirst—you can't—but you *will* become weaker, and weaker, until you literally cannot move. So I wouldn't advise trying to resist. You'll only become ravenous first, and that would be dangerous."

"I understand," I said. "Except—why blood? What—where did vampires come from?"

"Well, it seems you go right for the throat—in a manner of speaking," he said. "I'm joking," he said after seeing that I didn't get it.

"Oh. Sorry," I said. "I'm—I only want to learn everything I can. Anything you say I'm likely to take seriously."

"I wouldn't take *every*thing I say seriously," he cautioned. "In fact, it's best to assume everyone is a liar until proven otherwise."

"Do you think so?"

"It's been useful for me," he shrugged. "No matter. You wanted to know where vampires came from." I nodded, and he leaned forward and was silent in contemplation for a time.

"Oh, it was such a long process," he said, and then sat up straight. "It was such a long process that most of the details are lost to me. Let's just say it was a great mixture of a little magic here, alchemy there—"

"Magic and alchemy?" I said. "You know these things?"

"Oh, some magic, yes," he said. "But I've forgotten most of the alchemy."

"Then . . . then dark forces were used to create vampires," I murmured, "weren't they?"

"Dark forces?" he said. "That depends on your point of view. Remember that Christians came along and labeled anything that wasn't theirs, dark and evil."

"Well, I was taught that—that vampires are enemies of God."

"So are old women with love potions," he said, "if you believe everything they tell you." He paused, apparently so I could answer, and when I didn't, he smiled. "No matter," he said. "As I said, I've forgotten a lot of those dark forces. They served their purpose to me, and that was to achieve immortality. There was . . . there was a lot more to the process, but it's nothing anyone else need know now, for I've succeeded. What would be the point in duplicating it? I've been given the power to pass it on. The immortality, I mean."

"Then . . . you mean . . . *you* began all this?" I asked. "*You* created vampires?"

"I suppose you could say that," he said. "I'm quite certain I'm the first, either way."

"Oh, my," I gasped. "I—I'm honored. I mean—I had no idea that I'd met the very first vampire, I—and I've even been changed by him!"

"Tell me—have you *always* wanted to be one of us?"

"Uh—no, actually," I said. "I-I've just—well, I admit that my decision came very quickly, but—for so long now I've wanted to just—make my own choices. If I'm to marry again, for instance, I want to choose my husband."

"That will be difficult."

"Why? Don't I have the power to . . . to make others do my bidding? I notice you have that power over me."

"Well, that's something else."

"What is it, then? What is that strange spell you've cast over me?"

"What spell?"

"The other day—I mean night," I began, "When I was angry, you shouted at me, and—and I couldn't speak after that. All I could do was listen, and do what you said. And this spell makes me call you master, too. Must I call you that? Oh, Antonio, I admit that if you are truly the first vampire, you are far greater than I.

If you tell me what to do, I'll obey you, but please—must you have the spell over me?"

"It's . . . not exactly a spell," he said slowly. "It's also not something I can reverse once it's in place."

"What? You mean I'm going to be your mindless slave for—"

"No, no, not at all," he said. "But it's simply—" He stopped, and then sighed and leaned back. "All right," he said. "*You* I shall tell. It's just something I do to everyone I convert. You're no different than the others, that's all. But it can only be done while conversion is taking place. It can't be done afterwards, nor can it be removed afterwards. Understood?"

"Well, what can't be undone?"

"It's merely a . . . manipulation of the mind," he said. "Long ago, before I could perfect it, it resulted in mindless, dirty creatures who were savage, but obedient. But back then I suppose that suited my purpose. Don't worry, I've since destroyed the mindless slaves. But now I've perfected the technique, and . . . well, ever since some bad luck I had with one vampire, I've taken no chances. With *any* vampire I convert."

"But I still don't see—"

"All I've done to you, and to everyone else since the troublesome one, is to arrange your mind so that nothing has changed—you have all your memories, your thoughts, your intelligence—but when I so wish it, your will shuts off and—well, I trust you remember the sensation."

"Yes," I murmured, and looked down. For a long time I couldn't speak, until I heard Antonio.

"Tsk, tsk, now, Theresa, don't take it personally," he said. "As I said, I've done this to every vampire since . . . well, for a long time now. You're no exception."

"I thought . . . you'd trust me," I murmured, still not looking at him.

"And I also said earlier that it's best not to trust anyone until they've proven themselves."

"Then you don't trust me."

"You begged me to convert you, Theresa," he said. "I tried to talk you out of it. Are you willing to accept what comes of it or not?"

"I am," I said. "I *do* want to make this work. It's simply that—" Then I looked up at him. "You don't like me, do you, Antonio?"

"Oh, I like you," he said. "I like you very much. I even find you attractive. But it would be too dangerous for us to become involved, not here, not now, anyway."

"Then we can leave," I said.

"I'm doing just fine here," he said. "I'd have nothing to gain by leaving. And besides, Theresa, I do admire your courage. You walked in here one night and accused me to my face of being a vampire, and without fear that you were painfully lucky to get out of here alive. Unless . . . you didn't realize that."

"Perhaps I didn't," I said. "But I was frightened, nonetheless."

"Then you hid it well, and from a vampire that's quite a compliment. We have a talent for reading people's moods."

"Can we hear people's thoughts?"

"No, but our perceptions are better than those of humans," he said. "In some cases we might be considered mind readers. But you'll discover all this in due time. I trust you have no other real questions?"

"Only one, Antonio," I said. "The . . . troublesome vampire. Who was it? May I know, please?"

"Why is it important?"

"Curiosity, nothing more," I said. "I mean, apparently this person upset you enough to . . . to make every other vampire into a mindless—well, you do that thing to their minds.''

He was silent for a moment before leaning back into his chair and smiling.

''My, you *are* perceptive now,'' he said. ''Except, it's not really something I like to discuss.''

''Oh. Well, I only thought to ask.''

''I could tell you some, though,'' he said. ''The whole thing was a mistake. The only real mistake I've ever made, mind you. She was a . . . I thought she would come to understand, and appreciate what she was.''

''Oh. It was a woman, then,'' I said.

''Well, let's just say she didn't make much of an effort to love me, no matter what I did.''

''I see,'' I said. ''And . . . you also said something about avoiding married people these days. Was this because of the same woman?''

''Impressive,'' he said. ''I barely remember saying that. But yes—she was also the one who made me reconsider that position. She was married when I converted her, you see. Now I can see that was a bad idea.''

''May I . . . may I ask who she was?'' I said.

''I can't imagine you've heard of her,'' I said. ''If she had half a mind, she's changed her name by now, but back then I knew her as Mara.''

''Mara?'' I said. ''Is that all?''

''Oh, her last name was something like . . . Lattimus or something. Latrius? I don't remember.''

''I haven't heard of her, then,'' I said.

''I didn't think you would,'' he said. ''Besides, she'd have to be a complete idiot to live as long as she has and never change her name. Who knows? It's probably Beatrice these days.''

"Um . . . may I ask how long she *has* lived?"

"Well, yes, it's been . . . ohh . . ." he said, and stopped to start counting fingers. "I'd say about fourteen centuries now."

"Fourteen cen—?" I said, but was too shocked for a while to continue. "Sh-she's lived fourteen . . . *hundred* years now?"

"You needn't be so shocked," he said. "After all, we don't age, remember? This all happened a long time ago."

"But—that means that *you*—you're—?"

"No, *I'm* not fourteen hundred," he said.

"But—how could she—?"

"I'm closer to . . . five *thousand.*"

I let out a great cry and almost swooned at those words. Antonio thought it all very amusing.

"Don't believe me, do you?"

"No, I—! I do! I do, I *do!*" I gasped. "It's just—so incredible! Five thousand years? You've actually been on this earth for—since before Christ!"

"Oh, yes," he said, still smiling, "Never met him, though."

"Then—then you have lived through so much of human history!" I said. "Ohhh, the things you must know, the . . . the wisdom you must have!"

"Go on," he said. "I have no aversion to flattery."

"But Antonio," I said. "If you've lived so long, I—I'm surprised you aren't ruling the world by now. I mean, truly!"

He shrugged. "Ruling this world is something I decided to leave to others," he said. "I'm satisfied being fabulously wealthy, and living life by my rules."

"And that's what I want," I said. "To make my *own* rules."

"I know," he said, eyeing me strangely.

"But—this other woman," I said. "This, uh, Mara. Is she also one of the oldest of us?"

"I think so," he said. "Yes, I'd converted people before her, but they've since been destroyed. Some of them by my own hand. Yes, I'd say she's second only to me now."

"Do you know where she is, then?" I asked. He shrugged.

"Who knows?" he said. "But I would guess west of here. Possibly France or Spain. Maybe even somewhere in the British Empire."

"How do you know she's not dead?"

"That much I *would* know," he said. "That's the only link she's been unable to sever, not that it helps me much. I still know that she's alive. Nevertheless, should we ever meet again, I'll—well. Let's just say I'll have to finish some business with her."

"Oh," I said, not certain if I wanted to know about this business of his. I decided to change the subject.

That night Antonio also helped me with my appearance. At least then I'd look human again, if paler. There was still the matter of dealing with Frederico now.

"Please, Antonio, why won't you help me?"

"I've helped you in exactly the way I said I would," he said. "I've converted you and shown you what you can do now. By tomorrow you'll be gone."

"But I'm not ready to leave, Antonio!" I said. "I-I still have no plan to—"

"Is that my problem?" he said. "No, it isn't. You can go to your husband and tell him you're a vampire now, and—"

"But I—"

"—see what happens next, or better yet, what the *priests* will do to you," he said. "Won't *that* be lovely."

"But that's just it, Antonio!" I said. "I-I don't know what to do! I can't tell anyone what's happened to me, and if I go to him now, what reason could I give him to annul our marriage?"

"You could tell him you were unfaithful, and I'm sure he'd be glad to be rid of you," he said.

"I know," I said, "but I don't want it to be that way."

"Neither do I, to be honest," he said. "For if my name comes up in *any* way in this—"

"Oh no!" I insisted. "No, no, no, m-master," I said, trying to resist that, but in vain, "Must I call you master?"

"For now, yes," he said. "Until you've learned to stop arguing over silly things like this."

"Silly?" I said. "How can you think of this as silly?"

"Well, why don't you just kill him, then?" he said. "That's the only *other* way to obtain an annulment, you said!"

"But I would be executed!" I said. "Besides, I don't want him *dead,* I just want him . . . want him out of my life!"

"Well, then, you've solved nothing, have you?" he said. "Vampire or not, as far as everyone else is concerned, you're still married, so you haven't found any freedom after all, have you?"

"But there has to be a way," I said. "But wait! What if . . . what if I stayed out of sight for a long enough time? If he could never find me, wouldn't I be declared dead eventually, and then my marriage *would* be over?"

"I suppose so," he said. "But you're not staying out of sight *here.* It will probably take years before they declare you dead."

"Oh, my," I whispered, "I-I don't think I could wait for years. But where would I hide?"

"Good question," he said. "But, I have other business to attend to—"

"Antonio, please!" I cried, grabbing his arm. "I-I know I've been nothing but a burden to you, but you must be able to help me, I know you can!" He yanked his arm from me angrily and straightened his clothes.

"Leave me be, you prattling hen!" he said. "Have you no mind at all? Just fake your own death and be done with it!"

"What?" I whispered, but he was out the door by now.

Chapter 10

Antonio allowed me one extra night to come up with an idea. I had already learned some useful things about vampires, such as that we don't breathe very deeply when asleep. In fact, unless one is paying attention, we don't seem to be breathing at all. But no one was about to be fooled by my just lying there asleep. I had to make it seem as though I'd been killed, or even better, murdered.

Since I'd left Frederico at night some time ago, I came up with the idea that I'd been kidnapped. Antonio allowed me the use of a messenger to quickly and quietly drop off a threatening note to Frederico. I ended up including a ransom request and a fake location for money to be dropped off at. I didn't plan on actually checking the spot, but planned for him to find my lifeless body.

The lifeless part Antonio was gracious enough to explain to me. When I pressed for more advice, he relented and suggested that I stab myself with wood. Naturally I was reluctant to do this, until he called in one of his vampire servants (he had two, but the rest were human). Then he took up a big, sharp stick and stabbed him in the heart before my eyes! Then he pulled out the stick and bade me wait for a few hours.

I wasn't sure if I even wanted to see what was in store, but when we returned in a few hours his servant was not only alive, but completely healed, as well. After giving the man some blood, Antonio explained that vampires are only "dead" as long as the stick remains in place. We also don't breathe while it's there, but we're still alive. I agreed that that would be a very effective way to fool everyone.

Obviously this wasn't a foolproof plan. The worst that could happen would be if no one discovered my body until the morning, long after the sun had risen. I hadn't been burned by the sun yet, but took Antonio's word that it would be a very painful death. A permanent death, too. Also, there was the concern that I would be buried six feet under instead of being put in the family crypt. Or that the funeral would be open-casket and during the daytime. Or that no one would bother to pull the stick out, not even to prepare me for burial. But this was the best plan I could come up with in one day.

I expressed my misgivings to Francesca about so cruel a deception, but this was the choice I had to make. I wasn't about to go into hiding for seven years or more in the hope that I would perhaps be declared dead. This way would be quick and assured. But it would also hurt my husband, and most importantly, my family and friends. Antonio wasn't joking when he warned that I would be losing so much. But I still believed that I had gained much more.

The time arrived when I had to leave Antonio, but hopefully not for the last time. I had learned a great deal but I still felt as if I knew nothing. He had been terse, unsympathetic, and impatient with me at every moment, but he always had a look in his eyes that told me differently. Or perhaps it was a side effect to that mind-tampering he'd done to me—that I couldn't hate him no matter what he did. Looking back now, I believe that had been the case.

Antonio and I were in one of his guest rooms. I sat on the edge of the bed and stroked the covers while he bade me good-bye.

"I can do nothing else but miss you terribly, Antonio," I murmured. "You don't know what this means to me. All of it."

"If this works, you mean," he warned. "This will be a very dangerous ruse."

"I know, Antonio," I said, rising from the bed. "But it has to work. I know it will work. If I let my fear take over, then I'll never be free of anyone."

"Probably not," he said. I smiled and put my arms around him.

"Oh, Antonio," I said, but he backed away.

"Antonio?" I said, but he shook his head. "Oh, come now," I said softly. "Do you mean that after all this, you still hate me?"

"I don't hate you," he said. "I never did. It's only . . ."

"Only what?" I finished. "Oh, Antonio, I know I can't offer you wealth, or power, but . . . a woman has things to offer a man. I only want to repay you for all you've done."

"And . . . your offer is very generous, but—er—"

"But what?" I asked, touching his chest now. "You can't be afraid of *me*. I couldn't possibly hurt you."

"I'm not afraid of you, Theresa," he said. "Don't ever accuse me of that."

"Oh, Antonio, what harm could there be?" I said. "After all, I'm not exactly married now, if that's what you're worried about."

"Oh, you needn't worry about that," he said, taking my arms and running his hands all the way up to mine. From there he held my fingers and brought them up to his lips, and kissed them.

"Just remember that what I do, I do of my own choice," he murmured.

"Of course," I whispered, and leaned forward. He covered my mouth with his hand and cocked an eyebrow.

"I have no doubts you'll make your fortune someday," he said, keeping his face very close to mine.

"Grazie," I whispered, and shut my eyes to let him pull me towards him. Our kisses lit up the room all night.

Antonio had explained to me how to transform, but I hadn't had the opportunity to try it yet. I wanted to fly to Antonio's friend's in bat-shape, but I had too much to carry, such as some rope (which I didn't use, after all), the stake, a sash, and a note I'd had someone write for me (in case someone recognized my handwriting). It said, "Here is your change, *signor,*" meaning my lifeless body. Again, I knew this deception was very cruel, but faking one's own death doesn't allow for many niceties.

No one was around in the courtyard—it was the middle of the night, after all—so I tied the sash around my eyes and held onto the note. From there I took the stake and held it to my chest, and took a deep breath. I must have held it there for five minutes, thinking of nothing, until I took another deep breath and tried to whisper a prayer. It only gave me a headache. Crossing myself was out of the question, then. Another price to pay for my choice.

After another five minutes I took another deep breath, and another, and another, until I was almost hyperventilating, and then pulled on the stake with all my might. It was sharp, but it was no knife, and it began to go in, but not painlessly. In a way that's what I wanted, because then I had good reason to scream. I reached a point where I couldn't even hear myself scream, but could feel it, and with the last bit of strength I had, pulled the stake all the way in.

I felt blood pouring from my chest and heard (but did not feel) my body hit the ground before the approaching wave of excited voices faded into oblivion.

I felt a floating and sinking sensation for hours before opening my eyes to darkness. I tried to sit up and I hit my head on a board above me, so I sank back down and nursed my head. Feeling around me now, I determined that I had been put in a big box of some kind—a coffin, perhaps? That had to be it. It worked! I thought. They must have believed the whole thing, that I was dead. Now I was on a ship on its way to Naples; I had to be right.

I almost opened the lid right there, but decided that might be a bad idea. Unpleasant as it seemed, the only way for this to work would be to sit in there until they put me in the family crypt. Their crypt . . . Oh, my, now my memories drifted back to when I'd discovered my own family's crypt as a child. Needless to say, I'd tried to forget the whole experience. Now I was going to have to escape from the crypt. But that would be the only safe place for me to leave this box and go out on my own.

My plans for what would happen afterward were shaky at best. I'd decided that France might be a good place to try. Besides, French was the only other language I knew even a little bit of. Well, and Latin, too, but who speaks Latin but priests?

If I seem to be babbling, imagine what it was like

lying in a coffin for days on end. I thought of songs, poems, nursery rhymes, the latest fashions, anything that would make the time go by, when I wasn't trying to sleep, that is. It was also helpful to keep my mind off my increasing hunger. If this didn't end soon, I was sure to jump right out during the wake and attack everyone. So my endurance was stretched to the limit.

There were a number of times when the ride became bumpy. I heard voices during those times, meaning that people were probably carrying me around. My biggest fright came when the lid suddenly opened, so I had to shut my eyes and keep my breathing extra shallow. Fortunately it was the nighttime, or I was away from sunlight. Then I felt people lifting me up and heard voices. Ah, yes, it had to be the undertaker preparing me for burial. As long as they didn't embalm me or something, I'd survive. It was more of a challenge to keep my body stiff than you might think. I couldn't be completely limp, or they'd wonder what happened to the rigor mortis. So I had to keep stiff, but not so much that I seemed to be tensing my muscles. Vampires do also feel a little colder than humans, but in my opinion that just means our metabolisms are more efficient.

The idiots let my head hit the table at one point, which would have been all right if I'd been able to react in some way—*any* way. Finally the ordeal was over, and they'd dressed me in what was no doubt a lovely burial dress, and gave me a shroud. It made my nose itch, though. Then I was put back into the coffin, and the lid was shut.

Another time I was awakened from a sound sleep by people crying. I tried to shut it out, as tears were coming to me, too, but in the end I did weep some. This ruse was a terrible thing, but it would be even worse if

I sat up before everyone. Why, I'd probably be burned as a witch or a vampire.

Most of the voices were unfamiliar, until an eternity later some joined in that almost broke me. My sisters and brothers, some cousins, my father, and worst of all, my mother. I heard her throw herself across the coffin at one point, only to be pulled away by my brothers. It was all I could do to keep myself from screaming. This had to be my punishment for what I was doing; being forced to hear the lamentations of the people I hurt the most. I wondered if every dead person could hear their own funeral before ascending (or descending) to their final fate.

For some reason no one gave me a wake, which is just as well. I'd been to some where brawls had started, mostly because of the alcohol, but usually when the deceased had been a real scoundrel. Still, it would have been interesting to hear what my brothers and sisters *really* thought of me. But I knew that already, I'm sure.

For one last time I felt myself being moved. From the noise and movement I assumed that the coffin was on a cart. That meant they were taking me to the Caglioni crypt. The cart stopped, and people carried me now. I felt the thump of being placed somewhere, and after a moment heard a loud grinding of a big metal door shutting, and then locking. Locked inside—beautiful.

I waited about ten minutes before even breathing normally. This had to be it; this had to be the crypt. No one here now but us dead people. Taking a deep breath of, by now, carbon dioxide, I braced my hands against the lid and pushed. It moved a little bit, but that was all. I tried again and again, until it occurred to me that the idiots must have nailed it shut! Or maybe just padlocked it. Did they think I was going to try to escape or something?

My strength was hardly at its peak as it was, considering that I hadn't fed in far too long, but I mustered every bit that I had and pushed up. The lid jumped up about an inch before I had to let it drop again and recover. There went the bulk of my strength. No, I thought. This is stupid. I won't be stopped by *this*.

I tried to keep my wits about me and think of a real plan, but my hunger was unbearable now. I thought about what Antonio had said about being completely immobile from the lack of blood, and my strength was fueled by anger and panic as I pounded over and over against the lid. With one last burst of strength and a yell for support, I slammed my fists into the lid, which flew open and slammed into the side of the coffin. Cold, dry, stale air fell on my face while I fell back again, hyperventilating and eyes shut. My tongue felt my well-extended canines. If I could have drooled in hunger, I would have.

Antonio had explained to me what people's light blue glows meant after I'd discovered that he seemed to be purple. Apparently we can see the auras of living things when we're thinking about it, or when the light is right. The best light is the absence of it, so if anything was alive in this crypt, I would see it. I'd also learned that we can still see even if nothing living is around. In pitch darkness we can see, I figured out much later, the heat that most things give off. I hesitate to label it infra-red vision so as not to sound like some comic book, but that's apparently what it comes down to. My hunger strengthened my resolve to get out of there, not to mention a growing uneasiness. Just because I'm undead myself doesn't mean I like to hang out with the real thing. There was no smell of death—only dust, and I held my arms out and crept forward through the near darkness.

The Caglionis resting there weren't giving off an awful lot of heat, but I could see enough to avoid stumbling into any bodies lining the walls. I was one of the few who'd been shut into a coffin, which reminded me that I'd need to retrieve the thing later and fill it with dirt. More on that later. At last I reached a wall and felt my way along until I felt what had to be the door. As luck would have it, it was locked, from the outside. I almost lost my temper and started pounding on it. Then more of Antonio's teachings returned to me, and although I hadn't attempted it yet, I closed my eyes and tried to, as he put it, relax the world's hold upon me. A very disorienting sinking feeling began, but I dared not open my eyes. Eventually I didn't need to, for now I entered a world of pure senses and no body. Now I could spread myself all around the crypt if needed, every part of me in search of a way out. The door had openings, so I used them, and floated outside via hairline cracks.

Reestablishing the world's hold on me is a bit harder than relaxing it. In fact it was so soothing to be as mist that I wanted to remain that way for a long time, but even in that form the hunger is there. After a few moments of concentration I was my own self again. My hunger was worse in this form, but I couldn't very well satisfy it as mist, either. So with only a brief glance backwards, I snuck through the catacombs in search of food.

At this point even the rats looked good, but they all escaped into holes, as I couldn't get any of them to look me in the eyes. So I pressed on, wishing I could at least drool to ease my parched throat. There were a lot of spiderwebs and their makers along the way, but I wasn't *that* thirsty—yet. All the way through the catacombs I found myself looking behind me at every sound, as though I were afraid that my ex-in-laws' ancestors were chasing after me for mocking their burial grounds. I couldn't really dismiss my uneasiness as silly superstition, either, or I'd have to disbelieve in vampires, too.

The entrance loomed before me, once I'd dragged myself up the endless steps. The door was not locked, so I cast stealth aside and burst through, fangs bared and ready to rip through the first blood-filled thing I could find. Off in the distance was the Caglioni estate, and I saw lights on and heard muffled noises from within, so I broke into a run. Another opportunity to test my new abilities came when I tried to transform into bat-shape in midstride. That earned me a mouthful of dirt, but that wasn't about to stop me. Only half-transformed, I crawled up from the dirt, changing back all the way, and continued my run on foot.

There wasn't even a stray dog on the way. Despite what it seems, my intent was not to butcher my former in-laws, but to find an animal or perhaps a servant, if it came to that. The noises from within were very clear now; I recognized some voices as blood relatives. Their voices made me stop and listen, but I heard neither Mother nor Father. Some music coming from within led me to believe that this was my wake. Now this was a temptation—to stay and attend my own wake. I'd already been there for my own funeral, but after that experience, I'm not certain I could have handled any more of this. And the longer I remained there, the more likely I would be to attack my own brothers and sisters.

Forcing myself not to take backward glances, I ran around the house in search of the stables. After a few moments I reached the back of the house, but no lights were on, so I had to look at the heat and sniff around. The smell led me to a big building that was locked. I tried to pull off the lock but was too weak then, so I punched the door once or twice, then listened. There had to be animals inside, all right, so I hit the doors again, but was far too weak by this time. In frustration I let loose with a barrage of pounding and slamming my body against the door, when a lull allowed me to hear the approaching woofs of several big dogs.

Without hesitation I ran off in blind panic, giant hounds nipping at my heels. You forget a lot of things when terrified, such as that I was at least strong enough to handle these dogs, or that I could fly, or climb walls, or do any number of things to save myself. Nevertheless I led the dogs through a merry chase across the grounds until a big tree appeared as my savior. It could very well be that I ran straight up the trunk, I was so frightened. Once I was safe it worried me even more that these dogs would bring the whole household out to investigate. So far I couldn't see any new lights coming on from within. There was still the problem of these dogs trying to jump up after me.

I was breathing heavily out of fear, not tiredness, and as the dogs leaped and barked away to their merry content, my fear slowly dissipated as the hunger rose to intolerable heights. I looked at my fingernails, which had grown considerably, and I felt the needle-sharp teeth with my tongue. *Now* is where things came back to me. The fear became anger, and then rage, so I growled and leapt from my perch, landing on the biggest dog. I dispatched it with a solid swipe to the throat. Another one I locked gazes with and charmed it, but the third clamped its jaws around my leg.

"Kill! Attack!" I said to the charmed one, pointing to its brother. My faithful hound immediately clamped onto the third dog's throat and started shaking. It finally released its hold on my leg, so I nursed my wound while the two hounds tore each other apart. The first one was finishing its death throes; the smell of its blood became overwhelming, so I practically dove into the wound and started drinking. Normally I wouldn't recommend dog's blood, but under these circumstances it was a feast.

I'd hardly even wet my throat, when I heard somebody yelling, and looked up to see someone with a gun approaching fast. I thought about running away, but my hunger wouldn't let me. Instead I rose and threw the dog I'd been feeding from at my assailant. He couldn't see it coming and was knocked flat onto his back. He also dropped his gun, but by the time he started to scramble for it, I was on top of him. I couldn't tell who it was and didn't care by now; he was food.

In our defense, it ought to be repeated that we don't actually need human blood, as the blond lady was so fond of reminding everyone. What she neglected to mention was that we may not need it, but we will *always* prefer it. Always. Only the seriously repressed ones try to deny this. As a rule we limit ourselves to a butcher shop sort of supply, but I've found that there are many more people out there willing to donate to a friend in need than you might think.

Still, I cannot lie and deny that I killed a person that night. With the man I was allowed the time to sate the hunger, but I wasn't allowed to gather my wits. His yells had attracted others' attention; more lights from within appeared, and I soon saw light blue figures approaching. I drank as much more as I dared, then bolted in the opposite direction. Somebody heard or saw me and yelled. Fortunately they were still a good distance from me, and weak as I was, I could run much faster. They were losing me, but I figured it was time to try again, and concentrated on a transformation. I refused to fail this time, and shut my eyes and leapt up in midstride. Something happened now; I could feel limbs shortening and fingers growing, skin webbing out, my face flattening. When I opened my eyes again, the ground rushed by underneath me, and I soon felt myself sailing skyward. There was no opportunity to inspect my appearance, nor was I particularly interested in seeing my bat form.

I left the Caglioni estate far behind. Before dawn I would have to return to the crypt and prepare my coffin for departure, but in the meantime it was a good idea to stay away from the area until people had returned to bed. The whole place was sure to be in an uproar thanks to my feeding in their backyard. I was becoming rational again, now that I'd fed. I was sure I could walk amongst normal people in Naples.

Flying into town, I ducked behind a building and transformed, then strolled out casually onto the streets. The night had just begun, so there were plenty of people out and about. I strolled along the *strada* and nodded and smiled casually to the first group I came across, but they all backed off cautiously, then hurried away. I stopped and watched them scurry away, muttering amongst themselves and pointing. Others passed by me and gasped. Now I was worried. But my fangs aren't visible, I thought. A wipe across my mouth revealed no bloody messes on my face, so what was wrong?

When more people avoided me, I looked for the first reflective window around and had a nice surprise. My eyes blazed red and now my *ears* were pointy! Not to mention the fact that I was still wearing a burial dress, which made me a pretty creepy sight. I turned around and smiled sheepishly at some other skittish bystanders and bowed repeatedly while ducking into a convenient alley. Then I ran like a madwoman until spotting a nice corner to slump against. It didn't seem as though anyone had bothered to follow me, so I sat down and wrapped my arms around my knees. After a few moments of contemplation, I began to chuckle softly, until more than a few tears came forth. I didn't weep because I'd regretted what I'd become, but I regretted what I'd had to do that night, and was likely to have to do again. I knew I could survive what was to come, but that didn't mean I'd have to like everything I had to do in order to survive. I already had adultery, deception, and family betrayal on my conscience, not to mention the great affront to God that vampires are supposed to be. But that's according to human beliefs, and we all know how fallible those are.

I would have to find clothes if I was to walk around in public. But all of my things were at the Caglionis. I'd have to come up with a way to get in there and bring everything to the crypt before leaving Naples. Antonio had said something about being careful when entering homes uninvited, but he never explained what he meant. There wasn't much I could do about the dress for now, but I could fix my features. They had probably become ghoulish because I'd been hungry for so long.

After some time of skulking around the city, I found a small dress shop that was closed, but the owner was still inside, doing the books or something. I knocked on the door, but he waved me away. I was persistent, though, so he slammed his book shut and stormed over to the door, waving his fist. It was then that I turned on the charm, as it's said, and worked my way into his mind. Again, this was something I'd never done before, so I wasn't able to be very gentle about it. The dogs were just animals; humans aren't quite as easy to dominate. He winced in pain and tried to look away, but I stepped forward and forced my way in. It hadn't been as simple as Antonio had made it seem. He stopped shaking his fist and stood there with his mouth half open. Now that it was over, I encountered almost no resistance. I reasoned that charming others is more difficult than maintaining the hold.

"Signore," I yelled through the glass, "Please let me in."

Silently he unlocked the door and opened it wide. I brushed past him.

"Oh, *grazie, signore,"* I said. *"Grazie.* Please lock up behind me."

"Of course," he said, and did so.

"Signore," I said, "I know it is terribly late, but . . . as you can see, I'm not dressed very properly for the streets. I promise to pay you later if you will only let me have a dress now, *signore."*

"Of course," he said, and lumbered past me.

This was all a sham. I could have simply ordered him to give me a dress, but this was my way of pretending that I wasn't really stealing anything. Actually, at the time I did intend to leave him some money once I'd gotten my own back.

The owner stood still while I looked through his store and quickly pulled out various dresses that would suffice. It was a small store and didn't have the best selection. It seemed to me that he probably did mostly custom work.

"Have you a wife, *signore?"* I said, trying to make idle chitchat.

"Yes," he said.

"Is she pretty?" I asked.

"No," he said. I giggled. This was becoming an adventure, as I'd been finding opportunities all night to test my abilities. So far I'd transformed to mist, to bat-shape, had flown, and had charmed someone, all for the first time. But I had also killed for the first time and was still likely to be caught, if luck was against me.

The dressmaker had a small room where I could try on his clothes.

"I must say these are very fine dresses, *signore,*" I called from the room. I was starting to feel a slight strain from keeping my hold on him, but it was nothing I couldn't handle so far. Eventually I settled for a conservative red and black outfit and avoided the temptation of keeping all of them.

"I would like this one, *signore,*" I said.

"As you wish."

"I do mean to pay you back, but until then, you must forget that I was here."

"I will forget," he said.

"Do you have a back door?"

"Yes."

"I'll leave that way, then," I said. "And when I'm gone, lock up behind me, then go back to your work. Do you understand, *signore?*"

"Yes," he said, and led the way to the door. I smiled at him and kissed my fingers, then touched them to his lips. He didn't react.

"*Grazie, signore,*" I whispered, and walked away through the alley. I heard the door shutting and locking behind me, and smiled to myself. As I continued, though, I became more somber. Antonio had to have made his fortune in other ways besides stealing from people. That night I was experiencing fewer thrills greater than discovering my new abilities, but murder and thievery weren't what I'd had in mind when I said I wanted to make my own fortune.

Chapter 11

It's too bad I hadn't had much opportunity to see more of Naples before my conversion. I was seeing it now, but during the nighttime, which was now the only way I was going to see any city. Still, there were enough people out to keep things lively. There wouldn't be a repeat of what had happened before, either, now that I had real clothes on and a normal face. Pale, but normal.

Eventually I came upon a local pub from which much noise came. I was feeling a bit daring by now, so I went in. There was certainly no danger of finding anyone from my family here; this wasn't a place for the wealthy. More ale than wine was being passed around. Most of the noise came from a group of men with their arms around each other, swaying back and forth and singing vulgar sea chanteys. Some of them grabbed at the waitresses who passed by, but the girls were pretty experienced at avoiding pinching hands.

I stood a little from the doorway and took in all of this, when somebody's wandering hands grabbed *my* bottom. I jumped and turned to see an old salt who smelled of tobacco looking me up and down. He started to speak, but I ducked and ran past him into the crowd. From there I found a safe corner away from the mob of singing sailors. After waiting for some time, I realized I'd have to be aggressive to get any service. I banged on the table a few times, and a waitress came eventually.

"Only some wine," I said over the din.

"What?" she said.

"Wine! Some wine!" I shouted. She nodded and left me. Actually I didn't even feel like any wine, but I had to order something or probably get thrown out—literally!

This place didn't need to hire any entertainment, because the customers provided it. The sailors were such awful singers that they made quite a comedy of it. One of them on the end passed out and thudded to the ground. His friends just propped him up again and pretended he was still awake. Soon after that my wine came, and I sipped it, but it didn't taste quite right. No doubt it was the cheapest wine possible, but it still wasn't quite right. I started to contemplate it, when it occurred to me that I had no money with me whatsoever. It might as well have been Europe's finest wine; I couldn't pay for the spills the girls had to wipe up. So much for living the life of an honest vampire.

Somebody plunked down into the spot next to me. Fortunately it wasn't that old geezer who'd assaulted me before, but this one wasn't much of an improvement. This one smelled like beer and old fish.

"Eh, eh missy, why so lonesome over here?" he said, putting his arm around me and shaking me. "Come on," he said, slapping his thigh. "I'll keep you warm, eh?"

"I'm warm enough," I said.

"Ehhh, but I'll make you *warmer,*" he said, squeezing me tight. He looked away long enough to give a signal to some of his friends, who whistled and hooted their approval.

"Signore," I said, prying his arm from me. "A word with you, *signore.*"

"Hm?" he said, looking back. I locked gazes with him and found him much easier to dominate than the sober dressmaker. He loosened his grip on me and let his mouth hang open. I smiled and closed it for him.

"Buy a girl a drink, *signore?*" I said. He nodded dumbly and reached for his purse. I took it from him and pulled out enough for the wine, thought about it, then took a little more. Then I handed it back to him.

"Grazie, signore," I said. "Now go back to your friends. Go on, go back to your singing."

He nodded again and rose slowly from his seat, then turned to lumber back to his buddies. They seemed as confused as he was when he returned, but coming up with an explanation was his problem, not mine.

I decided to sip periodically at the wine and make it last that way. I'd finished about a third of it, when I started to feel a nice buzz coming on. Curious, I looked at the goblet, as though that would tell me anything about the wine, then shrugged and carried on. People don't get drunk off of one goblet of wine; besides, my family was famous for their tolerance of alcohol.

About halfway through the drink, though, the buzz was stronger, and I realized that I couldn't sit there all night. Most of the Caglionis and my family had to be asleep by now, and I had a lot to do. So I stood up and finished off my drink in a gulp, then left the money behind. Many hands reached out as I passed through the crowd, but I swatted most of them away. Then I reached the outside, took a deep breath of fresh air, and fell down.

I don't think that I passed out completely, but the ground did turn into pudding for a while. Someone hauled me to my feet and started dragging me along the *strada*. I was in no shape to offer any assistance. Eventually I was propped against a wall, where the person started patting my cheek repeatedly.

"Open up, *signorina,* get up now," a rough male voice said. I burped long and loud, then laughed.

"Oh, that's it, come on!" the man said, and I was yanked from the wall, only to fall down again. "Get on there, we don't need your sort on the streets!"

I was lifted up and tossed unceremoniously over his shoulder. He must have been a city guard or some other kind of authority figure. It was only after I reached a more sober state that I realized that I was probably being arrested as a prostitute. But before that time I only remembered that I was supposed to get home, so I began to struggle. He held on to me tighter, so I panicked and started flailing.

He made a noise in anger and flung me back onto my feet, then grabbed my shoulders.

"All right, you be rough, so now I'll be—*Madre!*" he yelled. I didn't understand it. I was only looking at him. Another officer came to assist and was equally taken aback.

"Zzzsssnorss, zzssso whz trbbl?" I asked, approximately.

"Madre!" the other cried. "And I thought I'd seen the worst of any drunk! Do you see those eyes?"

"Llllk nto my eyes," I said, falling forward. Charming them wouldn't get me anywhere. I couldn't have commanded a rock to lie still in this state. This, from one glass of wine?

My new friend tried to fling me over his shoulder again, but I pushed him away and started walking elsewhere. His friend rushed over to grab my arm, but I pushed him away, too. I discovered a little bit of my strength when he went sailing through the air, landing almost on the other side of the street. I remember being grabbed at again, and some sort of struggle erupted that ended with my throwing more people around and then running off into the night. There were people shouting after me while I ran, or rather, stumbled very quickly. I was overwhelmed with the urge to fly from them all, so I took a flying leap and somehow succeeded in transforming to bat-shape. Now nothing could stop me, until I hit a building. Thank God it had only been a wall and not a window in my way. Either way, I didn't feel the impact, but remember peeling myself from the pavement. Slamming into the wall did help me to sober up, though.

Later on, the cold wind in my face helped sober me up even more, but it was still a very erratic flight home. No lights were visible from within the Caglioni manor when I crash-landed into the garden. Fortunately the rose bushes were on the *other* side. A wave of nausea accompanied my transformation to human form, but that was as far as I let it go. If I ended up vomiting up blood, then I'd have to replenish it, and there wasn't time for that. So straightening out my dress, I staggered towards the house.

The easy part was getting there; the hard part was remembering where my room used to be. I remembered that it was on the second floor, which complicated things. Going to the front of the house, I tried the front door, which was locked. Doors at other parts of the house were locked, too. In fact, every door and window I tried was locked. That sounds very wise and normal these days, but the Caglionis were snug in their big, private estate and usually didn't bother with such things, as I recall. Then I remembered that there was a mad, vicious dog-and servant-killer on the loose, so now things made sense.

I remembered that Frederico's room was at the front

of the house, so I went back there and stood under what I believed was his window. I picked up a rock and cradled it a bit, then tossed it away. Waking him up wasn't the idea. There were a lot of trees and other plants near and on the building, so after some thought I shrugged and grabbed hold of some thick ivy. I might not have tried it while sober, but my climb to Frederico's window proved to be much easier than I dreamed. In fact, halfway up it occurred to me that I was barely even gripping the plants, ledges, and crevices for support. At my worst I only touched them, but hadn't fallen yet. Somehow I'd been sticking to the wall like a fly but hadn't noticed it right away. Very cautiously at first, I let go of one bit of ivy, and when I didn't fall, I took a deep breath and let go of the other.

I wasn't even slipping. After another deep breath I shuffled sideways and remained just as firmly attached as before. I dared to look down and realized that I was about thirty feet up, but that didn't strike me as a dangerous height anymore. Ah, the wisdom of the inebriate. I decided to take the ultimate dare and turn all the way down. I did so, and looked straight down at the ground. Even this didn't frighten me, for after all, I was a fly on the wall. Smiling to myself, I turned back around to face the sky, but decided to give the ground another look. From there it quickly degenerated into my spinning around and around in place, testing my limits by lifting up a hand here, or a foot there.

I was still so drunk that I didn't realize how dizzy this was all making me. By the time I stopped, I only had time for an uh-oh before plunging to certain bumps and bruises in the bushes below. Not certain death; it takes more than a short drop to do us harm.

Above me a window opened. I looked up to see Frederico poking his head outside, so I stayed absolutely still until he ducked back inside and shut the window. Then with a groan I rolled from the bushes, stood and dusted myself off. I considered trying another window, but decided not to, and started climbing again. In no time I was just under Frederico's windowsill, when I heard the front door opening carefully. Frederico emerged cautiously, dressed in a robe, and armed with his rifle. Antonio had assured me that neither steel nor lead will do us harm, but I decided not to take his word for it completely. Just then Frederico was devoting all of his attention to scouring the ground, so I took the opportunity to very gently and quietly pry his window open. This accomplished, I climbed up slowly and grabbed for the inside of the sill, and almost fell again. My arm wouldn't go inside. I checked, and yes, the window was open, but I couldn't reach inside.

Below me Frederico was apparently satisfied that he was safe, for he turned around and headed back for the front door. Almost panicking I tried to climb inside, but fell a few feet before grabbing the wall and stopping myself. By the time I regained my composure, a small light came from the window. Frederico had returned, so I froze against the wall and waited. Again he poked his head outside but didn't see me in the darkness, then shut the window again. A drunken idea came to me, so I climbed back up and peered inside.

In the darkness he laid his rifle beside his bed and ran his fingers through his hair. I reached up to the window, hesitated, and then knocked quietly. He almost hit the ceiling in fright and fumbled with his rifle. I stifled a laugh but did hiccup, then braced myself for the very serious task to come. Frederico knelt down and aimed his rifle at me, but I gathered enough concentration to look into his eyes and freeze him as he was. I fought off a growing headache and probed deeper into his mind. He lowered his rifle slowly and rose to his feet. I beckoned him to come forward, which he did, until he reached the window and raised it slowly.

"Frederico," I whispered.

"Theresa," he whispered back, "I dream of you . . ."

"What?" I said. "Oh! Yes, you're dreaming about me, Frederico. You . . . you must miss me terribly to do this."

"Yes . . ."

"But I cannot go to you," I whispered. "I cannot come inside."

"Come inside . . ." he whispered. "Come to me, Theresa . . ."

"But I can't, Frederico," I whispered, reaching out. My hand went inside. I pulled it back and stared it before remembering to keep my concentration on him.

"Um . . . um, I mean . . . help me inside," I whispered, and he obeyed. He shut the window behind me, then stood up and waited.

"Uh . . . uh, Frederico," I began. "You must tell no one that I was here. I mean, I was *not* here. You're dreaming of me."

"Dreaming . . ." he whispered, staring at me.

"Yes, dreaming, and um . . . well, I must go to my room now," I whispered. "Now . . . you should go back to bed. Go to sleep."

"Sleep . . ." he whispered, and went to his bed. I followed him and pulled his sheets back so he could climb in. Then I tucked him in, but hesitated before leaving.

His room was actually my room, too, but not my private little room that wealthy people often have. It took me a moment to remember that mine was right next to his. Not completely to my surprise I found that my things were being packed away. This was to my advantage, except I realized that I couldn't take very much of this junk with me—not if I was going to make it in one trip to the crypt. A big box was still mostly empty, so I spent some time dumping a lot of clothes and other necessities into that, then closing it up. At first I ended up with several boxes of "necessities" before deciding to grit my teeth and toss out two boxes. I ended up with something like a week's worth of clothes, all my jewelry, some toiletries, and things I don't remember now.

The stairs were past Frederico's room. I tried to pass right by, but hesitated again, and then set down my box entirely. I stood in his doorway for a long time, staring into his peaceful, sleeping face. Although I wasn't mad with passion for him I'd always had a real affection for him, even if it could grow to no more than a friendship.

After many moments I went to his side and touched his hair. He turned toward me, so I took hold of his thoughts once more and made him open his eyes.

"Theresa . . ." he said, and tried to sit up, but I stopped him.

"Shh, no, no, Frederico," I whispered, so he lay back down. "I'm not here, Frederico. I'm . . . I'm dead."

"No."

"Yes," I whispered, stroking his hair now. "Yes, I'm dead now, Frederico. You're still only dreaming that I'm here."

"Dreaming . . ."

"And . . . um . . . before I leave you always, I need to say that—I need to let you know that I'm sorry," I whispered.

"Sorry . . ."

"I never meant to hurt you this way," I continued. "I never meant to hurt anyone this way, especially not my family. My mother . . . um . . . but it's for the best,'' I said. ''I—I wouldn't have made you a good wife. You might think I would have, but I wouldn't. There are plenty of other girls for you; any one of them would make you a fine wife, Frederico. I . . . yes, that's what I came to say. Forget about me and find another wife, a better wife. You'll never see me again.''

''Theresa . . .'' he whispered, but I put a finger over his mouth.

''You're dreaming,'' I whispered. ''And keep dreaming. Dream about—whatever makes you happy. Dream about that.''

''Yes . . .'' he whispered, and let himself go limp. I stroked his hair a little longer before leaning over to kiss his cheek. Once he was in deep sleep I stood up and resumed hauling my things downstairs in silence. In spite of my drunken state I managed to carry everything out of the house without stumbling down the stairs or even waking anyone.

A chilly wind came about, making things bitter cold quickly. I could only trot at best. The box was very light to me but very bulky; I couldn't see over its top, and stumbled on just about every rock in my way. Almost every noise made me hesitate, until I decided to ignore anything except maybe a direct attack from some rabid animal.

The crypt door was ajar as I'd left it. I turned sideways to see better on my way down the stairs. There were still no lights within, so I had to see by what little heat there was. Once at the door where my own coffin was, I discovered that it was still locked, also as I'd left it. Oh, yes, I'd become mist to get out. Having no key, my only choice now was to yank off the lock or leave the box sitting outside. Neither choice was very wise, but I yanked off the lock anyway and tossed it into the box.

My former ancestors were still at rest within. Any

moment now I expected them to rise up and kill me for making so much noise. It was still only four hours into the night at best, but I'd had enough adventures for a first night. I opened my coffin, then groaned when I remembered that I'd have to fill it with dirt if I meant to take it with me. For the confused, I should say that in the legends I'd heard, vampires were always returning to their graves every morning. Either that or filling their pockets with graveyard dirt, sleeping in dirt-filled coffins, and so on. Antonio never answered my questions about why this was so, but he had always put me into a dirty coffin in the morning. I never did find out where he slept, though, so I only had my folklore-based knowledge to rely on.

Dumping everything onto the floor, I took the now-empty box with me out to the graveyard and got busy filling it. Then I reconsidered and dumped over half of it out, and hoped that would be enough. Back in the crypt I spread it all out nice and smooth and soft, then made a face before climbing inside and shutting the lid. I figured I could sleep the rest of this night off, too, besides the morning. Although it had been quite an adventure, I hoped that the next night would be a little duller. And that my inevitable hangover would be kind enough to go away quickly.

Chapter 12

It didn't seem likely that anyone had searched the crypts for the mad killer. I'd decided it to be wise to leave this place as soon as possible, as in, that night, but that wouldn't be easy. I could have carried the box to a port but not that damned coffin. A wagon would do that, but then I'd have to get back to the house to get one. Maybe some servant would let me borrow one, if I could only reach his mind before he ran screaming into the night at the sight of me.

I dragged the coffin across the catacomb floor up to the base of the stairs. If that noise didn't wake these dead, then nothing would. From there I crept up to the top and peeked outside. No one was working on any graves, so I left the crypt and strode confidently towards Caglioni manor. More lights and noise came from within. My family was still there, although why, I wasn't sure.

Again I avoided the temptation to stick around and went straight for the stables again. An empty cart that was the perfect size stood off to one side, so I started examining the front to figure out how to hitch up any horses.

"Hey!" a voice called from behind. I jumped about

two feet. "What are you doing there? What do— Oh! Forgive me, *signorina.*"

"What?" I said meekly, stepping forward. "What?" The servant before me stared right at me. He took off his hat and bowed hastily.

"Forgive me," he said again. "I—is there something I can do for you?"

"For—? Um . . ." I said, trying to relax now, "Oh, uh . . . I was only admiring your cart."

"Admiring, *signorina?*" he said. "It is only a cart. An old one at that."

"Oh, no, it's a very lovely cart," I said. "I mean, I need to borrow this. I have some . . . things to move."

"Things?" he said. "But, why would you want this one? Don't they have carriages for you? You . . . *are* with the families, aren't you?"

This was starting to make sense now. I'd never seen him before, either. That he didn't recognize me made me smile to myself, though.

"Oh . . . yes," I said. "Yes, I'm . . . Maria. Maria Allogiamento."

"Oh," he said quietly. "*Signorina* . . . I'm so sorry for the death of your . . . er . . ."

"Sister," I said. "She was my sister."

"Your sister," he said. "It's such a terrible thing, this. My master is—"

"Yes, he—he's very upset," I said quickly. "But, truly—I need this wagon. I'll pay you if I have to."

"Um . . . well, yes, but—"

"Excellent!" I said. "Then you'll begin hitching horses to it?"

"What, now?"

"Yes, right now!" I said, backing away. "I'll go bring my things."

"But *signorina!*" he called to me, and I stopped and ran back to him, looking at his eyes.

"Please, *signore.* Tell no one I was here," I said.

"No one . . ."

"I'll return shortly," I said. "In the meantime, please get the wagon ready."

"Wagon ready . . ." he said, and began his work. I backed away from him slowly at first, then turned and ran at full speed for the crypt.

I took the long way back to the stables in case anyone I knew was hanging around outside. I'd have to go back for the coffin, which would be a tricky thing to explain. It was getting tiresome having to charm practically everyone I met, but until I got out of there, it was the easiest way. The servant was just finishing hitching the horses when I arrived.

"Uh . . . oh . . ." he said, apparently confused to see me. *"Signorina?"*

"Yes?" I said, putting my box into the back.

"I . . ." he began, then shook his head. "Nothing, *signorina.* I think I must have been asleep or something."

"Hmm?" I said.

"Uh—pay me no mind," he said. Then, "Wait! You wanted this. What for? You couldn't be leaving, could you? Where is your family?"

In answer I only smiled and stepped close to him. Luckily he just sat there staring at me, so it was simple to enter his mind. I smiled and kissed him on the cheek, and so doing, felt the warmth from his face. I let my cheek glide down to his neck and smelled him. Now my mouth was watering, and I shut my eyes and prepared to take that night's meal, when my senses returned.

"No," I murmured, backing off some, "There has to be a better way than this."

"Signorina?" he asked. I looked him in the eyes.

"Uh . . . maybe you—" I said, then shook my head. "What is your name, *signore?*"

"Angelo," he said.

"Um . . . Angelo," I said, "We must go, quickly. Have you a blanket?"

"Yes."

"Then I'll lie down in the back, and you cover me with it. We must ride to the crypt first."

"Yes, *signorina.*"

He did as he was told and covered me with the blanket. I lay down and prayed that no one would come out to question Angelo. After a few moments we arrived at the door. I leapt out of the back and ran up to Angelo.

"Wait here for me," I said.

"Yes, *signorina.*"

It took some time to drag the coffin step by step up the stairs. I'd had to divide my concentration between carrying the coffin and keeping my hold on Angelo, which was becoming a bit of a strain. Once I'd dragged it through the door, the charming became easier.

"Angelo," I said. He turned. "Help me put this on the wagon."

"Yes, *signorina,*" he said, climbing from his seat and helping me lift the coffin onto the cart. That done, he sat around waiting for orders.

"Um . . . Angelo," I said, "Are these, um . . . are these easy to drive? These wagons?"

"Yes, *signorina.*"

"Not just for you, but for anyone," I said. "I've never driven one of these before. Is it simple?"

"I . . . I don't know, *signorina,*" he said. I shrugged.

"Well, I don't have much choice either way," I said. "It seems I'll find out soon enough."

"Yes, *signorina.*"

"Then I suppose . . . um . . . you should go back to the house now," I said. "Tell them, uh—well, don't tell them anything. Forget you ever saw me. If they ask about the wagon, well, you don't know about that, either."

"Yes, *signorina,*" he said, and started off.

"Er, wait," I called. He stopped in his tracks while I considered my situation. I planned to ride into port and hire a boat to France, if there were one. Meanwhile I wasn't certain if the boat would leave right away or in the morning. Either way made my hunting prospects shaky at best.

"Come here," I said, and he did so. I bade him sit down against the wall, then knelt beside him. Francesca hadn't died when I did this, nor had she been converted, so I was certain no permanent harm would be done.

"Forgive me if there's any pain," I said, and heard him gasp quietly when I began the feeding. I drank until I was sated, which didn't actually take as long as I'd thought it would. I'd had to feed from Antonio's other servants or animals before and noticed the same thing. Knowing that made the act much easier to bear, for it wasn't necessary to kill or convert under normal circumstances. My first night had been under extreme circumstances. Now that I think about it, the servant I'd attacked that night had probably been converted. Except I never came across him again, so I can't be certain.

Angelo was resting peacefully when I finished. I hoped that he would remember everything I'd told him—or rather, *not* remember anything. I climbed into the driver's seat on the cart, took up the reins and shook them a little. The horses ignored me, so I shook them a little harder. Frustrated, I yanked on the reins and hollered, and the horses took off with a jolt. I almost flipped into the back but held on tight and tried to bring the horses down to a manageable speed. After a lot of yanking and shaking I got a workable feel for what made them do what. It was still a bumpy ride into town. Before making it to the streets, I looked back at the Caglioni estate but saw no one chasing after me with any nasty weapons.

No one paid me any mind while I rode through the streets. Why should they have? Even the coffin was all covered up. I did have to stop once and ask for directions to the port, though. My second stop came after I arrived at the dressmaker's shop. I spent a long time staring at it before erring on the side of honesty and leaving an old brooch at the doorstep as payment. Then I quickly moved on.

The docks appeared to be closed, but some sailors were lingering about. I managed to get the horses to stop and alighted from the wagon. No one paid attention to me until I walked right up to one of the sailors.

"*Signore,*" I said, "Is there a ship here sailing for France?"

"Ummm," he said, scratching his chin, "That one." I didn't know which one he meant, so I made him take me to it. It was a small cargo ship—a schooner, I think. I've never been very knowledgeable about sea-going vessels. I got the attention of someone still on board and made him come down.

"*Signore,*" I said, "is this ship sailing to France?"

"It will be," he said.

"When?"

"Tomorrow morning," he said.

"Hmmm," I said. "Do you think it would be possible to leave earlier?"

"Like when?"

"Tonight."

He blew some raspberry and started for his ship again. I chased after him and grabbed his arm.

"Oh, please, *signore,* I—"

"Go on, missy," he said.

"No, no, I don't mean tonight," I said. "Truly, tomorrow morning will be perfect." He stopped and listened.

"What's this about?" he said.

"Oh, nothing, really," I said. "I just need to . . . well, I need a ship to France."

"Oh," he said. "Well, a passenger ship won't be here until tomorrow, maybe. This takes cargo only."

"Oh, that will be perfect, too!" I said. He eyed me curiously.

"I—I mean, that's what I have," I said. "Just cargo. You see, I—well, my dear sister has departed, you see, and—she's to be buried in France and—"

"What? You've got her box to take over?" he said.

"Well, yes," I said. "What else is she to go over in?" He was silent. "Well?" I said. "Have you no room? I'm certain you've carried worse things than somebody's coffin."

"Haven't, actually," he said, spitting out some tobacco. "All right, then, missy. I'm not doing this for free, you know."

"Of course not."

"So where is it?" he asked.

"Oh this way," I said.

"No, no, I meant the money."

"That, too, is this way," I said. He shrugged and followed me to the wagon.

"Just this, eh?" he said.

"Yes. That's it," I said. "The coffin, and some of her possessions. Uh—I have no actual money, but there is, um—" I said, and busied myself digging through my box. After a time I pulled out a few baubles and showed them to him. The sailor took them and examined them.

"Hmph," he said, "No money, hm? Your family didn't even give you any?"

"Taking care of her has been my job," I said. "Let's leave it at that."

"Oh," he said, then pocketed the baubles. "All right, this pays it. So what about you, then?"

"Just worry about this," I said. "I'm leaving later. Just make sure all of this is on board tonight. And—*please* be careful And as for her possessions, don't think I won't know if something's missing."

"What? You call me a thief?"

"I've called you nothing, *signore,*" I said. "I . . . only want to be careful. Forgive me if I've offended. But—do you think this will be brought aboard soon? When will your ship arrive in France?"

"A few weeks or so," he said. "Weather allowing."

"Day or night?"

"Weather allowing, missy," he said.

"Oh," I said. "But—this *will* be loaded soon, yes?"

"What's your hurry?"

"Um . . . I must be elsewhere soon," I said. "I just need to make sure it's safely aboard."

"All right, all right, missy," he said, spitting out more tobacco. "Wait around; I'll be back." He left me and headed for the ship. Luckily I'd parked in a fairly secluded place. I saw no people around, not even any auras, so I lifted up my coffin lid and ducked inside quickly. It's possible I could have asked him to load it first thing in the morning and just wandered around during the night, but I thought it wiser not to take any chances. What to do once I was on board would have to be dealt with later.

There were several voices approaching, and I heard my old friend Mr. Tobacco and some others. I'm not sure if it was for the best that I heard their conversation. A lot of it was about me in various terms—mostly about what he'd liked to do if he could have gotten me into bed with him. The others supported his ideas heartily.

I got the impression they were extra careful in carrying my coffin (and me) on board. No doubt they didn't want to drop it and spill its contents. It was a roller-coaster ride through the ship, until at last I was dropped somewhere on board. It seemed wise to stay where I was for as long a time as possible. Judging from the night before, it seemed that most of these sailors would be out on the town for the night and not on board. But after an hour of waiting I got bored and poked the lid open. I seemed to be in the cargo hold and had been placed high on top of some crates stacked almost to the ceiling. It would be a nice climb down, but nothing difficult for me.

It took forever to brush off all the dirt from my dress. That whole dirt-from-a-graveyard business made little sense to me, but I didn't want to take the chance and dump it all out. The dangers to vampires are few, but are always very severe when encountered. For all I knew I would have turned into a pile of dust if I'd traveled anywhere without my precious dirt.

No sailors seemed to be around on deck, either, so with great caution I climbed up from below and stood on deck. The night was warm and clear. I took many deep breaths of air and came to enjoy the salty flavor to it. Just then there was movement nearby, so I panicked and scrambled to safety down below. I poked my head up from below to hear some sailors returning to the ship. I was going to watch some more, when something crawled across my hand, and I gasped and fell all the way down the ladder. That was certain to bring some attention. Nothing seemed to be broken, even if it was a bumpy fall. A scan of the hold revealed that my attacker had been a large rat, and now several of them were scurrying around me. I kicked at them in disgust, when hurried voices from above spurned me to action. Like a maniacal cat I scurried up the sides of the crates to my box on top, threw myself inside, and shut the lid just as the sailors rushed down the ladder.

Well, this is going to be a thrill, I thought. Nothing more exciting than running for cover at every sound. But then I couldn't very well charm everyone on board, either, so that's the way it would have to be.

Even now I loathe rats and wish that they had no connection to vampires at all. To my extreme delight I discovered that we can summon them and make them do . . . something, I'm not sure what yet. Maybe they're supposed to attack people when we're in trouble, but the day I couldn't defend myself when rats could, hasn't come yet. They will serve as food in desperate situations, though.

I couldn't say if the old sailor had been right about the length of the journey. It seemed like months, but it may have been only a few weeks. By some miracle I was able to make it through without being discovered and without going mad. There were rats, but not an infinite number. To conserve energy, I tried to sleep as much as possible. Like any animal, the less active we are, the less fuel we need.

I was jarred out of sleep one night as I felt myself being dropped. After a brief panic attack, I came to the conclusion that we had finally landed, and the ship was being unloaded. Some sailors dropped me onto the docks with a loud thump, making the lid jump up a little, then shut again. I couldn't tell if the sun was up, but had to check sometime. I was about to open the lid to take a peek, when I heard some sailors chatting away.

"Here, here, what are you doing?" said one.

"I saw it open," said another. "No one nailed it shut."

"Ah, well, that— Here! You can't look in there!" said the first.

"Just a peek," said the other. "Who's to know?"

"What, and disturb who's inside? Don't be a fool!"

"Just a peek—"

"Hey!"

I had to freeze in place when the lid swung open. It was also nighttime, or you wouldn't be reading this right now.

"Hoo!" said the second sailor, "*Live* people should look so good." Then the lid was slammed shut.

"Idiot!" his friend cried. "Leave it alone, already, we have work to do!"

The unloading seemed to go on for hours. At one point I was dragged off to some much quieter place and left there. After another hour or so I couldn't take the lying around any longer and snuck out of my coffin. There were sailors hanging around still, but no one noticed me leaving the holding area. My first order of business was to get moving again. You try staying in bed for days on end and not feel stiff as a cement block.

The second order of business had to be food. I never wanted to see another rat again, not that that's been possible. Now that my rat-calling ability had surfaced, it was hard to keep the beasts away. I've since learned to do that, thank you.

So this is France, I thought, overlooking the streets ahead. It looked much like any city I'd been in, except perhaps Rome. This place was much dirtier. I wasn't likely to see the glamorous side as long as I stayed at the docks, either. Calling up as much dignity as possible, I stepped into town.

Since a number of hours had gone by, there wasn't much to see. The only open businesses were the inns, and the only people around were beggars and such. I decided that I should hire a room and started checking the inns. Eventually I found one that not only would accept baubles as payment, but where the innkeeper also spoke Italian. Food would have to wait; next was to hire a cart to load my things onto. Already this coffin was becoming a damned inconvenience, but that's the way it was. Luckily I still had plenty of jewelry with me, but this couldn't go on much longer. I needed to find a jeweler to appraise what I had and sell it. I was starting to get into the real gems now and not just the costume stuff.

Once the room and cart were secured, I loaded up my things from the docks and unloaded them through the back door. After securing my things within, I set out for the bar and caught the innkeeper before he retired. He gave me convoluted directions to a local jeweler, and I thanked him. All that was left then was the nasty business of finding food. No doubt there were plenty of stray animals roaming around, but seeing them was not the same as catching them. Cats and dogs seem to sense our presence and make hasty retreats, unless the dogs are in packs. Then they attack.

I went behind the inn to see if any dogs were around, but found none. After a time I became frustrated and resigned myself to feeding on some drunken sot, if one was around. There were plenty of them around, actually. The more I looked, the more homeless peasants I could see sleeping in alleys, curled up under rags or—if they were lucky—ratty blankets. Maybe Palermo had just as many, or Naples, or even Rome. If there were, I never saw them. But heightened perceptions lifted some of my haziness at every turn. It would still be some time before I had any sort of sympathy for them, though. For now they were just were the poor, useless ones, and no one would miss one.

Antonio had assured me numerous times that one of our gifts is immunity to disease—*all* disease. Still, it was difficult keeping my mind off plagues and disease while I bent over one of the solitary peasants. He awoke with a start, but I was ready for him, and stared long into his eyes. He relaxed and lay back down. He smelled like raw sewage, so I opted to feed from his arm and avoid his breath. Much better than rat blood, and the peasant would be weak for a few days at best. Unless he had some plague, in which case his death wasn't on my hands. It worried me that I might catch something from him, though. I certainly knew nothing of germs or viruses then, but at least it was common sense to stay away from sick people. Fortunately vampires really *are* immune to all diseases, and for those who still wonder, we don't carry them, either.

Now that was done, and my night was basically through. There were still a few hours until sunlight, though, so what could be done now? It seemed that living by night wouldn't be so romantic as I'd thought, because no one was up for very long at night. The only thing I could think of to pass the time away was to fly around the city and try to get the layout of the land. That was actually a wise decision, because I was able to find what had to be the local nobility at one end. I'd have to begin associating with them if I was to find my fortune. But that would have to wait, for the sky was becoming dangerously light now.

Chapter 13

The next night I tracked down a jeweler who appraised my things but could only buy a few of my cheaper items. It was the best either of us could do, considering that he spoke about as much Italian as I did French. Also that night I flew back over to where the wealthy lay. This would be my second glimpse of a nobleman's chateau, and it was just as impressive as before. It was still nothing, compared to the cathedrals of Rome. I already missed my old land—probably even more than I missed my family. But Antonio was right about it being a bad idea to stay there, at least for a number of years, anyway. Agelessness does have that advantage, that we can outlive any human who could do us harm. All of that would have to wait, though, for I needed a plan for the here and now.

It is far easier to cope with gaining sudden wealth than with losing it. The longer I stayed in town, the more I could see the disparity between those in the chateau and those in the street. The poor were very poor and the rich were very rich. I wanted to be with the very rich, and to hell with the poor who stood in my way. That was the way I thought *then,* anyway. Besides, nobody spoke my language and nobody was willing to help me learn his, either. My plan to hook up with some nobleman had to go on the back burner for a time while I tried to find my bearings. The meager bit of cash from the jeweler was running out quickly. Soon I was seriously considering moving my things into an abandoned shack or basement and working from there. At least I didn't have to spend money on food, but I still didn't have enough to hire anyone on a long-term basis to get any business affairs started.

People were tossing a lot of pamphlets around in those days, which gave me a lot of reading material to practice on. Mostly they just complained about King Louis and other powerful people. I ignored the content, though, and concentrated on just learning the language.

Meanwhile, every night I scouted the local chateau to see if anything was up, and lo, after a month or two of this, many carriages were pulling up to its front gate. From the looks of things it appeared that a party was being planned, so I dropped down in the darkness, transformed back, then wandered around to eavesdrop. From what few words I could pick up it seemed that the occasion was to be the next night, so I hurried back home and got busy preparing myself. My clothes were still in very good condition, and I also had a little fan somewhere. My trouble was that I didn't have a wig—but it would be no problem to find one.

I spent my last bit of money on a wig, but still had my fancy jewelry with me. Perhaps I could sell some to the rich folks at the party. So after getting all dressed up and wigged and all, I transformed to bat-shape and discovered that the wig and fan stayed behind. The stupid things wouldn't disappear to wherever normal clothing disappears to whenever we transform. So I had to hold on tight with my feet and hope nothing dropped into the mud on the way.

Upon arrival I discovered that the wig was a mess,

and a lot of the powder had blown away. It didn't seem to fit right, either. Oh, well, I thought. Maybe I can charm everyone in the chateau and make them think I look gorgeous. In spite of all this I held my nose in the air, spread my fan and stepped boldly up to the front door. Several snooty couples were ahead of me, and each was announced as they presented their invitations. Then my turn came, and the attendant held out his hand.

"Um . . . eh, forgive me, but I've misplaced my invitation," I said. "But, I am—"

"Quoi?" he said.

"Uh . . . I speak little French," I said in French. "I am from Rome. I have . . . er . . ." I said, and had to resort to a lot of hand waving. The attendant looked confused, and made as if to pull me aside, when a man behind me spoke up.

"You are from Rome?" he said in Italian. I turned around.

"Yes," I said. "And . . . I speak little French."

"What are you trying to tell him?"

"I, um—" I said, then continued more confidently, "I have misplaced my invitation, that is all. Please ask him to announce Maria . . . da Clovino. From Rome."

"Oui, *madame,* eh—what was it?"

"Maria da Clovino," I said. "From Rome."

The man stepped forward and explained my problem to the attendant, who eyed me suspiciously, until I practiced some subtle charming on him, and he agreed to announce me. He mispronounced my entire name, but at least I was allowed inside now. By this time I'd almost forgotten that strange barrier that I'd encountered back at the Caglioni estate. Fortunately nothing stopped me from entering this time.

I followed my new translator and his companion into

the main banquet hall, where food-laden tables lined all the walls, and a harpsichordist played. Some strings were seated near him, tuning up, apparently. My translator walked on, but I stayed behind to take in a little more of the scenery. Various couples walked by and looked me up and down, which made me nervous at first, but then I noticed that everyone did that to everyone else.

Before taking any real action, I wandered over to a mirror to look myself over. My wig was all right except for its lack of powder, but I spotted some people off in a corner getting repowdered. I also noticed that most of them powdered their faces, too. My pale skin helped me fit in better, then. I put the attendants to work at my wig before attempting any mingling.

Now I was free to walk amongst these people. At first I hung back and tried to eavesdrop, but could only pick up a few words here and there at best. From the tone of the women I listened to, they were probably gossiping, anyway. Come to think of it, the men probably were, too. After a time I overheard some men speaking in Italian. They were complaining about the king just as the pamphlets had—maybe that was the national pastime. I hung around until their conversation broke up, and then smiled and bowed slightly to the gentleman who remained. He returned my gestures.

"Madame," he said.

"Signore," I said.

"Ah, do you speak my language?" he asked in Italian. I fanned myself a little.

"I am from Rome," I said.

"Oh?" he said. "I was born there myself. But now I live here. And you are . . . ?"

"Maria da Clovino," I said. He took up my hand and kissed it.

"You grace us with your beauty . . . and presence, *signora . . . ?*" he said.

"*Signorina,*" I said, withdrawing my hand. "I am . . . not married."

"Oh?" he said. "A flower such as yourself? Why, that is—" He was interrupted by someone who cut in and addressed my companion in French. The two gave excited greetings to each other and kissed. Then they went on in friendly conversation before the Italian remembered my presence.

"Ah! Phillipe," he said, and then talked about me in French.

"Ahh! So you, too, are from Rome," Phillipe said in my language. "Then you must know the Vicomte Sargento's family."

"Uh . . . uh, no, forgive me, but I don't," I said.

"That's all right," Phillipe said. "No one else does, either!" After that remark the Vicomte Sargento slapped Phillipe on the shoulder before joining his friend in strained laughter.

"Ah . . . ah . . . forgive him, *madame,*" Sargento said. "The marquis is only very often such a donkey's a— . . . head." Phillipe wagged his finger at him warningly.

"Ehhh, what have I told you about your language in front of the ladies?"

"I said nothing," he insisted. "In fact I was kind to you as a result."

"Damned uppity Italians!"

"Eh! Watch *my* language?"

Well, at least they weren't as snooty as everyone else around there. Still, it was evident that the marquis had gotten an early start on the wine. Fortunately for me the manners of the wealthy were not as important to me as . . . well, as their wealth. Besides, I had no doubts that any one of my brothers could swear any of these people into the ground, so it's not as if I wasn't used to improper language.

This marquis was interesting, as a matter of fact. It was nice to have found another Italian, but I didn't want to cocoon with my own kind. This Frenchman seemed to be more open and lively than many of those surrounding us. In fact, it was rather refreshing to see a nobleman being loud and obnoxious to the point where he got a few stares.

During a rare lull in the conversation, I took the opportunity to inquire of our host. That is, I pretended to know who he was, but confessed that I had not yet seen him in person and needed him pointed out to me. He and the *signore* stared at me, and then laughed.

"Ahhh, well," Phillipe said, "uhh, actually, I couldn't say."

"You mean you've never seen him, either?"

"Oh, certainly, *oui, madame,* but only when I look in the mirror."

I stared at him confusedly for a moment, before two and two came together, and then I gasped and pointed.

"Oh!" I said. "Oh! You mean—*you* are the Marquis of . . . er—"

"Lyon," he said.

"Uh, of course, Lyon," I said in mock embarrassment. "Forgive me, I was about to say Rome."

"Of course," he said. "And . . . if this lout of a man had remembered his manners—"

"Eh? What?" Sargento interjected.

"—then he would have introduced us long before now," the marquis finished.

"Eh, you never gave me the chance to," his friend protested. "But so—*madame,* the Marquis Phillipe de Lyon. marquis, the *madame*—er, forgive me—the *mademoiselle*—forgive me again, but I don't know your title."

"My—?" I said. "Oh! Oh, yes, um . . . *baronne.*"

"Ahh, the Baronne Maria da Clovino," he finished. The marquis bowed slightly and kissed my hand.

"Enchanté, mademoiselle la baronne," he murmured. "But—I must say I don't recall inviting anyone named da Clovino. And I *know* I sent nothing to Rome."

"Oh!" I said. "Uh—no, I am only *from* Rome; you sent it to my home. Here."

"Here?"

"Well, I mean . . . Paris," I said. "You sent plenty to Paris, correct?"

"I sent two, actually," he said. "The *vicomte* and *marquis,* there, and there," he added, pointing to those guests. I started fanning myself nervously.

"O, well, *monsieur,*" I said, "I assure you I received an invitation, but . . . I misplaced it. Fortunately your attendant recognized me as a guest."

"Oh, he did, eh?" the marquis said, and looked me up and down a moment.

"Well!" he said. "It's fortunate indeed that I have such a . . . an astute servant. After all, this affair would be just another get-together without you."

Grazie, signo- er, *merci, monsieur,*" I said with a curtsey. "Really, I promise to master your language soon."

"Ahh," replied the marquis. "Well, good luck to you. But please take no offense when I say that no one save my countrymen can master the language."

"Well," I said in French, "I shall certainly try, *monsieur le marquis.*"

Our conversation was interrupted by some guests, who came to bid the marquis good night. I got the impression that most of these people would be staying there for the night. The chateau seemed large enough to accommodate everyone. For some reason I waited around until the marquis managed to lose them. During this time Signore Sargento took his leave to chase after some woman he'd apparently been chasing for some time.

"Some wine for you, *mademoiselle?*" the marquis asked as a servant brought over a tray. I smiled and shook my head. The marquis helped himself to two glasses.

"I'll drink your portion, then," he said, and finished both off. *"Mademoiselle,"* he began, "do you think you could accompany me outside for a moment?"

"N-now?" I asked.

"Oui. Now," he said, offering me his arm. I hesitated, then took it and followed him outside to his balcony. We reached the railing, so he let go and leaned against it, taking a deep breath.

"I only needed a little . . . fresh air," he said.

"Of course," I said. We weren't facing each other, but I could feel him staring at me.

"You know, this *is* a puzzle," he said after a time. Now I faced him.

"Why do you say that, *monsieur?*"

"Because . . . I did *not* invite you," he said, *"mademoiselle."*

"I-I'm sure you did," I said. "I would show you my invitation, but I—"

"Misplaced it," he said. "I know. But—what are you, then? A commoner?"

"Oh, certainly not," I said. "I . . . I am no commoner. My father is very wealthy."

"Oh, is he?" he asked, his eyes lighting up.

"Oh, yes," I said. "Very wealthy."

"Does he live here?"

"In France?"

"Oui."

"Oh, no," I said. "He, um . . . he is still in Sicily. I mean Rome."

"Ohh," he said. "I see. Well, *mademoiselle,* I'm not

sure how you got inside, but I am sure why you are here."

"Are you?"

"Of course," he said. "That's why I brought you out here."

"And why is that, *monsieur?*" I asked. He only smiled and put his arm around me. I shrank away, but he followed and brought his other arm around me.

"Wh-what are you doing?" I asked.

"That should be clear to you," he said. "Come: if you Italian women are half as passionate as Guiseppe says you are, then I should go to bed a *very* happy man."

"What?" I said, and was so shocked that I wasn't able to resist for a moment. But only for a moment. Without really thinking, I pulled one of his hands away and began to squeeze it. Soon he grimaced and tried to pull it away, but now my senses had returned to me. He dropped to one knee and pulled in vain.

"What are you—? Stop this!" he cried.

"I—am—no—*whore, monsieur!*" I hissed, then released his hand roughly. He became busy working the kinks out of his fingers.

"I am Maria da Clovino!" I continued. "I am no—no plaything for any man, no matter how—no matter what his title is! My sin to you was to join your party uninvited, but that is no excuse for what you tried to do!"

"*Mademoiselle,* I—"

"I will hear no apologies!" I said. "And I will leave this place. You needn't worry; I'll never sneak into any of your little get-togethers again!" I turned and made to leave, but the marquis grabbed my arm.

"Wait!" he cried, and I yanked my arm away.

"You will not touch me," I said.

"No, no, of course not," he said. "I won't—please

forgive me, *mademoiselle.* But what was I to think? You must understand that this sort of thing *does* happen."

"What?" I snapped. "Being attacked?"

"No, no, I mean—women who . . . go to these affairs . . . do you understand?"

"Yes," I said, "but I don't appreciate it."

"Of course not, *mademoiselle,*" he said. "I . . . you will forgive me. Yes?"

It did occur to me that under normal circumstances, he would never have apologized, least of all asked my forgiveness. My anger had made it difficult *not* to charm him, and while I hadn't quite dominated his mind, I had ended up, shall we say, staring him down successfully. I was too angry at the time to find out what his true reaction would have been, yet I still found myself attracted to him.

"Yes," I said. "I will forgive you."

"Ahh, *merci,*" he murmured, kissing my hand. I almost pulled it away, but then let him stroke it while he spoke.

"It seems strange to me, *mademoiselle,*" he said, "that you would come to my chateau at this time, and yet not be, eh . . . looking for handouts, so to speak."

"I suppose . . . you had some reason to believe that," I said.

"But since you are not, that still leaves the question of the reason you are here," he said. Now I pulled my hand away.

"I am . . . no commoner, *monsieur,*" I said.

"I'm afraid that you are, *mademoiselle,*" he said. "Unless your husband or father happens to be one of us."

"I have no husband," I said. "Nor . . . a father, either."

"No?" he said. "Then .. why are you—?"

"It was a mistake to come here," I said. "Forgive

me, *monsieur.* I've only caused you trouble. I'll leave you now."

"Wait," he said, holding my arm. "At least tell me why you are here, or how. Was it some . . . game to you? To pass yourself off as one of us, is that what it was?"

"How much truth you speak," I murmured.

"What?"

"Nothing," I said, smiling. "This night has all been a joke, *monsieur.* But only on me. I thought that—"

"Thought . . . ?" he prompted.

"I've wasted enough of your time," I said. "This is foolish, what I'm doing. *Au revoir, monsieur.*"

"You thought what, *mademoiselle?*" he called after me. I'd been walking away, but in spite of myself I stopped and turned towards him.

"What?" I said.

"You were going to tell me something," he said. "About why you came here, I think."

"I-I told you, it was only a joke," I said.

"On yourself, you said. What do you mean?"

"It's nothing that would interest you."

"Why not? Do you think *they* have anything better to say?" he said, gesturing towards the house.

"They . . . but they're your people," I said. "I'm only a commoner, as you say. What could I say to you?"

"*Mademoiselle,*" he said, stepping forward, "tell me why you came here."

"Uh—" I said, looking behind me, then back at him, "very well. I, um—actually, you were very close when you asked if this was a game to me. You see I—" then I laughed. "I'm afraid this might take some time."

He shrugged. "Why not?" he said. "The night is young."

"Is it?" I asked. "I thought it was rather late for you—I mean us."

"Then speak quickly," he shrugged.

"I'll try," I said, relaxing a bit now. "You see, I—well, this is my first time away from my homeland."

"You mean Rome?"

"Actually . . ." I continued, "I'm not *really* from Rome. Or not born there, that is. You see, my father—well, let's just say that I wouldn't be welcome back home."

"Oh," he said, nodding.

"Well, you might not understand," I said. "You see, I refused to marry the man my father had chosen for me."

"Now that wasn't very daughterly of you," he said.

"No," I said, "I suppose it wasn't. But there is another story behind that. To be quick about it, I would no longer be welcome back home, and—I decided to leave my homeland and make my own fortune. Oh, I have some money, of course, but I no longer—well, my father's wealth is not mine anymore. So you see what I mean when I say I am not a commoner, or rather not a *poor* commoner, because I am accustomed to wealth."

"So you had some . . . need to stay that way," he said. "To mingle with the wealthy. *Oui?*"

"Oui," I whispered. "But I see that this was a foolish undertaking. A—"

"I wouldn't say it was entirely foolish," he said. "But it was a great, uh—how do you say—*risk.* And . . . ambitious, yes, that's the word. You seem very determined."

"To do what?"

"Why, to regain your wealth, of course," he said. "And possibly to, eh, perhaps gain some more?"

"I . . . I'm not sure what you mean."

"Perhaps I mean nothing," he said. *"Mademoiselle,* if you still wish to leave now, then do so. But if you choose to stay, your . . . secret is safe with me."

"Truly?" I said in surprise. Genuine surprise, too, as I hadn't been influencing him in any way for some time.

"Truly," he said. "I suppose this one time, you have done no harm. But I must caution you on how fortunate you are. It's not often I allow intruders to remain here intact."

"Oh, I . . . I understand, *monsieur,"* I said. "I realize I never had any right to be here, but—it truly was such a challenge for me that—that—"

"I understand more than you think," he said. *"Mademoiselle?"* he added, offering his arm. I took it and followed him back inside.

The marquis still referred to me as a *baronne* when introducing me to people. I was very relieved at this, and ended up enjoying the remainder of the evening immensely. In fact, the only problem I had afterwards was when the marquis became insistent that I try his various wines and champagnes. Not drinking just wasn't in fashion back then, but I didn't want a repeat of that last time I drank. His speech slurred quite a bit when I finally took my leave of him and his friend the Viscount Sargento. Again, he kissed my hand, but before I left, he leaned close to me and whispered that I was welcome to come back, perhaps when there weren't so many people around? That sounded fine to me, but I only smiled and said something like, "We shall see."

Chapter 14

There was something Antonio didn't warn me about, and knowing his sense of humor, it makes sense. The marquis's party had taken place two nights before the full moon. This was actually the third full moon that had occurred since my conversion, but most of my first month was spent sleeping. There was a time when I slept very fitfully and had very, *very* erotic dreams, but I weathered that time well. During the second one, I . . . don't remember what happened, actually. But I did *not* wake up naked in the forest or zoo or some place like that.

For two days I noted that my libido was increasing dramatically, but didn't make any correlation between that and the full moon. Why should I have? I was a reasonable woman and wasn't going to spend my time worrying about what phase the moon was in. If I'd been a werewolf, well, yes, I would have.

The first night of the full moon I found myself flying at top speed to the marquis's chateau. I all but smashed the knocker through the door before that attendant showed up.

"*Oui?*" he said.

"You must tell the marquis that Theres-, Maria Allog-, Maria da Clovino is here," I gasped. My, my, he looks good, I thought. If the marquis isn't in, then he'll do just fine.

"Quoi?" the attendant asked.

"What?"

"Quoi?"

"Oh, let me through, I'll find him myself," I said, and shoved him aside. He grabbed my arm, but I yanked it away and pressed on. The attendant raised a ruckus behind me and gave chase, but I took off and outdistanced him easily. Some other servants passed by me in a blur as I picked up speed. I almost transformed into a wolf, but resisted. Where *is* he, blast it? I thought.

I stopped and started sniffing, ignoring the shouts of people still looking for me. There wasn't much rational thought behind what I was doing. Instincts were taking over. These were procreative instincts, mostly, and when you consider that vampires can't have children, it makes little sense that we should have such instincts. But we do. Believe me, we do.

I caught the marquis's scent just as some people came around the corner, so I raced up the stairs and ran full speed through the hallways until I reached the right door. I almost broke down the door, but retained enough intellect to knock, instead.

"Enter," a voice called, so I opened it quickly to see the marquis standing there with some attendants, apparently about to prepare him for bed.

"Oh," he said in quiet surprise, "Er—*mademoiselle?*"

"Maria . . ." I whispered, and stepped inside.

"Maria?" he said. "What do you—?"

"May I . . . speak with you alone? *Monsieur?*" I said. Just then a servant rushed up to the door, out of breath.

"Monsieur le marquis!" he gasped. Then he continued in French, and gasped and pointed at me. The marquis seemed confused, then calmed his servant and sent the

other attendants away. The last one shut the door hesitantly behind him.

"Now . . ." he began, "Mademoiselle—or Maria, what—?"

He couldn't finish, because I'd taken over his lips. He let me kiss him for a little while before pulling me from him.

"Mademoiselle!" he said. "What—?"

"I need you, *monsieur,*" I whispered. "I must have you, I-I cannot resist it any longer."

"Now wait a minute—"

"Take me," I said, "Take me now, Phillipe! I can't resist it!"

"Resist what?"

"I-I don't know," I said. "But whatever it is, I can't help myself! I must have you!"

"Now look here, *mademoi—*"

I couldn't waste any more time with words. Whatever was causing this couldn't be resisted, so I took his mind, then kissed him long and hard. He wrapped his arms around me and held on tight until I allowed him to let go. From there I started undoing his clothes, then became frustrated and tore his shirt open. We fell onto his bed and continued until both our clothes were all but rags. Phillipe blew out the candles beside him, and I came to my senses long enough to go to the door and lock it, then blow out all the other candles.

I finished removing what was left of his pants before a servant tried to come in. He started knocking and called to the marquis.

"Tell them that will be all," I whispered.

"That will be all!" he said in French. I finished with his clothes and dove under the covers with him. If I'd been able to think about it first, I would rather have worked on the relationship gradually, but it didn't work out that way. Perhaps it was best this way, too. Until that time I had had sex, obviously, but I had never had my expectations for it fulfilled—at least, not entirely. Frederico loved his sex, but it was nothing spectacular for me. Antonio had been better, but he was a bit too . . . mechanical to satisfy me. He was a very good kisser, though.

And now both of them had been topped by a man who wasn't even himself at the time. Most of the time he was under my control, but I'd like to think I wasn't just masturbating. The effect eventually became more like a mind-link, making it something that has to be experienced to be understood. For the first time my sexual expectations had been fulfilled. I achieved orgasms that I regret I have seldom duplicated since. Yet most of you would rather find out if I drained him dry. Perhaps to your disappointment, I did not. But his blood was part of the experience, I assure you. Even in this state I wasn't hungry enough to kill him, which was good, because it had never been my intention to convert him. He was going to remember me for a long time afterward, though.

The next night frightened me. My hunger had not passed; it had gotten worse. This time the marquis was there when I arrived at the front door. He was also already under my control, because I vaguely remembered wishing him to be there, ready for me. He escorted me to his bedroom, where the same thing went on, only worse. I'm surprised I didn't kill him this time, no matter how young and fit he was. Rabid wolves in heat were tame compared to this, yet I still didn't understand the cause. That's why I was so frightened afterward, as I had no idea why this was happening or how long it would last, or most of all, if it would get worse.

The marquis survived that night, and the next night, too, which thankfully was not as savage as before. I then returned to him a few nights later, now that my hunger had passed and I was capable of real thought. He looked terrible when I saw him, but I sort of expected that.

"May we speak in private, Phillipe?" I asked. He nodded and offered his arm, then led me out to the balcony where we'd talked before.

"I must—I must apologize for what's happened," I said.

"Apologize?"

"Yes," I said. "I—I don't know what came over me. I couldn't stop myself."

"But—neither could I," he said.

"True, but that's because—" I began, then shifted thoughts. "Oh, Phillipe," I said. "I'm very fond of you—truly—but I didn't plan on . . . rushing this so. Those last few nights were—well, suddenly I can think again, and—the more I think about it, the more I realize I behaved just like the—the whore that you thought I was."

"Why, I never thought that," he said.

"It's not my way, *monsieur,*" I said. "Never in my life have I been so . . . forceful. And believe me, I have always had an . . . affinity for men, but—never like that. Not like last night. Or the night before, or before. I only wish I knew what came over me."

"Madness?"

"It must have been madness," I said. "It *had* to be madness, for I was never in control of myself. And now that it's passed, I hate myself for what I've done, for I *despise* not being in control. I hate it!"

"I don't think you're mad, Maria," he said. "You're a woman who *does* have control. It is *you* who controls *me,* for I can't help thinking about you."

"What?"

"I dream about you; asleep or awake, I think about you always. It is *my* madness for you, Maria!"

"I-I don't think—"

"You mustn't leave me now, Maria," he said. "I need you now. I *love* you."

"You don't know what you're saying."

"Marry me, Maria," he said. "Marry me and you need never worry about your fortune again."

"Oh, Phillipe," I said. "If only I could tell you."

"Tell me yes," he whispered, kissing my hand over and over. "Say yes, Maria, that's all you need tell me."

"I can't," I said. "It's—"

"Why not?" he said. "I'm mad for you; I need you. Be mine, Maria!"

"Phillipe, you're—!" I said, pulling my hand away. "Marquis, I'm afraid it truly is madness that you speak of. You see, you're—"

"Marry me."

"Let me finish!" I said, and he waited. I tried to speak, but had to switch thoughts again. "Strange," I murmured.

"What's that?" he asked.

"Nothing," I said. "I'm only talking to myself."

Here was a strange dilemma. I was getting exactly what I'd been trying to get—a proposal from someone of the nobility—but now I wasn't certain how to deal with it. Was this what I could hope for? To escape one marriage, only to leap right into another one? How independent did I think I was, anyway? Still—the marquis *was* attractive to me, and if I did marry him, it would be because I chose to. And yet, I wanted the decision to be mutual, if possible. It was obvious to me that he was very much under my control, and paradoxically, I didn't have the experience to make him *not* that way. He was likely to dream of me night and day until he recovered from the bites, if ever.

"Phillipe, I . . . I'm very flattered by your proposal," I said. "But if you will, I would ask you to grant me some time to decide."

"Time?" he said. "But—how long?"

"Uh—a week?" I offered. "A week, *monsieur.* I must have at least that much."

"But I must know now—!" he protested, but I quieted him with a finger.

"You will grant me at least a week," I said. "Two, at most."

"Yes, Maria."

"Merci, monsieur," I said, then turned to leave. "Oh," I said. "It seems if I'm to live here, then I should be called Marie."

"Yes, Marie," he said, and I went over to kiss him before leaving. He didn't walk me to the door because I didn't want him to.

In almost two weeks I returned to the chateau. I had made an effort to learn more French and was able to announce myself properly to the attendant. He recognized me anyway, but I wanted to practice. Phillipe met me in the foyer, then escorted me to a sitting room. He looked much better, as I expected he would. His color and energy had returned. Now it was time to see if his senses had, too.

"I counted each day, each hour until you returned," he said after I'd been seated.

"Oh—really," I said in French. Afterwards our conversation would be a mixture of French and Italian while I practiced. Phillipe was patient with me through it all. Meanwhile he knelt before me and kissed my hand gently.

"Yes," he murmured. "Not a day went by that I didn't think of you. Or dream of you."

"Oh," I said. So much for his senses.

"As you requested, I gave you no more than two weeks to decide," he said. "And have you?"

"Uh . . . yes, actually," I said.

"Then tell me, I must know," he said.

"Now . . . now calm yourself, Phillipe," I said. "Have you considered the . . . well, the consequences?"

"What consequences?"

"Well, when people find out that I'm a va- . . . that I'm a commoner," I said, then sighed a bit in relief.

"Eh, they'll know nothing," he said. "You are a *baronne* from Rome as far as they know. And then you'll be a *marquise,* so what have they to complain about?"

"But—surely there must be some lady of *real* rank who's been—well, pursuing you."

"No," he said. "No one of consequence."

"Oh," I said, then was silent a moment. "Do you know," I began, "truly, you know so little of me. Perhaps it's best that you don't—"

"Marie!" he snapped. "I *must* know. Will you marry me?"

". . . I will marry you," I said, and he let me say no more until we'd finished with our kiss. So neither of us spoke for a long time.

"Phillipe, I—" I began, then just stared at him with my mouth hanging open.

"Yes?" he said. I just stared at him some more, then looked down and shook my head.

"No," I said. "No, it's nothing. Or—it can wait, for now."

* * *

He was very upset when I insisted on a small, intimate wedding. The last thing I needed was hordes of people around me. That, and I didn't want anything that would remind me of my first wedding, for fear that memories of family and friends would arise. The hardest part was arranging the ceremony at night. Perhaps my greatest concern was whether or not I could be married at all. I didn't think of myself anymore as some creature of darkness like all the stories depict us, but it seemed to me that there wasn't very much . . . holiness about us. Not as if humans are any better, but that business about crosses, holy water and so on has more truth to it than it should. At first, that is. Now the stuff doesn't bother me at all, but I've noticed for a while that new vampires are particularly susceptible to those things. I was no exception then—nice of Antonio not to tell me about that. So I was concerned that a church wedding might be too much for me.

My intention was to keep my vampirehood a secret from Phillipe for as long as possible. That was a little easier than it seems, at least while we were engaged, because I didn't move in until after the wedding. He wanted me to, but I gave him some story about being chaste. I also kept the suggestions up on him as long as I could. Oh, yes. "Influence" is our term for the old Renfield cliché, or forcing humans to do our bidding. It's a bit like charming, only on a long-term basis. It's a very rare thing these days; vampires who do that sort of thing are considered pretty vulgar. "Suggestions" then, is a very mild form of influence. I don't expect sympathy for keeping the suggestions up when I did. Obviously my beginnings were fairly shaky, and I was prone to use more extreme measures to accomplish things than I do today.

As an example, a lot of charming was used when I had my coffin brought in and secured in one of the basements. That one was then declared off-limits, even to Phillipe. The wedding took place the next night, followed by four days of reception. Believe it or not I ended up sleeping a good portion of the nights during that time. The main reception room was in the middle of the house and was away from any windows, so I was able to mingle with the guests during the daytime. It was there that I met the Comtesse du Pres, who must have been an old paramour of Phillipe's. If looks could kill, as it's said. Our confrontation never went beyond that, fortunately. In fact, I never saw her again after the reception.

Most people perceive vampires as very sexual creatures. Well, we are. Most of us, anyway. I discovered that trying to appear completely human during sex seriously reduces its pleasure potential, though. In fact, I'm not sure if its possible to climax as long as we're worrying about our teeth, eyes, ears, and so on all the time. This is how our wedding night went. Phillipe probably thought everything was fine, but I ended up lying beside him all night just wondering if this was going to work. I think I decided that, for the moment, I would just have to see how far it could go.

Unfortunately the first months stretched the limits of my control over Phillipe. I wasn't experienced enough to be terribly subtle, but I didn't want him to be a mindless slave, either. My whole intention in keeping the suggestions up was to see how effectively I could keep my secret from him. Phillipe wasn't the sort of man who could abide separate bedrooms or separate bedtimes for very long. When it got to the point where I had to start commanding him not to ask questions, I started to rethink the situation.

Part of my dilemma was that I had also grown to care for Phillipe. In fact, I was starting to love him, and with that feeling was the desire to keep him as long as I could. There is much truth in the old routine of "Let me give you eternal life." If you had the ability to keep you and your mate from aging, wouldn't you be rather tempted to do so? I wanted to give him eternal life, but I wasn't sure if I could convince him to accept it. I kept thinking about Antonio's "one great mistake"—the woman who'd never accepted his gift. I would have liked to have spoken with her.

Chapter 15

I started out the evening by calling him to me. Not yelling for him—*calling* him, as Antonio had done to me before. I hadn't actually done this to him until then, so he was disoriented, to say the least.

"Shh. Shh," I said. "It's all right, Phillipe. Sit down. I must speak with you."

"Er—very well," he said, and sat. I locked the door, then sat in a chair facing him.

"It's very important that I tell you this," I began, "which is why I—well, why I called you here the way I did."

"Called me-?" he said. "That was you? That—strange force?"

"Yes."

"But how did—?"

"Shh," I said. "I will explain, *chéri*. I . . . was hoping that I wouldn't ever have to, but I can see that this isn't working out."

"What isn't?"

"Our marriage."

"What?" he cried. "What do you mean, our marriage?"

"I don't mean our marriage per se, but—the way it

is now," I said. "It—I don't think I should deceive you any longer."

"Deceive me?"

"Yes," I said. "Before now, my entire life has been built upon deception. I've deceived everyone I've ever known, I'm certain. Including you. But it can't work forever."

"But—what have you done, *chérie?*" he asked.

"Only this," I said. "I've—" This wouldn't be as easy as I'd thought it would be. I stared at him a moment, then smiled and tried again.

"I am not what you think I am, Phillipe," I said.

"What do you mean?"

"I mean that—I mean that I am not—what you think I am."

"Yes," he said. "You just said that."

"Well, what I mean is—is that I'm not . . . a complete person," I said after a lot of silent gesturing.

"You still make no sense," he said. "Why don't you just tell me the truth?"

"Because . . . it's possible you'll try to kill me if I do," I said.

"What? Kill you?" he said. "Why on earth would I try to kill you? Why, not even if you were—now wait. You have seen another man?"

"What? No!" I said. "Of course not. And why do men always suspect that, anyway? Did you all meet long ago and agree to accuse your wives of that?"

"What are you talking about?" he said. "Are you going to tell me what's wrong or not?"

"Yes," I said, then took a deep breath. "Yes, I will. Forgive me, I've never had to do this before. And I fear for myself because of this. Phillipe, I am not—not human."

"Not—human?"

"No," I said. "I'm . . . the reason I must stay indoors always—at least when the sun is up—and don't eat very much, and . . . cannot drink wine is—is that I'm a vampire."

". . . What?"

"I don't say this to frighten you, Phillipe, but to give you a choice," I said. "You see, I won't—"

"A vampire?"

"Yes," I said. "But—in truth, I haven't been one for very long. Not even a year so far, and—"

"What are you saying, woman?"

"Now I know that there are many things that you've heard about us. Mostly horrible things, I'm sure, but—"

"My *wife* is a creature from Hell?"

"From—? No, no, Phillipe, I'm not—"

"Is this some joke?" he demanded. "To tell me that you're some horrible monster?"

"Horrible?" I said. "I don't think I'm horrible! And certainly not a monster, either!"

"Well, if you're really a vampire then you certainly are!" he said.

"Now it's not like that at all!" I insisted. "I-I admit that I, too, have heard many of those old—"

"But vampires are servants of evil!" he said. "Creatures of Satan, now, Marie . . . why do you tell me this? Please end this horrible ruse of yours and—"

Things had gotten out of hand now. I'd expected this but had hoped against it, but now I was forced to use charming to stop him in his tracks and make him listen. Once I'd dominated his mind, I kissed him gently and held both his hands while he had no choice but to listen.

I talked for a long time. I don't remember exactly what was said, but I know that the gist of it was the advantages vs. the disadvantages of vampirehood. I admitted that I loved him that night, which is why I wanted him to make the decision on his own. After I finished my speech, I released his mind and prayed that he'd remain calm.

"You . . . you did something to me," he said. "Something that made me unable to move."

"Forgive me, *chéri,*" I murmured. "I didn't want to, but you were becoming very excited. Your thoughts are entirely your own now, though. Do you . . . remember everything I said?"

"Yes," he said. "I . . . remember."

"Then . . . you won't try to kill me?" I asked.

"Even if I did," he began, "I'm not certain I'd know how to."

"Do you still believe me to be a . . . creature of evil?" I asked.

"I don't know," he whispered, then held both my hands. "Marie," he said, "you said that you love me. Didn't you?"

"Yes," I said.

"You don't know how happy that makes me," he said, "for I, too, have . . . grown very fond of you."

"Say it, Phillipe," I said. "If I can, then so you can you."

"Very well," he said. "Marie, I—I love you, too. Day and night, I think of you, I *dream* of you, I—"

"Phillipe," I said, "please, not that again."

"But it's true," he said, kissing my hands. "Ah, it's true, *chérie.* I don't think I could have lived without you. But—now . . ."

"Now you find that your love is not what you expected," I said.

"Oh, no, no, it's not—"

"Phillipe," I said, holding up a finger, "I will not hear this. You will speak only the truth to me, just as from now on, I will only speak the truth to you."

"Yes, Marie," he said. "The truth, then, is that I must think about what you ask."

"Then . . . you don't plan on destroying me?" I asked. "Condemning me as a servant of Hell?"

"I . . . I can't," he said. "But is it because you won't let me?"

I had no answer for him at first. I wasn't consciously keeping up suggestions, but maybe I wasn't able to control it. After all, my desire for him not to destroy me was terribly strong.

"No," I said quietly. "No, your will is your own, *chéri*. Just let me know quickly what you decide."

"I will," he said. "I promise."

To my dismay he decided to remain human—for the time being, that is. More important was that he decided to keep me as his wife. I admit that his knowing my secret relieved a lot of tension, but it was still a mixed marriage in a big way. Afterwards I thought I wouldn't have to worry about my teeth, eyes, and so on changing during sex, but he almost had a stroke when I let that happen one night. He thought I was attacking him. Up to that time I'd dealt with full moons by charming him throughout and showing whatever I pleased, because he wouldn't remember, anyway. Those were also the only times I ever fed from him. Even though he knew about me, I still had to charm him, and that was frustrating.

I didn't force the issue because I recognized that Phillipe was at a point where he needed to be able to conduct his affairs during the daytime. He didn't do much traveling when we first married, but later he started going to Paris for at least a few months each year. Those were always uncomfortable times for me, because for one thing, Phillipe had been my liaison between myself and his attendants. Most of them didn't know what to make of me, especially the stable workers who had to supply me with my nightly cup of animal blood. Try doing that each night while battling rumors that the marquis had married a witch.

A number of years had gone by, and Phillipe had still not changed his mind. I was getting more and more tempted to try some serious influencing. I didn't want him to be a doddering old fool before he finally decided to give agelessness a try. His stays in Paris were becoming longer, little by little, each year, and eventually I learned part of the reason why.

Phillipe had never actually been as rich as I'd hoped him to be. Most people picture the ruling classes as fabulously wealthy and without a care in the world. In truth, I noticed that the ruling class in France believed this of themselves, too, even if it was not always the case. France was losing money very quickly, and Phillipe was one of those noblemen who went to Paris to yell at the king. Actually, like most noblemen, Phillipe supported the king and didn't, at the same time. That is, he was all for there being a ruling class and wanted Louis to make sure there would always be one. Unfortunately the king had been letting things decline.

One time Phillipe returned in a particularly bad mood. I thought about cheering him up, but wanted to hear the news first.

"Hm?" he said. "Oh, don't trouble yourself, *chérie.*"

"Tell me the news, Phillipe," I said. "Obviously it wasn't a pleasant trip."

"Oh, the trip was fine," he said. "It's just Louis again."

"What happened?"

"Now he's gotten us into another damned war."

"Oh, no," I said. "Not against Britain, is it?"

"Of course," he said. "Who else? Now, I'd have

no problem with that, but this is a terrible time. Louis thinks the colonies will wear George out for us, but I doubt it."

"The colonies?"

"Of course, the—oh, yes, you wouldn't know, would you?" he said. "It seems George's New World colonists have attacked his troops."

"Really?"

"Yes, but now Louis thinks this is some grand opportunity to gain some glory. Surely, I would like to see George in ruins, but with farmers as our allies? What is he thinking?"

"But—what of everyone else?" I asked. "Do they support him? Or are they like you?"

Phillipe threw up his arms.

"It's all in chaos," he said. "I wish to keep my hands clean of the whole affair, but it won't be easy, I assure you."

"You mean, you might have to fight?"

"I will refuse, if it comes to that," he said. "I will—" then he stopped himself and sighed.

"Ah, my sweet," he said, taking my hand and stroking it. "I traveled all this way to forget Paris."

"I'm sorry," I said. "I only wanted to know what troubles you."

"I don't blame you," he said, and we kissed. I wrapped my arms around and held him there a while.

"Chéri," I whispered, "why don't we leave France?"

"Leave? But why?"

"Why not?" I said. "Things seem to be getting so bad lately."

"Oh," he said. "Have I gotten you worried? This will all blow over quickly, I'm certain."

"Oh, it isn't just that," I said. "It's everything. No one seems to be happy with the king, war or not. It seems it's only going to get worse, so why don't we leave?"

"Ah," he said with a wave. "Don't you worry yourself, *chérie.* Despite the king's faults, France is the greatest place to live."

"Well . . . personally I like Rome," I said. "Have you ever been there?"

"Yes. If you like, we can visit there," he said. "But only visit; I have no plans to live anywhere but here."

"I . . . don't think it would be wise for me to return there," I said. "Not this soon, anyway."

"Oh," he said in comprehension.

"Um . . . *chéri,*" I said, "speaking of which, do you think that things might have changed enough that—well, that you've changed your mind?"

"Ah," he said. "That again."

"What do you mean, that again?" I said. "Don't you know what this has been like for me? Don't you *want* to stay young, and strong, and—*hand*some?" I asked, thrusting my face close to his and giggling.

"But I *am* young, strong, and handsome," he said.

"I know that. And I want you to stay that way. Before you do grow old."

"Marie, I—I would but . . ."

"But what?"

"Well, you see what's happening now," he said. "Now I must go to Paris more than ever, and probably stay there longer, too."

"Oh, Phillipe. That's not fair at all," I said. "What is it you can do now, now that it's begun? What else will it be when this is over?"

He looked me straight in the eye for a while, as if daring me to charm him. I restrained myself, and he brought my hand up to his lips and kissed it gently.

"Chérie," he murmured, "I must thank you for not using your powers against me for all these years."

"I didn't think it'd be fair," I said. "And . . . it's been suggested that it's a bad idea to force conversion upon others. At least, that's the impression I got."

"I'm glad you got that impression," he said. "But . . . perhaps now I've been unfair to you. Still . . . this is a bad situation that we're in. I would like to be able to go to Paris and make myself heard."

"Well, you still can," I said. "You just have to be very careful."

"What, and ride to Paris in a coffin?" he said. "That's what I'd have to do, wouldn't I?"

"Um . . . well, perhaps you wouldn't be able to, then," I said. "It just seems like this is only one more thing to get angry about, that's all. Why can't you just get angry from a distance? Surely there are plenty of those who only send letters to the king and don't visit in person."

"Oh, yes, there are plenty of those," he said. "I was just hoping I wouldn't have to be one of them."

"Then . . . your answer is still no," I said.

"No?" he said. "No, Marie," he whispered. "My answer is yes."

Chapter 16

"Marie," Phillipe said shortly after waking, "do you miss the sun at all?"

"Do you?"

"You must answer me first."

"Why is it important that you know?"

"It's not important," he said. "I was only curious."

"Oh," I said, then sat up and stretched. "Actually . . . I try not to think about it anymore," I said, watching the last bits of daylight disappear from the sky. "It's not wise to dwell on things like that. Things we can't change."

"I know," he said, sitting up in his casket. "But, even after all this time, I couldn't help but ask."

"Yes, well . . . time to start another night," I said, and climbed from my own casket. He watched me dress for a while, then dragged himself from bed.

He was right about "all this time." I'd converted him a number of years before. Since then we'd been living the lives of reclusive, eccentric nobility. I was pleased that Phillipe neither despaired of nor gloated over his new existence. He had come to accept his situation, even enjoy it, but as indicated above, he had occasional reservations. After all, it wasn't always easy being a creature of evil and servant of Satan; at least, that's the impression we got. But the servants kept whatever reservations they had about us to themselves. We'd decided it would be wise not to feed from the servants and we stuck to living off of the livestock by rotating our donors.

I may have been his master, but Phillipe had been a vampire for about as long as I had. That meant that I'd had about as much to learn as he had. But together we discovered our abilities—even some that I hadn't been aware of yet. For instance, we learned of the telepathy that vampires share when in nonhuman form, and we discovered what it's like both to transform into mist and literally to become one entity. The union that human lovers achieve has nothing on that, believe me.

We'd come to rely a great deal on our friend Giuseppe Sargento for news from Paris. As I'd expected, things had gotten worse. There were probably no rich people left anywhere, but the upper classes still insisted on living high on the hog. We were no exception. Phillipe and I had never known anything but wealth and were determined to keep it that way, although I think I had a better grasp of our situation than he. The problem was that there didn't seem to be much that I could do, as this debt was a national problem.

It had been years since we'd ventured out into town, and even then, things had not been promising. Phillipe was as fair as he could be for a lord, but he gathered dirty looks and hostility whenever he went into town. Finally, he never went into town. The last time I accompanied him, the sight of all those wretched, destitute people pulled at my heart, but I didn't know what to do for them. Not for all of them; there were just too many. By now my feelings for them had risen from contempt to ambivalence. I pitied their lot and wanted to help while also believing that most of them created their own problems. In truth, Phillipe and I were probably just as poor as they but just didn't seem to notice it.

Giuseppe had brought news of some makeshift Assembly that had formed on a tennis court. I thought he was joking, but Phillipe was very upset that he was unable to be a part of it. Somehow we'd successfully kept our secret from Giuseppe; we'd pretty much convinced him that Phillipe was now too perpetually ill to travel. I still wanted to leave France and suggested that we stay at Giuseppe's estate in Rome, and damn the risk of running into Antonio again. Phillipe still wouldn't hear of it.

Giuseppe ran in like a wild man one night, shortly after we'd risen and dressed. He was ranting in Italian so quickly that even I could barely understand him. Phillipe managed to calm him down enough to make some sense out of him.

"The Bastille . . ." Giuseppe gasped, "The Bastille . . ."

"The Bastille?" said Phillipe. "What about it?"

"They've taken it . . ." he said. "Unbelievable . . ."

"Who? What? What are you talking about, man?" Phillipe demanded. Giuseppe eventually explained that a mob of enraged peasants had stormed the Bastille and armed themselves, and as far as he knew, Paris was in flames. This was unexpected news for us all, to be sure. Well, not entirely unexpected.

"Why am I not as surprised as you?" I said. "Didn't we discuss this before?"

"What are you babbling about, woman?" Phillipe snapped while Giuseppe talked to himself. Both of them were pacing.

"I told you the peasants were angry," I said. "Ready to riot at a moment's notice. They've been following the colonists for years now! Didn't I once say that—"

"Will you be silent?" Phillipe barked. "Enough about the damned colonists! What's happening there, man?"

"I've told you all I know," Giuseppe said. "Paris is probably in flames, destroyed by now."

"By peasants?"

"Completely armed peasants," I reminded him.

"They're after the king, Phillipe," Giuseppe went on. "They're after the lords, they're after *us!*"

"You mean you were there?"

"No, thank the Lord," said Giuseppe. "But many of us are fleeing. What do we do, Phillipe? What about here? Have they risen up here?"

"I . . . I don't know," he said.

"Let's get out of here," I said. "We'd be foolish to stay here now, even *you* must see that!"

"And what do you mean by tha-"

"She's right, Phillipe!" Giuseppe cried. "Who knows how far they'll go?"

"You don't think this will spread, do you?"

"I don't know anything," Giuseppe said. "All I know is that I'm afraid. Very afraid. No one is happy here. No one *has* been for so long now. They'll only be inspired by this! Your own people could be plotting to burn *you,* too! We've got to get out of here!"

"But—"

"We must leave, Phillipe," I said. "We must leave *now.*"

"Yes! Listen to me, man! Listen to your wife, we must leave!"

"Where shall we go?"

"Rome! Spain! Even England, does it matter?"

"But . . . I . . ."

"Enough indecision!" I said. Enough suggestions,

too. Now I was commanding him. "We will leave here immediately, Phillipe, especially while it's still dark."

"Yes, Marie."

"Giuseppe," I said, "you'd better bring as many carts around as you can."

"Yes, yes! Immediately!" he said, and raced from the room.

"We'd better pack as light as we can," I said.

"Yes, Marie."

"But how will we manage our . . . beds?" I asked.

"We'll manage."

"Then we must *really* pack light," I said. "No more than bare essentials."

"Yes, Marie."

It took me about an hour to cram my real essentials into several bags. Phillipe was wasting time with niceties when I went to check on him. I ended up pulling out some of his things and tossing them onto the floor when Giuseppe finally returned.

"Have you finished?" he asked. "I have my things packed away already."

"Good," I said. "We'll be ready any moment. Is there any news from the town?"

"None that I heard, or could see," he said. "That's a good sign."

"It is," I said. "We should hurry, then."

"Where are we to go?" Phillipe asked.

"I think we should go to Rome," Giuseppe said. "We can stay at my—"

"But Rome will take so long," I said. "What about Spain? Won't that be a shorter trip?"

"Probably, but as long as we're away from here, we'll be safe," Giuseppe said. "Besides, we'll simply stay with my family, and—"

"I think . . . Spain would be best," Phillipe offered.

"But why?" Giuseppe asked, perplexed.

"My wife is right," Phillipe said. "The journey will be shorter."

"Why is that so important?"

"Um . . . well, we have some . . . crates that are difficult to travel with," I said.

"Crates? Full of what? We can't afford to—" Giuseppe stopped as Phillipe began moving towards him. Giuseppe was confused, not afraid. "What are you doing?" he asked. Then Phillipe stopped in front of him, and looked back at me momentarily.

"What's wrong?" Giuseppe asked. "Phillipe? Are you—*Madre!*" he cried as Phillipe stared him down, then clamped down hard onto his friend's neck. This took *me* by surprise, too.

"Phillipe!" I said. "What are you doing? You're not converting him, are you?" That got me no answer save a wave of the hand to silence me. I could have pulled Phillipe away, but that probably would have resulted in a torn throat for Giuseppe.

Giuseppe went limp in Phillipe's arms, and I could see that conversion was not his plan. He carried his friend over to a bed and set him down gently.

"I'll see to our caskets," Phillipe said. "You see that he's all right."

"Was that necessary?"

"You know we don't have time to explain things," he said, and left. I held Giuseppe's hand until he revived. It occurred to me that Phillipe wouldn't want him fully alert, so I kept Giuseppe in a half-conscious state until Phillipe returned.

"Everything is almost loaded," he said. "Let's get our bags and Giuseppe and go." I grabbed all I could carry, and Phillipe brought in a servant to carry his things while he carried Giuseppe.

Most everything was ready outside. Phillipe lowered his groggy friend to his feet.

"Giuseppe," he said, "Giuseppe, you must listen to me."

"Yes?"

"We're all leaving now," he said. "We're leaving for Spain."

"Yes."

"I know some people there, and they'll see to our safety," Phillipe said. "In the meantime, you must never—I mean *never*—question us about any of the strange things we carry with us. Not our caskets, not anything."

"Yes . . ."

"I'm sorry to have done this to you, my friend," he said. "Best friend or no, there are just some things that . . . It's best you not know everything about me."

"I understand."

"We must leave, Phillipe," I said.

"Yes . . ." he said. "Of course, Marie."

Servants that were still awake had gathered around the entrance. We told them we had to leave on a brief trip. Better than telling them we were leaving before people like them decided to kill us. Phillipe wanted to bring some along, but I talked him out of it. The fewer bodies, the better, and for the moment we had Giuseppe enthralled. I could only hope that that would be temporary, as I was very fond of him and didn't like seeing him that way.

After the packing was done, we all hopped into the carriage and sped away. Phillipe was angry that I was taking my books along, but I wasn't about to leave my babies behind. I won't ever be able to have any real babies, so I might as well have some sort of substitute. Besides, many of those books were quite rare and are even rarer today.

The ride to the docks would take us through town;

this was sure to be a risky trip. Phillipe made Giuseppe sleep for most of the way.

"I'd really rather go to Rome," I said.

"So would I, but didn't you say it was dangerous for you?" Phillipe said.

"Um . . . I don't know, actually," I said. "It would probably be risky, but not nearly as bad as staying here."

"Well, this should all come and go very quickly," he said. "In the meantime, I believe the people I know in Spain will give us sanctuary."

"But how will we manage there?" I asked. "I don't even know Spanish. Do you?"

"No," he said, "but don't worry, *chérie.* We won't need to."

"Well, I don't want to live somewhere if I don't speak the language," I said. "And I'm not sure I'll be able to learn another one."

"I told you, this will blow over soon," he said. "And we'll be able to return, you'll see."

"What, just like those upstart colonists against Britain?"

"They only won because *we* were there!"

"Yes, but you were against fighting Britain."

"Oh, I'm in favor of putting Britain in its place, and I'm glad we won, but don't you start thinking a bunch of farmers could have taken it down alone!"

"I never said that," I said. "It just seems to me that this might turn out differently than people think. I'm just trying not to underestimate them. After all, they're all well armed now that the Bastille has been taken."

Phillipe sighed loudly and turned away, muttering something like "Women." I frowned at him but didn't make any further ado. He knew that I could dominate him at any time but chose to let him flex his ego muscles—when there was no harm to it, that is.

There were more people out tonight than usual. They must have heard the news about when we did, and that made me nervous. I kept expecting them to start tearing the wheels off and pummeling us with stones the moment our carriage appeared. As we passed through the town I scooted close to Phillipe, who wrapped an arm around me. We both made it a point of not looking outside, but after a time curiosity got the best of us. Phillipe poked his face up to the window first, then stuck his head all the way out. He looked from side to side, then sat down again.

"Is anyone armed?" I asked.

"Hm? No, no, of course not," he said. "It's very quiet, actually, as you can hear."

I stuck my head outside and looked around, too. People were watching us pass by and seemed very tense, but no one was carrying any weapons that I could see. Then I looked behind us, and saw a small group of people following our caravan. Occasionally someone joined in, but otherwise it didn't seem to be a mob. Still, I was nervous. Phillipe pulled me back inside and held me even closer. I wrapped my arms around him and shut my eyes.

"We'll be safe, *chérie,*" he said. "There's nothing to worry about."

"Oh, of course not," I murmured.

We made it through the town intact. I think everyone, even the peasants, were too shocked from the news to act upon it immediately. There was a pretty big crowd at the docks watching us load up everything, but we got little more than glares, some curses, and people kicking loose pebbles and whatnot every now and then. People's auras tend to shift around in intensity and sometimes color when emotions are particularly intense, but this crowd's auras stayed fairly steady. Finally we got everything hauled on board, including our coffins, and ordered the crew to set sail. Ordinarily they might not have, but I think the crowd was making them nervous, too. Of course, *we* were the cause of that crowd.

I take it back. Soon after the ship had begun sailing, someone threw something on board that we later learned had been a dead rat.

Chapter 17

Phillipe's acquaintances in Spain did agree to take us in. He was also right about our not really needing to learn Spanish. There were plenty of French around who'd also decided to take an extended vacation; I even recognized some of them. This was fortunate, as three appears to be my limit on languages. Not that I didn't try to learn Spanish. Our hosts had also loaned us their guest house, which made hiding our condition from them very easy.

Guiseppe helped us settle in and didn't try to convince us to return to Rome with him. Nothing would have made me happier, except that Antonio might have been less than pleased if I ran into him again. I would have to stay away for a human lifetime before it was wise to return. So we bid Guiseppe a tearful farewell while he left to tend to his estate. We promised to meet in France, once things had calmed down.

Our hosts, the Cardenases, were wealthy but not noble. In fact, they were sympathetic to our plight but understood the other side, too. Nobility was fine, but only if it was well-managed, and France's wasn't, according to them. Phillipe and Señor Cardenas got into many heated arguments about this, some of which I listened in on. Phillipe's rage against the uprising only got worse as more news came to us over the years. The younger *señor* had been to France, but left quickly when he saw the carnage there.

"They are not discriminating, *señor,*" he told us once. "They behead mostly your kind, but also their own people."

"Behead?" I asked.

"Yes, with their new beheading machine," he said. "The . . . geeteen? Gee-oh—well, I don't remember the name but it—" Then he stopped and made a shivering sound.

"*Señor,* it is not for the faint of heart," he finished.

"It sounds horrible," I said.

"Horrible is not the right word," he said. "There were lines and lines of people, all to wait for the blade to fall. A platform covered with blood, so many heads had fall-"

"That's, um . . . that's fine," Phillipe said. He was probably bothered by the mental images of blood flowing everywhere, just as I was.

"Ah—I'm sorry, *señor,*" the younger Cardenas said. "I never meant to upset. But the horrors there . . . It's barbaric."

"Barbaric is right," Phillipe said. "But sooner or later it must end, and France will return."

"As what? As a graveyard?" I asked.

"The way things are going, it may," young Cardenas said.

"Is there no sign of respite?" Phillipe asked.

"Respite?" Cardenas said. "*Señor,* I am *not* returning there, not for a *long* time."

"Oh, Phillipe, this is terrible," I said. "Why don't we stay here?"

"In Spain? Not forever!"

"Forever, indeed!" I said. "What has France to offer you now?"

"It's my home!" he said.

"And Sicily is mine!"

"You mean Rome," he said.

"I was born in Palermo and hoped to die there," I said. "But all our dreams don't come true, do they? So this silly devotion of yours is tiresome!"

"Tiresome?"

"Yes, tiresome!" I could see that young Cardenas had decided to leave us two lovebirds alone, and was inching his way from the room. "We can go anywhere we wish, within reason, so why don't we?"

"Because I don't want to!"

"Why?" I said. "Must you be standing in line to be beheaded before you decide to live elsewhere?"

"I don't want to return *now,*" he said. "I meant after this is over. *Then* we return."

"Oh, glorious," I said. "Return to a country that's executing every duke and baron they can get their hands on. And just imagine what they've done to the king!"

"We can return," he said. "We'll simply have to renounce our heritage."

"Far easier for me, as I'm not noble by blood to begin with," I said. "Personally, I'm willing to take the chance of returning to Italy rather than return to that bloodbath."

"Will you stop saying . . . that word?" he whispered. "It makes me think about it."

"So go kill a rabbit, then," I said. "I don't wish to discuss this anymore."

"You began this, as usual," he said. "Yet you never finish anything."

"I do so," I said.

"Do you?" he said. "Then why does it seem that you always—" he leaned close to me and whispered,

"—use your influence on me to make me agree with you?"

"I do not!"

"You do," he said, "for I can feel it when you do."

"W-w-well I only do that when you're being impossible," I said. "Like right now."

"Oh, you're going to send me away now?"

"Of course not!" I said. "If you leave, you do so on your own. But I am leaving."

"So I will have free will to follow you," he said.

"Don't tempt me, Phillipe," I warned.

"A-ha!"

"If you have the means, then use it!" I said. "If there are times when nothing I say gets through to you—and that happens more than you think—then . . . then yes, I *will* do what I can to end it! Is that a sin?"

"I couldn't say, as it's nothing a *human* could do," he said. "And all those rules were made for them."

"Well, you see?" I said. "Our rules must be different, then."

"Yes, but who are we to make them up, hmm?" he said.

"And what do you mean by that 'hmm?' "

"Am I to be sent away because I annoy you?" he asked.

"Of course not," I said. "You . . . you do what you wish, I don't care. I'm only your wife, remember? A man must be his own master, yes?"

"Yes," he said, and there was silence for a while. I had turned away from him, until I felt him nuzzling my neck.

"No," I grumbled, pushing him away. "I want none of that tonight."

He let his chin rest on my shoulder for a bit before standing up straight.

"I'll be in my study," he murmured, then left. I

returned to my own study and tried to read, but sat and thought all night.

Perhaps Phillipe had spoken some truth. He was a stubborn, opinionated sort who only became more so after being converted. Over the years he'd become a bit spoiled with his ability to convince others of his positions, and perhaps I had, too. Whenever he seemed to be getting out of hand, I always reined him in with a little convincing of my own. Rarely in front of others, though. But perhaps I'd started doing that unconsciously, such as whenever he'd just been getting on my nerves and little else. It made me wonder if the happiness in our marriage wasn't due largely to that power I had over him. Just before Phillipe returned, I promised myself to make a conscious effort not to influence, suggest, charm or otherwise use powers upon him, except human ones. That promised to be difficult, but I would at least try it first.

My brief experiment did suggest what I feared. Phillipe and I were starting to argue more and longer. Our opinions on the uprising were becoming more disparate every day. I was starting to appreciate what the people were trying to accomplish, while Phillipe persisted in seeing them as ruthless barbarians. It got to the point where he seemed barely the man I'd married. It made me wonder if perhaps he couldn't accept my gift of immortality—or, more likely, vampirehood as a whole. I may never know, because very shortly before France's new little emperor attacked Spain, we had gone our separate ways.

Phillipe was planning his return to France when I left, and I honestly haven't seen him since. We'd had an official human wedding ceremony, but, neither of us being human, we decided that it would have to be up to us to annul our own marriage.

I was going to return to Italy, but decided to take

my own argument to heart. If Phillipe's unyielding devotion to France was silly, then why shouldn't mine to Italy be? I decided to give England a try for several reasons. One was curiosity. I wanted to see on my own just how evil this evil empire was. Another reason was spite. Phillipe hated England, so I'd figured I'd go there just to annoy him.

While in Spain we'd managed to regain much of our lost wealth, so I had plenty with me when I left. I also had that damned coffin with me, and my book collection, which had grown a bit.

It's too bad Mara and I never actually met while we were both in London. According to her, she was supposed to have been a whore or something around this time, which I just cannot bring myself to believe. But whatever she was, I think we could have been friends if we'd met at a different time.

As you know, when I arrived I spoke no English. No one I met knew Italian, but there were those who spoke French, particularly in the financial district. This is where I needed to be, anyway, as I needed someone to help me invest my money. I found someone named Pennywise—isn't that perfect?—who took care of my daytime finances. I never learned his first name; it was a very formal arrangement. I hired him without benefit of tasting him, either. I also wasn't interested in speculation, but just wanted steady investments, which he gave me.

At the time I had no interest in coming across any other vampires. If Phillipe and Antonio were any indication, conversion just magnified men's natural arrogance. In Antonio's case he had some leeway, considering that he *was* the first of us. He'd also had me under his thumb, thanks to that spell he'd put on all of his convertees, including me. Fortunately I seemed to be the only one in London with a purple aura, except perhaps the unseen Mara.

England had taken a beating from the colonists but still had a nice empire. Another hired hand found me a nice townhouse, and I was able to live off the interest from my investments. I hired a housekeeper who came to accept her mistress's unusual habits. Actually, I learned that I would have to hire new housekeepers every few years or so, to disguise the fact that I wasn't aging along with them. I also had to start resorting to other standard ruses for ageless people. It's a good idea to move every fifteen or twenty years no matter where we are. We've also learned to do such things as will our money to ourselves under a different name, or just pretend to be so-and-so junior or the third or whatever number. I've fallen into the pattern of changing my name about every thirty years.

I forgot whatever Spanish I'd learned in order to squeeze in English. I would have forgotten French, but I have a lot of books in French, so I can brush up on it still. But I *did* forget Italian, believe it or not. That's because I'd grown up speaking the local dialect and only learned Italian to speak with everyone else. So as of today I speak Sicilian, English and French and have no accent for any. I must not—since people are always surprised when they learn I'm not a native.

Once again I'd sworn off men, which lasted a number of years. How I dealt with full moons is no one's business but mine, but if you must know, no one was converted. I came to believe around then that conversion was something not everyone was worthy of. A person can lose a lot of blood before dying, and there was no reason I should bloat myself on the men I came across for some time. Normally we don't need that much, anyway.

So I spent a lot of time trying to add to my library. For the curious, it should be obvious that most of my reading material concerned the occult. I wanted to learn as much as I could about us and our origins. It would have been incredible if I could have found Antonio's diary, but now that I think of it, he wasn't exactly the sort who *would* jot down his private feelings. And even if he had been, he probably would have used some language I'd never even heard of.

The number of books on vampires alone might surprise you, though. Unfortunately all I had at the time were ones written by humans. Those were almost no help. I picked up another interest while scouring bookshops, and that was primarily Eastern meditation. I'd had it with Western meditation, which I'd always been taught had to be prayer. I've always had a desire to better myself, and bringing out my inner strengths through real meditation has definitely done that.

It's a bit more complex than it seems. Eastern meditation was beneficial for me because it helped me control my urges, and I don't just mean for blood. Full moons affect all vampires to a certain extent, and my goal was to lessen that. Craving sex doesn't bother me. I hate not being in control. Meditation helped retain some control—to a point.

I also spent a number of years trying to discover and hone my abilities. I didn't learn this until later, but our power increases almost entirely from age as opposed to experience. It can be boosted artificially, such as through various magical tokens, but nothing beats age. I can only imagine what level Antonio had gotten to, or even Mara, for that matter. Too bad she never tested herself. But in the meantime I was frustrated by my lack of real energy. I discovered a latent telekinetic ability, but at the time all I could do was make very light objects quiver a little.

* * *

I suppose I seem to be skipping through history a bit, but what's to tell? The Industrial Revolution only afforded me more opportunities for investments. Appropriately enough I did invest in a slaughterhouse and packing plant and a lumber mill. You might remember Mara talking about how the slaughterhouses sold cups of blood to people in the morning. People seemed to think it was good for them. It's good for *me,* anyway. Since I was a major stockholder, I was able to have quarts of the stuff delivered to my doorstep. I also went through a couple of uneventful marriages, one of which ended when my husband killed himself because he couldn't handle vampirehood. Like I said, immortality isn't for everyone. I blamed myself for a long time over that one, until I successfully reminded myself that he had asked to be converted. And I did try to help him through the transition.

My decision to go to America was the result of various considerations. One was that it seemed to be the place where a lot of people from other countries were going when times were bad. Two was that I was bored. England is fine but the people are just so . . . *dead!* Formalities, manners, proprieties—they'd been with me all my life, and these people were sticklers for them. If you'll pardon the expression, I needed to see some new blood.

Shortly before leaving, I found a public sale of somebody's belongings. I was told that they'd belonged to some man who'd gone insane and tried to kill his girlfriend. Sounds like my kind of fellow. But what was interesting is that he'd had about as many occult books as I had, and a lot that I'd never seen. The best finds by far, though, were his books on magic. I don't mean about magic; they *were* magic. This guy had had genuine spell books, so I bought every book there and packed them away. I tried to ask a bobby more about this man, but he couldn't tell me anything. I decided not to track him down in the asylum, though.

The trip across the ocean was a bitch, but I survived. This boat wasn't one of the cattle-car deals with the babushkas who speak no English. I went over with the bankers and industrialists. As for food, there were rats on board that I only sampled at best. Amongst the passengers, I did help bring about a new fashion trend of thick neck scarves. Nobody died because of me, though. A major obstacle occurred when we arrived at Ellis Island in the daytime. Somehow my coffin was sent through customs intact, but I woke up in the unclaimed baggage area. I'd debated taking my last housekeeper with me, but that would have meant revealing my secret to her. She didn't want to leave England, anyway. So I went alone and toughed it out.

Ellis seemed to operate at all hours, so the crowds hid my climb from the casket. I gathered all my things together and went through the lines like everyone else. By this time I'd become a British citizen, so only my green card was necessary. From there it was another luxurious cruise to Manhattan.

My ties to Europe had not been entirely severed. I'd sold my house but kept my investments. My broker had already contacted someone in New York so I wouldn't be left dangling. I had to find my own hotel, though.

Chapter 18

I consider myself very fortunate that I seem to have been gifted with good timing. I'd arrived in New York about ten years before the flood of immigration began. And speaking of hotels, mentioned earlier, I'd ended up marrying the owner of one of the hotels I'd stayed at while getting my bearings. Then he ended up selling it and buying an apartment building, where we both lived comfortably. Ever since my experience with Phillipe, I'd never been comfortable with the idea of staying with a human. After what I felt was an appropriate time of courtship, I always revealed myself and left it up to my man to decide his own fate. Not all my men said yes, but, difficult as it was for me, I could not stay with them if they refused me. I also didn't want them remembering my secret, so a bit of charming served to erase that part of their memory. George, the hotel owner, after he went through the usual business of disbelief and so on, was quite willing to go through with it.

As far as my marriages went—as with most vampires, marriage was a common-law agreement. Most of us don't feel comfortable with the idea of a church wedding, so about half use a judge and the others just live together. In my case I can't feel truly close to a man unless he's ageless like me. He doesn't even have to be a vampire, as long as he won't grow old and die on me. My exception has to be werewolves. I don't know how they came about, but something about them and us doesn't mix well.

By the turn of the century we'd seen the coming of horseless carriages, nickelodeons, and the book *Dracula*. I snatched it up right away, once I found out what it was about. It was a good story but it had a lot of inaccuracies. The count struck me as being very much like Antonio. Stoker could have met him, for all I knew.

What's more interesting is that soon after *Dracula* came out, I found another book in a basement bookshop. It was called *A True History of Vampiredom* and looked like a self-published effort. In fact, no author was listed. It was just there. I read it and finally found something that was worthwhile. This was something that had to have been written by another vampire, but who? I never did find out, but it clarified some of the things Antonio had told me about our origin. I don't think he wrote it, though. It didn't seem to be in his voice, if that makes any sense.

This book talked a lot about what we can do, and ultimately, our place in the world—according to this author, anyway. I say this because I didn't agree with everything that was written. He (She?) held more of the "new and better breed of life" sort of thought than I did. Oh, I do believe that we're superior to humans in various ways, but I'd rather not live on a planet populated entirely by vampires. In truth I like being in a minority.

The book also mentioned "elders," or vampires who'd been around a while. Antonio was described, but I thought it strange that his name was never mentioned. He was simply called The First. That may be because the book went on about how The First could be summoned by calling his true name. I cursed myself for never trying to find that out myself. He probably wouldn't have told me, anyway. Dracula was never mentioned or described, by the way. Other vampires were mentioned by name, such as Degh, Liu Yu Chen, and Ivan the Red (I wonder why?). I think they were destroyed somehow; the book is very vague at times. Then Mara was mentioned in better detail. It seemed to corroborate what Antonio had said—that she might have been the second oldest vampire around. Now these were the sorts of things I'd wanted to read about for a long time. It didn't say where she lived, though.

My husband George and I moved to mid-Manhattan soon after World War I began. We'd tried to be good landlords, but the neighborhood was falling apart around us. It was hard to keep up a good building when the tenants kept trashing it, or keeping far too many people in one room. So we got back into the hotel business and lived in the penthouse.

I know that regular people hate the rich, but I've just been gifted with good investing instincts. Not all of my money was in stocks, thank goodness, but the ones that I bought almost always brought in good money. I'd sold a lot of my European stock to reinvest it in things like the Staten Island Ferry, Edison's company, and other rather lucrative ventures. George put his own money into the war economy, but I stayed out of that. Our hotel brought us a steady income, and our penthouse life made it easy to hide our little secret. The staff had to accept us as the eccentric owners who couldn't ever be disturbed in the daytime. I had small holdings in an American slaughterhouse, but pulled them out when trying to get blood from it proved impossible.

Even after the hundred years or so that I'd been around, the only vampires I ever came across were

Antonio and the ones I myself had converted. This was frustrating for someone like me, who wanted to mix with my own kind. I perceived the problem to be in our small social circle, so George and I made an effort to find new faces. It seemed to me that any other vampires around would be "upper crust" like us, since we have the time and resources to find our fortunes. Unfortunately, after a lot of "upper crust" get-togethers, we found no one else.

On a lark I talked George into crashing a flapper party with me. Actually, we couldn't crash it unless someone invited us inside, but we finally made it in and mingled immediately. We ended up separating, so I wandered off into the loudest room. The people there were dancing their hearts out, beads and pearls flying all over the place. It was a stereotypical flapper party, but it was happening. Like us, most of these people were rich, but our usual acquaintances were stuffed shirts compared to these folks. I hung back and observed at first, scanning the room for any purple people, if you know what I mean.

And finally, after all this time, smack in the center of it all was a woman whose aura was distinctly purple. She was quite the wild dancer and seemed to be the belle of the ball. I waited until the music stopped, but it started up again as I made my way through the crowd. She'd jumped right back into her Charleston when I stood beside her. She glanced at me but went back to the dancing. I had to dodge her a bit before tapping her on the shoulder. She stared at me, but kept dancing.

"Um . . . I'm sorry to bother you, Miss . . . um . . ." I shouted over the din.

"Gloria!" she yelled.

"Miss Gloria!" I shouted. "I was wondering if I could speak to you a moment?"

" 'Bout what?" she shouted back.

"Well . . . I can't say here!" I shouted. "Please, only for a moment!"

She kept dancing, then shrugged and followed me to a less-crowded room. Throughout our talk she kept bouncing to the rhythm, making me a bit nervous.

"This is a lovely party," I said.

"Yeah," she said. "You ain't never come here before, aintcha?"

"Huh? Oh, no, no, I've, uh . . . I'm here with my husband," I said. "That is, we saw all this and just couldn't resist, um . . . joining the fun."

"Yeah," she said. "Didn't think you were dressed for this."

"Oh, well, um . . ." I said, looking at my outfit, "I can see I'm not, either. But—maybe someday I'll get the sort of outfit you have."

"Yeah," she said. "So, uh—what's the news?"

"Pardon?"

"Why'd you drag me out of there?"

"Oh!" I said, embarrassed. "Um . . . well, maybe this isn't the place to say, but—"

"Say, what kinda accent is that, anyway?" she asked.

"What?"

"The way you talk," she said. "I can't tell where you're from."

"I'm from . . . well, I'm from a lot of places," I said. "England, um . . . France and Italy. Sicily."

"A real mutt, huh?"

"Sorry?"

"Sorry," she said. "Didn't mean that. Go on."

I looked at her a moment, then had to suppress a laugh. This was proving more difficult than I'd expected.

"Um . . . well, actually, I was sort of curious as to where *you* come from," I said.

"Brooklyn," she said.

"Originally?"

"Whadda you mean, originally?" she said. "I said Brooklyn."

"Oh, of course, Brooklyn," I said. "What I really meant then, was, um . . . well, when you look at me, what do you see?"

"I don't know," she said. "Some Italian lady. You're Italian, right?"

"Sicilian, originally," I said. "But what I meant was . . . was . . ."

"Look, just tell me what you want!" she demanded.

"Yes, yes, of course!" I said. "Forgive me. What I want to know . . . um, Miss Gloria . . . is . . . do you believe in vampires?"

Her ordinarily devil-may-care expression became somber.

"Music's kinda loud, lady," she said. "What'd you say again?"

"I said," I said, leaning close to her ear, "do you believe in vampires?"

"So you asked for it, huh?" Gloria said.

"Yes," I said. "It seemed to me the only way out of my predicament."

We'd retreated to the garden outside. The music was very muffled inside, but the party showed no signs of dying out yet.

"What, marrying a rich guy?" she said. "You got a weird idea of what a predicament is." I smiled.

"It's not quite that simple," I said, "but yes, I can see how people would think that's crazy."

"Or dumb."

"Look, it was my way out," I snapped. "I haven't regretted it yet."

"Okay, okay," she said. "You musta done what you thought was best. But me . . . I dunno. Sometimes I really like this, but a lot of times I don't. Like . . . when I gotta eat."

"I know what you mean," I said. "But there's consolation in that we don't need all that much, nor do we have to take from people."

"Yeah, but it's small consolation," she said. "When it comes to people, I'm scared to death of . . . you know, hurting them. Getting clumsy or something, and tearing them open. Brrrrr," she said, shivering. "I can't even think about it, sometimes."

"Then . . . you must have been forced into this," I said.

"Yeah, kinda," she said.

"Kind of?" I said.

"Well, I couldn't really figure what was happening," she said. "See, I met this fella at another shindig, and we really hit it off, if you know what I mean."

"Mm-hm."

"Well, he didn't do nothing that night, but I kept seeing him over a few days. I mean nights," she said. "You know I could only see him at night." I smiled and nodded.

"So, um . . ." she continued, "Well, you probably know the rest. One night he figured I should be an ageless beauty queen. And that's okay by me. I got nothing against being young forever."

"How long ago was this?" I asked.

"Oh, it was . . . ten years or something," she said.

"Really? Then it hasn't been that long," I said.

"I guess not," she said. "I figure not aging won't mean nothing till I'm eighty."

"I suppose in a way, it won't," I said.

"What about you, then?" she asked. "How long for you?"

"Oh . . ." I said, a little embarrassed for some reason, "I'd say it's been about . . . a hundred and fifty years now."

"A hundred an'—" she yelled, then stopped and looked around. "A hundred an' fifty years?" she whispered. "You're joshing me."

"I swear to you that I'm telling the truth," I said. "But you'll see someday. Why, I know a vampire who's five thousand years old."

"Skiddoo, lady, who's that?" she asked.

"Believe it or not, he's the very first vampire," I said. "In fact, he converted me."

"What'd he do?"

"Converted," I said. "You know—made me a vampire?"

"Oh," she said. "Is that what it's called?"

"That's what *he* calls it," I said. "And he ought to know."

"Who is this fella? Where is he?"

"I don't know, actually," I said. "That is, I met him in Rome but he could be anywhere now."

"He's not, um . . . oh, what's that fella's name?" she asked, snapping her fingers. "You know who I mean. Starts with a *D.*"

"Dracula?"

"Yeah! Him," she said.

"No," I said. "Well, I don't know, actually. Maybe he did some things that inspired someone to write about him. If I ever see him again, I'll ask him."

"Fine," Gloria said. "Maybe I'll ask him a few questions myself."

"Um . . . but tell me," I said, "I may have lived longer than you, but . . . you seem to have a wider circle of friends than we do. My husband and I, that is.''

''Husband?'' she said. ''You had a church wedding and everything?''

''No,'' I said, ''no, it was more by mutual agreement. But tell me: would you happen to have seen any other people like me? Like ourselves?''

''Bloodsuckers?'' she said, then swayed back and forth as though thinking about it. ''Mmmmm, well, yeah, I might have,'' she said. ''You mean besides the fella who, uh . . . converted me?'' I nodded. ''Yeah, converted me. I left him, I should tell you.''

''Well, then, I won't ask to be introduced to him,'' I said.

''I hope not,'' she said. ''Well, there's Charlie, but he hates being called that. A real snob.''

''Where is he from?''

''Don't know,'' she said. ''Maybe English. I'm no good at figuring out accents. Too many people from too many places.''

''That's true,'' I said. ''Er—I suppose that includes me.''

''Nah, you're okey dokey,'' she said.

''Oh, I'm . . . glad to hear that.''

''Listen, maybe we can gab later,'' she said. ''Get together or something. You said you got a husband? Is he, uh . . . you know?''

''A vampire?'' I said. She nodded. ''Yes,'' I said.

''Probably don't dance, huh?'' she said.

''Who? He?''

''Both of you.''

''Oh,'' I said. ''Well, we do dance, but not, um . . .'' I said, gesturing towards the party.

''Don't Charleston?'' she said, rising. ''Come on, I'll teach you,'' she said, holding her hand out.

''Well, I'm sure it's a fine dance, but—'' I said, but

was yanked to my feet after I'd barely touched her palm. Gloria laughed and dusted me off.

"Hey, what's your name, anyway?" she asked.

"Me?" I said. "Oh, um, Constance." Yes, that was my name at the time. Gloria seemed to consider it, then nodded in apparent approval.

"Okay . . . Constance," she said. "Let's get back to the fun."

One thing about the Charleston is that you can't do it unless you're dressed properly. It was designed for long pearl strings and tight dresses. I had on a long, thin dress, but that was the extent of my flapperness. Gloria, on the other hand, returned to being the life of the party. People were very pleased to see that she'd returned. I consider myself a passionate woman, but couldn't lose myself in that jumping and flailing dance. I excused myself by waving to Gloria, who waved back but kept up her dancing.

In another room I spotted George easily through this crowd of blue people. He had his back to me; when I got close enough I discovered that he was fondling some woman's neck. From the looks of her it didn't seem as though her mind was her own. I watched this for about half a second before grabbing George and whirling him around. His eyes had a red tint, and so did those of his lady friend.

"What—what—" I sputtered, then covered his eyes.

"Hey!" he said, yanking my hand away. "What—"

"Stop this!" I said. "What do you think you're doing?"

"Nowww, nowwww, li'l muffincakes, I'm, uh . . . see, it's not what—"

"You're drunk," I said in disbelief.

"Me? Whaaaat, you accuse me of—"

"What did you drink?"

"Ahhhh, only a—maybe this . . ." he held up his fingers to indicate a tiny amount. Then he widened the space. "Maybe . . ."

"Oh, for goodness sake, George, this is inexcusable!" I said. "You know how alcohol affects us! And how did you get any of that, anyway?"

"*She* gave it to me!" he said, pointing to the woman. "Swear to you on the Good Book, she *made* me—"

"Oh, stop this!" I said, yanking him away from his friend. She was still entranced. "Well?" I said. "Aren't you going to send her away?"

"Huh?" he said. "Oh, yeah, sure," he mumbled, then leaned over as if to bite her. I yanked him away again.

"Not that, you—! Oh, go cover your face!" I said, and pushed him aside to stare into the girl's eyes.

"Forget you ever saw this man," I said.

"Forget . . ." she said.

"Go on," I said. "Back to the party with you." She wandered away and snapped out of it once she'd passed us.

"We were just talking," George said on the way back. I was concentrating on finding a taxi.

"You weren't," I said. "You were about to taste her."

"Wasn't!"

"At a *party*, George," I said. "Right in front of everyone, looking like a ghoul!"

"Ghoul?"

"*You* didn't see yourself," I said. "You can't see yourself now, either. Can't you do something about yourself?"

"Hey, you ain't always a beauty queen yourself, you know," he slurred.

"I'll forgive that because you're drunk," I said. "Now I'm talking about fixing your eyes and ears. And put away those teeth or keep your mouth shut!"

He blew me a raspberry instead and started falling, so I let him.

"Who the hell put this wall here?" he shouted at the pavement. Just then I found a ride, and worked at dragging my husband into the car.

"Casey Hotel," I said to the driver. He gave George an interesting look.

"My husband is sick," I said.

"Oh, yeah, sick, sick, sick," George said, leaning against me.

"Quiet, dear, or you might upset your stomach again," I said.

"Sure you don't want the hospital, lady?" the driver asked.

"Oh, no, it's just a bout of . . . the flu," I said. "He'll manage."

"Flu!" George shouted. "I don't have any damned flu."

"Just hang on, dear," I said. "We'll be home soon."

"Why didn't we fly home?" he asked. *"Ow!"* he said after I elbowed him in the ribs.

"Sorry," I said.

"Look, uh, lady, driving crooks around isn't my style," the driver said.

"Crooks? What are you talking about?"

"Got the flu, huh?"

"I do *not* have the flu!" George said. "According to her, I'm drunk!"

"Will you shut up?"

"But I tell you, sir, that I am *not* drunk!" George

continued. "For imbibing is illegal, yes, a violation of the Constitution itself, and *no one* loves the Constitution more than I! So, sir, do not accuse *me* of being a crook."

I'd had enough of this, so I put my hand over George's face and made him sleep.

"Please, sir, my husband truly is ill," I said to the driver.

"Hallucinating, I'd say," he said. "Look, the other boys'll take just about anybody, but I tell you I don't like . . . er . . ."

He'd been glancing over his shoulder sometimes to speak, allowing me to make the briefest of eye contact.

"Please, sir," I said. "We just need—*watch the road!*" He looked back just in time to keep from slamming into somebody's carriage. The sound of screeching tires made the horses jump. Then the respective drivers got into a brief shouting match. We were about to continue on our way, when I tapped our driver's shoulder. He turned around.

"What?" he demanded.

"Please, sir," I said in my most soothing voice, "we only need a ride home. No questions, no more trouble."

"Yes, ma'am . . ." he said, then turned around to take us home.

Chapter 19

George could nurse his own hangovers—and fold his own clothes and tie his own ties. One of the sore points in our marriage had begun when I'd joined up with the suffragettes a few years back. Suffrage for women made perfect sense to me, but not to George. Sometimes I wondered if I was ever going to find a man who didn't have an ego the size of Asia. And these were all men who knew—who *knew* that I could literally make them do anything I wanted them to, at any time, but they *still* thought they were God. To be fair, none of the men I've known could hold a candle to Antonio's arrogance, but there were frustrating times, believe me.

Actually, George and I got along quite well until the suffragettes showed up. He knew that I was well educated, but figured that I was exceptional. My feeling was that there were just as many stupid men as women, and I still believe that. But afterwards George started making an issue out of my lack of housekeeping. That would have been all right, except that I hadn't been doing housework before it all started, either. The only way I survived those stormy times was to ignore him most of the time and call up room service. It wasn't as if he could claim to be the sole breadwinner. Maybe that's what had bothered him so much. All along I'd been bruising his poor ego.

I'd made contact with Gloria again and asked her to bring over all the vampires she knew to our penthouse. George wasn't too keen on this. I admit some hesitation about bringing in strangers sight unseen, too. But this was my first opportunity to really mingle with my own kind and not have to watch everything I say and do.

Gloria had come over alone before the big gathering. It was a few months before her friends could synchronize their schedules. Gloria came through with about five others. She told me that she'd wanted to bring her boyfriend, but he was human, and she'd gotten the impression that this was an undead-only affair. She'd told me about him before, but I'd always assumed he was one of us.

"Yeah, well," she said, "he knows about me, but he sees it as more like a disease, you know? I tell him to quit calling it that, but it's better than him . . . you know, being afraid of me. Besides, making him—I mean converting him would be kinda like getting married, dontcha think?"

"Yes," I said, looking at George. "It is about the equivalent of marriage for us."

"Yeah," she said. "Besides, I'm not sure if I wanna do that to him. Know what I mean?"

"Um . . ."

Gloria's friends, including Gloria, were anything but rich. Gloria herself was a phone operator or something, and the others were all working stiffs themselves. I had to make an extra effort to make them feel at home, then. At first they all seemed intimidated by our opulence, but then became quite taken with the room service. Naturally we got the fastest service, being the owners.

I'm not sure if these people were even used to gatherings like this. Once I reasoned that this was probably the first time they'd ever been to an all-vampire gathering, it became easier to break the ice. Most of them had come up with terms and phrases on their own for various vampire phenomena, so we started out with a definition game. This was the first time I'd heard about "putting suggestions on," and I taught them "converting." Some terms we worked on together, such as "misting" and "transfusing." The latter is a sexual term for something that probably only vampires can do. Or should do. Obviously we talked about sex at times. Some of those people had hysterical stories to share, especially the ones about vampire-human sex.

As the night went on, we shared our individual conversion stories. Apparently I was the only one who had asked for it. Even George had taken some convincing. Some of them preferred their new existence, but the rest just seemed to accept their fate. Gloria was like that. I was the oldest amongst us; second was the woman approaching seventy. George and another named Jonathan were the only males among us. And yes, even now, women seem to be the most common victims of other vampires. That's frustrating when you'd rather date fellow vampires and there just aren't enough men.

As the evening was winding down, we'd finished playing our version of charades. The ability to transform made for some interesting clues. When it came time for the guests to leave, we presented them with our tokens of appreciation, or one blood-donation bag each that we'd bought from the Red Cross. No blood-bank robbing jokes need apply. Just buying them was enough excitement for us. Our guests were thrilled, to be sure. We all promised that we'd have to get together again, and one woman said she could bring more people next time.

Most of us did find ways to get together sporadically. Gloria became a good friend, although we've been out of touch these days. She still had to work for a living, though, so one Christmas I gave her a hundred dollars (a hell of a lot back then) to spend or invest as she chose. I convinced her to invest it, though. She knew nothing about the markets, so I just put it in with my own holdings.

It was a nice gesture, but a brief one. Not all of my money was in stocks and bonds, but enough was there to leave me considerably poorer come '29. Gloria lost all the money I'd invested for her, and almost lost her job, but prevailed in the end. George lost whatever he had in stocks, but we still had the hotel. Then the income from that quickly became barely enough to squeak by on. We had to lay off half of the staff and worked doubletime ourselves, except in the daytime, of course. We could do it no other way, unfortunately. Small consolation was that we could save money on food and rent. Big consolation was the fact that our bank was one of the few that had survived the notorious runs at the beginning.

In retrospect I realize I should have been more aware of the imminence of the economic collapse, but so should the rest of the world have been. The important thing is that we were never forced out into the streets, but we did come close to being honest-to-God poor for a while. Gloria lost her apartment, so we let her live with us as long as she contributed what she could afford to the arrangement.

The president's reforms and new programs were fine, but things didn't really charge up until the forties. The economy picked up nicely, but then George had some strange notion of leaving Manhattan and running off to California to look into those Hollywood studios. Motion pictures were a big deal, and actors were being worshipped as gods, so he had the idea to invest over there. Investing in a studio was all right with me, but I didn't want to move there. Then George admitted that he was getting tired of running a hotel, so I encouraged him to sell it and get into some other business, as long as we didn't have to go chasing after flighty get-richer-quick schemes. Besides, movies were no good since they'd started whitewashing themselves. The sex comedies had always been my favorites.

George was pretty set on this. Then I learned that Gloria wanted to try being an actress. I'd never seen her act, but she was quite a dancer, so I didn't bother arguing with her. She and George became very excited about going West and didn't listen to me. New Yorkers were loud, chaotic, nervy, and just plain crazy even back then, but I liked them. I liked the city even more, and these two wanted to turn up their noses at it and pack up the covered wagon. After a few years of this I agreed to join them only after they made a solemn oath to return to Manhattan if their plan backfired. Just in case, we left almost all of our holdings in New York.

We arrived just in time to see *Casablanca* the next night. I was thrilled that the movies' whitewash was peeling, but I was still not convinced enough to throw my money at the things. George talked me into investing the same amount that he did. Fortunately I'd talked him down from almost all of his money to about one quarter. We found and bought a small place, and Gloria got to work trying to be an actress. More like a waitress, in the end. Hollywood made movies during the daytime, and no amount of charming was going to convince studios to reorganize their schedules.

What happened then is that my attention was caught by the growing real-estate development around us. George was right about movies being big business, but I was more interested in the people coming in droves to live there. Gloria and I huddled often and came up with the idea of buying and selling prime real estate. George thought this was just as dumb as I'd thought his studio thing was. Gloria had no real money, though, so I loaned her some in order to get a cosigner. I scouted around and found a banker willing to deal with us at night, and the loan was clinched at my house. We started with one Hollywood Hills place, fixed it up by ourselves for nights on end, then put it back on the market. It sold quickly, and profitably.

A very simple idea that's risky, but it worked. Remember what I said earlier about good timing. People wanted real estate, and we provided it. Gloria had long ago paid me back my original loan and was at my financial level by the time we sold our tenth place. This was getting to be fun, to say the least. George's movie investments were fine, but now I was making a lot more than he was, and so was Gloria. And all this time beforehand, he'd refused to invest in our ventures. That became his problem, then. Once again his poor ego was getting stepped on because the wife was more successful than he. That, and we both came to the conclusion that we'd been married too long.

George and I parted on amiable terms. There was no business about alimony or palimony or whatever. Both of us were more than capable of taking care of ourselves. Shortly after this Gloria and I decided to go legit and we formed our own real-estate company. We insisted upon keeping it small but busy, as the fewer humans we had to keep secrets from, the better.

And speaking of humans, Gloria and I had gotten so involved with our dealings that we hadn't really been looking around for our own kind. Once we'd as much as possible settled into our business, we took time off for a bit of social life. George knew some Hollywood types, but none of them were vampires that I could see. Still, we'd met enough people through him to gain admission to a party or two. From there we could get other invitations.

We both met our share of actors, producers, and so on, but Gloria was much more taken by the glamor of it all than I was. There is a difference between being genuinely self-confident and just being a snob. I should know, because I've been both. Gloria still wanted to be an actress in her heart of hearts, but knew that her current profession was the reality. There were a lot of fun parties, though.

We finally came across another vampire, but she'd been converted by George, so she didn't count. She told me that she'd had a very brief fling with him that ended with her conversion, and now she was trying to adjust. I offered assistance but was rebuffed. I saw her a few times afterwards throughout my time in Los Angeles, but her disappearance after only a few years made me wonder if she hadn't watched the sun rise one morning. Killed herself, I mean.

Gloria found her own convert, finally. She was still with him the last time I saw her. Meanwhile I went through my period of beating them off with a stick, until I became interested again. If the above sounds confusing, one of our mixed blessings is an extraordinary attraction to whatever sex we happen to prefer. It doesn't matter if we're even interested at the moment; all vampires are pretty much walking pheromone factories. Even the prissy ones have to fight them off. Sounds just great until you consider that for every winner, we fend off a thousand slobbering butt-scratchers. My curse is attracting extremely arrogant men most of the time. Maybe it's because I'm petite and look young.

We were still living quite comfortably by the time the sixties came around. I'd bought myself a very big house because I like space, and because it had such a nice library. My books filled almost all the shelves when I first moved in. After a while I needed two rooms. I like books. I also had a small pool and sauna.

Up to that time I had also located more vampires, though it wasn't easy. I hadn't converted anyone since George, so they didn't come from me. As usual I worked at getting as many as I could together. Sometimes it worked and sometimes it didn't, but very, very slowly we were finding more common grounds than just our mutual agelessness. As with any group, a clique formed here and there, but the whole could still be perceived. Obviously Gloria and I remained good friends, but she spent most of her time with her husband for a while. Like she had been, he was a blue-collar worker who lived mostly on her money. Gloria could always relate to the working stiffs, unlike me, who had never been one. I tried, though.

Jackie helped me there. We first met during an anti-war demonstration that I admit I was really only observing. I saw a purple girl taking pictures of the tent-dwelling protesters and I followed her discreetly.

"Hello," I said after she noticed my presence. She looked me up and down.

"Hi," she said, then focused on a friend who was giving her the peace sign. She looked very young, but I knew better than to assume how old one of us was. She was Asian, was a little shorter than I, and she had long, straight hair held in place with a headband. Most of the people had their hair about that way, too, but her clothes weren't quite as hippie-style as theirs. It was quite obvious that I belonged to a completely different part of society.

"Are you a photographer?" I asked once she'd finished.

"Not the kind that makes money at it," she said. "I figure I will someday, though."

"Oh," I said, nodding. "Good luck, then." She turned and looked me up and down again.

"Something wrong?" I asked.

"I don't know, is there?" she said. "I mean, you're just hanging around."

"Oh . . . well . . . actually I was just passing by and—well I'm just observing all of this. This is a protest, right?"

"Uhhh, yeahhhh," she said.

"I mean, of course this is a protest, I knew that," I said. "What I meant was, I've never actually taken part in one."

"I can dig that," she said, then turned to leave.

"Listen, um . . ." I began. She stopped. "I was . . . wondering if I could talk to you about something. Privately, I mean." She looked around, then back at me.

"About what?" she asked.

"Um . . . well, as I said, it needs to be in private."

"Why? You the fuzz or something?"

"The—? Oh! You mean the police?" I asked. She nodded. "No, of course not. It's simply that . . . well, looking at you I can see that we have something in common. Something very . . . unusual in common."

After that I remember that she stared at me for a long time.

"No shit!" she said. "Is that why your light's darker than everyone else's?"

"And so is yours," I said. She had her own little tent off at one end.

"Wow," she said. "That's heavy."

"Um . . . I take it this means that you've never come across anyone else like me?"

"Uhhh—" she said, scratching her head, "I dunno. I've probably seen other dracs before, but I never noticed, I guess."

"Dracs?"

"Yeah," she said. "You know—dracs. Like Dracula."

"Ohhhh," I said.

"That's just my nickname," she said. "And you know, before you explained the, uh, the aura thing, I just thought it made me psychic. Winter says I'm in tune with the universal oneness."

"Is she a vampire?" I asked.

"Wha-? Nah, she's normal. She's blue. I thought about telling her about this, but—I dunno. It worked out just letting her think I was psychic. Too bad I haven't been able to tell the future, though. Can you?"

"No, not that I know of," I said. "I'm not sure if that's within our scope."

"Well, shit," she said. "There goes my fortune telling business."

"Mm-hm," I said, amused. "Um . . . tell me, uhh—you know, I forgot to ask your name."

"Jackie," she said.

"Jackie," I said. "I'm Theresa." Gloria and I had changed our names when we'd begun the company. I'd thought it was time to go back to the beginning. Jackie and I shook hands.

"But tell me, Jackie," I said, "I was wondering if I could ask you something personal."

"Like what?"

"Well, like how old you are."

"Oh," she said. "How old do I look?"

"Well, I don't try to guess from physical appearances."

"Well, do it anyway."

"All right, um . . ." I said, looking her over, "I suppose you look about seventeen."

"Shit," she said.

"Well, that's what you seem to be physically," I said. "I mean, I'm sure that you're older, but—"

"You're lucky, you know," she said. "You look like you're about . . . twenty-five or so, but me! I've been seventeen since the fifties and I'll *always* be seventeen!"

"The 1950s?" I asked.

"Yeah, what other fifties did you think?"

"Well, you see—um, sorry," I said. "Don't let me interrupt."

"There isn't much else to say," she said. "I got vamped in '55, and here I am. I'm a teen in my thirties. Heavy, huh?"

"Yes," I said. "Heavy. But, um—you really haven't met any other vampires until now?"

"No," she said. "Well—except the guy who did me in."

"Oh," I said, noting her bitter tone. "Do you . . . want to talk about it?"

She was silent for a while, and started to fidget with her camera. Then she sighed loudly.

"What about you?" she asked. "You're not twenty-five, right?"

"Well, twenty-three, actually," I said. "Physically, I mean. But I was converted close to two hundred years ago."

"No shit?"

"No shit," I said, smiling. "Then, Jackie," I continued, "do you think you'd be interested in meeting other people like you? Like us?"

Again, she was silent in contemplation.

"I don't know, man," she said quietly. "I don't—this is like a trip, you know? You come out of . . . nowhere, and—really, I don't know."

"That's all right," I said. "I can understand how you'd be apprehensive. Not all of us are willing to mingle, as we say."

"How—many other of us are there, anyway?" she asked hesitantly.

"Um . . . probably not as many as you might think," I said. "Or maybe more. But I assure you that you'd be more than welcome to join us."

"Join us," she echoed. "You make it sound like some . . . club or something."

"Well, nothing so formal," I said. "Really, I meant just—well, meeting others of our kind. That's all it is, really. We're not asking for membership cards."

"So it's just a bunch of you guys hanging out together?" she asked. "Going shopping together at the blood bank?"

"It'd be nice if we could, but no," I said.

"These are just vampires," she said slowly. "Right?"

"Um . . . well, so far, yes," I said. "But that's the whole point of it. As I said, it's nothing formal. It's just that I—and a lot of us—see the importance of sometimes . . . just escaping, and staying away from people and . . . being ourselves. To talk about things that we can't talk about in front of humans. Do you understand? Can you dig it?"

She laughed and rolled her eyes.

"Yeah, I can dig it," she said.

"Oh, you know what I mean," I said. She laughed

again, then was somber and went back to fidgeting with her camera.

"This is heavy," she whispered.

"It is," I said. She looked at me.

"Sounds groovy," she said, "But, um . . . I can't answer you right now. This is something I have to think about."

"Take your time," I said. "And you have plenty of *that.*" She smiled sadly.

"Yeah," she said, "I guess I do."

I'd given her my phone number that night but had forgotten to get hers. That was just as well, as it was more important for her to make the first move.

About a month later I heard from her again. She called me up in tears and was so incoherent that I could barely understand her address well enough to fly over there. I arrived at a rundown hotel and ran up the stairs to her apartment door. It was locked, but I could hear her sobbing and knocked on the door. She wouldn't come; in fact I had to convince her that it was me so that she'd open the door and invite me inside.

The door finally opened, and what a sight greeted me. Jackie's face looked like it was stuck in some half-transformation, then it started shifting again. I rushed inside and shut the door quickly, then held her tightly and tried to calm her down. Her features were only shifting more. She cried out as though in pain, and when words couldn't calm her, I tried a link out of desperation.

Her thoughts were utter chaos. She was drowning in distorted (or maybe not?) memories, thoughts, and feelings. It was all I could do to batter my way through that mess and achieve a complete linkup.

The walls started breathing. I looked down and saw blood pouring through the window, filling up the room past my head in a few seconds, then rushing away and pulling me along with it. I opened my eyes to see a black ceiling, until the ceiling started shifting, and formed into a huge, evil face that screamed. I felt it picking me up in its teeth and chewing me up into so much oatmeal before spitting me back out again. Then I found myself chained to a sofa and surrounded by fanged munchkins from the movie of *The Wizard of Oz*. They danced around and around and chanted some voodoolike spell, then jumped on me and tore my skin off. More things followed before the last thing I remember seeing was Antonio, dressed up as Dracula and laughing.

When I opened my eyes next, the table in front of me started shifting, but when I looked at it closely, it went back to normal. I heard a clock ticking, and stared at the wall for God knows how long before I heard a quiet sobbing next to me. I was afraid to look after that, but after gathering up the courage I saw that it was Jackie, sitting next to me, curled up into a tight ball and crying quietly. She didn't seem aware of my presence.

"Jackie?" I murmured. She stayed where she was.

"Jackie?" I said again, reaching out to her. When she didn't take my hand, I let it rest on her shoulder.

"Jackie?" I said, shaking her gently. She shifted, but didn't look at me. "It's me, Jackie," I said. "It's Theresa. Can you hear me?"

She nodded quickly. I scooted closer to her and turned her a little toward me.

"Jackie?" I said. "It's all right now. Whatever . . . whatever that was, it's over."

"Trip," she whispered.

"What's that?"

''Bad trip,'' she whispered.

''Um . . . yes,'' I said, not comprehending. ''Bad trip. Jackie? Jackie, come here,'' I said, pulling her towards me. She still wasn't looking me in the eyes, but let me pull her towards me into a loose hug.

''It's okay now,'' I whispered. ''Shhhh, it's okay.''

''Shit,'' she whispered.

''Can you tell me what happened, Jackie?'' I asked. ''Can you tell me . . . what that was?''

''Bad trip,'' she said.

''You said that before, honey,'' I said. ''But what caused it? Did somebody do something to you? What was that?''

''Bad trip,'' she said.

''Jackie,'' I said, holding her face in my hands, ''please tell me what happened, besides bad trip. You called me up; you were very upset, and when I tried to link with you . . . well, all hell broke loose. Will you please tell me what happened?''

''I called you up?''

''Well, yes,'' I said. ''You called me . . . a half an hour ago, maybe? Don't you remember?''

''Huh,'' she said, then was quiet.

''Look, um . . .'' I said, ''um, Jackie. Was it something . . . something you took, maybe? Something you, uh—'' My eyes had been wandering, and at this point they fell onto the clock on the wall.

''That's not right,'' I whispered, then looked at my watch. ''What?''

''What?''

''But that isn't right,'' I said, and grabbed Jackie's arm to look at her watch.

''What?''

''But how can it be so late?'' I said.

''What?''

''It's almost three o'clock,'' I said, shaking my head.

"But—you called me at around eleven o'clock, and I got here right away. But it couldn't have been so long! Not for . . . three hours!"

"Three hours," she echoed. "Fuck. Fuck!" she cried, standing up. I followed.

"Fuck, fuck!" she kept saying. She was pacing now.

"Jackie, please!" I said. "For God's sake, will you calm down and tell me what the hell's going on here?"

"Winter did this," she muttered, then threw up her arms and fell back onto the couch. "Aaaaoooohhh, fuck," she said. "Winter—uh, a long time ago she gave me some . . . well, you know. Stuff."

"What stuff?"

"Aaaaaaccciiiiid," she said. "LSD. You know."

"Oh."

"Yeah, well—I didn't take it," she went on. "At least . . . not until tonight."

"So that's what it was," I said. "That was your bad trip. And mine, it turns out."

"You had some, too?" she asked.

"Well . . . indirectly, yes," I said. "You were so distraught when I got here that I tried to link minds with you, and . . ."

"Had your own bad trip," she said. "Jeez, Theresa, I'm sorry. Really, I—I didn't mean—"

"Never mind that," I said. "I'm okay now. I hope *you're* okay now."

"Yeah," she murmured. "I'm okay."

"But . . ." I said, sitting beside her, "that still leaves us with why you took the stuff in the first place."

She was quiet at first, then leaned forward to fumble with her cigarettes. She lit one for herself, and offered me one. I declined. Then she tossed the pack and matches onto the table and ran her fingers through her hair.

"Jeez, I don't know," she murmured.

"There had to be a reason you did that," I said. "And I doubt if it was just curiosity."

"Maybe it was," she murmured. "Fuck, I don't know."

"You know, um . . . I know you're upset right now, but—did you notice that you swear a lot?"

"I smoke, too," she said, giving me a sharp look. Then: "Sorry. Really, I'm—I've been thinking a lot. Since you left that night I just kept thinking and thinking about your invitation and all that shit. Sorry; there I go again."

"It's all right," I said. "Keep talking."

"There's nothing to say, I guess," she said, then took a long drag and blew out the smoke. "I guess maybe I *should* meet your friends. That's all I've been thinking about, all this month since you left."

"I didn't realize my invitation would have such an effect on you," I said.

"Oh, it's not your fault," she said. "I'm the one who's f—messed up. I never smoked before this. Wasn't even interested in it."

"You mean . . . before you met me?"

"No, I mean before . . . you know," she said. "Before getting vamped."

"Oh," I said. "You know, we call it converted. But whatever term you prefer—"

"Okay, converted, then," she said. "You know, it's not like I was prom queen, or even popular at all when I was a kid. When I was in school. I was, uh . . . one of the weirdos, you know. One of the *chinks.*"

"I see," I whispered.

"So it's not like I was losing a bunch of friends when I got converted," she said. "So I've always been a loner. But then this happened, and—well, I hang out with the others. With Winter and Sam and, um . . .

Rainbow and those guys. But there's only so much I can do with them. So much I can tell them . . ."

"That's exactly it, Jackie," I said. "That's why I've made an effort on my own to find others like me. Other vampires. Like you, I suppose I've been a loner myself, but then when it comes down to it, we all need to be with others. Especially others like us. I suppose I needed some . . . proof that I wasn't the only one."

Jackie nodded vaguely and took another long drag.

"You know what held me back before?" she said.

"What?"

"I guess I was . . . scared of seeing him again."

"Who?"

"The guy that bit me," she said. "I suppose you could say I had a hit-and-run."

"Oh," I said. "Yes, um, there are a few of us who had that sort of conversion. But you see? These are people you'll be able to . . . talk to, and share with, and—"

"Yeah, yeah. Okay," she said. "Okay, I can dig it now. If there's all these vampires around like you and me, and—well, even if I see him again . . . maybe it'll work out okay. If I see him again, I'll just kick him in the balls."

I laughed out loud, and she joined in. I leaned over and hugged her tightly while we calmed ourselves.

"Welcome to the club," I said.

"Yeah, the guys'll be *thrilled* with that," she said. "Telling them I've joined some members-only group. Some establishment jokers."

"We come from every kind of background, and occupation," I said.

"Yeah, I know. I know," she said, then we were both silent for a time. She looked at her watch.

"Jeez, you should probably get home," she said. "How far away are you, anyway?"

"Oh . . . it'll take no time at all," I said. "It took about a half an hour maybe, flying."

"No shit, you flew over?"

"It was the fastest way," I said. "You sounded pretty desperate."

"Huh," she said. "You really flew. You mean . . . flew?" she asked, flapping her hands. "Did the bat thing and everything?"

"Yes," I said, laughing. "Don't tell me you never have—?"

"Yeah, I've, uh—done all that," she said. "Not very much, though. Sometimes it freaks me out too much."

"Like a bad trip?" I asked. She smiled but shook her head quickly.

"Nooo, nooo, not even close," she said. "Fuck, no—uh-uh. That was it for me, man."

"And for me, I hope."

"You said it, man," she said, then looked at her watch again. "Well, hey, jeez, I didn't mean to do this to you—"

"Really, it's all right—"

"But listen: if it gets too late you're, um—well, you can crash here."

"No, no, really—"

"Hey, it's cool, really," she said, rising. "Come on, I'll show you the rest of this rat hole."

"Really, it's quite all right—"

"Some hostess I am," she said, flipping on lights here and there. "I drag you over here, make you share my bad trip, then don't even show you around. The kitchen there, obviously. And the bathroom . . ."

"What's all this?" I asked, looking at the black paper covering the walls and jugs all over the floor.

"Oh," she said, "see, I made it a darkroom, too. For pictures?"

"I see," I said.

"And the bedroom," she said, flipping on the light. "As you can see, I've got plenty of room if—"

"What—why do you have a bed?" I asked. She stared at me.

"Because . . . it's a bedroom?" she asked.

"No, I mean—well, you have a bed in here instead of a . . . you know," I said.

"I-I guess I don't," she said. "Instead of a what?"

"Well, do you keep your casket somewhere else, and just have the bed out for effect?"

"Effect?" she said, and stared at me. "No, I . . . actually sleep in it. But as you can see, I got the window all covered up tightly, and I stuff a towel under—"

"Wait, wait," I said. "I'm confused here. How can you sleep in a bed?"

"How could—? Well, what do *you* sleep in?"

"Well, a coffin, of course," I said. "That's what we've always had to sleep in. A coffin, and filled with—oh, I see," I said.

"See what?"

"You sleep in a bed, but you fill the mattress with dirt instead of foam, right? Oh . . ."

"What the fuck are you talking about, girl?"

"What?"

"That's a mattress," she said. "That's a bed! Look!" she added, and went in to push down on the bed several times.

"Look, springs!" she said. "Foam! Sheets! Pillows! This is a bed!"

"But I . . . I . . ."

"You mean you—you really sleep in a—coffin?" she said, approaching me again. "And you fill it with dirt?"

"I . . . if I could just borrow your sofa a moment," I mumbled.

"Sure . . ." she said softly. "Sure, Theresa. Let me help you . . ."

Together we got me to the couch safely. I sank into the cushions and shut my eyes.

"Hey . . ." Jackie said, "hey, you okay? You're not tripping again, are you?"

"Two hundred years," I whispered.

"You want some water?" she asked. "Theresa, talk to me! You okay?"

"Yes!" I said, grabbing her shoulder. Then I opened my eyes and looked at her. "I mean . . . no," I said. "No, I'm not all right at all."

"Do you . . . can I get you something?" she asked. "You're tripping about that bed, aren't you? You thought that you had to . . . you really thought vampires are supposed to sleep in coffins?"

"Two hundred years, Jackie," I muttered. "Two hundred . . . fucking years!!" Then I cried out long and loud before jumping to my feet again.

"Jeez I'm sorry, Theresa, I mean—no shit, I didn't even think about that, I just did it, dig? I had no idea that—"

I stopped her by grabbing her shoulder.

"You've done nothing wrong," I said, then let go and looked at her. "It's nothing you've done, Jackie, I promise you that. It's just that—a very long, and cruel practical joke has been played on me. Hell, on just about every vampire except you! Do you realize that we've *all* been sleeping in those things?"

"Well, shit, maybe *I'm* the one who's wrong."

"No. No, absolutely not you're the one who's *right*. Aaaaaaack!" I yelled again. "No. Sorry. Sorry, I can't take my anger out on you. On your poor neighbors who are trying to sleep."

"Ah, they're all shitheads, anyway."

"Still, believe me, Jackie, if anything I should *thank* you," I said. "Thank you over and over and *over* for what you've done for me tonight. For *all* of us."

"Uh . . . well, thanks, I guess. I mean you're welcome."

Chapter 20

Shortly after that incident I took a year-long leave from the business and traveled the world. Gloria and her husband weren't interested in joining me, so I asked Jackie. It took me about two months just to convince her to come. She didn't like the idea of not being able to pay her own way, but I was feeling generous and insisted that it was a Christmas/birthday/whatever present. Even today she probably thinks she owes it all back, though.

Why the trip? A lot of it was to celebrate my freedom from that damned coffin. Now I could go wherever I pleased without dragging a casket around. Funny how I'd thought myself oh so worldly and wise, only to learn a thing or two from someone who'd acted out of ignorance. It had never occurred to Jackie to scrounge around for a coffin, nor had she heard of that dirt business.

I was also rather hoping to run into Antonio again and have a few words with him. I had asked him—*asked* him directly about the coffins and dirt, and he'd just smiled. He never showed me where *he* slept, either, so this guy, first vampire or not, was a bona fide asshole. And I had been like an advice columnist to so many vampires since. It wasn't until I told everyone I could think of, that I learned that a few others were sleeping in regular beds, too. It had just never occurred to them to say anything about it before, which is understandable, I suppose. People usually don't go on about how they sleep.

So I used the trip to gather my wits and blow off steam. I wasn't much interested in Europe, but Jackie was really stuck on the idea, so we spent a lot of time there before moving on to other continents. She refused to go to China, though. It wasn't exactly the best place to be at the time, but I'd hoped she'd be interested in discovering some of her heritage. It became pretty obvious that she was still in a rather rebellious stage. She wanted to find the real Jackie, but apparently not by dwelling in the past, as she put it. She also wasn't interested in meditation, even though her friends had tried to talk her into it, too. I soon discovered that she used photography as her meditation, as far as that could go. And smoking.

Jackie was more restrained around men than I was. The trip helped rejuvenate my interest in men. France, even though I'd been reluctant to return there, became a rewarding experience in more ways than one. For one, I found myself actually enjoying the men, arrogant though they were, and secondly, I picked up some new books. Somebody dumped his copy of *L'Etranger* (i.e. *The Stranger)* by Albert Camus on me, and I was hooked. My new friend then gave me his copy of *La Peste (The Plague),* and I still needed more. Jackie probably didn't enjoy France so much once I started drowning in every book I could find by Camus, and then Sartre. I read *Nausea* and *No Exit* and wanted to curl up into a corner and not move afterwards, but I loved them!

Without going into a long boring treatise, suffice it to say these works did *not* give my life new meaning—

that would have been contrary to the idea of existentialism. Actually, the movement had come and gone by the time I read the books, but it was new enough for me. I came to the conclusion that life is wasted on the living, as was said in a radio play. What those works really did for me was clarify what I'd felt unconsciously for a long time, but couldn't have put into words: life has no meaning but what you put into it. I differed from the authors in that I *do* believe there is an afterlife, and that there *is* a God. Vampires, of all people, should know that, since many of us have felt His power firsthand. But I don't believe that human beings are even a twentieth as important as they think they are. On the other hand, I also believe that vampires exist because Antonio worked very hard at making sure they did. But I never believed that we shouldn't enjoy ourselves.

Now most of you may be surprised to learn that I never trashed the coffin. I almost went so far as to soak it in kerosene, but then put it off until later. Later came, and the coffin was still intact. Part of what made me hesitate is that, even if I hated the thing, it had been with me so long that I'd become attached to it. We'd been through quite a lot, after all. Another reason was that all during the trip I slept in hotels, motels, hostels and so on, and it had always been such a hassle light-proofing the rooms. Granted, once my room back home was fixed up, I wouldn't have to deal with it anymore, but I didn't *want* to fix it up. I didn't want to plaster over the windows, or hang dark, heavy curtains, or any of those things. So damned if I didn't end up keeping the coffin. They're small, cozy, and light-proof. When humans came by I just showed them the guest bedroom and said it was mine. The real room was locked during such tours.

Shortly after the world tour, Jackie decided to return

to school and finish high school. Night classes only, of course. One night she called me and said that one of her teachers was a vampire, but had forgotten her name. I said "Oh, good," or something, and suggested that she introduce me to her. Jackie is a bit more subtle than I when it comes to such things, so it took a while for her to get her teacher alone. At one point they went to a humans' costume party together, but Jackie said it ended up disastrously when her teacher got drunk accidentally.

Michael, one of us wealthy ones, was having a get-together. I was anxious to attend because Jackie said she'd be introducing her teacher to me. When I arrived, Jackie was with a very befuddled-looking, tall, blond woman with Princess Di hair. I went to Jackie immediately.

"Hi," I said, tapping her shoulder.

"Oh!" Jackie said. "Hey, Theresa! What's up?"

"Nothing new, actually," I said. "Just business as usual."

"That figures," she said, smiling. "Oh, yeah, this is Mara, the teacher I told you about. Except classes are over now, so we're allowed to be friends."

"Um, hello," Mara said, extending her hand.

I pride myself on keeping my composure under almost any conditions. So naturally I started acting like a blithering idiot.

"Wha—Ma—yee—wha—" I babbled. Mara looked at me quizzically, but kept her hand out. Finally I managed to take it. It was the lamest handshake I've ever given. Jackie looked at me like I'd turned fluorescent green.

"Um . . . it's Theresa, right?" Mara said. I nodded.

"Are you, um . . ." I said, forcing my brain to wake up again, "Are you—*the* Mara?" She widened her eyes and cocked an eyebrow. Leave it to me to put people at such exquisite ease.

"Well, I'm, uh—I'm *a* Mara," she said finally. My eyes blinked a few times.

"Oh!" I cried. "Yes! Of course, what am I—? Of course you're *a* Mara, but I meant—" I stopped and ran my fingers through my hair. "Can we try this again?" I asked.

"You're insane, Theresa," Jackie said.

"Oh, hush."

"Okay, one more time, then," Jackie said. "Theresa, this is Mara. Mara, Theresa." Now we both put our hands out at the same time. I shook hands heartily.

"Very glad to meet you," I said. "Very *very* glad to meet you."

"Um . . . thank you," Mara said, but she still looked uncomfortable.

"Obviously I owe you an explanation after that . . . outburst before," I said. Jackie nodded heartily. "You see, I'm . . . well, I've always been somewhat of an . . . historian."

"Well, hey, you two should get along great," Jackie said. "She taught the history class."

"Oh, you teach history?"

"Um . . . Western history, mostly," Mara said. "My specialty is English history."

"Makes sense," I said, nodding. "Er—I mean, you sound English. Your accent."

"Oh—yes," she said, now comprehending.

"But anyway—what the fuss was all about, was that I'm sort of an amateur historian myself," I said. "Except that *my* specialty is . . . well, us."

"Us?"

"Us vampires," I said. "Over the years I've been trying to compile a . . . well, a good sense of where we came from. And of course every history needs its . . . figures."

"You mean historical figures?" she said. "As in, famous vampires?"

"Something like that," I said. She shrugged and smiled.

"It doesn't seem that there are a whole lot of famous vampires," she said. "Except Dracula, perhaps. And various, vampirelike people, such as the Countess Bathory."

"Well, that's part of our history, I think," I said. "But famous might be the wrong word. A better definition might come from . . . well, who the original vampires were. The oldest ones."

"Oh, I see," she said. Jackie left Mara's side, apparently to gather some hors d'oeuvres.

"For instance," I said, "did you know that according to my books, there are only *two* vampires left of any . . . well, of any real maturity?"

"You mean any real age," she said. I nodded. "No, I didn't know that," she said.

"Um . . . well, according to *them,* anyway," I said. "Perhaps . . . you'd like to look at them sometime. Oh, but; a lot of them are in French. Do you know French?"

"No, sorry," she said.

"Well, maybe I can translate them for you," I said. "A lot of them are *quite* fascinating."

"Oh, I wouldn't want you to go translating a whole book for me," she said. "Besides, aren't there any English versions?"

"I doubt it," I said. "You see, I suspect that some of the books I have were written by vampires themselves, and not by hunchbacked scholars."

"How did you manage to find them?"

"I suppose I've just been very fortunate at looking

in the right places," I said, shrugging. "But some of those books—well, two, actually—mention some of the elder vampires."

"Such as?"

"Oh . . . well, they both mention the first vampire, but never by name, and—is something wrong?" I asked. Mara seemed visibly disturbed.

"Hm? No," she said quickly, "no. Go on."

"Uh . . . it also mentions a Chinese vampire, and one called Degh, and—"

"Never heard of them."

"Well, according to those books, they were destroyed, or just haven't been seen for centuries."

"Oh," she said, and seemed to be contemplating this.

"But—there was also a Mara mentioned," I said. "Of course, that's only a name. I mean, you may have just picked this name for yourself long ago and—"

"What did it say about her?" she asked.

"Oh . . ." I said, "only what it said about the others. That is, that she's very old, and very powerful. My experience has shown me that the older we get, the more powerful we become."

"I suppose that's true," she said.

"Am I interrupting?" Jackie said after rejoining us.

"No, not at all," I said. "We're just chatting."

"Jackie, is there any coffee over there?" Mara asked.

"Yeah, I'll show you," she said.

"Excuse me," Mara said, and I nodded. I watched her and Jackie return to the snack table. I worked at getting Jackie's attention discreetly. She returned to my side while Mara was busy with the cream and sugar.

"Were you waving at me?" Jackie asked.

"Yes," I whispered, glancing over at Mara.

"What's up?"

"Mmmm . . ." I said, still glancing back and forth.

"What are you looking at?" Jackie asked, starting to turn, but I caught her shoulder and brought her back around.

"Nothing," I said. "Um . . . Jackie?"

"What?"

"Is Mara the sort of . . . ? No, that's not it," I said.

"What isn't?"

"I'm . . . I'm not sure," I said. "I just think . . . well, I get the feeling that she doesn't like me."

"You guys just met, how's she supposed to hate you already?"

"It's just a gut feeling," I said. "Or . . . oh. You're right; I'm just being stupid."

"You said it, not me."

"Well . . . maybe I could join you two," I said. "Do you know where you're sitting?" Jackie shrugged.

"Anywhere, I guess," she said. Mara rejoined us, coffee in hand, and looked at both of us expectantly.

"Do you wanna sit somewhere?" Jackie said.

"Sure," said Mara. I followed their lead. Michael's house was even bigger than mine, so we soon found some nice sofas to lounge on in a corner.

"So, Mara," I said, "I understand that you've been . . . well, alone for most of the time."

"I've led a fairly solitary life, yes," she murmured.

"Then it must have been quite a surprise to you to find out that there were others like you," I said. She glanced around the room, then nodded.

"It is a bit of a surprise," she said. "And in a way, it's a nice feeling, but on the other hand, I was rather hoping there *wouldn't* be others like me."

"Why do you say that?"

"Well, only that I wouldn't wish this to be inflicted upon others," she said.

"You mean . . . immortality?"

"I mean being a vampire."

"Oh," I said, then thought for a moment. "But then, you'll see that not everyone dislikes this existence. Myself, for instance. I rather enjoy it."

"You like being a vampire?"

"Of course," I said. "Now, I admit, there are disadvantages to everything, but overall I've been much happier this way than as a human. In fact, I asked to be converted."

"Yeah, but most of us didn't, remember?" Jackie said.

"Of course, of course," I said, patting her hand. "I admit that I'm hardly the rule."

"Well . . ." sighed Mara, looking around again, "I suppose I shouldn't jump to conclusions, then. My experience with other vampires has been a bit . . . limited."

"May I ask you a personal question?" I asked. Jackie groaned.

"Ohh, noo, here she goes," she said.

"What?" I said.

"Well, you're gonna ask her how old she is, right?" Jackie said.

"Well it's . . . of interest to me," I said. "Besides, I wouldn't warn them first if I didn't recognize it as a personal question, would I?"

"Never mind," Jackie said. "Go on."

"Is it . . . was that the question?" Mara asked. "You want to know how old I am?"

"Only if you want to say," I said.

"Ah . . ." she said, "thirty-one."

"Thirty-one?" I said. "Is that . . . including your human years?"

"Those *are* my human years," she snapped.

"Oh, but I meant your vam—ah," I said. "So you

don't want to say." For an answer she only smiled, then sipped at her coffee.

So what an auspicious introduction that was. Throughout the evening I couldn't shake the suspicion that not only did she take an instant dislike to me, but had come to despise me by the time the night ended. And I'd done my best to be as friendly, open, and engaging as I could be. Who knows? Maybe that's exactly why she didn't like me. Up until then I had never met such a close-lipped vampire as Mara, saving perhaps Antonio. She had to be the one he'd mentioned—his "one real mistake." If she were the same Mara, I assumed that she'd simply gone back to that name as I had mine. It wasn't until I read her own book that I learned otherwise.

Interviewing her was out of the question, then. Not that I was obsessed with the woman, but I'd gotten to a point where I wanted to compile my own history of vampiredom. Actually, more like a series of insights into our psyches. So having a heart-to-heart talk with the second oldest vampire so far was high on my wish list. But that never came to pass.

After years of contemplation, I came to a possible answer. She had probably sensed her creator's presence in me. My senses and sixth senses are acute, but no doubt couldn't hold a candle to hers. That's why she fascinated me so. The things that I was certain she could do, yet never did, proved a little frustrating to me. Never had I met anyone who despised her vampirehood as much as she. In fact, it really made me wonder at times why she'd never just watched the sun rise or something. The problem is that, celebrity or not, her hatred of her vampirehood tended to make her seem like a real snob. My closest friends had a hard time feeling comfortable around her because she was so . . . self-righteous, for lack of a better word. The others and I liked being open with each other about ourselves, but couldn't be when she was around. Not that she was around us very often, as she hated me, but you get the idea. One of us eventually gave her the nickname Mara Poppins. Never to her face, though.

In spite of all this, I did have tremendous respect for Mara, whether she believes it or not. Much of it was that, even if she hated her vampirehood, she *had* survived for almost two thousand years. And no, she didn't strike me as being overly intelligent, but she probably made up for that in instinct, or even sheer power. It used to bother me that she hadn't built herself a financial empire in all that time, but I've come to realize that not everyone thinks it important to have piles of money. I couldn't count myself with that group, though. Another thing is that I feared her. Yes, I said feared her. We're talking about someone who could make a building blow up through willpower alone, and she was very sensitive. I wasn't terribly interested in pushing her too far, then.

Life went on as usual for a number of years. Gloria and I survived the ups and downs of real estate quite prosperously. In fact, it was very difficult keeping the staff as small as we wished, so we were considering splitting it up. Gloria would then manage our companion office, while mine would remain the headquarters. I never did find out how lucrative that would have been.

I'd been having daymares for almost a week. They all involved being paralyzed and hearing someone coming closer and closer, until I could feel his breath on my neck, and then someone in front of me shoots me with a crossbow. I never woke up screaming, but after the same dream day after day, things got a little tense. Jackie came through for me when she asked me to go out for a drink with her. Not alcohol, of course, but sometimes we went to dance-places and watched the crowds. Every time, guaranteed, someone would approach us, but we didn't always feel like dancing.

Jackie chain-smoked and drank her Coke while I sipped my iced tea. Our conversation was quiet and sparse that night. I guess we were both just in that sort of mood. As we expected, we got glances, smiles, and stares sometimes, but weren't much interested in them. Besides, Jackie and I usually had a policy of dating only other vampires. Most of us are that way, actually.

Some boys waddled over to us and tried to get friendly. They had their beers in hand, and one of them had one of those giant blue beer cans that are still made of tin. I don't remember the brand name. They were a bit drunk and wouldn't take our subtle hints to go away, so I settled for an unusual approach.

"Tell you what," I said to the blue-can boy, "how about if you let me have the rest of your beer? Then I'll see what we can arrange."

"Well, hell, I'll get you a whole new beer," he said, and tried to call over a waitress, but I stopped him. Meanwhile, Jackie had a concerned look on her face.

"No, no," I insisted. "That's all right. Really; I'd much prefer yours," I said in one of my more seductive voices. The good ol' boy smiled and handed it to me. I swished the can around a little, then emptied it into a water glass.

"You're supposed to drink it, lady," he protested. I only smiled at him, put my hands on either end of the can, and crushed it. His own smile faded as I took his hand, turned the palm up, and put the can into it.

All he could do was stare at it while Jackie and I got up from our seats.

"Hoooooly shit," we heard one of them say behind us. Once outside Jackie laughed and hit my shoulder.

"Jeez, Theresa, that was awesome!" she said. "Why the hell haven't I thought of that?"

"Well, I didn't feel like wasting a good charm on them," I said. "Besides, it's a good thing that some of those cans are still made of tin."

Just then I had the very distinct impression that we were being followed, so I whirled around. There were people behind us, but no one that I knew. Or that seemed to know us. Jackie tapped my shoulder.

"Hey, Terry!" she said.

"Theresa," I corrected. "You know I hate Terry."

"Well, I said Theresa about five times," she said. "Terry got your attention, didn't it?"

"Fine, but don't do that anymore," I said, and continued on, glancing behind me a few times.

"What is it?" she asked.

"Um . . ." I said, glancing back for the last time, "oh, nothing, I guess. For some reason I thought there was someone behind us."

"There's a whole bunch of people behind us."

"Well I meant—oh, never mind," I said. "It was nothing."

I hope, I thought to myself.

The daymares continued after that, and became even more graphic and bloody. Finally I was afraid to sleep altogether, so I climbed out of the casket and sat cross-legged on the floor. Usually I can reach my REM state through meditation in a matter of moments, but this time it took me about ten minutes.

My pulse was at its slowest, when I felt a slight

breeze of cool air, and then my name being whispered. I opened my eyes and scanned the room, but saw nothing unusual. After some thought I transformed my ears to bat-shape and listened. I heard nothing, but felt a growing pressure in my chest that made me stand up, clutching the edge of the casket for support. The pressure increased until it was starting to hurt, then a low, low hum began. It stayed as it was for a while, then increased in volume. The pain in my chest was becoming unbearable. I shut my eyes and held on tight, but the pain kept up. I started to weep, and sank down slowly to my knees, sliding along the coffin edge all the way.

Soon after I'd been reduced to a sobbing heap, a deep, clear voice said:

"Theresa."

I looked up quickly, but there was still nothing to see.

"Who—is—that?" I wheezed.

"Who do you think it is, my sweet?" it asked.

"An—Antonio?" I gasped. At that, all the pain left me, and I could breathe again.

"A prize for the lady," his voice said.

"Antonio?" I said, rising slowly to my feet. "Is—where are you?"

"Not there," he said. "Not in body, anyway."

"But—but where have you been?" I asked. I heard him chuckle.

"All over," he said. "Just as you have."

"What? You mean . . . you were following me? All that time?"

"I wouldn't waste my time on that," he said. "You know that I can keep tabs on you whenever I wish."

"But Antonio—"

"Close your eyes, Theresa," he said. I did so, immediately. He'd worked that damned spell on me again!

"Relax your arms now," he said, and I did. "Relax your body, but remain standing. Clear your mind." It was cleared.

"Breathe slowly . . . deeply," he said. His voice was clearer—almost as if he were in the room. "Keep your thoughts clear," he said. Now he sounded as if he were right in front of me.

I would have gasped when I felt his hand touch my cheek, but I wasn't allowed to move unless ordered to.

"Ahhh, my little *signorina,*" he said. "I see that you've done well for yourself. And of course, you have me to thank in large part for it. And you'll have the chance to return the favor, but I won't tell you about that just tonight. But for now, tell me: you've found her, haven't you?"

"Who?" I asked.

"Why, the witch, of course," he said. "Have you found Mara?"

"I've found . . . *a* Mara."

"And what, she's never told you about me?"

"Never told me . . . anything," I said. "Hates me."

"Hates you?" he said, incredulous. "Why, you've always been such a charming one, no pun intended. But of course she knows about you and me, right?"

"You . . . and me?" I said.

"Why, that I converted you, of course," he said. "Or does she still think I'm dead?"

"I . . . I don't know," I said.

"Who would know?"

"I don't know."

"Hmmmm," he said, and then I felt him bring his hands to the sides of my head. "You must be my eyes, Theresa," he whispered. "Be my senses, learn about her, flush her out."

"Don't understand . . ."

"You don't have to," he said. "Just do it. Find out what she knows about me, get her to talk about me. Get her to say my name aloud."

"Your . . . name?"

"My real name," he said. "Or in her case, the name she knew me by."

"But I—"

"You knew me as Antonio, Theresa; you can do no more for me. Except in this. I will . . . need you both, and soon. Get her to speak, Theresa." His voice was becoming distant. "Make her speak." he said, then vanished.

I was free to move on my own, so I opened my eyes immediately, only to see nothing.

"Antonio?" I said. "Antonio! Antonio, please! Tell me what you're doing here? Was that you who's been giving me those daymares, then? Antonio, please!" Still no answer. Now I was furious. "Antonio, you son-of-a—a—a horse! Get back here and tell me what you want! And why you wouldn't tell me about the goddamned coffin!"

Chapter 21

My first opportunity to carry out Antonio's orders was detailed in Mara's own book. It happened pretty much as she said, so I won't bother going over it again just to present my point of view. I will say, though, that at the time, I thought it had been entirely my idea to go alone to the strip joint where I eventually ran into Mara. Now I suspect that Antonio had given me some little suggestion to go there. Once I sat with Mara and company, though, I found that I'd lost my nerve. She had a way of looking at me that made my energy drain away, so I couldn't gather the courage to ask about such a touchy subject. Spooking the performer with an impromptu show of mist didn't help, because Mara dispersed it. Such a party animal.

It was then that Antonio showed his disapproval by blasting her with a headache. I got the impression that he was only trying to scare me, not punish me. And to give Mara a taste of what was to come, no doubt.

I'd been a bit hesitant to try meditating again after that last time, but I'd been very tense lately. I wonder why. Soon after achieving REM, that hum and pressure began again.

"Antonio," I said under my breath, "please, just come, if you must, but please, no more pain!"

"Oh, very well," his voice said. I expected to be paralyzed at any moment, but nothing happened. I stood up slowly.

"Are you here, Antonio?" I asked. "Are you here in the room? Or will it always just be your voice?"

"The voice, for now," he said. "I'm not actually in Los Angeles, you see."

"What? You mean . . . you're not even here . . . at all?"

"I'm *alive,* if that's what you mean," he said. "At the moment I'm actually in San Francisco, so if you don't mind, this is a bit of a strain, so no delays."

"Oh, uh—o-of course not," I said, looking behind furniture here and there. Well, just to make sure.

"You need to try harder," he said. "Get her to talk."

"It's not easy, considering that she hates me," I said. "Why don't you pick on someone whom she actually likes?"

"Don't get catty with me," he said.

"And why not?" I said. "Have you ever, at any time, treated me with even the . . . the slightest bit of respect? After all this time, do you still see me as your . . . little *signorina?* Your toy and puppet? Eh?"

"There won't be time for this sort of thing when I arrive, so listen carefully," he said.

"No, *you* listen—!"

"Theresa," he said firmly. I felt a stiffness in my body, but I could still move. My heart rate about tripled.

"There will be no arguing right now, so listen carefully," he said. "Now that I'm so much closer to her, I can sense her. But just a little bit. I can tell that she's very upset about something. Find her, tonight. Find out what's disturbing her, and exploit it! If she's vulnerable, use it! Get her to—"

"Why won't you tell me what this is all about?" I said. "Antonio, is this for some sort of revenge?"

"In some ways, yes," he said. "And oh, what a glorious revenge it will be!"

"But *I* have no bones to pick with her," I protested. "Why do *I* have to tempt her wrath? I have better things to do, you know. I *do* have a business to—"

"Because *my* wrath will make hers seem like a baby's tantrum, that's why," he said. I was silent.

"I hope that's clear to you," he said. I was still silent.

"Well?" his voice boomed.

"Yes!" I said angrily. "Crystal clear! Now go away!"

I found Mara that night at Jackie's place, wallowing in self-pity over coffee. Rather pathetic, actually. That, too, was laid out in detail. Jackie had told me earlier that Mara had gotten involved with a human. I wasn't surprised, considering that her own kind were beneath her. Apparently she was still trying to keep her secret from him, which—I'm sorry, but that would drive me out of my mind. There's no way I could take "Um . . . well, no, dear, I'm just one of those night owls, ha ha" for much longer than a day.

That night was also the first time I'd seen her even hint at what she could do. I got her so riled that she almost shook Jackie's apartment to pieces. The woman had some serious problems about Antonio, and thanks to him, I was stuck in the middle of it. You'd think he would have allowed them to go off somewhere and throw mountains at each other, but he always had to have others do his dirty work.

"She told me she was happily married before you

converted her," I told Antonio's voice the next time it showed up.

"I suppose she was," he said tiredly. "God knows she kept reminding me of it."

"Well, why did you convert her, then?"

"I have no time for this foolishness," he said. "You must try harder. Get her to—"

"Say your name, say your goddamned name, I know that! Enough!" I yelled. I expected to be blown to bits where I stood or something worse, but there was a long silence.

"I'll be arriving very soon," he said.

"Well, *I'm* not picking you up at the airport," I said.

"Suit yourself," he said. "I expect you to be ready, nonetheless. And Mara."

"Ready for what?" I cried. "Will you please tell me what's going on?"

"Tell me, has she ever been into your house?"

"What does that have to do with anything?"

"Answer me."

"No!" I cried. "If it's so important, no!"

"Then you've never invited her inside?"

"Well, of course I—" I said, then thought a moment. "Uh—well, no, I don't think I ever have. Since she hates me, I just—well, I assumed that she'd be insulted if I *did* invite her."

"This may work out just fine, then," he cooed.

"Why?"

"Ahhh, no doubt you've never entered a house uninvited," he said.

"Well, of course not, there was always that . . . barrier blocking the way. So how could I have?"

"We'll discuss that later," he said. "Meanwhile, I need you to keep her on edge, on the defensive."

"What? Bother her even more? Do you know she

almost wrecked her friend's apartment because I pissed her off? I don't think so . . ."

"Tell me, does she have a lover that you know of?" he said, ignoring my comments, as usual.

"Um . . . I don't know," I said. "Last I heard, she was with some human. Why?"

"A human?" he said, his voice dripping with disgust. "*Please* tell me she plans to convert him."

"How the hell should I know?" I said. "I mean—I don't know, Antonio. You'll have to ask her when you get here."

"I might just do that," he said.

As I promised, I did *not* pick him up at the airport. Knowing him he probably flew on his own, and from San Francisco, no less. All I know is that the night before Hallowe'en, I was overcome with the urge to check my front door. I opened it slowly, and who should be standing there but Antonio in all his glory. My eyes went round as plates, then narrowed into a hard glare. He threw his arms out wide and smiled. I stepped quietly over the threshold.

"Hello, Theresa," he said, kissing me on the cheek. "It's been some time, hasn't it?"

I slapped him in the face as hard as I could, turned, went back inside, and shut and bolted the door. I was safe for the moment, as he was yet to be invited in. I looked down at the floor while stepping slowly towards the hallway, and ran smack into somebody. I started and looked up.

"Whoops; you need to watch your step," Antonio said.

"Eep—wha—yuh—h-hoo—" I said, pointing all over the place.

"Why, don't you remember?" he said. "You invited me in."

"Wha—What?" I finally gasped.

"You mean you don't remember?" he asked. I forced my head to shake. "Oh," he said. "I guess I must have charmed you into doing it, then made you forget. But that's old news. I understand that—"

"You!" I sputtered. "You—you—you asshole! How dare you do what you've done to me?! Have you no respect for me whatsoever? Do you?"

"More than you think, Theresa," he whispered. "Much more."

"Well, then, *show* it, you poor excuse for a—a vampire!"

"Now, Theresa, please, I can understand your anger," he said. "But believe me when I say circumstances forced me to contact you the way I did. If I could have talked to you in a more . . . comfortable way, believe me, I would have."

"A telephone would've been just fine," I said.

"But not as cheap."

"What?"

"It's only a joke, truly," he said, and tried to take my hands into his. I pulled them away. He looked hurt.

"Oh, Theresa, please don't be this way," he said. "Don't you see that I need you right now?"

"You also said that you needed Mara," I said.

"Mara—?" he said, then smiled. "Oh, I do. But . . . not completely in the same way as I need you."

"Antonio," I said, "when I needed *you,* you refused me. Now you return here, causing me great pain—literally—and tell me you need me. Now how would *you* respond if you were in my situation?"

He looked at me for a long time, then smiled.

"I sensed this in you," he said. "From the moment I saw you, I could feel it. That intelligence. That ambition, that . . . hunger to survive, and prosper. I'm not surprised you've done as well as you have, and in fact, I know you could do so much better."

"Well, I'm content at this point," I said. "Or I *was,* until you started tormenting me with those daymares."

"As before, there was no other way that I could contact you," he said. "The daymares were some . . . side effects of my return to you."

"What are you?" I asked. "Have you gone beyond being merely a vampire and become something else? What are you?"

"With age comes power, you know that," he said.

"Yes, but—"

"But you're right, in a way," he said. "I'm the most powerful vampire there is, but I've discovered a way to become something much, much *more* than that!"

"Something . . . more?" I asked. He then went on to describe some spell that he'd been searching for in the course of a few millenia, and had finally found it. It sounded to me as if the caster would become something second only to God, or something equal to the Devil, I'd wager. I had great doubts that Antonio would use this power as a force for pure good. I knew that refusing him would be pointless, though. I could become his mindless slave at a moment's notice. He admitted that Mara would prove somewhat of a challenge, but not really, in the end.

"That's why I need your help," he said. "That's why I need *both* of you. I need . . . two others who are bound to me by blood."

"But . . . we're not related to you," I said.

"Bound to me by *blood,*" he repeated. "Normally that *does* mean relatives, but you and Mara—"

"—were converted by you," I finished. "By blood, ohhh, I see."

"That's why I need you," he said.

"But, Antonio," I said, walking around him, "what are *we* supposed to gain from this? So we help you become . . . well, whatever this spell will do, so what will happen to us? Will we share this power?"

"If you wish," he said. "If it works, I can make you a goddess."

"*If* it works?"

"Well, of course it will work," he said. "After all this time I know that *this* is what I've been looking for."

"So . . . this spell, you say, will give you almost unlimited power," I said. "And you claim that it will do the same for us."

"You can share my power," he said, "but yours will never be equal to mine."

"Naturally," I said. "But, I thought you wanted revenge on Mara."

"I do," he said. "I never said *she* would share my power. Once it's over I'll show her what it means to know *real* pain."

"All this just because she didn't want to be a vampire?" I asked. Antonio stiffened and shut his eyes. I had the feeling I'd asked the wrong question. He clenched his fist so tightly that it shook, and I glanced about the room to see various small objects start to quiver. A deep rumbling was building beneath our feet.

"Uh . . . uh, Antonio," I said, "I'm sorry I asked that. Really, you don't have to—"

"You have no *idea* what that woman put me through!" he hissed, whirling about to glare at me. His eyes blazed red, and a vase fell from a table.

"I-I'm sorry, Antonio!" I said. "Please; please, it's all right! I take it back; truly, I never asked that!"

He unclenched his fist and took a deep breath. The room began to quiet down. I put a reassuring hand on his arm.

"I'm sorry, Antonio," I said. "Forgive?"

"Yes," he said. His eyes were normal again. "I see that you were only curious. Suffice it to say that *she* will know."

"Of course," I said, glancing around the room again.

I attended Michael's Hallowe'en party alone. Antonio assured me that he would be there one way or another, and I didn't press for details. I hadn't been to Michael's Hallowe'en deals in a while, as he had a lot of human friends and encouraged the rest of us to bring ours. That way it usually ended up with about half of the guests being human, and the other half being vampires who had to watch what they said and did. Obviously that was something we had to do throughout our lives, anyway, but on Hallowe'en of all nights I prefer being with my own kind.

My orders were to find Mara and her human, and toss some wrenches into the works. Now, granted, I like men, but stealing others' men away is *not* my style. Antonio wanted Mara on the defensive so she'd be easier to deal with, though. Meanwhile I'd probably be the one to get my head pulled off.

But this was all part of his big plan, which was scheduled to go down that very night. Somehow I was supposed to get Mara started in the direction of my house. Antonio said he'd take it from there.

Antonio sent me some brief headaches when I started lagging behind schedule. Well, it wasn't easy stealing her man away as long as she was attached to his hip for most of the evening. He was an average-looking fellow. Sort of goofy-looking and shorter than she, but appealing. I had no way of knowing if she'd marked him yet. Bitten him, that is. With her it was hard to tell.

Finally the two started mingling on their own, so as soon as Mara wandered off to get some coffee, I headed his way. He was sitting around with a bunch of others, so I scooted into an open spot. Fortunately most of the others were vampires I knew. I was able to jump into the conversation easily, but always kept my eye on Mara.

"Yeah, that's when Mara asked me here," he said at one point.

"Oh, do you know Mara?" I asked. He seemed to blush.

"Ohhh, yeah, I guess you could say that," he said.

"Oh, yes, that's right, I saw you arrive together," I said. "I'm Theresa."

"Jim," he said, offering his hand. I shook it heartily.

"Jim?" I said. "Ahh, so *you're* Jim. She's told me a lot about you."

"Who? Mara?" he said.

"Yes, we're friends, you know," I said. "Hasn't she ever said anything about me?"

"Uh . . . well, no, sorry," he said. "Actually, I'm kind of . . . well, she has kind of . . . different friends."

"Different?" I asked.

"Well, I don't mean different, I mean kind of like—oh . . . it's hard to say," he said. I beckoned him closer to me.

"Do you mean that they're . . ." I whispered into his ear, "vampires?"

He leaned away and stared at me.

"Uhhhh . . ." he said. I put a gentle hand on his arm.

"It's all right, Jim," I said reassuringly. "She's

probably told you all about how you have nothing to be afraid of."

"Uh . . . I don't, right?" he said. I laughed.

"Of course not," I said. "Look around you. We're here; humans are here. If we were dangerous like all the movies say, then this sort of party couldn't exist, now, could it?"

He looked at me in the eyes for a long time. I debated influencing him, and perhaps just thinking about it made it happen, but finally he broke eye contact and laughed.

"Right," he said, then looked at me, "yeah, I mean—right, of course."

We both laughed after this. The others were engrossed in their own conversations and paid no attention to us. I patted his hand and smiled.

Off in Michael's makeshift ballroom, another song started. Jim listened and smiled.

"Whoa, I love this song!" he said. "Do you see Mara around?"

"I don't think so," I said. "What's wrong?"

"Oh, nothing, I was just wondering . . ." he said, squinting off into the room. "Oh, yeah, there *are* people dancing. I wonder if she wants to?"

"Well, I don't see her," I said. "But—*I* like this song. *I* could dance with you."

"Hm?" he said. "Um . . . well . . ."

"Oh, she wouldn't mind, would she?" I said, standing. "Besides, she doesn't like to dance." That was a guess on my part.

"Uh . . . well, usually not, but one night she . . ." he said, then blushed again and stood up. "I should track her down, anyway."

"All right," I said, and followed him. So we tracked her down. The look on her face when she saw Jim with me was . . . scary. Jim might have been the only thing that kept her from belting me on the spot. I swallowed and gave her the "He won't be stolen for long" line attributed to me.

A song that neither of us liked followed, so we thanked each other for the nice time and left the room together. I meant to chat with him some more, but Jim made a beeline for Mara. I decided to hang back and observe. Mara looked as though in a trance when he tapped her on the shoulder, and what followed then was probably the greatest and *loudest* lovers' spat I'd ever heard. That anyone else had heard, either, because the room came to a dead stop while she bawled him out for dancing with that hussy. Jim was thoroughly bewildered, and even Jackie was afraid to intervene in this one.

I was engrossed in the whole show, when someone tapped me on the shoulder.

"Antonio!" I said. "What—?" He put his finger to his mouth.

"What's going on?" I whispered. "How did you get in here?"

"Pay attention there," he said, pointing at Mara. "That's my doing."

"What do you mean?" I said, watching them again. "Did you—?"

"She won't even remember this fight," he said. "Now, when it's over, I'll need—wait! Stop the human! Don't let him follow her! Keep him here!"

"What?" I said, but Antonio wasn't there. I was hit by a twinge of pain, so I ran over to Jim, who was following after Mara. Jackie was in hot pursuit, too.

"And I hope somebody bites you!" Mara bellowed before storming through the door. "Storming" is right. The whole house was quaking, and I could have sworn Mara was starting to glow. That's a bad sign.

Jim didn't even see me until he slammed right into me. I held my hands out.

"Jim," I said, "Jim, you better let her go."

"Will you excuse me?" he said angrily, and pushed me aside, but I rushed in front of him again.

"Listen to me, Jim," I said, staring into his eyes, "it's best that you stay here."

He stared back at me for a long time before relaxing his arms.

"Yeah . . ." he said. "Yeah, you're right."

"You'd better come with me."

"So tell me, Jim," I said, guiding him to the bed, "how does Mara treat you?"

"Treat me?" he said. We'd snuck into one of Michael's guest rooms during the commotion.

"Yes," I said, sitting beside him. "How does she treat you? Is she kind to you?"

"Yes . . ."

"Does she show respect for you?" I asked, putting my hand on his knee.

"Respect?"

"You know . . . respect," I said. "For your feelings. For your *man*hood."

"Respect . . ." he whispered, but said no more. I sighed and looked at the door as if at any moment, it would be blown off its hinges. Antonio better be right about taking care of her, I thought.

"Tell me this, then," I said. "Has Mara . . . offered you her gift?"

"Gift?"

"Yes . . ." I said, leaning close to him, "her gift. You know about her vampirism, don't you?"

"Oh, yeah," he whispered.

"And is it something . . . something that interests you?" I asked.

"She told me . . . she'd never hurt me," he whispered.

"And has she?"

"Never make me like her . . ." he went on. I sighed again.

"So you mean to say," I said, "that she's promised never to make you a vampire?"

"Yes . . ."

"But that's so unfair," I said.

"Unfair?"

"Well, of course, Jim," I cooed, rubbing his knee. If I survive this night, perhaps I'll go to Antarctica instead of home, I thought.

"It's unfair because—well, think about it," I said. "She loves you, doesn't she?"

"Yes . . ."

"And you love her, don't you?"

There was a pause. Then, "Yes . . ."

"Well, then, it only makes sense that you would want to be together forever."

"Forever?"

"Of course," I said. "Or as close as you can get to it. Now Mara can never be like you again, but *you* can be like her. You, too, can be immortal, Jim."

"But . . . she said she wouldn't . . ."

"You mean she refuses to let you live forever?" I asked. He nodded. "Well, that's very cruel of her. Very selfish."

"Selfish . . . ?"

"Tell me this, Jim," I said, "and you must be absolutely truthful. Do you *want* to be with her forever?"

"Forever?"

"Yes," I said. "If you stay with her, wouldn't it bother you that she never ages, yet you grow older year after year? You'd be an old man in no time, and there's Mara—young as ever. Wouldn't that bother you?"

"Yes . . ."

"Well, then," I said, draping my leg across his lap, "is that fair that she *wants* you to age?"

"No," he said, then looked at me. "No, it isn't."

"Then let me do what she won't, Jim," I said. "Let me make you ageless."

"Ageless . . ." he whispered, bringing his arms up. I took them and put them around me.

"You can be with her forever, Jim," I said, and started leaning back onto the bed. He followed me. I scooted along the mattress to rest on the bed properly. Jim crawled over to me and tried to kiss me, but I put a finger over his lips.

"Lie down," I said, and he did so. Then I bent over him and undid some of his shirt buttons.

"Make me ageless," he whispered.

"I will, I will," I said, glancing at the door. He reached up and started to bring his hands up into my blouse, but I grabbed them and kissed the knuckles.

"Patience," I whispered. "Wait for me."

I busied myself undoing the rest of his buttons, then stared at him a last time before diving into a kiss. He was a good kisser. For his sake I hoped that Mara equalled him. Then I broke away from his lips and worked my way along his cheeks, then down to the neck. He arched his head back and sighed long and loud. I kissed him several times on the neck, and looked back at the door one last time. Now I hoped that she wouldn't find out for a different reason, and that's that I was beginning to enjoy myself. Jim was good at finding the places where I liked best to be touched; again, he deserved someone equally good. I don't know about Mara, but I knew that I could show him the best time he'd ever had.

Jim stiffened and flinched. His eyes shot open, and he started to struggle.

"Ohh, no, no, no, my sweet, there's nothing to be afraid of," I cooed. His arms shot out, so I took them and tried to bring them down, but he resisted.

"Ohhh, it's all right, Jim—"

"I—! She—!" he gasped, then really got violent. A fist glanced at my jaw, but didn't hurt, so I grabbed his arms hard and tried to bring them down. Then I knew that this wasn't human strength I was fighting against. Oh shit, I thought, and almost panicked, but then something came over me. Maybe it was Antonio. Or maybe it was that old love of a good challenge that took hold of me. Whatever the reason, I smiled to myself and forced Jim to look me straight in the eyes.

"It's all right, Jim," I said, "you're with *me* now. There's nothing to fear."

"I have to go!" he cried.

"Go?" I asked. "Go where? *Here* is where you want to be. Where you *need* to be."

"I—need—" he gasped. "She needs me! Let me go!"

"But *I* need you, Jim," I said. "Fight it, Jim; resist! I'll help you!"

"Oh, God, it hurts!"

"Shhhhhh," I said. "There is no pain. There—"

"Mara!" he cried.

"Mara's not here!" I said. "Look at me, Jim! Fight her! Remember that she won't give you what you want; I will! Fight—"

"I have . . . to go to her!" he gasped. "I'm—being—*caaallllled!*" he cried before launching into a blood-curdling scream. I covered his mouth and watched his eyes turn up into his head before he stopped and collapsed into a sweat-covered heap. I got up from the bed and ran to the door, hesitated, then ran back to Jim and rubbed the sweat from his brow.

"Shhhhhh," I whispered. "It's all right, Jim; it's over now. We can go on. We can finish this, Jim!"

"Help . . . me . . ." he groaned.

"Yeeesss," I whispered, crawling back onto him, "yes, I can help you, Jim." I let my teeth grow. "Let me help you, Jim. Before she returns, I can . . . give you . . . what she won't . . ." As I said that, I'd been feeling my way around his neck, had found the vein, and was about to taste him, when somebody yanked me away by the back of my neck.

"Somebody," indeed. I knew who it was; I *expected* it, so why did I keep going? Antonio no doubt had a lot to answer for. Or maybe it had been me all along. Nevertheless it was clear I had gone a step or two beyond too far.

Mara's brightly-glowing figure held me aloft by my throat. Her eyes were solid black, and every object in the room—including the bed, and even Jim—was shaking violently. From the rumbling beneath the floor I expected the walls to cave in at any time.

"Mara," I squeaked, "you'd probably like an explanation!"

"NO" her voice boomed, and I don't remember much else. According to her I was slugged in the face, and judging from the imprint I left in the wall, that's probably true. I came to to see Michael hovering over me, furious, but not even close to what I'd just seen. And Antonio's wrath would be worse? Actually, it would have been. *He* wouldn't have left me alive.

"What the hell happened here?" Michael demanded, helping me to my feet. "Theresa, what do you think you were doing in here?"

"Thank you, Michael, I'm fine," I whispered.

"What did you do to my wall?" he asked.

"Pay for it," I muttered.

"What?"

"I said, I'll . . . I'll pay for it," I said, now conscious enough to look him in the eyes.

"Well, *some*body will, and it won't be me!" he said. Just then Jackie rushed in.

"Jesus Christ, Terry, what happened here?" she cried.

"Please don't call me Terry," I said. A crowd was gathering in the doorway.

"Get home, and get home *now,*" Antonio's voice boomed.

"What?" I said, looking around.

"Mara just stormed out of here like—shit, I don't even *know* like what!" Jackie said. "What did you say to her?"

"I said get home now!" Antonio's voice boomed again, and I broke away from the others and rushed to the door.

"Where do you think you're going?" Michael yelled after me. The crowd in the doorway fell over itself to make room for my exit. I could feel that my teeth were well extended, so I covered my mouth and ran like a madwoman for the window.

"Theresa!" Michael and Jackie called out in succession. I wanted to stop, but couldn't. Now *I* was being called.

"She's on her way now," Antonio said, ushering me inside.

"I hate you," I muttered.

"Follow me to your library," he said.

"She almost killed me," I said. "She—she was glowing . . ."

"Come on," he said, and yanked me along after him.

I gasped when I saw what he'd done to my study.

All the furniture had been shoved to the walls, and books I'd been organizing had been tossed around haphazardly. In the center of the room was a huge, painted circle with a seven-pointed star in it.

"What—the hell—have you done to my library?" I demanded.

"This is part of the whole thing," he said, gesturing to the circle.

"How dare you do this to my floor?" I said. "Now you paint hexes in my rooms?"

"It's not just a hex," he said. "It's a very important part of this. Now, she's going to arrive here soon, so—"

"No," I said, throwing up my arms and backing away, "no, I've done all I can possibly do for you, Antonio. Now you ask too much of me. Get rid of this—now."

"I don't ask anything of you, Theresa," he said somewhat threateningly.

"Please, Antonio," I said. "Please just—just go. I want no part of this anymore. Surely there must be others who are joined to you by blood. There must be other vampires you've created, somewhere. Why don't you—?"

"I will tolerate no more disobedience!" he roared, and my body went stiff. He glared at me, then started circling me slowly.

"I've put up with your complaints long enough," he growled, "and you still don't understand. You have no other purpose to me other than this. Mara, on the other hand, should provide me with some . . . entertainment. When you first came to me you made a very serious mistake to think I would forgive you your transgression. Nobody *demands* that I share my power. And while I don't think it was a mistake to let you live, keep in mind that anyone who demands immortality of me had better know his place. Or *her* place. Is that clear?"

"Yes," I whispered.

"Good," he said, fiddling with my hair. "Then you won't argue with me anymore?"

"No."

"And you'll answer the doorbell that's about to ring any moment?"

"Yes."

"Then you'd better go," he said, and let me move again. "Ah," he said, stopping me. "*Don't* invite her inside."

"Don't?"

"No," he said. "When she *does* enter, it *won't* be under her own power."

So Antonio's real name was Agyar. That's what Mara called him, anyway. I like Antonio much better, but maybe the other name was popular back then. The sight of Mara flying through the barrier after Antonio pushed her from behind was . . . well, spectacular. A brilliant flash of light, and then Mara's completely powerless body flopped to the floor. I thanked the stars that no one had ever pushed *me* into any doorways.

Antonio made sure that I kept my promise by shutting down my will again. Together we dragged Mara and Jim into the library, and things went on about as Mara had described. Mara had power, but Antonio left her far behind. Why he kept her trapped inside the heptagram, I may never know. She called him a coward, and that may be part of it. Still, if I'd been him, I wouldn't have taken any chances, either. In that brief struggle, he kept me under his power, maintained the heptagram, and even managed to possess the boyfriend and *charm* Mara through him! Now *that* was power, so

I can only imagine what that spell would have done for him.

I would like to say this. Antonio was using Jim to charm Mara, and then talk her into converting him. And it may be that nobody wanted Jim to live forever more than she. That may be why she was the most repressed individual I've had the misfortune to come across. Within moments Antonio had reduced her to a quivering, sobbing heap who could have sucked Jim dry in a few seconds. Or rather, *she* reduced herself to that. For God knows how long she'd been denying that hunger that everyone has—and I mean humans, too—and I shudder to think what she would have become if Antonio had succeeded in bringing it all out *permanently*. Possibly an even more dangerous creature than he. But then she broke down and started moaning "Gaaaahh" or something, and all hell broke loose.

Antonio dragged us all into the center, and began the spell before we knew what hit us. It must have been the sort of spell that draws in everyone around it, because we all found ourselves chanting the same words. Antonio was probably the only one who even knew what he was saying. Then I felt energy flowing through me, and basked in it until I started becoming weaker. As Mara explained before, this thing was taking *our* energy along with wherever it got the rest from. Before I knew it I was dropping to my knees, and opened my eyes to a slit to see that Mara was still standing, but shakily. Antonio, meanwhile, was having a ball. The last thing I remember was a long, loud laugh followed by a scream, and then someone threw a bomb at me.

Chapter 22

Voices filtered in and out for days on end. I think they were days. It could have been only one hour. Time became difficult for me to interpret. I felt, saw, smelled, and tasted nothing; hearing was my remaining sense, and perhaps it sustained me—briefly, anyway.

I heard someone who might have been Jackie, so a thought occurred to me to open my eyes, but nothing happened. I wanted to feel my way around, but nothing moved. Nothing at all. Not an arm, or an eyelid. Not even a breath, I'm certain. There was a brief time at the beginning where some words filtered through, like "friend," and "miss her." My name might have been thrown my way a few times, too. Then some thumps and creaks followed for a bit, followed by a soft, scraping sound of something falling onto . . . wherever I was.

After that I felt, saw, smelled, tasted and heard *nothing*. Complete and total nothingness, save the occasional thought that flashed into my mind. I wasn't sure I was still alive. I could have been in hell. Why not? Complete deprivation is a pretty effective punishment. Absolute nothingness save thought, but without any means to apply it. That would make a better hell than a lot of flames and lava. An eternity of isolation. It would be enough to make the mind that remains go mad, don't you think?

After what seemed like a millenium, one hint of a sense returned. Taste, I think—or smell, I'm not sure. After another millenium the sense got a little stronger, and I decided that it probably was taste. It wasn't strong enough to tell me if it was a good taste or not, but something had made it fight its way back. I found myself focusing all thought on making it stronger. It did get stronger—strong enough so that the merest hint of smell followed, and then touch. I felt something that seemed like the wing of a fly on my mouth, but was far from being able to brush it away. After several centuries I felt something moving across my lips, then down my throat. This happened again a few decades later, then again a few years later. Now it was happening at intervals of months. Things were entering me through my mouth, and at first I was terrified. Was this an added torment? Were things invading me to mock my helplessness? But my senses were returning to me; this *had* to be good. Right?

Something very big forced its way down my throat. I felt it squirming and kicking, and for the first time, something moved on its own. My tongue flinched once, then was still. A few weeks later it happened again. Something large, and this time I felt hair, squirmed its way down my throat. And the next thing moved—my jaw. Now for the first time, hearing returned when a squeak reached my ears, then was silent. Something warm and wet washed over my dried-up tongue, replenishing it just in time for me to recognize the last drops as it rushed down my throat. Blood. I had bitten down on something, and it was alive!

Now I remembered who I was, but didn't know *where*

I was. My arms were still immobile, but more things followed the last one. Except I was beginning to taste these things. Do I have to describe what I was tasting? Is it really necessary to go into detail about what worms, or cockroaches, or slugs or beetles or ants or even rats taste like? I will *not* describe them. Let the ones who wonder find out for themselves, because I won't go into it again.

I'd swallowed a mouse, when a finger moved again. A snail had gone down when my whole hand flinched. And on, and on, and on until I'd created an endless stream of bugs, spiders, slugs, rodents, and anything else that could make its way to me. My eyes could open, and my arms could move, and now it was clear what had happened. The stuff that Poe had made his living by writing—stories about people being buried alive!

Buried alive? A vampire? Buried alive? Antonio had only hinted at what happens when we don't feed to the point of losing all strength. We cannot move, he'd said, we cannot speak, we cannot do *anything,* save think. Lie there and think, because we won't die. God knows I wanted to die. I even tried praying to Him, and *begging* Him to release me from this, once I'd decided that this wasn't the afterlife, after all. I'd been completely drained of all strength for eons. Now the most repulsive living things I could think of were the only things that could save me.

Rat after rat gave me the strength to feel the lid of my coffin, and push. Nothing happened, and I was exhausted already. Each time I tried, I had to replenish with more creatures. Very slowly, though, I was requiring fewer things to get my strength back up. When it got to the point where I could try over and over again, the lid budged open about an inch, and then no amount of shoving did any more. I felt along the sides and noted that it was open just enough for me to feel the dirt on the outside, so I started scraping. Eventually the scraping became digging, and then . . . I hope you understand what happened.

I was digging my way out of my own grave. My strength always gave out until something replenished it. I considered it a treat whenever something like a gopher came across my constant summonings. After several decades of digging, the coffin lid opened almost two feet, so I really dug in along the sides and started making a nice tunnel. A crowd of rats joined the fun, making it easy to feed whenever I needed to. More were sure to replace the ones I ate.

The ground above me was soft and pushed up easily. I took a long, deep breath more for effect than air, because there wasn't any, shut my eyes, then stood up. The ground gave way and piled off to the side as I pushed and squirmed my way to a rush of cool, almost-clean *air!* My tunnel was filled up like a vacuum after I made the last climb to the surface. Exhausted, I slumped across the dirt and breathed in my first breath of air in an eternity.

It was no surprise to find myself in a graveyard. Nor was I surprised to find my own tombstone. My date of birth was wrong. To my good fortune it had been night when I finally burst from the earth. That would have made a fine shot for any living-dead movie.

Chapter 23

We all go a little crazy sometimes. A long and wide succession of animal and yes, human mutilations followed my return from the dead. I might have had a rational thought when I first set out to renew my strength, but I doubt it. I remember that there were a lot of images flashing through my mind, though. Most of them were of faces. Some of the faces made me feel good, while others drove me instantly into a blind rage whenever they appeared. And I didn't even know whose faces they were yet.

Most prominent were the faces of a thirtyish, dark-haired, malevolently handsome man, and a blond, green-eyed woman, also thirtyish. I killed most often and most violently whenever they appeared.

My first conscious thought occurred when I passed by a newspaper vending machine. I'd passed dozens of them before, but now it occurred to me to stop. For a while I stared at the paper inside, then smashed through the glass and dragged the paper outside. Blood spurted from my wrist and started splattering onto the paper. I killed a passerby, then wandered off somewhere where I could read.

It took me a few nights to start comprehending what I read. The first thing I remember understanding was the date, but I wouldn't believe it at first. If this paper was accurate, I had been indisposed not for eons, but for eight years. My eternity had lasted me only eight years! That should have comforted me, but it didn't. All I could think of after that was, if eight years had felt like *that,* then any longer, and I would never have been able to read anything at all, ever. Or know reason or rationality ever again, either.

My next memorable moment occurred after I'd regained the ability to go where humans go and not drool in anticipation. I had no money, nor anything else of any worth, because it never occurred to me to steal from any of my victims. But I wanted to browse, anyway, so I browsed in a convenience store and observed how little consumerism had changed in eight years. I was rather hoping to find a brave, new world so to speak, but it was business as usual for the humans. Except that it was likely that things had only gotten worse.

Bored, I was about to leave, when I spotted one of the tabloid papers. In huge, black letters, it read "Vampire Has Baby!" and showed a picture of a blond, green-eyed, thirtyish woman smiling and holding a newborn baby in her arms. I stared at that picture so long it seemed to be coming towards me, so I blinked my eyes and looked away. Then I looked back again, but nothing had changed. That woman was still there. I grabbed the paper from the rack and started walking away with it. After I reached the door, I heard a voice behind me but ignored it. Then a rough hand whirled me around, and the counterman was yelling at me. I stared at him a moment, then pushed him through the plate-glass door. I heard him scream, but ignored that, too. Other humans were running towards me, so I tucked the paper between my legs, spread my arms, and flew. I heard someone shout, "Hey, that's a fuckin' vampire!" before I went flying out of earshot.

More reading showed me things I never could have imagined in a lifetime—a vampire's lifetime. I *was* in hell. Everywhere I looked, there was something about vampires. People knew about us now. People *know* about us now. Not as villains in movies or books or dreams, but as real beings. Dracula was dead, and for real this time.

But that's not the worst news. That was only bad. The worst news is what people were saying about us. We weren't villains in fiction anymore, because now we could be *for real.* I read about how vampires were responsible for AIDS. How they were carriers of just about every other disease, including social ones like greed, lust, anger, pride, sloth, envy, and gluttony. Television told me about vampires being suspected of every murder that was committed, including the latest rash of animal and human mutilations. They were creatures of evil and of the Devil himself; read your Bibles, the Anti-Christ has come. There were articles and stories and items about Vampire Act this and that. Should vampires be allowed to get blood? Should they be allowed to marry, and if so, even adopt? Should they even have any rights at all?

There was too much happening now, too much to assimilate. My rage was building, and I needed some way to vent it, something to focus on, and it couldn't be humans. I looked at my tabloid again. There she was, in all her glory. Smiling. Happy. But with a child? The article revealed nothing, save that one Mara McCuniff had given birth to a little girl.

I never sought out any of my old friends or acquaintances. Not even Jackie. How could I? Was I to expect her to support my plan? Obviously not. For all I knew she might have been having babies herself. *All* vampires might have been having babies. At least one that I knew had.

I kept seeing her face outside of my mind's eye more and more. Once I saw her on television talking about how wonderful it was to be a human again, and you can be too, if just follow these simple steps! Now the world *was* crazy. I'd had no part in it, either, because I'd been in a hole in the ground the whole time.

A year after I escaped from the grave, I browsed through a bookshop and caught sight of another one of those vampire paperbacks. *The Vampire Memoirs,* it read, and I would have moved on except for two things. One was the cover. I remembered that I'd long ago wanted to write my own history of vapiredom. It was possible that someone had actually found my sparse notes, pieced the story all together somehow, and published it, using an old picture of me as a model for the cover. It looked more like some "glamor-photo" of me, but it was a good enough likeness to invite plenty of comparison. But then I saw the byline of one Mara McCuniff and someone I'd never heard of.

By this time I had money and the ability to function normally amongst humans. In a daze I took the book to the front counter. After the purchase I returned to the ratty hotel basement that I called home and curled up by candlelight.

Suffice it to say that I felt my characterization was exaggerated. I've also never read a more self-pitying, melodramatic bit of tripe in my life. But now at least I had a purpose in my life, and that was to eliminate the one responsible for this mess. It seemed so obvious that Mara's little diary was what brought about all this against us. She had handed the proof of our existence to them on a platter. Now she was having babies. And smiling. That wouldn't do at all.

For those who wonder, I had already tried to return to my old house. I couldn't even enter it. Strangers were living there—*human* strangers. I hovered around my house for weeks, watching them, until one night all but one seemed to have left. Their ratty teen boy, it was. After the rest of them left I snuck up to the doorstep and knocked on the door. Antonio said he'd done this to me, so maybe it would work. To my surprise, his voice came from an intercom.

"Hello?" it said. I started and stared at this new intrusion.

"Uh . . ." I said, poking at various buttons, "can you hear me?"

"Yeah, who is this?" he said.

"I'm, uh—I've been locked out of my house," I said. "Do you think I could use your phone?"

"Isn't anyone else home around here?" he asked. How hospitable.

"No," I said, "no, I don't think so. Please—just for a minute. It's a local call, too."

"Well, okay," he said, and the intercom clicked. After a moment his heavy footsteps sounded in the hallway, and then the curtains on the door moved aside. I smiled. The boy finally opened the door.

"You're locked out, huh?" he said. I smiled and charmed him so fast that his mind was a blank when I entered it.

"Invite me in," I said.

"Come in," he said, and stepped aside. I held out my hand, and when it touched nothing, I stepped through the doorway.

"Is anyone else here?" I asked.

"No . . ."

"Wait here, then," I said, and ran into my old library.

I cried out in bitter frustration and anger when I saw what had happened. All my books had been removed, and one wall had had the shelves themselves torn out. Where my desk had been stood a giant entertainment center. The walls were lined with videotapes and those new CD things. A big sofa had been plopped in the middle of the room, and a fridge was off to one side. They even had exercise equipment in there.

After stepping all the way inside I noticed that *some* of my books remained, but none that were of any use to anyone. In a growing rage I stormed from the room and rushed back to the entry. I grabbed the teen hard by his shoulders and shook him.

"Where are my books? *Where are my books?"* I demanded.

"Wha—I—uh—!" he said, and I shoved him away and paced.

"Gone," I grumbled. *"Gone,* all of them sold or—or given away! To whom, boy? Tell me!"

"I don't—I . . ." he said, so I made an extreme effort to calm myself and not tear his throat out.

"Now, wait," I said to myself, taking deep breaths, "now, now—all isn't lost. All can't be lost. All—shit! Shit, shit, it *is* lost! Do you realize how many of those were one-of-a-kind?"

"No . . ."

"Of course you don't!" I yelled. "You probably don't even know what a book *is!* None of you—you *humans* do! Even if I told you which ones I needed most, you couldn't help me!"

"Help you?" he said.

"My house," I muttered, looking at their so-called

decor, "I have no house now. Because you *stole* it from me! You stole my things from me! Where are they, boy? *Where?*"

"I . . . don't know . . ." he said, backing away.

"Did you sell it all?" I asked. "Give it away? I had books that—I had books of *magic* in there! *Real* magic! What have you—?"

"Magic?" he said.

"Yes, magic," I said. "Not that any of you would recognize it. Tell me, boy, what—"

"I have . . . something . . ." he said.

"What?"

"Mom and Dad don't know," he said. "Some books I have. The old owner left them . . ."

"What books?" I asked, grabbing his shirt. "You mean you still have some of them?"

"In my room . . ." he said.

"Well, show them to me, boy! Bring them out!" I said, releasing him. He turned and headed for the stairs. I made him go faster until we reached my old parlor—I mean *his* room—where he fell to all fours and looked under the bed. I'd heard about typical teens' rooms, but was disgusted with what I saw, nonetheless. The least he could have done was get rid of the food lying around.

"Well?" I said. "Hurry it up, boy!"

Silently he reached under the bed and pulled out clothes, food, shoes, and other junk, until he reached back and pulled out some very familiar tomes. He'd barely even brought them out when I snatched them from his hands. Yes! I thought. *Yes!* These were exactly what I needed. Bless the boy's immature fascination with the occult! I kissed the dusty covers and went to the doorway. Then I turned around and looked at the room again.

"Forget I was ever here, boy," I said. "I was never here."

"Never here," he said.

"And, uh . . . clean up this room, will you?" I added. "Make it spotless."

"Spotless . . ."

It took me about a year to track down Mara's house. I didn't want to rush into things, either. My blind rage had gradually shifted to a cold, calculated plot for revenge. I was going to make sure that she suffered slowly.

Mara was usually not alone. There were always kiddies and a husband running around in there. How many babies was she having, anyway?

A possible opportunity came. After several hours of watching from across the street, I saw that no one but Mara seemed to be inside. Normally they kept their curtains closed, but this time they were open. Throughout the evening I watched her paint her nails, watch television, drink coffee, and wander around aimlessly. She went into her bedroom a lot, too, or somebody's, anyway. A real wildwoman. Then she settled down to read a book, so that's when I began.

First I needed to cast the spell that I'd nicknamed the cone of silence. It involves tracing around an object with various materials, then reciting a spell that keeps all sound within. In this case, the focus was on Mara's house, so once the spell was in effect, an H-bomb could hit the place, and no one would hear a thing. I don't think it affected trying to make a phone call, for instance, but that would be easy to take care of.

The spell was completed, and so far no one seemed to have called the police about the stranger skulking around their neighbor's house. I love big-city folks. I snuck back around to the front porch and looked in the window. Still reading away. I froze in position until, at last, Mara yawned and stretched, set the book aside, and stood up. Then she went back to that bedroom door and peeked inside. It occurred to me that someone else might have been home, after all. Maybe that baby?

My chance came when Mara went up to the window and grabbed her curtains. She started pulling them across the window, I counted to three, then stood up and lit up my eyes. She looked right at me, called out and jumped back. I misted quickly and watched her peer back outside, until she came back to the living room and started turning lights off. Come back! I thought, but of course she didn't hear. Then the porch light was flipped on, so I transformed and crouched down. I could sense that she was leaning closer to the window, peering outside, and when the time was right, I stood up again. This time it would work.

It was known to me that Mara's willpower was second to none. Even Antonio had had trouble with her. But she was human now. I could hardly believe my eyes when I saw her in the darkness, but it was true. A nice and strong, blue aura. But it wasn't light blue like that of a normal human. That discrepancy would have to be contemplated later, though.

I watched her arms drop to her sides and her green eyes fade into that nice warm red that all charm-ees share. For a moment all I could do was stand there and marvel at how easy it was. Then, I gestured to her to head for the door. I knocked, and after a moment, locks and deadbolts were undone, and the door swung open.

"Hello, Mara," I said. "It's been such a long time, hasn't it?"

"Yes . . ."

"Well?" I said. "Aren't you going to invite me in?"

There was a brief hesitation, then she stood to one side.

"Come in," she said, and I bowed and passed through the doorway.

"Shut the door behind me," I said, scanning the place for signs of others. I heard it shut. "Lock up," I said, and the locks and deadbolts were locked and bolted. She waited for more orders.

"Anyone else here?" I asked, facing her now.

"No . . ."

"You sure about that, now?" I asked. "Give me the names of everyone in this house, right now."

"Mara . . ." she said. "Theresa. Je—Jennifer."

"Jennifer?" I said. "Who's that?"

"My daughter."

"Where? How old?"

"Asleep," she said. "In her bedroom. She's . . . almost two."

"Ahhh," I said, nodding. "Well, maybe you'll let me meet her soon."

"Meet her."

"So tell me . . ." I said, taking her left hand and examining it. "Oh, married now, huh?"

"Yes."

"Happily?"

"Yes."

"Very, very happily?"

"Yes."

"To whom?"

"Jim," she said.

"McCuniff?"

"Yes."

"Figures you'd take *his* name," I muttered, then looked around some more. "Shut the curtain," I said, and she did so. "Now turn the lights back on." That was done, too.

"So where is everyone else, dear?" I asked while she worked at her tasks. "Where is Jim darling and any other kiddies you have?"

"Chicago," she said.

"When will they be back?"

"A week," she said. "We're to join them tomorrow."

"Why the delay?"

"Jennifer . . ." she said. "Ear infection. Airplanes are bad for them."

"Oh, yes, the air pressure and all," I said. "Of course. You're just being a loving, concerned parent to wait."

"Try to be."

"I'm sure you do, Mara," I said, walking up to her. "I'm sure you do."

She looked down and rubbed her eyes. I leaned against the sofa and waited for her to look up again. As expected, she yelped and jumped back. I smiled but said nothing.

"Oh!" she cried, regaining her composure. "What are—who—wha—"

"What's wrong, Mara?" I asked. "Don't you remember me?"

"But you're—how did you—I thought we—" She was flustered. I smiled and stood up straight, then walked towards her. She backed away at each step I took.

"Oh, I'm sorry to have startled you," I said, "but you *have* to remember *me.*"

"Tuh, tuh, tuh . . ." she said, and backed all the way into the wall.

"You mean you *don't* remember me?" I said, catching up to her and putting my hand next to her. She scooted along the wall until she came to a corner.

"Theresa!" she cried.

"Shhhhh . . ." I said. "You don't need to shout. Your baby's trying to sleep, remember?"

"My—my baby?" she said, and pushed past me. She ran to the bedroom door and went inside. I shrugged and followed her. She had the kid in her arms when I reached the doorway.

"What have you done to her?" she demanded.

"Nothing," I said. "All I said was that she's trying to sleep. If she starts crying it'll be *your* fault."

"Wh—what do you want with me, Theresa?" she asked. "Wh-what happened? I thought—we *all* thought you were—were—"

"Dead?" I finished. She nodded quickly, and her kid started waking up.

"Yes, I got that impression," I said, straightening a picture on the wall. "In fact, that's something I wanted to talk to you about." Mara hugged the kid tighter to her.

"Then . . ." she said, "you were—were buried alive. Weren't you?"

"Yes, I was," I said. The kid was starting to grumble. "Your daughter is fine, Mara," I said. "I suggest that you put her back in bed."

"I-I think I'd like her close to me, thanks," she said.

"Oh, you don't seriously think that I . . . that I've done anything to her, do you?" I asked.

"Wh—well, of course not, it's just—um . . ."

"You know, she's a cute kid," I said.

"Th-thank you," she said. "We—w-we think she'll be very pretty when she gets older."

"Just like her mom," I said, smiling. She blushed.

"Th-thank you," she said.

"May I hold her?" I asked, stepping forward. Mara held the kid closer to her instead.

"Uh . . ." she said, "uh that—might not be a good idea. Sh-she's not feeling well, you see. Ear infection. Sh-she needs her rest."

"Ohhh, yeahhh," I said, nodding. "Well, then, we'd both better let her sleep. Why don't we just talk out here?"

Mara stared at me a long time, then looked at her kid and kissed her on top of the head.

"Rest well, Jennifer," she whispered. "I love you." Then she put Jennifer back into her crib before she was disturbed any more. I backed away to let Mara leave the room and shut the door tightly.

"So that's your very own kid, huh?" I whispered. She nodded quickly, then stepped away from me. "One you gave birth to and everything?" I asked, following her.

"Uh . . . y-yes," she said, then turned to face me. "You know, I—you can't imagine how glad I am that you're—well, that you're—"

"Alive?" I finished. She nodded. "So am I," I said, smiling.

"Then, ha-have you—have you talked to anyone else?" she asked. "T-talked to Jackie, perhaps?"

"Jackie?" I said. "No. No, actually, you're the first person I've contacted since I . . . busted out."

"Busted out," she said, laughing nervously. "Yes, i-it—it must have been awful. I mean—I-I've only imagined what—what it must be like, but . . ."

"Maraaaaaa," I said, putting an arm around her, "why do I get the feeling that you're nervous?"

"D-do I seem nervous?" she asked, wiping her brow. "Oh—I—a-actually I've had sort of a hectic day."

"Oh, I'm sorry," I said.

"Yes, well . . . Jennifer being sick and all and—th-the family away, and, um—"

"You know," I said, "maybe I came at a bad time. Would you like it if I came by at some other, more convenient time?"

"Oh," she said, "would you? I-I mean, not that I'm not *glad* to see you again, I mean—well, Jackie will be ecstatic. B-but maybe you should let me break the news to her."

"Oh, don't worry, it'll be better if I surprise her," I said. "But, Mara—I'm so glad I had this opportunity to see you again."

"Uh, yes, um," she said, fumbling to undo her locks and bolts, "r-really, this is sort of a bad time, but—oh, *do* feel free to come by again."

"I'll do that," I said, and held out my hand. Mara looked at my hand, wiped the side of her thigh, smiled nervously, then grabbed hold.

I gave her my best, most hearty, most viselike handshake I could give. She groaned, then winced in pain and started pulling at my hand.

"Tuh—Theresa," she grunted, dropping slowly to her knees.

"What's the matter?" I asked.

"You're—hurting me!" she gasped. I frowned.

"Oh," I said, "am I shaking hands too hard? I'm sorry. I guess I'm used to people with *my* strength."

"Please!"

"I had no idea it would hurt you so much, Mara," I said. "I would *never* want to do that." I brought my knee up hard into her belly. "Would I?"

While she was doubled over, I picked her up from below and heaved her somewhere behind me. I must have had a bad grip on her, because she only made it to the top of the sofa. Her body hit the sofa back halfway, so she flipped over entirely, to land between the couch and the dining room table. I casually locked and bolted the door, then sauntered over to her.

She was on her hands and knees by the time I came by, making it easy to grab her by the back of her pants and slam her into the wall. The back of her head smacked against the wall, so I grabbed her by the throat and pinned her in place before she could collapse. It was a good grip—the sort where any violent moves will snap the neck, but it was not blocking the arteries or veins. I didn't want her passing out on me yet.

"Do you have any idea how long I was in the ground?" I asked rather calmly, actually.

"P-please," she wheezed, "didn't—know!"

"Didn't know what, Mara?" I asked, pushing her up against the wall. She was about a foot taller than I, so I couldn't push her up very high, as I'd wanted to.

"Didn't—know you were—alive!"

"So you say," I said. "Now that's something that puzzles me. Maybe you can explain. Hm? Maybe you can explain exactly how it is that you, and my *friends,* would believe that a VAMPIRE was dead just because she wasn't breathing." I slugged her in the gut. "Ehh?"

She was too busy coughing to answer, so with a yell I picked her up again and threw her across the dining-room table. She skidded along the top then slammed into a chair at the other end, falling backwards into the corner. She screamed in pain then started sobbing uncontrollably.

"Help me!" she cried. "Somebody—please help me!"

"Yes, I saw that movie, too," I said, picking up a chair and breaking it into several pieces. "They had to *kill* him at the end, didn't they?"

"Please!" she sobbed. "Please don't hurt me anymore! Don't hurt *her!*"

"What? Who?" I said.

"M-my baby!" she said. "Please don't hurt her! Kill me if it's what you want, but let her live!"

"You, my dear," I said, reaching down and yanking her to her feet, "have been watching too many *movies!*" At that I had slammed her against the wall again. Then I grabbed one of her hands and forced her to take one of the chair pieces.

"Here," I said. "You haven't been a challenge at all so far. You might need this."

"I don't want to hurt you . . ."

"You're not likely to, but that's just in case you change your mind," I said, and beckoned her forward. "Come on," I said. "You want to finish what you started, don't you?"

"I started nothing," she whispered. "Please—none of us knew, Theresa. You had no aura. You had no life-signs, you had nothing!"

"And what about Antonio? Did you kill him, too?"

"Yes! I-I mean, no!" she blubbered. "I mean—I wasn't the one who did. Don't you remember what was happening? To both of us? He was—"

"How—did—he—die?" I demanded, stepping forward with each word. She gripped the chair leg tighter, but shrank back into the wall.

"He-he was—" she whimpered. "Jim killed him. My husband. It was difficult for me to see, but he managed to wake up and stab him in the back with . . . well, with one of these," she said, indicating the chair leg that she held.

"I find that *very* hard to believe."

"But it *is* true!" she said. "Um . . . i-if you think about it, he was almost immobile . . . you know, while casting his spell, and um—" she stopped then as her lips began to quiver. I was getting bored with her.

"H-he's dead now, Theresa," she said. "He's finally dead! Isn't that—doesn't that make you happy?"

"Hmph."

"But I thought that you . . . that is, h-he treated you just as terribly as he treated me. Don't you feel . . . free from him now?"

"Yeah, just like your book said," I said.

"M-my book?"

"Yeeeeess, your *book,*" I sneered. "Didn't think I could read, hmm?"

"Well, of course I did, but—"

"You said you used to be some great warrior, too," I said. "Give me a fucking break."

For a moment it looked like she might have actually conjured up some of those old fires that she claimed to have had. But just for a moment.

"Theresa," she said, setting the makeshift stake down, "if something in there offended you, I—I'd like to—"

"Offended?" I said, "You use a word as mild as 'offended' to describe how I felt? How I feel *now?*"

"But what did I say?" she cried.

"Pick up that stake!"

"I don't want to fight you!" she said. "I—! I can't fight you. I'm human now, it would be futile to fight you hand-to-hand."

"Coward."

"If that's what you think, then yes, I'm a coward."

"Don't you *dare* condescend to me!" I yelled. *"You* made this world that I woke up to! *You* betrayed us! *You* handed the proof of our existence right into their hands!"

"But that's not the way it was!" she said.

"Who hated vampires above all else?" I said. *"Who* despised everything about us and everything we are? Who?"

"But it wasn't my doing! My book proved nothing to anyone! I-it was thought to be fiction at first, I swear it!"

"At first, you said! So then, you went on talk shows, right?"

"No!" she cried. "No, I swear I'm telling the truth! Th-the proof of our existence came completely independent of it! I-it was somebody in a hospital, another vampire—"

"Who?"

"I-I don't know," she said. "Believe me, no one thought my book was real until long after we became known!"

"So of course your book made things so much easier for us," I said. She stared at me a moment.

"I-I can't say that," she whispered. I sighed and shut my eyes for a moment.

"Death is too good for you," I growled. "You'd die without ever knowing what you've done."

"H-how do you know I don't?" she asked. "Theresa, please, you've gone through an experience that—that no human could have survived! You've—"

"Then death would have been the best thing for them," I said, stepping forward. "Don't you think?"

In spite of her promise Mara grabbed the stake and twisted it in her hands.

"W-w-we can talk about this, Theresa," she said quietly. "Murdering me won't help you. C-can't you see that—that this is the way Agyar would have done this? Y-You don't want to be like him, do you?"

With a yell I rushed forward, grabbed her by the neck, and slammed her hard against the wall.

"Don't—you—*ever* accuse me of being like him!" I hissed. Now that I was close she didn't have the leverage to get me with the stake. I leaned in her face.

"No, no, of course not," she whispered, trying to turn away. "I-I'm sorry, Theresa. Truly, I'm sorry . . ."

"You know," I said, "it's too bad a simple apology won't undo the damage you've done. Except, I might almost have forgiven you for it, if you hadn't put *me* on the cover!" On the word "me" I slammed my knee into her groin. She tried to double over, but I held her up.

"What the hell were you thinking, girl?" I demanded. "It may not be exactly me, but I think people will get the idea!"

"Tried to"—cough!—"tried to—make them change it," she gasped. "Wouldn't do it. Couldn't do it."

"What the hell are you talking about? It's your goddamned book!"

"Don't know what happened," she wheezed. "I'm telling the truth. I could do nothing about it!"

For an answer I slammed her head against the wall again. She groaned, and her eyes started rolling up into her head, so I slapped her face over and over.

"No, you don't," I said. "Not yet, you aren't." I ended up supporting her entire weight while I fought to keep her awake. Eventually some strength returned to her legs, so I pulled out a chair and made her sit there.

"And you prefer this existence?" I asked. "You like being human? Being weak?" Her response was unintelligible, so I grabbed her chin and made her look at me.

"Is this your answer, Mara?" I asked. "Being human again is the answer to your problems? Is that what you think?"

"Happy," she whispered.

"What? Did you say happy?"

"Happy," she said louder.

"So you think you're happy now because you're human and you're married and you're dropping babies all over the place? Eh?"

"Please go . . ."

"Answer me!" I roared. The kid was crying from her room again, this time louder than ever. "And why don't you shut that kid up?" I yelled.

"Cry, Jennifer," she muttered. "Cry, and maybe someone will come to help us."

"I'm afraid I've arranged things so that no one will hear us," I said. "And you *still* haven't answered me, Mara."

"What," she mumbled. "Whaaat?" she cried, standing up. "What do you want from me? An apology? My death? Why won't you leave me alone? Why won't *anyone* leave me alone? Why can't anyone leave me in peace?"

I was surprised by the speed with which she snatched up the stake and tried to impale me. I caught her hand with the point just touching my chest, then brought her arm up behind her back.

"Goddamn you!" she screamed. "Goddamn you, why don't you leave me alone!"

"Such language," I said, and threw her against the wall. She slid down to her knees and groaned. Meanwhile I rushed into the kid's bedroom and picked her up. I reached the doorway when Mara was just pulling herself back up.

"Such language in front of your own child, Mara," I said, and she whirled around and screamed.

"Don't you touch her!" she screamed. "I swear, if you do *any*thing, I'll—!"

"Then *do* it, Mara!" I said over the kid's cries. "You've been no threat to me at all, so *do* something! Fight me to get her back!"

"Give me my child!"

"I said *fight* me to get her back!"

"And you said you weren't like him!" she cried. "That you weren't like Agyar! Well, this is *exactly* his way! Using innocents to—"

"Careful what you say, Mara," I said. "I might get too angry and—maybe lose control of my strength."

"You wouldn't *dare!*"

"Wouldn't I?" I said. "How far would *you* go to save your kid, hm? Do you think I haven't lost precious possessions of my own? Things that *can't* be replaced?"

"She's just a baby, Theresa," she pleaded. "Please, your rage was meant for me, not her. Just don't hurt her."

"I'm only going to say this one last time, then I'll count to three," I said. "You'll have to fight me to get her. One." She grabbed the stake and held it tightly.

"Please, Theresa . . ."

"Two."

"Let her go . . ."

"Three!"

"No!" she roared, and rushed at me with stake in hand. At the last instant I knelt down and clutched the girl close to me, sending Mara sprawling over my back and into the room. I shut the door behind her and stared at the girl, trying to get her to look me in the eyes. Mara slammed against the door, then flung it open in a rage. She stood there with her fists clenched and teeth gritted, shaking with rage. I wonder what the house would have looked like afterwards if she had still been a vampire.

"If you touch my daughter," she growled, "I will kill you. Even if it takes my last breath, I will kill you."

"Now *that's* the spirit," I said, and smiled. Then I held the kid out to her. "Better put her back to bed, then." With near-vampire speed she snatched the kid-from my hands and ran for the front door. It was simple to jump ahead of her, though.

"Ah-ahh," I said, throwing my arms out. She spun around and made for the back door, but I blocked that exit, too. She cried out in frustration and turned around and around, apparently trying to decide where to go. Then with a yell, she ran back into the kid's room and slammed the door shut. I tiptoed over to the door, and was about to listen, when the door flew open again, and Mara hurled herself right at me.

I was surprised that she managed to send me sprawling, but now the next move was mine. She picked up a chair and smashed it into my torso as I was getting up, though, knocking me back down. It almost hurt, too. She whacked away at me, until I managed to catch part of the chair and yank it out of her hands. Then I threw it back at her and knocked her down. We both got up at the same time, and I let her throw the first punch across my jaw. Rage seemed to be making her particularly strong; either that or there was still some trace of her power in her, human or not.

I let her throw punch after punch and kick after kick, mainly to see what my limits were. It seemed that she was starting to remember those old fighting tactics that her dead husband had taught her, because now she was hitting sensitive spots. It would start to hurt if I let her keep up, so I caught one of her kicks and twisted the leg, forcing her around and down onto her knees. She started to struggle, so I gripped her by the hair and yanked her head back. Then I made a fingernail grow, and held it at her neck.

"I think I've had enough fun for tonight," I said. "Time for you to apologize."

"Theresa . . ." she whispered, "none of us knew. We all thought—I swear we didn't—"

I yanked her hair to get her attention.

"I don't think we're connecting here," I said. "I said *apologize.* I want a good, sincere, heart-felt apology, for all those lovely things you said about me, and vampires in general, in your book."

"Y-you don't understand all that's happened here," she said. "How the world really *has* changed. It isn't as bad as—AH!" she cried as I yanked at her hair again.

"Oh, I'm sure a vampire will be elected president any day now, but *you haven't apologized yet.*"

"I'm sorry!" she squeaked. "I—I didn't mean to—I had no idea you'd see it as—"

"Do you have a death wish or something?" I cried, but didn't yank the hair. "I said apologize!"

"I'm sorry!" she said, then started crying again. "I'm sorry, I'm sorry, I'm sorry, I'm sorry, I'm sorry . . . Please, Theresa, if killing me is what you want, then please stop toying with me. End my life, but please let my family live!"

"You know, you bore me," I said. "In fact, you've always been a very boring person. Look at you, Mara. Look at this *place!* For all those years . . . Jesus, all those *centuries* . . . has this really been your goal? To be a happy housewife who cooks happy meals for her happy husband and happy kids? Well, is it?"

"I—I love my family . . ."

"You could have given them so much, Mara," I said. "You could've given them . . . them anything they wanted! *You* could have had anything you wanted, but you never used your talents! Never!"

"I'm happy," she whispered. "I'm content. I'm—I love them. I love them all. I don't want it any other way . . ."

"Oh, *please,*" I groaned.

"I never asked to be what I was!" she cried. "I fought it every bit of the way! Second oldest and most powerful. The First, moving mountains, bringing any man to his knees. I never wanted those things! Never!"

"You never deserved them."

"Theresa!" she said. "If it makes you any happier, I'm terrified, all right? You've proven that you're better than me, that you're—you're stronger than me! What difference will it make to let me live? *I'll* age now, *I'll* die, and *you'll* keep on, *you'll* survive! And then even you could go on to be the oldest and most powerful of us all! But right now . . ." she said, sobbing again, "right now, for the first time in . . . in centuries, I'm happy. I'm content now that I finally have a family; I finally have my humanity!"

"And I have nothing, Mara," I said.

"You've succeeded before, certainly you can do it again!" she said. "A-and you have all the time in the world to do it! I don't! I'm going to grow old and die now!"

"You sound almost happy about that."

"I-I am, in a way," she said. "It's been so long, Theresa. Sixteen hundred years is a long time."

"So is two hundred," I mumbled.

"It is," she said. "Theresa; I-I understand your rage more than you think. I-I know you read my book, so you must know that—that I haven't had the most pleasant life, either. Please, Theresa; y-you need to talk to someone. Find Jackie, find . . . find any friend, and talk to her. This isn't the way . . ."

There was a long silence while I contemplated her words. My grip on her was starting to relax, and I felt her reach up slowly and try to pull my hand away.

About that time a wave of anger rushed over me. She was tricking me, I decided. She was breaking down my defenses and tricking me into sparing her! I had to give her credit for cleverness.

"No!" I yelled, then held on tightly as ever and

pulled her up to her feet. Then I shoved her into the wall and brought my face right up to hers.

"You *liar!*" I spat, and threw her against another wall.

"I'm telling the truth!" she cried. "I meant every word, Theresa!"

"Shut up!" I said, slugging her once across the face. She grunted, lurched to one side, then almost stood up again. When she kept swaying back and forth, I slugged her again on the other side, and she fell.

I waited for her to get up again, but there was no movement.

"Get up," I said, nudging her with my foot. Still nothing. I flipped off the nearest light to check her aura, which was as strong as ever.

"Get up!" I yelled, almost kicking her now. Then a memory returned; it was of Antonio, screaming and kicking at her while she lay helpless. It made me hesitate long enough to hear that kid blubbering and wailing from her crib.

"Shut up!" I yelled, as if that would make her stop. When she didn't, I rushed into the room and hovered over her.

"Shut up!" I roared, and smashed away one side of the bed. Wooden shards flew across the room and littered the floor, and I grabbed the kid by her pajamas and brought my hand up. She screamed and tried to pull away, and I tensed up, ready to tear the kid's throat out, but couldn't make my arm move.

The girl cried and cried, until I stared long and hard into her eyes, and her tears stopped. My arm had lowered itself almost without my realizing it. I let go of the girl's pajamas and backed away a few steps.

So now I'm killing children, I thought. The bitch's little girl or not, she was still an innocent. She didn't deserve death—not like her mother did. What had happened wasn't *her* fault.

I picked the girl up slowly and looked at her face. There was so much there that I *could* hate—Mara's eyes, and nose. Her hair, even her expressions. It was as if I were holding some two-year-old version of Mara. But it still wasn't her fault. I cradled her close to me and stepped through the doorway to stare down at Mara.

"You don't deserve her, Jennifer," I said. "I'd be doing you a favor."

I walked over and nudged Mara again. She rolled over onto her back, where I could see the bruises forming on her face. On a whim I set the girl down beside her mother, then pulled out of her mind. She rubbed her eyes and started to snuggle up to her mother.

"Mommy," she said, shaking Mara. When there was no response, she started to sniffle a bit. "Mommy?" she said again, then started groaning. By the time I picked her up again, she was crying. She screamed when I pulled her away.

"Mommy!" she cried, so I turned her over and made her look at me. After a few moments she was quiet again, so I probed deeper. The girl's aura was the same color as her mother's, which was odd. I didn't know what to make of it. I also sensed something different about the usual mother-daughter bond—something I couldn't name or understand. There was more to what I'd thought about Mara than it seemed, but I came to the conclusion that it was probably bad. Even now I couldn't say what the extent of this bond was.

No matter what I sensed, I couldn't bring myself to leave the girl alone with this woman. I have Mara to thank for this idea. She'd written something about forming a special mind-link with some little girl she'd known. It seemed like a good idea to me. I went even further into the girl's mind, found the loneliest spot I could, and slowly formed a picture of me there. I put some of my pleasant memories, thoughts, and feelings there, and made them permanent. If Mara could leave her essence with someone, so could I.

"You might need a friend sometimes when you're alone, Jennifer," I said when it was done. "I doubt if you'll ever see me again, but I'll always be with you." Then I kissed her on the forehead and brought her over to the couch and laid her there.

"Sleep now," I said and she did.

That left my other problem. I went over to Mara, who was still resting uncomfortably, and knelt beside her.

"Maybe you never were worth it," I said. "What good is killing you if you don't even know why you've died? You'll probably go on through life, having nightmares about this, telling your analyst about this, and not once will you ever know why this happened.

"I could probably live with being your faceless monster," I continued. "Because you're right; you *will* die eventually, while I could go on until the sun burns itself out. Actually, without the sun around, I'll probably go on even longer. Wouldn't that be nice? I knew you'd think so."

I put my arms under her and lifted her up. Her arms and head fell back limply while I brought her over to the other couch. Then I laid her down and headed back for the kitchen to grab some paper and a pen. My message was brief: "Changed my mind.—Th."

Then I took my note to the living room and put it on the table next to Mara. Hmmm, doesn't look right, I thought. So I grabbed her left hand, but stopped and looked at it again. Then I took off her ring and set it aside. I stuck the note in her hand. After this I went over to Jennifer, who slept comfortably, and picked her up again. She snuggled close to me, and I kissed the top of her head.

"The worst is yet to come, Jennifer," I whispered, "but I can tell you're a survivor. It'd be nice if I could see you years from now, and see how you turned out. But then, I hope I've arranged it so that you'll be seeing me in your dreams."

Then I set the girl down on Mara's chest, and wrapped her mother's right arm around her. Such a picture-perfect scene. But I couldn't provide for the girl any better than her real mother could—not at this time. Taking Mara's ring, I squeezed it together, then dropped it into her left hand with the note.

Before leaving, I poked around her house, looking at family photos and such, when I discovered an unfinished manuscript on her desk. She'd written about two hundred pages so far, so I took it with me. Hadn't she done enough? I'd thought. What I read didn't look very useful for curing oneself. I think that's what it was for. It started out about some custody battle that Mara had had with one of her kid's natural parents. She said it made a lot of headlines, so I assume most of you know what I'm talking about. Then all the stress of it led her to a nervous breakdown. From there the manuscript just gets weird. It read like some fantasy novel, so I learned nothing from it about how to become human. Now I wish I could give it back to her, but I ended up burning it in frustration. Apparently she hasn't rewritten it, because I haven't seen any other books from her.

As for my departure, I couldn't very well leave without tasting her blood. Mara had good, healthy blood. She was very generous to donate a pint to a friend in need.

Chapter 24

It's been quite a few years since I've written in this journal. The next few years were just so hectic that I didn't have time. Now, about twelve years later, I've settled down enough to have time for this. A hell of a lot has changed since, but I've decided not to change a word of what precedes, because nasty though it was, it was the truth. I haven't been brought to human justice for my crimes. I emphasize "human" because vampires have ways to make penance that few humans could tolerate. The human legal system can't even handle its own kind, so in most cases we've been allowed to deal with our own, our own way—including punishments for severe crimes, like killing humans. It isn't defined as murder, because murder refers to killing our own, meaning other vampires.

Before this time I sought refuge the human way. I never saw anyone else in Los Angeles after that night. Los Angeles was no longer safe for me. I don't think any of my friends would have given me refuge. Certainly not Jackie, not after doing what I did to her best friend. Even Gloria would be without me forever; she'd probably been doing just fine with the business, anyway. Right away I spent most of my money on a ticket to the Bay Area, where I remain at this time.

I left at night and arrived at night, and spent some time wandering the streets, looking for shelter. With no money, I had to resort to petty theft through charming, until one night another vampire discovered me. He took me into his home to let me get back on my feet, but I left when I discovered that his lack of morals made me look like Mara Poppins. He and his friends saw themselves as rulers of the night or something, and while they didn't cut a bloody swath of death and destruction through the city, some of their activities were . . . questionable. I was only one against several, so I wasn't about to take the law into my own hands against them.

My experience with that group led me to thinking about my own crimes. But how could I do penance for them? Not through God—my very existence was an affront to Him. Or maybe it wasn't anymore. Holy symbols didn't bother me anymore. I could have hung crosses all over my house if I'd wanted. Maybe that was a sign that He would welcome me back.

Since I couldn't make the usual daytime hours, I had to knock on a rectory door until the housekeeper appeared. A plump, elderly Italian woman appeared.

"Buona sera, signora," I said, bowing my head but not quite looking her in the eyes. "Is—is the *padre* in?"

"Yes, he is," she said. "May I tell him who's come?"

"Well, actually, I—I wish to see him in there," I said, pointing to the church. "I-in the confessional."

"Well, his usual times are posted here," she said, pointing to the door. "Unless you called him before? Does he know you're coming?"

"Uh, no, I—uh . . ." I said, fidgeting, "Please, *signora.* I-I can come at no other time."

She gave me a hard look, then looked behind her.

"I-I will wait in there for him," I said, and started backing away. "In the first one."

"I'll tell him, but it's up to him, miss," she said. I turned around and ran into the church. Once inside I ran for the confessional, but stopped at the entrance. There was so much to say, but would any of it be forgiven? Is vampirism a sin? Nothing is said of it in the Bible except a little about drinking blood. But vampires have no choice.

I was given a long time to change my mind, but stayed where I was in the confessional. I'd knelt down, but couldn't bring myself to cross myself. I heard someone enter the church, then walk along the aisle. Eventually a knock came at the door.

"Si," I said, shutting my eyes. The priest entered his own booth and opened the screen. "Forgive me, *padre,* for not coming at the proper time," I whispered.

"That's all right, my child," he said. "God is always ready to listen."

He listened, but it took me a while to speak.

"Forgive me, *padre,* for I have sinned," I said.

"Go on, my child," he said.

"I have—I have not been to confession for many years now," I said. "There is . . . much that I've done."

"Yes, my child."

"In fact, I . . . I have not been a Catholic for many years now, either," I said.

"Do you wish to return?" he asked.

"I'm not sure I can," I whispered. He was silent.

"I don't think the Lord approves of my kind," I said.

"The Lord approves of everyone," he said.

"Yes, that's what we're taught, I suppose," I said. More silence.

"I . . . I tried to hurt someone," I said. "I tried to hurt someone . . . very badly."

"Go on, my child."

"I tried to—I tried to kill her, *padre,*" I said.

"Is she . . . ?"

"Dead?" I said. "No. I didn't succeed. Or rather, I stopped myself before it happened."

"Why did you do this, my child?" he asked.

"I was . . . angry with her," I said. "She'd . . . written some things about me and some others that made me . . . a little crazy, I suppose."

"A little crazy," he said. "And this person," he continued, "have you made amends with her?"

"No, *padre,*" I whispered. "I . . . She doesn't know where I am."

"So you run from her now," he said. "You run from what you must face."

"Do I?" I said. "I'm not sure."

"Do you feel remorse for what you've done, my child?" he asked.

"I know that what I did was wrong," I said.

"But do you feel remorse?"

I was silent for a moment.

"I don't know," I said. "I—I want to make amends, but—that anger that made me do this before . . . much of it is still there."

"Are there . . . any others you've tried to hurt?" he asked.

". . . Yes," I said after some time. "But not for the same reasons. I-I wasn't quite myself then. I'd been through—a great ordeal. One so terrible that it made me mad for over a year."

"Have you . . . seen anyone about this?" he asked. "A doctor? Someone who helped you overcome this?"

"No," I said. "Perhaps I should have. But then, normal doctors can't help people like me."

"People like you?"

"I'm . . . different than most," I said. "I doubt if you'd understand."

"God understands all things, my child," he said. "You have committed some grave sins. But without true remorse there can be no penance. These people you've hurt—do you truly regret what you've done?"

"I . . . I don't remember exactly what happened to most of them," I said. "As I said, I wasn't myself. Am I truly accountable for them, then?"

"What your mind may not have done, you body did do," he said. "If you truly hurt those people, you must give restitution to them."

"Could I not be absolved of any of these things?" I asked.

"Without true penance?" he asked. "You must face those you've hurt, my child. You must ask their forgiveness, and probably more."

"Such as?"

"To do whatever you can to undo your sin against them," he said. "If they needed a doctor because of you, then pay their doctors."

"What if I have no money?"

"That's simply a suggestion," he said. "Let them decide what they need of you. But you must face them again."

"What if—what if she doesn't forgive me?" I said. "What if she tries to have *me* killed?"

"Do you believe that will happen?" he asked. I was silent a while.

"I don't think so," I said. "Sue me, probably, but not kill me."

"You must face those you've hurt, my child," he said. "And if not, you must go to the police and tell them what you've told me."

"The police?" I said.

"Yes."

"And . . . if I don't, you won't go to them yourself," I said, "right?"

"I cannot break my silence," he said, "but you must make restitution somehow."

"But what if I'm not forgiven?" I whispered.

"Then . . . God will know you made the effort," he said. "You must place yourself in His mercy, my child." Again, I was silent, but for a long time.

"I don't think I can," I whispered.

"Then . . . I cannot give you absolution, my child," he said.

"I didn't think you could," I whispered.

"Not until you find it in your heart to be truly repentant," he added. "Not until you're willing to face what you've done. I'm sorry, my child."

"Forgive me, *padre,*" I whispered. "I—I think it was a mistake to come here."

"Coming here was no mistake," he said. "But it will be a mistake to die never having been absolved of your sins."

"Yes, I—I suppose it would," I said. A long silence followed.

"Padre?" I said.

"Yes, my child."

"Do you think you could—well, wait for me to leave before opening the door?" I asked. "That is, don't get out until I'm gone?"

"If you wish, my child," he said.

"Thank you," I said, and opened the door.

"Go with God, my child," he said. "May He have mercy on you."

"I hope so, too."

So the human way was a bust. For a long time I wandered the streets with no real focus, save survival. I was able to run into other vampires here and there, and the generous ones let me crash for a time. I usually moved on quickly, as I didn't like being a burden. This was a strange world I'd woken up to. Vampires were still wary about revealing themselves to humans, but many of them did so, and tried to work through the consequences. Many of them seemed relieved that they no longer had to hide. One of them showed me a new census questionnaire that asked if you were a vampire, and if yes, asked other questions. What was next? Indicating if you're Caucasian, Black, Asian, or Vampire? We can't be considered a race, because there are vampires of all races already.

I learned that there's some organization called VamPT, which stands for Vampires are People, Too. Apparently it started out as some self-help or support group for vampire yuppies, then went on to become a major lobby group. I'm sure they have some very admirable goals, but I wish they'd change that name. *I* can barely take them seriously.

There seem to be a lot more vampires here than in Los Angeles. That, and the so-called liberal atmosphere this place is famous for, has apparently made this the best place for vampires. I'll have to see miracles before I believe that. I also shudder to think what it's like for vampires elsewhere.

I shouldn't complain, actually, because I have been able to form my own business again, and this time a lot of people knew about me along the way. Not that that's the way I'd wanted it, though. I own a workout center that caters especially to vampires. Most of the members are humans, of course, but even vampires like to keep in shape. I don't know of any other facility that provides weights over two thousand pounds. There are two members here who like to show off for the humans by bench-pressing their maximum of three thousand pounds. And remember that our strength increases with age as well as with working out. I wonder how much Antonio could have lifted?

You may be wondering how all this came to pass, and how I ended up doing penance after all. Most human justice systems are based on some physical punishment as their penance. To try a vampire by a human system doesn't bring about much justice. Execution could be possible for severe crimes, such as mine, but what's the punishment? I prefer being alive, but I've lived long past a human lifetime. No one would be cutting my life short by any means; I've already buried the victim, *and* his ancestors. Death would probably be welcome to more of us than you might think. Life imprisonment? That seems ironic, considering that we'd never leave, but then, the prison hasn't been built yet that can hold one of us. I mean that, too.

I've learned firsthand that, if there's to be a punishment, let it be psychic. I fell in with a rather spiritual group of vampires who'd found that empathy was the true path to goodness. Humans can only try to put themselves in another's shoes, but we actually can. By charming, of course, or in this case, linking. I came to like these people, and then trust them—enough to confess some of what I'd done to my closest friends among them. Their judgment was that I should find people who were suffering in the same way as I'd made others suffer, then link with them. Only that way could I understand what I'd done.

I found most of these people in emergency rooms. For months I was made to keep a vigil there, visiting patients by sneaking into their rooms and linking with them after the medics had finished with them. I learned of a different kind of pain and fear than I'd known while buried. In fact, after the first night, I told my friends that I wouldn't do it again, but they wouldn't allow that. Earlier I would have scoffed at them and walked away. Things had changed, though. As mentioned above, I did this night after night for several months. I went to different hospitals, too, as not every night yielded any real emergencies, fortunately. My true test came when I linked with someone who was dying. I wanted to pull away, but something made me hang on to the end. Our link only ended when his thoughts did. When it was over, I found myself crying for the first time in years.

I'd like to think that I provided a service for those patients by offering them some small comfort. Eventually my friends saw enough change in my temperament to allow me to stop. Perhaps I should have kept up my vigil, but linking is a very draining experience, physically as well as emotionally.

I'm well aware of the controversy surrounding allowing vampires to police their own, so to speak. Many humans will read the above and still be left speechless with righteous rage and indignation, and may even be tempted to hunt me down and destroy me like the dog I am. Please try to keep in mind that the above punishment was the most minor of what I ended up doing to rehabilitate myself. Our system of justice is designed with the vampire psychological makeup in mind. Humans always have believed and always will believe that pain and suffering are the best way to rehabilitate. I stand corrected—execution is the best way. It may surprise you to know that vampires have been shown to be biologically human, but the rest is still being debated. *Vive la différence!*

My friends all figured that I'd made amends, but it turns out I hadn't. The priest had been right about one thing. It was still necessary—for my own personal rehabilitation—to ask forgiveness of my victims, especially one specific victim. Since I'd been out of my mind when I'd hurt the others, I couldn't seek them out individually, but I made amends in other ways.

I'd become very good friends with a vampire named Chris. She helped me get back on my feet and kept me from sinking into the gutter. She more than any other showed me the ropes of vampire living in human society. I still prefer keeping a low profile. It's no one's business what I am. Not all of us feel that way, obviously.

I worked at somebody else's workout center before I came up with the idea of opening my own. The other ones didn't stay open long enough. I could only work part-time there and part-time in other places for that reason. Once again, I tried for a business loan and promised Chris a job if it worked. My timing hasn't lost its touch, I guess. My climb was slow and rather shaky at times, but I think the center has caught on pretty well. Of course I hired Chris, who turned out to be a good instructor. Vampires can work out for hours before even sweating, so our aerobic sessions go at a superhuman pace. Humans aren't allowed to sign up, period. They like to watch, though. Myself, I don't even have time to use my own center. Don't think I'm not in shape, though.

Chapter 25

It had been about eleven years since the incident in Los Angeles. The center was thriving by then. It seems that a lot of humans preferred those late hours, too. There were always as many humans as vampires working out at early morning hours. I think some of them just like to watch us break world weight-lifting records, but that's fine with me.

Chris had mentioned needing a part-time towel-girl and gofer, so I let her handle the hiring. She let me know when someone had been hired, but I never met the girl until about two weeks later. Talk about turning-points. Read on.

Chris greeted me in a bad mood as soon as I walked through the door. She insisted that I talk to the new girl, and dragged her over to us. Chris kept talking after she brought her over, but I didn't hear her. The new girl was a typical-looking sixteen-year-old. Blond hair, green eyes, tall for her age, plain but could be pretty if she tried. And I knew exactly who she was.

The girl took some time before looking me in the eyes, but when she did . . . same reaction. We had met before, and we both knew it.

"Vanessa?" Chris asked me. Yes, another name

change. But even that's a pseudonym for my real one. "Are you listening?"

"What?" I said, tearing myself away from the girl's sight. "What was that?"

"I just told you what happened," she said. "I found her sleeping in one of the closets tonight. I think it'd be best if you talked to her."

"Um . . ." I said, "yes. I think I should, too." I pulled Chris aside to go over some business before returning to the girl.

"We'll be in my office, Chris," I said. "I'd like you to take care of my calls, though."

"Got it," she said. We walked through the back hallways and up the stairs to my office. I fumbled for my keys.

"Um . . ." the girl said, "she called you Vanessa, right?"

"Yes," I said, working on the lock, "that's my name."

"Oh," she said. I opened the door and flipped on the light.

"Is that bad?" I asked.

"Oh, no," she said. "It's just that—for a minute I thought we'd . . . met before. But I don't know any Vanessas."

"Oh," I said, ushering her inside quickly and shutting the door. "Sit," I said. "Make yourself comfortable."

"Thanks," she mumbled, and pulled up a chair. She folded her arms and looked down. I rearranged my desk before sitting down, and then I watched her for a time before speaking.

"Chris tells me you were sleeping in one of the closets," I said quietly. "Is this true?"

She kept her gaze downward and bit her lip.

"I . . . I told her I'd just dozed off," she murmured. "That's all I did."

"Are you sure?" I asked. She shrugged.

"I guess I was just tired tonight," she said. "I—I told Chris I was sorry. But she made me talk to you."

"Have you . . . ever done this before?"

"What?"

"Dozed off anywhere at the center?"

She unfolded her arms and shifted around in the chair.

"No," she murmured.

"What?"

"No," she said louder. I sighed and leaned back. There was a silence while I stared at the window and turned my chair from side to side.

"Am I in trouble, ma'am?" she asked. "Really, I didn't mean to do that. It won't happen again, I promise."

"You're not in trouble, uh . . . uh, sorry, I was never told your name," I said.

"Jen," she said. I stopped turning.

"Jen?" I asked. "As in Jennifer?"

"Yeah," she said. "Am . . . am I going to lose the job? I'd like another chance, ma'am. I like working here. I like the people, I like—"

"I don't think you need to lose your job over this, Jennifer," I said, smiling. "Jennifer?"

Finally she looked up at me tentatively.

"You don't need to be afraid of me," I said. "I'm not angry with you." She smiled nervously.

"Oh, good," she said. "I mean, Chris kinda made it seem like—well . . ."

"Oh, Chris gets that way sometimes," I said with a wave. "But—Jennifer; before you go, I think it's only fair that I ask you some questions."

"What—kind of questions?" she asked.

"Well, the sort of questions that are . . . very important—you should answer as truthfully as you can."

"Like, what kind?" she asked.

"Well, for one thing," I said, taking a pen and doodling aimlessly, "I think it's only fair that you tell me some things about yourself, like—how old you are."

"I'm . . . sixteen," she said.

"Yes, that's about how old I'd say you were," I said. "But I want to know how old you actually are."

"Well, I said, I'm sixteen," she said.

"Do you have a driver's license?"

"Um . . . no, I haven't gotten that yet," she said. "But I'm working on it."

"How do you get to work?"

"Um . . . bus, usually," she said. "Sometimes I have to walk, though."

"How far?"

"Uh . . ." she said, shifting again, "about . . . th-four miles maybe."

"That's a good walk," I said, nodding. "And you work until . . . ?"

"Um, usually until eight," she said. "Sometimes you need me later, but I don't mind. I'm only part-time, you know."

"Yes, I know," I said. "Then . . . tonight you worked until . . . ?"

"Oh, um, the usual," she said. "Eight, I mean."

"Did you miss the bus, then?" I asked.

"The bus?"

"When did Chris find you in the closet?"

"Oh . . . that," she said. "Uhh, nine, I think. Really, I was just tired, and I was just sitting in there, and the next thing I knew—"

"It's all right, honey," I said. "Really, I'm not angry with you."

"See, I-I was just waiting for my . . . my parents to come and pick me up, and—"

"Oh, do they pick you up, too?" I asked. "That is, besides taking the bus or walking."

"Oh, yeah, and my parents," she said. "I forgot. Well, actually, it was just for this one night."

"Oh, then they could be here right now, wondering about you," I said, picking up a phone. "I'll ask Chris."

"No, no!" she cried. "I mean, they already called me, and said they'd be late. Like around ten-thirty or so. But it's only nine-thirty right now."

"I see," I said, putting the phone back. "Then . . . your parents know you're here."

"Oh, yeah, of course," she said. "They're just gonna be late. That's all."

"Jennifer," I said. "I'm going to ask you this again, and I mean it when I say I want the truth. How old are you?"

"I told you I'm . . ." she said. "Thirteen," she finished very quietly.

"So you're thirteen now," I said.

"I-I've always been thirteen," she said. "But people always think I'm older, so . . ."

"So you say it, too," I said.

"Yeah."

"So that leads us to another question," I said. "Do your parents know you're here?"

"Well, yeah, I said they were coming, but kinda late," she said.

"Jennifer."

She was about to protest, then looked down and around. She mumbled something.

"Pardon?" I said.

"No," she said. "No, they don't know that I . . . that I work here."

"Is there some reason why they don't know?" I asked. "Some . . . trouble at home? No, forget that one. That's none of my business."

"Um . . . well, I just haven't told them, that's all,"

she said. "I mean, they probably wouldn't mind that I have a job and stuff, but . . ."

"They don't even know you're here at all," I said.

"Not here at the center, no," she said.

"Jennifer," I said, "I meant *here.* In this city, right?"

"Well, no, it's not like that," she protested.

"So your parents do live here?" I asked. "In this city, I mean."

"Uh . . . well, not *this* city," she said. "Actually, they're kinda . . . south of here."

"Oh, you mean like in San Jose?" I offered.

"Yeah," she said, "Like there."

"Or are they *farther* south?" I asked.

"F-farther?" she said. "You mean, like, uh . . . ?"

"Monterey?" I offered.

"Yeah, like that," she said. "That's where they are."

"I see," I said. "Of course, Monterey is quite a commute to here. And you said you were only a few miles away."

"Well, I am," she said. "I mean we are."

"Jennifer," I said, "I'm no longer going to ask you. I'm going to *tell* you to tell me where your parents live, or where you live, or I'm going to have to assume that you don't live with them."

"You don't have to assume," she mumbled. "I-I've kinda been out on my own for a while."

"How long?"

"Um . . . about a month or something," she said. "But I guess you're going to call them now."

"I'm afraid I'm going to have to call them," I said. "But I won't do that this minute. It won't kill us to wait until early tomorrow night."

"Night?" she said. "I figured you were going to say morning."

"I sleep in the morning, Jennifer," I said. "In fact, I sleep all day." She said nothing.

"But tell you what I'll do for you right now," I said. "I can let you sleep at my place. But I—"

"Huh?" she said. "At *your* place?"

"I expect there won't be any problems with that," I said.

"From me? Well, no, it's just—no, I-I'll find someplace."

"Jennifer," I said, "you're my responsibility until you're with your parents again."

"No, you're not—"

"I won't have you arguing with me," I said in a tone that she knew wasn't best to contradict. "And I think you should consider the alternative. At my place, you'll be warm, comfortable, and most importantly, *safe.* You're probably hungry, too, right?"

"Oh, I can get some stuff. I'm—"

"Well, then, I'll pick something up on the way over," I said.

"But I—"

"I said, don't argue with me. Now in exchange for this, I expect you to, um . . . tidy up the apartment. I haven't had much time to keep up my housework lately. You can do that, can't you?"

"Oh, yeah," she said, apparently relieved. "Yeah, sure, I'll clean everything if you want."

"Fine, then," I said. "I'll take you over right now, but I have to come right back here to work. I have a pull-out bed for guests, so you'll be quite cozy, I assure you."

"You really don't need to do this—"

"I do, Jennifer," I said, looking straight at her. "Believe me, I do."

"Th-thank you," she whispered.

"You're welcome," I said. "And Jennifer . . ."

"Yeah?"

"I'll have to call your parents," I said, and she sulked, *"but*—I promise I won't call them until we've discussed this some more. All right? Deal?"

"Yeah. Deal," she said, still sulking.

"I can see you're not too happy about that," I said, and she shrugged, "but I don't think running off again will solve anything. At least with me you'll be safe. Please, Jennifer, don't get back on the streets. Even after a month you must have seen what's out there."

"I've seen some bad stuff," she whispered.

"So I hope you understand that I'm trying to help you," I said.

"Yeah, I do, Vanessa," she murmured. "Um . . . are you sure we haven't met before?"

"We'll talk, Jennifer," I said. "I promise."

"I do love my family," she said. "And I guess I miss them, too. Especially my dad."

"But you ran away for some reason," I said. "Do you . . . want to talk about that?" Jennifer shrugged.

"I guess it's 'cuz of my mom," she said. "I mean, we—" She sighed and looked down.

"You don't have to tell me anything if you don't want to," I said.

"No, I'll tell you," she murmured, looking up. "I-it's kind of stupid, actually. I mean it's not like what some people had to go through. It's not like anyone beats me, or . . . or does drugs or anything. It's just . . . you know for most of my life, my mom has—she's—"

"Take your time, dear," I said.

"Thanks," she said. "I guess it's that—most of my life, my mom has—" She stopped when her eyes started misting up. "She thinks I'm a freak, Vanessa," she finished. Tears were starting to form now. I got up from my seat and sat next to her.

"No, I'm okay," she sniffled. "I do this all the time. I hate it."

"Oh, it's only salt water," I said, putting an arm around her. She laughed a little.

"It's kind of hard to explain," she said.

"Well, why would your mom think you're a freak?" I asked.

"She's never said that to my face or anything," she said. "But all my life, I've just . . . always been to doctors and stuff. People have always been poking at me, and doing tests on me."

"Well, why would they do that?" I asked. "Do you have some . . . medical condition? Now you let me know if something's none of my business, you hear?"

"No, it's okay," she said. "I mean, maybe you've even read stuff about me. Or about my mom, too. Or maybe you won't even believe me, 'cuz it's pretty weird."

"Try me."

"Yeah, well," she began, "it all kind of ties in with when people found out about vampires. You know, the real thing, and not just the people who are into blood and stuff."

"I know what kind you mean."

"See—my mom's kinda famous," she said. "She, um . . . she even wrote this book a long time ago, and it kind of caught on when everyone found out about vampires."

"Maybe I read it myself," I said. "What's the title?"

"Uh . . . *Vampire Memoirs,*" she said. "See, my mom *used* to be—um, I'm probably getting off the track."

"You're doing fine to me," I said. "And . . . by the way, I *have* read that book."

"Then, I guess you know who I am, then," she said.

"I think I should let you tell your story before we get into mine," I said. "But, to my understanding, your mother used to be a vampire."

"Yeah," she said. "Then she changed back somehow, and, um . . . then had me."

I waited for her to continue. In the meantime, the more I watched her movements and expressions, the more reminded I was of her mother. This was more than just some mother-daughter resemblance. Jennifer looked like a thirteen-year-old version of Mara.

"After that," she continued, "there was test after test of me. Her, too, 'cuz no one had seen a vampire change back before."

"That's true," I said. "But . . . something confuses me. If your mother went through so much testing herself, and all that publicity and exposure that she must have had because of her book, well . . . why do you say that she treated *you* like a freak?"

"It's kinda hard to explain," she said. "See, I'm . . . I *am* human. I know I'm not a vampire, but for some reason—maybe 'cuz she used to be one—I'm . . . *like* a vampire. Do you know what I mean?"

"I'm not sure," I said.

"Well—they've done so many tests to me and stuff," she said. "I've had blood tests, skin samples—which are the worst—hair and nail samples. They even did a gene test a bunch of times. My mom had all that, too."

"You mean like chromosomes?" I asked.

"Yeah," she said. "They said we were both human, but—I don't know if you're gonna believe this, though."

"Again, try me."

"They said that—that we have the same genes," she said.

"The . . . same genes?" I said, not quite understanding.

"Well, yeah, we have the same—the same pattern of . . . well, you know about twins?" she asked.

"They're . . . people that look the same," I said.

"If they're identical twins, yeah," she said. "Except, the reason they're identical, is 'cuz they have the same, uh . . . same gene pattern. The same DNA."

"So, you're saying that . . ." I said, fighting for the words, "that you and your mother are twins?"

"Something like that," she said. "Except, in our case, we're not twins. We're clones."

When I didn't answer, she sighed in frustration.

"Yeah, I didn't think you'd believe me," she said.

"I never said I didn't," I said. "Believe me, I've seen much stranger things than . . . than clones. It's just . . . difficult to understand. Why would you and your mother be clones in the first place?"

"Hell if I know," she said, throwing up her hands. "Except, all I know is that now they say that my dad isn't even my dad, and I've been—shit," she said.

"It's okay," I said, squeezing her shoulder. "Do you want to talk about this later?"

"Nah, I should at least finish this much," she said, her eyes tearing up again. "See, they—they told me that—that now I'm some freak, because I wasn't even born normally. They found out that I'm my mom's clone because I'd been sitting in her womb for so long."

"Well, how long do you mean?"

"Promise you won't say I'm making it up?"

"I wouldn't think you'd make any of this up," I said. "How long, Jennifer?"

"Um . . . something like . . . sixteen hundred years," she said. We both sighed and leaned back.

"And I'm not making that up," she murmured. I shut my eyes.

"I believe you," I whispered. "In fact," I said, looking at her, "this even answers a question that all vampires have had for a while, even if unconsciously."

"What question?"

"Well, Jennifer," I said, sitting up, "it's known that vampires aren't able to have children."

"Can't they?"

"No," I said. "And it's sad at times, but that's how it is. Except—some of us—"

"Us?" she said. I smiled gently.

"Us, Jennifer," I said, but she gave no reaction. "Some of us have wondered," I continued, "what if—what if someone were converted, while she was pregnant?"

"I guess she'd be walking around with a big belly forever," she said, laughing nervously.

"Not if she were only a few weeks pregnant," I said. "Or even a month, or two months. No one would ever know. Not even she."

"That's what they said," she said. "Mom was pregnant for as long as she was a vampire, and didn't know it. And—and meanwhile, I just sat there. Like some . . . parasite that wouldn't go away."

"But you didn't," I said. "She changed herself back, and then you were able to grow again. But that's wonderful, Jennifer."

"Yeah, wonderful," she mumbled. "And what if she hadn't? I'd still be . . . just sitting there."

"Do you . . . have memories of this?" I asked. "From the womb?"

"How could I?" she asked. "I was just a fetus."

"I think you'd be surprised what the mind can do," I said. "After all, you were in there for so long. It must have left *some* impression on you."

"I wouldn't be surprised," she said. "Maybe I do remember stuff."

"And, if so, maybe that's some of what's caused you to have trouble with your mother," I said. "Um . . . what sort of relationship do you have with her?"

"Not the best," she said. "Ever since I could remember, she's always been—I don't know, completely freaked about me."

"In what way?"

"Well, she's always been real . . . protective, I guess," she said. "Maybe it's because of all the doctors and stuff, but I always felt like—like she just wished I'd never been born."

"Oh, I'm sure it's not that way at all," I said.

"Isn't it?" she asked. "Then why did she get so freaked when my powers showed up?"

"Powers?"

"Yeah," she said. "I know it sounds corny and stuff, but I have . . . powers. That's the only way I can describe them. I mean, what else would you call being able to look at people and—and see right into their heads? Sometimes read their minds, and sometimes even make them do what I want?"

"How about charming?" I offered.

"Well, I heard that's something that vampires can do," she said.

"We can," I said.

"We?" she said, staring at me for a long time. "Vanessa . . ." she began, "you're—the real thing, aren't you? You're a real vampire."

"I am," I said, rubbing her shoulder. "But I'd like to hear your story first." We looked at each other for a long time before Jennifer suddenly looked away.

"Um—yeah," she whispered. "Yeah, my story. Um—well, the first time it started, my mom and I were fighting about something, like school, I guess, and I just looked at her, and—I wanted her to leave me alone, and I even *said*, 'Leave me alone!' Then she just stopped, and went kind of stiff, and went downstairs without another word. And it was like—I don't know, like I was the one who made her feet move. Like it wasn't her going downstairs."

"I think you've come extremely close to describing just what charming is," I said.

"Have I?" she said. "Is that what you do, too? I mean, you can do that, too?"

"All vampires can," I said. "And it's made me think of something. A hypothesis, I suppose. I suspect, Jennifer, that you—probably because you *were* in your mother's womb so long, that—that maybe her own powers somehow leached into you. I mean, you say that you're actually her clone."

"That's what they tell us," she said.

"Then that means there had to have been some . . . I don't know, some . . . cleansing going on," I said. "As her child, you weren't quite—fully formed, so maybe being inside of her for so long made you . . . made her, *your* blueprint. As though you stopped sharing your mother's and father's genes, and flushed out his to take on hers. Am I making sense?"

"Yeah," she said. "Yeah, I think that's what some doctor guessed, too. You know, you're really smart, Vanessa," she said.

"Thank you," I said. "I try to keep my knowledge broad. But don't you take that as gospel. I'm just throwing out ideas."

"Well, it makes enough sense to me," she said. "Except . . . the trouble with that is, if it's true, then . . . well, then there's nothing left of my real father in me. There's nothing of my present dad in me. I'm just . . . Mom."

"You know, that's supposed to be every daughter's

worst nightmare,'' I said. ''Turning into her own mother.''

''Yeah, well, this is *real* for me,'' she said.

''I'm sorry,'' I murmured.

''And that's what I hate!'' she said, standing up. ''It was bad enough before with Mom all . . . all scared to death about me being like a vampire! Now my life is hell because . . . because I can't even get away from her! I can't even look in a mirror without her staring at me! Now I'm told I'm not even me, I'm my mom!''

''Maybe . . .'' I said, ''maybe this news has affected her the same way. Didn't you think of that? And maybe your pseudovampirism frightens her because she's afraid she—or even you, for that matter—might not be as human as she thinks.''

''Oh, we're human,'' she said, waving me off. ''We *are.* But Mom is like . . . okay, she says when she was a vampire, she wanted to become human again more than anything else, right? Well, now that she is, she's like . . . like it's not enough, you know? Like she doesn't want anyone else to be a vampire either, you know?''

''I think I do,'' I said.

''But I guess sometimes she thinks that I want to be one,'' she said. ''Except I don't. Maybe I can do all these weird things, but—I'm not a freak, Vanessa,'' she said, sniffling. ''I'm not a freak!''

''Shhh,'' I said, standing and holding my arms out. ''Come here,'' I said, and she let me hold her tight. ''Of course you're not a freak, Jennifer. You're not a freak at all, in fact you're—you're a very *special* girl.''

''No, I'm not,'' she mumbled.

''Yes, you are,'' I said. The phone rang then, but I ignored it.

''Better get your phone,'' she said.

"I have a machine," I said. We parted and sat down again.

"What if it's work?" she asked.

"Oh, Chris knows better than to call me on my day off," I said. "Besides, we're not done here. You're not a freak, Jennifer. You're a very special young lady."

"Whatever," she said.

"But I'm curious," I said. "Does your father treat you the same way? Your siblings?"

"Not so much, I mean not really," she said. "My sister and brother are like, ten years older than me. And Dad . . . well, I love him and all, and—if I regret this, I never wanted to hurt *him.* It's Mom I had to get away from. Especially after finding out about that clone shit."

I nodded, but let her continue.

"All my life I felt some kinda . . . I guess you could say bond with her, but it was a kind that I didn't want. It was kinda like . . . like she was always in my head. Like I couldn't get rid of her. And I hated that. Then I turned eleven and started being able to do weird things and—"

"Jennifer?" I interrupted. "Oh, I'm sorry, dear."

"What is it?"

"I was just wondering if . . . you can transform yourself," I said.

"Like in what way?"

"Ohhh . . ." I said. "The way vampires can do. Transforming our bodies, I mean."

"You mean like into a bat or something?" she asked. I nodded. "No," she said. "Nothing that major. But I can make my teeth grow. Mom wants me to file them down, but I won't. They come in handy sometimes. Like when my food is tough. Stuff like that."

"I know what you mean," I said.

"You really are a vampire, aren't you?" she asked.

"Yes, I am," I said.

"Wow," she said.

I smiled. "That doesn't bother you?" I asked.

"No," she said. "I've been around them a lot. mean, Mom still has some vampire friends. Like, Jack ie's been like a big sister. She used to baby-sit some times. I guess she sometimes baby-sat Jerry an Elizabeth, too."

"Your brother and sister?" I asked.

"Yeah," she said.

"Speaking of them," I said, "I was curious. No . . . your mother gave birth to you, but that was righ after she became human again. But you said that you siblings were ten years older than you?"

"Oh, they're adopted," she said.

"Ah."

"Um . . ." she continued, shifting in her seat, " guess it's time for you to call them, huh?"

"Your parents?" I asked. She nodded. "Well, to b honest, Jennifer, I don't know. I'd like you to tell m something first."

"What?"

"If I call, and they come and take you back, whic I'm sure they will, do you . . . think anything will hav changed?" I asked.

She looked at me quizzically, then looked away.

"You've been gone for . . . what, a month?" asked.

"Sssomething like that," she said, shrugging.

"Do you think, if you see them now, that you'll b able to talk to them?" I asked. "The way you've bee talking to me?"

"I tried to before," she said. "To my mom, any way."

"And your father?"

"Like I said, he's okay," she said.

"Well, why would he let your mother . . . be the way she was around you?" I asked. "Didn't he ever say to her, 'Hey, she's not a freak. Leave her alone'?"

"There was never anything like that—it's hard to—like I could *tell* she was afraid of me."

"I see," I said. "Through that bond you had with her. But in the same way, could she sense how *you* felt?"

"I don't know," she said. "At least, she never really acted like she could."

"Hm," I said, and we were both silent for a bit.

"Jennifer," I said to break the silence, "do you . . . *want* me to call them? Do you think you're ready to go home again?"

"The truth?" she said.

"Yes, the truth," I said. "The truth as only your heart can tell you. Are you ready to face them again? Could you face your mother right now?"

There was another long silence while she thought about it.

"No," she said very quietly. "I don't think I'm ready."

I leaned over and wrapped my arms around her, and kissed her on the forehead.

"I won't call them yet, then," I whispered.

"You won't?" she asked excitedly. "Really, you—?"

"Shhhhhh," I said, and she was quiet. "Not tonight, no. But you shouldn't run from them forever. You *can't* run from them forever."

"I know, Vanessa," she said.

"If you like, I could help you get ready to face them again," I said.

"But you're all busy with the center and stuff," she said. "And I've just been a lot of trouble for you."

"You have no idea what kind of help you can give me, Jennifer," I said. "Until you're ready, I can give you a home, and you can help me . . . help me work out some of my own problems."

"How could I help *you* with anything?" she said. I was about to give her a hint, but then smiled.

"Well, I could use someone to keep things in order around here," I said. "I can make this deal with you: I know you'd like to work for the center, but really, you're not old enough yet."

"But—"

"Let me finish," I said. "Instead, I *can* offer you room and board in exchange for your housecleaning, uh, gardening, mmmm, I suppose even washing my car when it needs it."

"You mean, you're gonna let me live here if I just do the dishes and laundry and stuff?"

"But under the condition that you end up trying to work things out with your mother," I said. "So don't think I'm going to be adopting you. Because even if—even if you've had problems there, you still have a home, and a family. Take my advice, girl—don't turn away from them."

"Maybe . . ." she said quietly, "maybe I should go home right now, then. I mean, you don't owe me anything. I'm just some runaway."

"You mean a lot more to me than you think, Jennifer," I said. "Believe me, you do."

Chapter 26

Jennifer proved to be an adequate housekeeper. Her appetite was small so there wasn't much grocery shopping to be done, either. She ate strange food, though, like peanut butter and pickle sandwiches, salted apples, and ketchup on her eggs. Or maybe that's what everyone eats. Obviously I don't have much need to keep up on food trends.

Even after two weeks Jennifer wasn't ready to go home. I avoided trying to convince her either way, because, to be honest, I wasn't ready to call home. Mara and her husband would no doubt be at my place in a day at most, and then what? I could have avoided it all by being at work when they showed up, but that would just be more hiding, wouldn't it?

After two weeks I did decide that the next step towards my reformation would be to confront my youngest victim—Jennifer herself. I wish I'd been allowed more time to prepare exactly what I was going to say, but my business had been taking up a lot of my time around then. This was the time that I was working on opening a companion workout center in another bay-area city. The plan was for Chris to manage that one for me while I took over the first one. I hated to see a good instructor like her leave, but she had some people in mind to replace her.

So I winged it, and hoped that Jennifer wouldn't react like a normal person, meaning in blind terror.

"The place looks nice tonight," I said, setting the latest groceries on the counter. I let Jennifer take care of the unpacking, as she could figure out where all that food was supposed to go.

"Thanks," she said. "I just figured maybe I should get down and wipe out all the corners, and clean windowsills and stuff like that."

"It shows," I said, nodding. "But, um, when you're done with that," I continued, "or, rather, after you've fixed something to eat, I'd like to talk to you about something."

"Oh," she said, "you sound kinda . . . is it bad?"

". . . I think it might be," I said. "I hope not, though."

"Well, what is it?" she said. "I can listen this way."

"No, no, I don't want any distractions," I said. "But for now, forget I said anything, and do what you have to do. Fix yourself some dinner."

"Well, if it's important, I can—"

"Just—get something to eat, okay?" I said. She looked at me as though a little afraid.

" 'Kay," she said.

"Um . . . I guess this is about calling my parents now," she said after settling in.

"That'll come up at some point, I'm sure," I said. "But before that, I have to tell you something very . . . well, disturbing."

"Like . . . what?" she asked nervously. I looked in her eyes and even opened my mouth to speak, but had to lean back and think some more first.

"You know, Jen," I began, "I know you must have heard this a million times, but the more I look at you, the more I think of your mother." I'm not the sort of person who shortens names, except she'd said she prefers Jen.

"Yeah, I have heard that a lot," she said.

"Of course, I mean it a . . . different way than most," I said. "In fact, when I first saw you as a little girl, I . . . I saw it even then. I saw your mother."

"Little girl?" she said. "You mean, we *have* met before."

"Yes, we have," I whispered.

"Well, why didn't you tell me before?" she asked. "Why didn't you—?"

"That's . . . what you'll find out when I tell you this," I said. "You see, um . . . yes, it's true that we *have* met before. But you only met me briefly. You see, uh . . . well, it's . . ."

"Theresa," she whispered, but more to herself than to me.

"What?"

"That's who you are," she whispered. "You're Theresa. Now I remember. You're—but I thought you weren't real . . ."

"Has—did your mother tell you about me?" I asked.

"She told me about someone . . . someone named Theresa," she said. "Someone who was a vampire, and tried . . . to hurt her. She says she tried to hurt *me,* too."

"No, no, that's not it at all," I blurted out before I could stop myself. I covered my mouth, but Jennifer had already figured it out.

"You mean—" she said, standing, "You mean you're—? You're—?"

"Oh, shit, oh, no," I said, standing up, too. "Wait,

Jen, i-it wasn't supposed to come out that way. I-I was supposed to—supposed to lead in, so I could explain things—"

"But you can't be Theresa!" she said, backing away. "You can't be the one Mom was talking about! Because—because you're my friend!"

"Yes, I *am* your friend, Jen, I *am,*" I said. "Please let me explain myself. I promise you, I won't hurt you. I would *never* hurt you."

"You were in her book, too," she continued. "You were—you were that one she didn't like. Were you?"

"Please sit down, Jen," I said. "Please—let me talk to you. I'm going to explain *everything,* I swear I will."

"You're lying to me," she said. "Or she was. Who's lying to me? Mom? But you were my friend whenever I was lonely! You were the one I always talked to! How could you be that other Theresa?"

"Please sit, Jen, and we'll talk about this," I said, and there was a pause. "Please?"

I gestured to the sofa, and after some consideration, Jennifer sat down again, but far at the end and without taking her eyes off me.

"Thank you," I said, and she nodded. "I . . . guess I should start at the beginning," I said. "First of all—first of all, yes, I am that Theresa that your mother told you about. I'm . . . I'm the one who tried to hurt her."

"She says . . . you tried to kill us," she said. "When I was just a kid, you tried to kill us."

"I never meant to hurt *you,*" I said. "Never. But—as for your mother . . . I-I suppose some of what was said about me in her book was true. But, as in any story, we only get her side of it. All anyone could know of me is what she lets them know. What she lets them see. I mean, I read it, and . . . and I suppose I was . . . upset about it. But—"

"Wait a minute," she said. "You can't be the same one from her book. I mean . . . you're supposed to be dead."

"Supposed to be dead?" I said.

"Well I meant—it says you died," she said. "Like, you were drained or something."

"That, too, was a . . . trying time for me, to say the least," I said. "Um . . . I guess to make things simple, I wasn't quite as dead as people thought I was. But—that's something I'd like to put behind me."

"Oh. Sorry," she said.

"No, no, it's all right," I said. "The problem is, though, is that I was also trying to put—what I did behind me. What I did to your mother."

"Maybe . . ." she said thoughtfully, leaning forward, "maybe it isn't fair to hear only her side. Maybe she did kinda . . . distort things. Mom does that a lot."

"Well, thank you," I said. "I-I'm so glad that—thank you for letting me talk first. Except—maybe what I have to say won't make things better."

"Uh-oh."

"It's not so much uh-oh as—you see, at the time, I thought of what I did as . . . justified," I said. "I thought that—that after I read the book, that your mother had—betrayed us. That she'd betrayed her fellow vampires by revealing that we exist."

"I thought that all started when some guy was found in a hospital or something," she said. "At least that's what I was told."

"Well, now that I've been able to . . . get back in touch with things, and find my own kind again, I've . . . I've been told the same thing," I said. "Now I see that your mother—even though her book didn't entirely *help* things—can't take all the blame for what's happened to us since."

"I remember that, growing up, there were always

people trying to talk to us,'' she said. ''Reporters and TV people. For years and years they wouldn't leave us alone. Mom says she even had a nervous breakdown at one point, and that had to do with her changing back.''

''So I read,'' I said, ''I mean, so I've heard. And then shortly afterward, she had you.''

''Yeah, me,'' she said. ''The freako.''

''Now you stop this freak business,'' I said. ''You have a gift that sets you apart from both human *and* vampire. You have the best of both worlds, Jen.''

''I'm not so sure,'' she said.

''I hope you'll let me help you with that,''I said. ''But, after this, you might not want to be anywhere near me. And if so, I won't blame you.''

''Then . . . you really did try to kill us,'' she said.

''Her,'' I said. ''Never you, I—'' I stopped and sighed. ''This isn't my way,'' I said. ''I've been trying to make this easy—to make it seem like there's something ultimately good about this. But I can't. I have to tell you the truth, Jen, and it won't be easy.''

''Can I say uh-oh now?''

''Be my guest,'' I said, ''because here it is, Jen—in the end, there is no justification for what I did. I went to your house when you were a little girl, and with the sole intention of killing your mother.''

''Shit,'' she whispered.

''But never you,'' I said. ''No matter how much of an animal I become, or how out of control or beyond hope, I don't think I could ever bring myself to kill a child. And if anything, you were the one to teach me that.''

''Me?''

''Yes, you,'' I said. ''Because . . . towards the end, I found myself ready to . . . ready to kill you, too. But—I couldn't. Not a child. Not an innocent.''

"You were going to kill me?" she whispered. I looked down; almost unconsciously my hands went into a praying position, and I shut my eyes.

"Like I said, there's no justification for what I did," I said. "Jen . . . this is likely to be a futile effort, but I need to ask your forgiveness." My eyes were still shut while I waited for her answer. I kept them shut even when a few minutes passed by before she even sighed.

"Jesus . . ." she said softly. "I don't know what to do. I don't know what to say, I don't know what to *think!* This is like . . . too much . . ."

"I understand that this is a lot to ask," I said, opening my eyes. "But maybe I should tell you more before asking again."

"Yeah," she said distantly. "Yeah, keep talking."

"As I said, I couldn't bring myself to do it," I said. "I couldn't kill you, Jen. Because . . . seeing you there . . . You were just a baby, not even three yet . . . And I wondered, is this what I've become? Have I become the monster everyone says vampires are supposed to be? It made me think, here I am, trying to kill your mother because I thought *she* had betrayed us, but what was I doing? I wasn't doing any better. So I . . . I put you on the couch, and brought your mother over there, too, and—basically I just changed my mind. But I guess, if anyone saved both your lives, it was you, Jen. I didn't kill your mother because of you, either."

"Because of me?" she said. "But . . . she never told me this."

"She didn't know this herself," I said. "All this happened after I'd knocked her out. And I didn't stick around to explain things to her."

"Jesus . . ." she murmured again. "She told me . . . she said she just found some note afterwards saying you'd changed your mind. God, that was always so freaky. No wonder Mom freaked out on me."

"About what?"

"About Theresa," she said. "About my friend. Except—she wasn't really a—*real* friend, not like physical or anything. She was more like an imaginary friend."

"Tell me about her," I said.

"Well, it started when I had dreams about this lady," she began. "She looked like—well, she looked like *you.* That's why I'm so confused about this. I had these dreams about Theresa, and later I sort of . . . made her real to me. See, like I said, my sister and brother were a lot older than me, so we didn't really have much in common, you know?"

"I know."

"It was a lot like being an only child," she said. "And it was hard to make any friends when I was with doctors and in hospitals all the time, you know? So, when I kept dreaming about Theresa, I just kind of made her my imaginary friend. When I was lonely, I'd think about her, and most of the time it was like she was really there. Usually I'd just think the stuff we did, but sometimes I'd talk out loud. Mom heard me once and thought I was weird. She hates it when I do anything at all that isn't normal."

"Plenty of people talk to themselves," I said. "They certainly do *here.*"

"Yeah, well, I guess it ties in with my mom trying to make me normal, whatever that is," she said.

"Yes, what is normal?" I asked. "But go on."

"Um . . . well, that's about it, really," she said. "Oh, yeah. Except—one day I made the mistake of talking about you. I talked about the imaginary friend and told them she was Theresa, and it was like, they totally freaked out. They said 'No, no, please don't call her that!' and I said, 'Why not?' and that's when they told me about the Theresa who attacked us. But you said that *you* were the one. But you look like Theresa!"

"I think," I said, "I think I should explain some more, then. First of all, did you ever read your mother's book?"

"Yeah," she said.

"Well, do you remember what she did with the little girl, Elizabeth?"

"You mean my sister?"

"No, no, I mean, that little girl in the Middle Ages," I said.

"Oh, her, yeah," she said. "What about her?"

"Well . . . if you remember, your mother did a sort of . . . mind-link with her," I said. "Where she placed a part of herself in—"

"Oh, yeah, I remember that," she said. "She left her essence or something, as Mom says. What about it?"

"Well . . ." I said, shifting around, "I suppose you could say that I . . . did that, too. But with you, Jen."

There was another long silence.

"You mean," she said, "that it *was* you who attacked us, but before you left, you . . . you did the same thing to me? When I was a kid?" I nodded.

"That's . . . essentially it," I said. "And in the end, that, too, is part of what saved you. You see I—"

"You bitch," she muttered.

"What?"

"How could you do that to me?"

"Well—a-at the time it seemed a—it seemed a good thing to do," I said, my voice faltering.

"I can't believe you'd—you'd fuck up my mind!" she said, jumping to her feet. I stood up, too. "You invaded my mind and stuck yourself in there? Do you know how much that fucked things up for me?"

"I—I can see how that would upset you—"

"Upset me?" she cried. "Goddamn you, do you

know how much trouble I got into just saying your name to my parents? Well, do you?"

"Jen, please let me explain—"

"Explain what?" she demanded. "No—no, I'm out of here. You tried to kill me, you tried to kill Mom, you—God, you said *your* place is safer than the streets? I should call the cops! Would you like that?"

"We have our own police—"

"So I'll call the vampire cops, then!" she said, heading for the phone. I started to follow, so she ran, but I overtook her easily and grabbed the phone away.

"Jen, please listen—"

"Get away from me!" she cried, backing away to the stairs. "You just—don't touch me!" Then she ran upstairs, yelling, "Get away!" I ran after her.

"Jennifer, no!" I yelled. She had reached her room and slammed the door shut by the time I reached the top.

"Don't you touch me!" she yelled from inside. "I'm getting out of here, and I want you out of my head, too!"

"Jennifer, please don't do this—"

"Just leave me alone!" she yelled. She continued with words to that effect while I thought for a moment, then misted my way under the door. I reformed right behind her. She was busy packing up her duffle bag while shouting.

"Jennifer—"

She screamed, whirling around and trying to run. I caught her, and she struggled furiously to escape.

"No! No! Let me go!" she screamed. *"Help! Mmmph!"* I covered her mouth, but she bit my hand and actually made it bleed. She wasn't kidding about making her teeth grow. I tried to make her look at me, and when I did, her red eyes weren't what I'd expected. For a moment I felt my thoughts swimming, but I shook it

off and stared her down. First she stopped screaming, and eventually stopped struggling, as well. Finally, she was calm.

"I'm sorry," I whispered. "Forgive me, Jen. I guess I shouldn't blame you for *your* hating me, too. I guess . . . I guess I deserve all of this. With Mara—your mother—it's certainly too much to expect her forgiveness, but you . . ." I sighed, turned away, and fought off tears. "I-I guess . . . I guess I figured that I was making things easier by doing the linkup. So, if I saw you again, maybe I could use that bond to . . . to soften the blow. Well, that's certainly a wash. But if it helps, I never meant to hurt you, Jen. I—I've come a long way since that night I attacked Mara, and have changed a lot, too. But until now I guess I've never done *real* penance for what I did. Human or not, it seems that priest was right."

I released her from my hold, but kept my back turned to her.

"Theresa?" she whispered finally. I turned around slowly. "Or . . . is it Vanessa? What should I call you?" I sighed.

"I'd like to be called Theresa again," I said. "That's always been my real name. But . . . I think I should say Vanessa is right."

"Then, Vanessa?" she said.

"Yes," I said.

"I'm not sure what to say now," she said. "Maybe I owe *you* an apology."

"Oh, please, not even close," I said.

"No, really," she insisted. "I-I think I do. I think . . . yeah, what you did was wrong, and—shit, *very* wrong. You tried to kill somebody. That's about as wrong as you can get, next to actually doing it. And you did that thing to my head, that made me get into trouble whenever I talked about it."

"God, I'm sorry, Jen," I said. "Truly."

"Well, I only got into trouble when I said my friend's name was Theresa," she said. " 'Cuz, that's when they told me about what happened, and tried to make me change the name. And I did try, but—nothing else was any good, except Theresa. It made me feel bad after hearing all that, but I couldn't come up with any other name. She had to be Theresa."

"I see," I said.

"So you did end up messing things up that way," she said, "but then, Theresa *was* my friend, too. Maybe only an imaginary friend, but she was my best friend. I guess that sounds kind of pathetic, that I couldn't even have a real best friend."

"I think it really just worked out to your being your own best friend," I said.

"Something like that, I guess," she said. "So maybe . . . maybe I was pretty unfair to you just then."

"Oh, God, no," I said. "I'm the one who needs *your* forgiveness, remember?"

"Well, if that's what you need, I guess I forgive you then," she said. "I mean, hell, you've been real good to me with all this, too. Letting me stay here, and all. Talking to me."

"Just trying to help," I said.

"So . . . the thing with my parents, then," she said. "All this time you've been afraid to talk to them, too."

"Something like that," I said. "I seriously doubt it they'll be as . . . willing to listen as you."

"Well, maybe I can do something," she said. "I mean, we both need to talk to them. All of us need to talk together. Maybe you and me can help each other deal with them."

"I think I'd like that, Jen," I said. "You know, for being so young, you're very . . . old. Wise beyond your years, that is. I don't mean old."

"The hell you don't," she said.

"What?"

"I *am* old, remember?" she said. "Sitting around all those centuries in my mom?"

"Er—well, I didn't mean—"

"I know what you mean," she said, smiling. "But maybe you're right about my remembering things while I was there. I think most people think I'm older because I'm tall for my age, but if I've been sitting around for hundreds of years, well—I've got an old soul, too."

"You know," I said after a while, "you may be right."

There was more delay in calling the parents. I told Jennifer of my concern that, should she return, she would never have any training in how to work with her abilities. I convinced her to let me help her explore what she could do. Like Mara, she had a blue instead of light blue aura, which made me hypothesize that both of them were in some transitional state. Or it could have been a state all its own.

Jennifer's powers were mostly psychic. She'd already demonstrated her charming capabilities, and after using myself as a guinea pig, she became rather adept with them. They weren't quite at a real vampire's level, but she certainly had an advantage over humans. Part of her training involved learning how not to abuse it, either. For one thing, subtlety seemed to be beyond her—people were either mindless slaves or they weren't. She agreed that her lack of subtlety was a limitation.

She also had the latent telepathic abilities that vampires have. We can communicate mentally when in animal form, and so could Jennifer. Or to rephrase that,

Jennifer could not physically transform, but she coul communicate with me when I did. She said she' learned about that as a child, when Jackie had trans formed to amuse her. Apparently that was anothe thing that Mara had been concerned about—instead o being happy about.

We went to the center to test her physical limits. I turns out that Jennifer can become one hell of an ath lete if she wants. For a thirteen-year-old, she can d pretty much everything at twice the capacity of othe teens. Strength, endurance, agility—as I said, prett much everything is exceptional, including her fiv senses—which is why all of the above only proved m suspicions—that Jennifer was something better than normal human.

Lest we forget, Jennifer shares DNA with he mother, the most unambitious being on earth. I shoul be kinder, actually. What I mean is that both wome share an almost inhuman desire to be . . . normal. T be absolutely unexceptional. It should be obvious i Mara, who hated being a vampire and just wants t keep on being a typical housewife, with a husband kids, house and two cars. Jennifer was going to need lot more help than I could give her to convince her tha her abilities didn't make her a freak. More than any thing she just wanted to be a regular, dumb kid an more importantly, just herself.

To help her be herself, I tried to help her reduce th resemblance to her mother, but that was met with op position. Jennifer wasn't all that willing to endure an radical transformation to her hair or clothes or what not. Makeup wasn't all that important to her, eithe (nor was it important to her mother, as I recall). That' fine, because to be honest I'm glad she wasn't int dying her hair or chopping it all up, because she reall does have naturally pretty hair. I finally got her to ar ange it nicely, since it wasn't going to be permed. And, like her mother, she had some nice dimples whenever she smiled and naturally big, round eyes. Their almost-emerald green color didn't hurt, either.

I'm beating around the bush some. The biggest reason both of us were stalling at calling her parents, was that we didn't want to be separated. I should only speak for myself, actually. I didn't want her to leave so soon. I'd come to enjoy Jennifer's presence and companionship. Home had more meaning now than just a place to sleep. I wouldn't go so far as to say that Jennifer was like a daughter to me, because she was very much a friend, too. But being with her reminded me of some old promises I'd made for myself when I was human. Like having children, for one.

I've never stopped liking children. But from the beginning, I must have been repressing my desire to have any—to protect me from the fact that I *couldn't* have any. Sometimes I'd stare at mothers holding their children—stare for a long time before even realizing I'd been doing it, but then all feeling would go numb, and I'd get back to business. But now I understood much better what motivated Mara to adopt that girl in the Middle Ages, and even how she felt when she learned she'd have to give the girl back to her family. I suppose if I envy Mara anything, it's that she had had the opportunity to experience motherhood, and even now had been given a second chance. That's when I realized that the stalling had to stop.

"But I'm not ready to go home, Vanessa!" Jennifer said, her eyes misting up. "You still need to help me practice, right?"

"You've learned enough that you can practice these things on your own," I said. "And besides: your mother has vampire friends, right? Like Jackie?"

"Well, yeah, but she's got her own stuff to worr about," she said.

"And I don't?"

"Oh, I didn't mean it that way," she said. "I ju . . . don't think I'm ready, that's all."

"It's time, Jen," I said. "Your family misses you.

"Well, I miss them, too," she said.

"So?"

"So . . . I'm still scared, I guess," she said quietl "I'm still scared that nothing will change."

"It will change," I said, taking her into a hug. "It' change because, because it'll have to. They'll have t see that you ran away for a reason."

"What if they don't?"

"Jen," I said, looking her in the eyes, "you sto this, now. Even I'm afraid to call them, and you kno why, but I have to. We have to talk to them."

"You'd think I could just stay with you," she grum bled. "Hell, we fugitives need to stick together."

"We probably do," I said, smiling, "and we wil once they get here. We can lean on each other. Bu you know that I couldn't give you as good a home a they can. And besides, what am I supposed to do whe your face shows up on a milk carton?"

She thought that was funnier than I did.

Chapter 27

Jennifer had talked me into getting a Christmas tree, which is something I'd never done before. Vampires can celebrate any holiday they please, but in general, we keep things fairly subdued. In fact, except for Halloween and birthdays (for the ones who can remember theirs), we don't even exchange gifts. This year was a very special Christmas for both of us, then. Jennifer made me a card and gave me a small, framed picture of herself, and I gave her a set of stationery and some decent clothes. Simple gifts, but they were enough to reduce both of us to tears.

I went into my den while Jennifer made her call. It was Christmas night. I tried not to overhear, but it wasn't easy ignoring the shouts that came from the other end of the phone when her parents answered. Jennifer kept calm but couldn't get them to quiet down for a long time. After that it was easier to mind my own business. I had told her to go ahead and give them my address, but not to reveal my real name. I prefer doing things face-to-face. Afterwards she told me that they'd be on the first flight out. I could tell she'd been crying, too, but I said nothing about it.

Now we had to be ready for a visit at any moment. The center was open the day after Christmas, but I

took that day off, too. Too bad I couldn't sleep tha
day. It isn't easy tossing and turning in a casket.

I'd barely come out of the room at sunset, whe
Jennifer came racing up the stairs excitedly.

"They're here!" she shouted in a whisper. "Thei
flight got here this afternoon!"

"What?" I whisper-shouted back. "Wh-wh—you
parents? When did they get here?"

"About an hour and a half ago!" she said. "Com
on, I've already talked to them and—"

"W-wait!" I said, resisting. "Wait, you mean—yo
mean they know who I am?"

"Yeah, they know your name's Vanessa," she said
"Come on, they want to talk to you!"

"B-b-but I'm not ready!" I said. "That is, I can'
go down like this! I look like a dog's breakfast!"

"Ohh, you look fine," she said. "You *always* loo
gorgeous."

"Well, thank you, but—please, Jen, tell them, I'll–
uh, be down soon," I whispered. "Please?" Sh
smiled.

"You're still afraid, too, aren't you?"

"Jen?" came what could only be Mara's voice fror
below. "Is everything all right?" My heart almos
popped out of my chest.

"Dya, dya, Jen, just—just tell them I'll be righ
down, okay?" I said, backing up the stairs, then whirl
ing around to run back into my room.

"Vanessa!" Jennifer called after me, and knocke
on the door.

"I'll be right there!" I said, and heard her go bac
downstairs. Then I fell onto my couch and rubbed m
eyes. Ohhh, I thought. Beautiful.

I went to my windows and pulled aside all the cur
tains. The last vestiges of daylight were fading away

And I was only two stories up. I could easily make it, or better yet, fly.

No, no, no, I thought, shaking my head. This is ridiculous. Who are they? A bunch of humans. They're just humans! And I've lived longer than—well, at least longer than *two* of them put together. On second thought, I'd lived longer than one of them. Maybe not any of them, actually. Even Jim was supposedly the reincarnation of Mara's dead husband, according to her book. Well, so much for that argument, then.

I gave myself the fastest makeover in history, tossed half of my clothes around the room looking for the right outfit, and was finally ready. As far as I was concerned the mirror said I still looked like shit, which only proves that mirrors must have been originally intended as torture devices.

There was a lot of excited chatter in the living room as I made my way downstairs. Jennifer had apparently made her peace. Too bad I had slept through the whole thing. I made it to the bottom, took a deep breath, let it out, and went around the corner.

All three were seated around the coffee table, smiling and chatting. Mara had her back to me, so Jennifer saw me first and rushed over.

"Oh, Vanessa!" she said, taking my arm, "It's about time you showed up!"

Jim was already facing me, and Mara turned around.

"Dad! Mom!" Jennifer went on, "This is Vanessa. I tell ya, I'd be turning tricks if it hadn't been for her."

"Now, Jen," her father protested, and he and Jennifer went back and forth some about that. I didn't hear what they said, though. Somehow I doubt Mara did, either.

This wasn't quite the way I'd planned things. They were supposed to show up long after I'd gotten up, and had practiced to the mirror what I would say, and then curled up in my chair and slippers, waiting patiently for them to come. I was supposed to have heard them and Jennifer reconciling, and maybe even caught a glimpse or two of their hugs and tears before revealing myself.

Eventually Jennifer and her father resolved their disagreement, and Mara and I were still staring at each other. Then, on some reckless whim, I thought of a little joke.

"Mara," I said quietly, "you'd probably like an explanation." I got the feeling that Jim finally remembered who I was, too. He had the same look his wife had.

"Mom? Dad?" Jennifer said very softly. "Vanessa's my friend. She . . . took good care of me."

"Did she?" Mara whispered.

"Yeah, she did," Jennifer said. "In fact, she—" I held my arm out to stop her, and shook my head slowly.

"But—"

"Jen?" I said, still shaking my head. "Now it's my turn to talk to them, remember?"

"Yeah," she said, and backed away. I watched her a moment, then looked at Mara and smiled slightly.

"Mara," I murmured. "Jim. Like I said, you probably want an explanation."

"You're damn right we do," Jim growled, but Mara held up a hand to quiet him. That only irritated him.

"Mara, do you know who that is?" he asked.

"Of course I know who it is," she murmured, then looked at me and bowed her head slightly. "Vanessa?"

"I think . . ." I said, walking along the wall to the far sofa, "I think it would be best if we all recognize that I'm Theresa."

"Theresa . . ." Mara said, but then was silent.

"You've got a lot of nerve," Jim growled. "You've got a lot of nerve to do what you did, and do what you did to our *daughter,* and now you come out here and—!"

"Dad, you don't understand!" Jennifer said.

"You have no idea what happened, Jen," he said. "We told you what happened, but you weren't there—"

"*She* told me what happened, too!" Jennifer cried, pointing at me. "I know *exactly* what happened! She said—"

"And what *did* what she say, hnh?" he demanded. "Since when do you think *she'd* give you the real story, hnh?"

"So how do I know *your* story was the real one?"

"How do—?" Jim said, and was speechless with anger for a moment. "Look, young lady, you were too young to remember, so you didn't see what she did to your mom! I did! Even Jerry and Elizabeth did, goddamn it, so I don't want to hear any—"

"Hold it! Shut up, both of you!"

Surprisingly enough, that came from Mara. Jim was too shocked to argue. Mara had both hands up and her eyes shut tightly while father and daughter calmed themselves. Then she opened her eyes and looked right at me. I would have stopped it all before that, but I'd thought it important to hear what I was up against. I doubted if I'd even heard a fraction of it.

"Mara?" Jim said quietly. She looked at him briefly, then back at me.

"Theresa has asked if we'd like an explanation," she said very quietly and calmly. "I think we ought to allow her the opportunity."

"Give—?" Jim said. "Mara, you're kidding, right?"

"I am not," she said, her gaze never straying from me. She bowed slightly. "Theresa?"

"Er—"

"Mom, she really did tell me everything," Jennifer broke in. "I *know* about—"

Both of us moms held up a hand to stop her, but this time I think it was Mara that Jennifer heeded. She bit her lip and backed out. Mara turned her attention back to me, gesturing grandly.

"Theresa?"

"Thank you," I whispered, and cleared my throat. "I—it means a lot to me to . . . be able to talk to you both like this. To clear things up, mostly, but—"

"Clear—things—up?" Jim asked warily. "As in, there's something ambiguous about what happened?"

"I-I never said there was," I said. "That is, you're right about that. There isn't a whole lot that—that can actually *be* explained about what happened. I was . . . wrong to do what I did. I-I was crazy, I was—I wasn't getting all the facts, I—"

"Oh, Jesus, I don't believe this," Jim groaned, pacing behind his wife. "Mara, Jen—we're getting out of here."

"Dad!"

"But Jim, I wanted to—"

"I said now!" he yelled, trying to gather them together. "Come on; Jen, get your things, Mara, you, too, come on, let's go, come on—!"

"Dad, no!"

"I said *now!*" he roared, and Jennifer yanked herself from his grip. He reached out again, but she kept out of his reach.

"What the hell are you doing?" he said. "Come on, let's go!"

"Goddamn it, Dad, she's trying to talk to you!"

"Now, don't you swear at *me—!*"

"Uhh, Jim?" I said. "Mara?"

"You're not even *trying* to listen to her!"

"Yeah, yeah, we'll all listen to her a lot later, but—

Jennifer!'' Jim yelled. ''You get over here immediately!''

''I for one would like to hear an explanation!'' Mara's voice boomed, and all was quiet again.

''Mara . . .'' Jim whispered, ''this is—this is *her*. This is Theresa! You know, the one who—''

''I know bloody well what she did!'' she snapped. ''Do you think I've forgotten or something?''

''Well, no, but what makes you think we're safe here, huh?''

''Hey, I was safe!'' Jennifer said.

''What did you look like afterwards, huh?'' he pressed on. ''How long were you in therapy because of her?''

''Jim . . .''

''Well? How long?''

''Four years!'' Mara cried. ''I know that! You know that! Everybody knows that! Stop treating me like a bloody child!''

''Oh, for God's sake, I'm trying to get us out of here alive!'' he protested. ''Jen?''

''No . . .'' she said, backing away. ''I'm not going home with you.''

''What?'' we all said.

''Not if you guys are gonna be like this all the time!'' she said, tears welling up. ''Not if—not if you're just gonna freak out about everything as usual!''

''Jen, you don't under—''

''I do too understand!'' she shouted. ''Dad . . .'' she sniffled, ''why are you being like this? I-I've never seen you like this. You were always the one who—who listened to me. And Mom . . .'' she continued. ''You were always the one who didn't want to hear anything. And now you're the only one who even wants to listen. I know what happened. You think she told some . . .

some whitewashed version, but she told me everything!"

"Everything?" Jim said.

"Everything, Dad," she sniffled. "She—she told me about—about how she tried to kill you, and how—"

"And you," Jim interjected. "Did she tell you that, too?"

"That's not what it was, Dad," Jennifer said. "She wasn't trying to kill me at all. See, she—"

"So you *did* get the whitewashed version," he said.

"Jim," Mara said. He frowned and folded his arms.

"Mom . . ." Jennifer began. "Vane—Theresa told me about what happened. She also told me what you *couldn't* know, 'cuz you were knocked out, right?"

"I was . . . unconscious for a time, yes," she said, looking at me.

"Well, she told me about—"

"Jen?" I said, holding up my hand. She stopped, but reluctantly. "Thank you, honey," I said. "I think it's best that I tell the rest."

"Oh, yeah," she said with a nervous laugh. "I'll shut up now."

"Thanks," I said, and looked back up at Mara.

"I told her as much of the truth as I could," I said.

"Your truth, Theresa?" Mara asked slowly and quietly. My heartbeat fluttered a bit, and I took a deep breath.

"*The* truth," I said. "I don't believe in whitewashing things. Not in this case, anyway. Not that I explained in gory detail what happened, but yes, she understands that—long ago I did attack you, with the intention of killing you. And . . . as for her, I admitted that I came very close to killing her, too. I suppose that was the turning point, too."

"She didn't kill you because of me, Mom," she interrupted, then realized her mistake and shrank back. I smiled a little, though.

"I suppose that's one way of putting it," I said. "But, yes, that moment where . . . where I looked at Jen, and actually . . . thought of killing her, that I realized what had happened to me."

"And what *had* happened to you?" Jim asked defiantly. For a moment I could only laugh, though.

"Ahhh, I can give you no reasonable explanation for trying to kill her in the first place, yet I'm supposed to have one for *not* killing her?" I asked. No one else but Jennifer seemed amused, though, so I put on my somber face again.

"If I could give a reason," I said, "I would have to say . . . that no matter what we vampires may be . . . We are not animals.

"We are not baby-killers," I continued, and looked down to become lost in my thoughts. "When we reach the point where we kill only for sport, then that's when we've lost. It's a stupid saying, but there's much truth to the notion that with great power comes great responsibility. There's so much that makes us better than humans, but I suppose . . . I suppose if there's some reason I didn't kill anyone, it's that—that no matter what, we have to acknowledge our humanity. No matter what, we have to remember that we all started the same way. We have to hold on to that, or we'll be worth less than a cow's ass to the world. We're not baby-killers, Jim. *I'm* not a baby-killer. But the fact that I almost was . . . that terrified me."

When there was only silence, I looked up. Mara seemed to be looking at my feet. I looked closely at her for a long time. She seemed . . . old. Her human age had been thirty-one, but now that had changed. Ten years had gone by. Wrinkles had come, and more were sure to follow. White hairs—very few just then, but sure to increase—were peeking out from amongst the yellow ones. It was then that I was reminded that I could no longer imagine bumping into her every hundred years or so. After another thirty years or so, no one would ever bump into her. The oldest vampire will be gone. And whether she believes me or not, the world will be a lot emptier without her.

"I always tried not to think about what would happen if I ever saw you again," Mara said, and looked me in the eyes. "I . . . I tried not to bring back the nightmares by dwelling on the past. But of course, that only made things worse."

"I know," I murmured, remembering my own daymares.

"Do you know I . . . I went through four years of therapy after that night," she continued. "Mostly to . . . to see if it was possible to know why? Why did you do what you did? Why would you come only to *me* for . . . for revenge, I suppose. After four years, that's all I could assume. But now you tell me there *wasn't* a reason."

"I wouldn't say there *wasn't* one," I said, "but I would say there wasn't a . . . rational reason. If you like, yes, it was for revenge. Revenge after waking up from having been—literally—buried alive for eight years. Revenge after seeing your book, and what it—"

"B-b-but my book," she said, throwing her arms out. "How could—? What exactly *did* I say about you that was so terrible? I-I looked at it over and over, and still couldn't find anything that—that was really all so libelous as you made it seem!" I smiled a little and started to pace slowly.

"I couldn't say that—it was so much what was said about *me,*" I said. "After all, you couldn't have known the real story about Antonio and myself. So, naturally, I came across as rather . . . shall we say, manipulative?

But . . . whether or not I decide to tell the whole story on my own is still up in the air, I suppose. But I'm surprised you still don't understand, Mara. If I was angry about anything, it was the *principle* of what you'd done. It was the idea that—that any of us even *would* write something like that, and least of all publish it!"

"That's something I wrestled with for a long time, you know," she said.

"Then why do it after all?" I asked. She looked at me, then sighed loudly and looked down.

"That's a good question," she said. "In fact, I think now, that if I could go back, I probably wouldn't have done it."

"Mara," said Jim, "what's happening here? Why are you trying to justify anything to her? Nothing that you said or did in that book justified what she did to you!"

"I never said it did, Jim," I said.

"The hell you haven't!" he said. "You've just finished telling her about the principle of the thing as though that's an excuse!"

"That's what my excuse was before!" I said. "Right now is where I'm telling you that it *wasn't* an excuse! All I can do is plead guilty! I was insane then, remember? Or do you think lying in a grave for eight years is like a little nap?"

"You've never even paid for what you've done, have you?" he asked. "You've been hiding out here all the time, haven't you?"

"I haven't been hiding out anywhere," I said. "And as for never paying, you do of course remember that vampires have their own justice system?"

"Something which I'm against, mind you," he said.

"And Mara?" I asked. There was a delay before she looked up again.

"Separate courts?" she said. I nodded, and she sighed loudly again.

"There's still such a controversy about it," she murmured.

"But how do *you* stand, Mara?" I asked. "How do *you* feel that, legally, I've made restitution for what happened, but through our system and not that of the humans? Or is something more required of me? Specifically, Mara—what do *you* require of me?"

"You've been . . . tried and convicted?" she asked. "According to your laws?"

"*Our* laws."

"I can't be judged by your laws," she said, shaking her head. "I'm human now."

"So you say, but to me you'll always be one of the elders," I said. "But you haven't answered my question. Mara McCuniff: what do you need from me in order to see justice?"

Both she and Jim seemed surprised that I had asked that. Jennifer looked at me nervously, and I shrugged and smiled back at her weakly. Then Jim knelt down to whisper with Mara as though in conference.

"Come on, honey," he said, "think about this. Did you hear that? What do we need?"

"I—I don't know . . ."

"Don't know?" he said. "Think of all the—think of what she did! Think of the hospital! Think of what could have happened to you, or Jen, think of the years of—!"

"All right, all right!" she said, throwing up her hands and standing up. She was breathing heavily when she looked at me again, then calmed herself.

"Theresa," she began, "what sort of sentence were you given? And was it carried out?"

"My sentence consisted of many things," I said. "Most notably, empathy was one of my requirements." Mara nodded in comprehension. "That I did for several months solid. Also, there was . . . another few months of nonentity."

"Total?" she asked, apparently surprised. I nodded.

"No acknowledgement from anyone," I said.

"My."

"Then of course, no doubt out of homage to human justice, dismemberment," I added.

"Dismemberment?" she said. I nodded and showed the limbs that had been removed, only to grow back after a year or so. That had been a challenging time, to say the least.

"I think I don't need to hear more," she said.

"I do," said Jim. "I don't even know what the hell you're talking about."

"Well, I'll explain them all later, honey," Mara said gently.

"Then, that's all you think is necessary?" he protested. "Having an arm cut off? She grew the damn thing back, anyway!"

"Mara," I said, ignoring the husband, "I agree with him that what I did wasn't enough. You see, before I sought out our own justice, I sought . . . a priest. A human priest, probably out of some . . . vain attempt to recapture the religion I'd lost. Well, I have lost it, but he told me I needed to face the people I'd hurt, and ask their forgiveness. And, at the time, I . . . couldn't. I wasn't ready; I was *afraid* to. But I can't be afraid any longer.

"Mara—Jen—Jim—" I said, looking at each in turn, "I ask only your forgiveness for what I did. Whatever you ask of me, I'll do it, but—it should be, from the bottom of your hearts, what is truly necessary for *you* to have peace of mind."

There was another long silence. Then, a very quiet voice spoke up.

"Theresa," Jennifer whispered, "you know that I've already forgiven you. You don't have to ask me again."

"Shhhhh," I said, and waited for the others. Jim looked like he had plenty to say, but he was apparently giving Mara first crack at me.

"There's nothing," Mara began softly, "there's nothing you could physically *do* to . . . to undo what was done. Most people would ask for . . . money or something, as though that was supposed to solve things I suppose it would be only fair to make you pay for my total doctor bills, and . . . my therapy, too, I suppose."

"And getting your ring fixed," Jim said. "Don't forget that."

"Oh . . ." Mara said, twisting her ring around "Yes, I—that, too." From the look on her face, I got the impression that that of all things hurt her most That's only a guess, of course.

"That would be fair," I said. "But that's not what's really needed, right?"

Mara shrugged and seemed to grasp for the righ words.

"Jen?" she said softly, "Could you come here a minute?"

Jennifer didn't answer, but went to her mother They were almost the same height already. Mara held her by the shoulders and looked at her for a long time before pulling Jennifer slowly towards her into a tigh embrace.

"I'm so sorry, honey," she whispered through tears "I—I just—"

" 'S okay, Mom," came the muffled response. After a moment Jim leaned over and squeezed the two of them. I looked away until they'd finished.

"Your hair looks nice, Jen," Mara said, brushing her hair around.

"Thanks," Jennifer said. "Theresa did it." Now if only Mara would let me fix that poodle cut of hers . . .

"Oh?" Mara said, looking at me. She moved her daughter aside gently and stepped towards me. I had no idea what to expect when she stopped right in front of me.

My body stiffened involuntarily when Mara suddenly flung her arms around me and held on tight. I looked at Jennifer, who seemed as shocked as I. My eyes probably still looked like ping-pong balls when Mara finally let go.

"Thank you," Mara whispered, wiping away a tear. Then she went back to her absolutely baffled family.

"Did I see," Jim said. "what I think I just saw?"

"Yes, you did," Mara said, "though I can hardly believe it myself."

"Does this, uh . . ." I managed to say, "does this mean I'm . . . forgiven?"

Mara wiped away some more tears and sniffled. She looked at Jennifer, then back at me and nodded quickly.

"Uh . . . why?" I said. "I-I mean—I'm *glad* you do, but—uh . . ."

"Maybe I've just gone mad," she said. "Or maybe, I just started to think that—that you've brought my daughter back to me. You've helped us become a family again. For that alone we owe you our utmost gratitude. And no, there may never be any justification for what you did, but I suppose . . . there can be justice. I realize that—you've never been one of my favorite people, and I'm certain you knew that."

"Believe me, I did," I said.

"But then, different though we are, there are some

. . . similarities," she said. "You do have many goo
qualities."

"Gee, thanks," I said.

"Well, what I meant was . . . was that you too
someone in off the streets, and—God, I'm just so happ
you're back, Jen!" she cried, and dove into anothe
hug.

"Y-yeah, me, too, Mom," she said, still confuse
"Um—About all the stuff I can do . . ."

"Stuff?"

"Yeah, you know, my powers and all?" Jennife
said. "Well, Theresa's been helping me practice wit
them. You know, learn how to control them? Isn't tha
cool?"

I got the impression that Jennifer had asked that t
test her mother. To learn if there was the possibilit
that things *were* going to change.

"Yes," Mara said after a while. "Yes, that is good."

"Mom . . ." Jennifer began, "I never asked to b
the way I am. I don't even like having these powers
But I'm not going to pretend I don't have them, be
cause I can't. I may never use them, but they're alway
gonna be there."

Again, there was a long silence.

"Of course," Mara whispered, fixing Jennifer's col
lar. "Yes, I—I recognize that. Believe me, Dad and
have—well, obviously we've had to do a lot of think
ing. Trying to figure out what happened to make yo
run away. And he doesn't agree, but—but I'm certai
a lot of it is my fault. I-I'm certain I was too . .
protective of you, especially at a time when—well
when you're starting to outgrow that."

So maybe there was hope for the tall lady after all.

"Mara?" I said quietly.

"Yes?"

"I was wondering if I could ask you something,"

aid. "Let me know if it's none of my business, but ou should at least answer it for yourself."

"What is it?"

"Jen says that everything came to a head about the ime she learned that you were . . . well, twins," I aid.

"Yes, something like that," she said, then to Jenifer, "Perhaps we shouldn't have told you, honey."

"But you did, so it's done," I said. "Which means hat you knew about it yourself for, how long?"

"About . . . well, since she was a little girl, really," he said.

"I see," I said, nodding. "Then my question to you as to be: Do you think that because of what you knew, hat maybe—just maybe you weren't as frustrated by he knowledge as Jen was?"

"Um . . . frustrated?" she said.

"Well, in the sense that—if every daughter's nightnare is becoming just like her own mother, well, vouldn't it sort of be in reverse, too? Wasn't it a nightnare of your own to know that your daughter was—quite literally—*you?*"

"You have no obligation to answer," I added when here was another silence.

"It's hard for me *to* answer right now, that's all," he said. "It's not something . . . that people are usully conscious of. Meaning, you've asked me a very good question. And I think it's something I should vatch for, once we've arrived home.

"But still, when I first learned that, I couldn't help out think that—after all those years . . . centuries, I'd oeen carrying myself in my own womb. Before, half of ner was me and the other half was Gaar, and when I ound out what had happened, well—I found myself rying. I'd thought that Jim and I had a child of our own now, or even . . . that after all those centuries, I

still had something that Gaar had left me. But . .
there was nothing of him left in her anymore. It wa
just . . . me."

"My God," I said. "That's exactly what Jen tol
me."

"Did she?"

"Just about, Mom," she said.

"My goodness," Mara said. "I had—no idea."

"You do now," I said. "It seems to me that ther
ought to be a little more communication between yo
two from now on."

"I can see that," Mara said, looking at her daugh
ter.

"And what about you, Jim?" I asked.

"What about me?"

"Has this been a problem for you, too?"

"How? Why?"

"Well, again, you needn't answer except to yoursel
but—knowing that Jen isn't biologically your daughte
after all, well—isn't there some resentment?"

"You're right," he said. "It *is* none of your busi
ness. We've got two adopted kids already, and they'r
mine just as much as Jen—"

"Peace, peace," I said, throwing up my hands. "It'
none of my business, I'm—I'm sorry."

"Accepted," he grumbled, but I doubt if he mean
it.

"You know, I've never had kids of my own, Mara,"
I said. "Not even adopted ones. Why am I giving *yo*
advice? *You're* supposed to be the earth mother, no
me."

"Good question," Jim said.

"You have good instincts," said Mara, ignorin
him.

"Then, I suppose I could try another bit of advice,"
I said. "Jen isn't you, Mara. She isn't you any mor

than a twin is the same as her twin. She only shares your genes, not your soul. There's no reason for you two to fight each other."

"There isn't, no," Mara said.

"And . . . before you all go, you ought to keep something else in mind," I said.

"What?"

"Oh . . ." I said, "you just ought to keep in mind that some of us like being what we are."

"What are you talking about?"

"I mean vampires," I said. "You can't imagine how happy I am for you, if being human has truly made you happy. But as for everyone else, it's best to keep in mind who really does want to be human again, and who doesn't."

"Theresa, I . . . I can't see why you're bringing this up," she said. "I don't know what this has to do—"

"Never mind," I said, throwing up my hands. "Forget it. I'm babbling. There's only one thing that's important right now, and that's that you're with Jen again, and vice versa. And that you all make it as a family again. That's what's important."

"Um . . . yes, that's the important thing," she said warily.

Chapter 28

I offered them beds at my place for the night, but they went the motel route instead. So we had to say goodnight that night. Once again, I offered my hand to Mara, but in friendship this time. Understandably, she was hesitant, but it turned out well, in the end. Even Jim ended up trading handshakes. As for Jennifer . . . well, let's just say we didn't let go of each other for a long time. Her parents can think that I was faking my tears, but I know better, and so does Jennifer.

I told Mara that I'd been working on my own book. She didn't seem very happy about that, but I explained that it was more of a diary than anything else. And it was, at first. Originally I started it as an outlet for my frustration and anger, and partly for revenge, too. I was supposed to write some acidic, scathing diatribe against Mara and the rest of the world, but it didn't end up quite that way.

It occurred to me when I began writing this again that I could go back and sanitize a lot of it, and remove most of the anger. I decided that doing that would be at the expense of the truth, or the truth as I saw it then. Besides, I haven't changed *that* much. One could say that I've mellowed with age, though. I've come to accept that humans learning about us was inevitable, and if it hadn't happened now, it likely would have in a hundred years or so. It was just quite a shock to wake up to this, to say the least. Things are a complete mess right now, but it ought to work itself out in oh, a thousand years or so. Hopefully I'm joking.

In the end I find it strange that someone so different from me could be so intertwined in my life. Practically from the beginning Mara and I have been connected, even if only because we'd been converted by the same person. Incidentally, I, too, am glad he's dead, if he really is. If he isn't, he could be reading this and plotting to kill me, too. Maybe, except I'd tell him the same thing to his face, and he knows that, too. At least I'll have died fighting.

But I do have this to say in Mara's favor. Again, she doesn't strike me as terribly bright, or ambitious, or even imaginative. But she is one of the more sincere people I've ever known. She's more the sort who, if she hurts someone, does so out of ignorance as opposed to malice. That is, she had no idea what Antonio was making me do, so of course I came across as a manipulative bitch. Not that I'm not that way at times, but you get the idea. She may be uptight and self-righteous at times, but she also has a hell of a lot of love to give. Probably a lot more than I have, and I'd like to think I have a generous soul. In the end, then, I suppose I shouldn't begrudge her the yearning for normalcy in her life. The happy housewife's life is often just an illusion, but in her case, I think it's real. I think that she really is one of those women who needs little else but a family, home, and a little job. She could very well be happy as a clam that way; I couldn't say, but if so, I wish her luck in keeping all of the above until she dies. Still, she and her daughter have got to learn to stop worrying so much about everything. I get the feeling that none of the above would have come about if they'd just learned to take things slow and easy. If Mara's human again, she shouldn't waste her remaining years letting things raise her blood pressure. Old bats like us need to have fun sometimes.

Jennifer isn't allowed to call me, so I haven't tried stirring things up by calling her, instead. So we correspond when we have the time. She wrote about the minor tiff that her parents had on the flight home. It seems Jim took Mara to task for dismissing my crimes so readily. Jennifer was quite relieved when Mara declared the case over, and so am I. I miss the little vampette, but this is the way it has to be. I offered to remove my essence from her before she left, but she asked to be able to think about it first. As of this writing she hasn't answered me yet.

If Jennifer's letters are any indication, things have improved at home. She had piles of Christmas gifts waiting for her at home, plus a huge Welcome Home banner that her siblings had made. Afterwards she and her parents, particularly Mara, set aside some time to talk, which is nice to hear.Last time she wrote they were considering family therapy or something. And I'll clobber her if she doesn't keep me updated on that, too. Jennifer's a good kid and deserves a good family. Maybe that therapy thing will help her work out her own personality; after all, twin or not, she isn't exactly growing up in the same environment her mother had been in.

That family thing I'm not paying for, but it was arranged that I should send monthly payments to them to reimburse them for the doctors, Mara's therapy, emotional damage, and yes, the repair bill for her wedding ring. It's actually quite a nice ring. I wish one of my husbands had given me something like hers. Even the one her dead husband gave her centuries ago is in good shape. That, and it's a genuine artifact, I'm sure. Hell, it's from the fourth century, isn't it?

For the curious, you'd better believe I'm grateful for this arrangement. I forgot to mention Mara's greatest quality: her capacity for forgiveness. I recognize that what I asked of her was too much for anyone to forgive, but . . . she did. To make matters worse, I doubt if I could have, had our roles been reversed. So much for my bid for sainthood. This is why I'm so grateful with how this turned out. Like her mother, Jennifer, too, has this capacity. I can only hope that that therapy doesn't talk her into abandoning her best qualities.

At this point I'm practically up to present time, so I'll stop here before this deteriorates into some day-by-day update. By now I've decided that I ought to publish this. It won't be under my actual name, but I've given the amateur sleuths all but my home address if it's really so important to them to track me down. Some people just have too much time on their hands. A better question for them to ponder would be: why am I doing this? If Mara's second autobiography—the one I'd trashed—taught me anything, it was the price of fame. She asked me if I'd taken it, which I admitted, and to my surprise, she thanked me. She thanked me for keeping her from making the same mistake twice. All that publicity from the first book, not to mention just about everything else in her life, had made her life more of a hell than paradise, so this is a risky venture at best. But then, I still like challenges. If this ruins me, cosmically speaking it will be for fifteen minutes, because in the end I'll outlive everyone who ruins my life, anyway. Unless they're vampires, of course.

—Maria Theresa Allogiamento

Dear Reader,

Zebra Books welcomes your comments about this book or any other Zebra horror book you have read recently. Please address your comments to:

Zebra Books, Dept. JAS
475 Park Avenue South
New York, New York 10016

Thank you for your interest.

Sincerely,
The Editorial Department
Zebra Books